RETURN

TO

CHARLOCK

By Leah Moyes

Return to Charlock is a work of fiction. Names characters, places and incidents are either the product of the author's imagination or are used fictitiously. Any resemblance to actual persons, living or dead, events, or locales is entirely coincidental.

First Printing: ISBN 9798514526260

Cover Design by Molly Phipps/WGYC Book Design

Published by: SpuCruiser Media
Email: Leahmoyesauthor@gmail.com
Website: https://www.leahmoyes.com/
Facebook @BerlinButterfly
Twitter @authormoyes

Acknowledgements

Over the last year, I've had the opportunity to meet with new authors and book clubs and one of the first things I tell them is that I could not have accomplished what I have without my critique team. They are my right arm in the writing process and many times help mold my novel's direction. Each member brings unique insights and strengths, and I am forever grateful for their perspective. Though not all were able to contribute this time around, their friendship continues to mean the world to me. Thank you, Dawne Anderson, Taylor Brown, Maria Carrasco, Wendy Hargrave, Melisa Harker, Stacy Johnson, Greg Moyes, Susan Provost, Lani Taunima and Lina Taunima.

A very special thank you to Dawne Anderson and Taylor Brown for your editing skills and insights. More than once you've had to jump in the ring and stop me from strangling the blasted comma. Thank you for taking my lump of coal and creating a gem.

To my writing buddies, Jennie Durkee and Stacy Johnson. Thank you for your friendship and support and to many more getaways to come!

To my family for their support. love, humor, and mounds of chocolate through my writing journey.

Thank you, Greg for always taking care of me and the house when I'm tethered to my computer. You are my greatest love and support!

"What of the other hindrance? Has it been taken care of?" Her Papa muttered.

"You mean Jacob?" Josiah asked tentatively.

"Shhh. Don't speak his name ever again."

Margaret held her breath. *Jacob?* The mere mention of his name prickled her skin. She leaned forward to grasp what followed.

"He'll be taken care of, I sent Harker this time. He won't return again." Josiah announced, his voice dripping with satisfaction. "You've got to hand it to him though, he never gave up—always believed he had a chance."

"Well, no daughter of mine will ever marry a tradesman, that's for sure."

"To the future Lady Gentry." Another clink and swallow.

"Damn that girl, where is she off to?"

In an effort to stay well hidden, Margaret took a small step backward, only to find that her shoe slipped clumsily down a step. She clawed at the frame of the door, grasping for stability, but made no connection. With a helpless cry, she launched into a full free-fall down a set of stone cellar stairs.

Chapter 1

The Gilford Estate

Thursday, 12 May 2011

The ripe mustard scent of the Charlock bloom caught in my throat the moment I stepped out onto the veranda. Pausing, I allowed the warm sunshine to bathe over me as I plucked a cluster of the bright yellow flower off a nearby vine. Twirling the stem through my fingers, I glanced toward the empty breakfast table nearby and fought to keep the hollow pang in my stomach from expanding. Trenton's business took him to London a week ago and although he came to Charlock as often as work allowed, his absence always left me sad.

"Miss Shelton?" Gretchen walked out to meet me, both hands gripping a different vase with competing flowers. "Do you prefer the roses, or the lilacs, in the master suite? I can't recall."

I laughed. I could barely see her head over the bounteous bouquets. "The roses go in the master suite for Trenton's parents and the lilacs in all the other guest rooms."

She nodded, confirming the decision. "Oh, and the additional maids you hired for the next two weeks are arriving in an hour. Would you like me to notify you when they get here?"

"Yes, Gretchen, thank you. I'm going to take a walk, but I won't be gone for long."

She nodded and rushed inside with her heavy load. I took the steps to the gardens sluggishly, though I had no real reason to be disheartened. Since the night of the wedding "ball" last July, and my first kiss with Trenton Gilford, our lives drastically changed for the better. While I still carried on as the curator and Trenton managed his family businesses, we became attached and somewhere along the way—fell in love.

I studied the ring on my finger. The sunlight caught the diamond's perfection at a stunning angle. My heart stirred. After tracing the unique oval cut, I touched my neck out of habit. My skin lay bare, having removed the necklace the day Trenton asked me to marry him. It hung from my bedroom mirror as a reminder of the link between my past, and my future. The only surety of my forthcoming journey came with the knowledge that I wouldn't be facing the unknown alone.

With understanding beyond my comprehension, Trenton never pressured me to move on, knowing how much Jeff meant to me. He encouraged me to bare my soul, share my fears, and in return he made promises. Promises to respect, and love me always, but most of all, he allowed my heart to heal. *"Kat," he said one night on one of our moonlit walks. "I never intend on replacing that part of your heart, just joining it."*

The searing pain that once tore through my chest after Jeff's death slowly subsided over time. I had not forgotten him but found that I could *feel* again, and the affection Trenton poured out to me became the soothing answer to my fragile wounds.

He was not the only one.

Merritt, Trenton's third great-grandfather who I had met back in 1878, played a substantial role in my healing process. Both he and his sisters, Lizzy and Abby, taught me a great deal about love and friendship, and I missed them immensely. The time travel experience, though never forgotten, was only spoken of when Trenton and I were entirely alone. We both knew the consequences of what others might think of me if they ever overheard.

As I maneuvered through the beautifully manicured gardens being prepped for the next wedding, my hands gently glided over the buttery daffodil stalks and sweet briar roses with captivation. I hesitated beneath an arched trellis where the lilac hued blooms of wisteria suspended from the notched wood, compelling its passers to inhale the sweet musky fragrance. Taking in the breathtaking scene, I chuckled. No matter how much I had resented weddings in the past, this next one could *not* be missed—for it was my own.

Walking along the path toward the river, I sidestepped the haphazard puddles from yesterday's rain showers. The heavy dampness that settled into the peat moss and leaves left the air brimming with a trace of mint from the numerous birch trees. By the time I reached the edge of the Thames, the earthy scent enveloped me from all sides. I located my grassy oasis, though I could no longer call it mine, for Trenton and I shared many special occasions here—the most memorable being the warm autumn night Trenton proposed.

A fervor of delight coursed through my veins with the mere recollection and left a ridiculous grin across my face. Lanterns lit with soft flames, outlined the edges of this very spot where Trenton expressed his truest heart and dropped to one knee. His generous and kindhearted words that night profoundly imprinted on my soul.

Everything I adored about Trenton intensified in the months of our engagement, and every time he departed Charlock Manor, his absence invoked acute loneliness.

Watching the water swirl around the rocks reminded me of that first morning we happened upon each other, here, after I criticized him severely for his announcement of selling Charlock. He startled me, and I slipped off a stone and landed partially in the water. My irritation for Trenton and his arrogance in the beginning has now become a source of our playful banter.

I chuckled at the memory, then frowned at the ensuing emptiness. Even with his return later this afternoon, our time alone wouldn't come for a full ten days.

Guests would begin arriving this afternoon and our serene tranquility would be sparse, if we were privileged to have any at all. Trenton and I both agreed during the planning stages of the centuries-old Gilford tradition of a full wedding week that we hardly wanted the first few days spoiled from jetlag, so we extended the festivities to a week and a half. With the majority of guests arriving from international destinations, our parents and best friends included, we believed the extra time would be worth it.

Trenton's parents, though we weren't entirely sure of where they would be flying in from, would be amongst the first family to arrive tomorrow. The very thought heightened my anxiety. I had never met them—even *after* we became engaged.

Despite Trenton being an only child, he often claimed to have an odd relationship with his parents. This concept was strange to me, especially with the closeness of my own family. With a deep determination, I fostered a desire to rectify this. Last Christmas, we invited both sets of parents to Charlock for the holidays, nevertheless, Mr. and Mrs. Gilford were regretfully detained . . . apparently for months on end. Now I would be meeting my new in-laws during the pre-wedding revelries, mere days before we wed.

A stick snapped nearby and I startled to the sound. Whipping around, I found Trenton hunched several yards behind me.

Though he must have discarded his suitcoat somewhere along the way, he still wore his stylish dress shirt and slacks.

His countenance betrayed him.

His lips curved into a playful smile, and the roguish arch of his eyebrow exposed his intent to surprise me. Jumping to my feet, I shortened the distance in a heartbeat. The very sight of him initiated chills throughout my body. Eagerly throwing my arms around his neck, I nearly bowled him over to the ground in the process.

"What are you doing here? You're early!" I managed to ask before his mouth met mine. His profound touch matched my longing as his hands wound through my hair and pulled me closer. The kiss lengthened from one to several, propelling a fervent pounding of my heart into rhythm against his own.

With labored breath, we released but remained close. Between the fine lines bordering his eyes and the silver streaks against his deep green irises, they mirrored the happiness I felt.

"I finalized the project as quickly as I could." His hands moved to my waist and squeezed lightly. "I've missed you."

I smiled back. "I've missed you too. The house is so empty when you're gone."

He glanced at his watch, the same gold band I'd grown used to seeing since that fateful interview two years ago. When his eyes met mine again, they conveyed the very thoughts I had considered earlier, only now confirmed with his next sentence. "With our friends arriving soon for the *hag* party and the others tomorrow, we will rarely have a moment alone."

When Trenton and I first talked about a bachelor and bachelorette party for the first night of our wedding week, Trenton kept referring to them as a *stag* and *hen* party, but when we opted to do a dinner together, the titles combined to a *hag* party. I teased him relentlessly at first, since in America the word *hag* doesn't exactly bring about the best image.

One of his eyebrows arched mischievously, and his lips lifted into a rascally grin. "That is, until our honeymoon . . ."

With my hands steady against his chest, I raised up on my toes and kissed his cheek. "I can't wait."

"Neither can I." He chuckled. "It's been ages since I've been on the boat."

"That's the only reason?" I wrinkled my nose.

His head flew back into a full laugh. He teased me relentlessly. Both his hands cupped my face, and he grew serious before he leaned in. "No, of course not," he whispered with his lips tickling mine. "I know a far better reason."

My smile grew.

He planted a quick kiss on the tip of my nose, and took me by the hand, and led me over to the grassy bank. As we sat down, he settled easily behind my back and wrapped his solid arms around me, drawing me to his chest.

"I'm glad you arrived earlier than expected." I nestled deeper into him. "You're welcome to sneak up on me anytime."

Moving my hair aside with his chin, his lips reached the tender skin beneath my ear and kissed. The sensation singed every part of my body. "Helen said you missed breakfast again." His breath warmed my neck. "You must stay nourished, love. This week is sure to be exhausting. Are you well?"

I nodded weakly. "Oh, just simply feeling sorry for myself."

"Is that so? Whatever for?"

"I was lonely."

"And who were you pining for?"

"My devilishly handsome fiancé." I threaded my fingers through his. "He left me a week ago and my heart . . . and body have been longing for him ever since."

"Hmmm," his lips now went to the nape of my neck and brushed the curve enticingly. "What a fool to leave such a devastatingly beautiful woman alone. I must amend that at once."

"And what did you have in mind?"

He placed his hands on my waist and twisted me around on his lap to face him. My eyes scanned his undeniably striking features from his dark wavy hair to his angular jaw, then lingered precariously at his inviting lips. The lips that tempted me on sight. Without hesitation they were upon me once more. His hands cupped my neck as he thoroughly kissed me. Once I surrendered, he leaned back to answer my question. "I will kiss you forever." I clutched his shirt and pulled him back to me for more.

"Ten days, love . . ." His lips tickled mine when he whispered. "Ten days, then you're all mine."

Those words—those beautiful, enticing words sliced through me with scarring precision. Suddenly trembling, I scrambled to my feet as if the wind was knocked out of me from the unforeseen assault on my memory. Moisture surfaced on my hands as I pressed them weightily against my chest—their presence seemingly required to hold the pieces of my heart back together.

Fragmented images of mangled metal, debris, and a lifeless body underneath a white sheet, emerged. Gasping, I couldn't stop the emotional onslaught.

In the two years since Jeff's death, I felt myself healing—the nightmares had tempered, the anger subsided, and now, even the weddings did little more than incite a stir . . . so why did these very words suddenly shake me to the core?

Because Jeff said something similar the night before he died.

"Kat?" Trenton stood up and moved behind me. My sudden reaction appeared to startle him as much as it did me. "What's wrong?" His hands rubbed my shoulders tenderly.

My eyes blinked repeatedly, keeping the tears at bay as my lungs fought for steady breath.

"Please, tell me what's wrong."

Trenton gently reached for my wrist and spun me around to face him. He brushed the tears off my cheeks as they fell, then held me until my chest stopped heaving. When I finally released and peered upward, his eyes revealed overwhelming compassion.

With my emotions barely under control, I whispered, "Please, Trenton . . .please promise me you won't get into a car this week."

"A car?" His eyes fixated on mine until they turned a lighter green. Understanding dawned on his face. "Oh, Kat . . ." His arms pulled me in again and pressed me against his chest. The rise and fall of each breath he took enveloped and sheltered me. Both the steady pace of his heart and the vibration of his voice pulsated against my ear. "Nothing is going to happen to me, I promise."

My tears soaked his shirt as he soothed. I tried to make sense of my panic when the sudden realization struck me—it was no longer about Jeff and his death. My torment centered solely on the fear of losing Trenton. "I don't know if that's a promise you can make," I mumbled.

He kissed my forehead and nudged my chin upward. "I will not leave you." His eyes portrayed his seriousness. Then he smiled to lighten the mood. "You're stuck with me, I'm afraid." He lowered his lips to mine and kissed the tears that settled there. "Seriously though," he spoke through his kisses. "All of our events are here on the grounds. I'm not leaving until after the wedding and only with you in my arms."

I leaned back. "But what about the horses and the games?"

"All perfectly sound, love. I've been riding since the age of four. As far as archery, I can compete with the best of them, and I'm certainly not daft enough to stand behind a target. Fishing is harmless, I suppose unless someone is foolish with a hook. That leaves the cricket game and you are going to see this one-time *almost* professional athlete whoop my former teammates with a tiny flick of the wrist." He held my face in his palms once more and lowered his head close. "Nothing is going to happen to me." Then kissed me gently until I forgot the reason for my distress in the first place.

I wrapped my arms around his neck. "Thank you, Trenton. Thank you for loving me."

"It's hardly laborious." He chuckled, then grew serious. "I became the luckiest man in the world when you said yes." He held up my hand and rubbed my diamond ring with his thumb. When he glanced toward the direction of the house, he sighed with a hint of regret. "Now, I suppose we must delay our passion momentarily and see to the needs of our home." The way he said *our home* drove a rash of tingles across my skin. Could Charlock Manor truly be *my* home? He continued without hesitation. "The staff will need to be addressed before the guests arrive. And, well, I'm certain I'll need some form of therapy before and after my relations materialize."

I laughed easily and met his hand as he guided me away from the river. "Your family can't all be that bad. You've met half of mine and survived."

"Your parents are normal, Kat!"

I snickered. "Normal? Do you even know what that means? My dad argued British law versus American law, snored through Christmas dinner, and mom wanted to do your taxes."

He squeezed my hand. "I love that they want to be a part of our lives and that they enjoy our company. I can't truly say the same about mine."

"Well, that will be my new challenge." I lifted my chin. "I'll work hard to win them over."

Trenton smiled. "Well, if they don't love you, they couldn't love anyone."

We reached the steps leading to the veranda and he stopped me once more. Since our first kiss the night of his friend's wedding, a sweet ritual transpired. We never passed this spot without a sizzling repeat.

"Whatever happens this week love, just remember, in ten days we are getting *hitched*, as you Yanks like to say, and nothing will stop that from happening . . . not even my parents."

When Trenton finally released me from another delicious kiss, he smiled wide and led me up the stairs and back into the house to face reality once again.

As I entered, I reflected on his choice of words. Was it possible I hadn't met his parents yet because they didn't approve? Or was it possible that they might try and stop us from taking our vows? Shouldering the Gilford name was not only exhilarating, but intimidating. The noted attachment to Merritt, Lizzy, and Abby was not only wished for, but about to be realized.

Maybe Trenton's parents didn't believe I deserved the esteemed honor that that entailed.

Though this new fear wanted to wrestle to the surface, I pushed it away. *Not now,* I insisted in my head. The only thing I needed to concern myself with was becoming Mrs. Trenton Gilford in a little over a week.

Chapter 2

"Gilford!" The deep voice boomed through the vast entryway with deafening precision. Trenton and I had returned from the river an hour before and met with the staff. A dozen new faces appeared on temporary loan from neighboring estates to accommodate the twenty-two guests invited to the *Gilford Games*, but the arrival of our first guest stole all our attention.

"Hastings!" Trenton met the man with a robust hug. Another man swiftly squashed him from the side. They laughed as they tried to squeeze the air from my fiancé, only to release him before he passed out. They weren't as tall as Trenton, but both could claim an inch or two in shoulder width over him. "Marlowe," Trenton squeaked out as he struggled for oxygen. They doubled over in laughter at a jest I imagined happened often.

Trenton straightened and flashed a quick smile in my direction. The men didn't miss Trenton's target and immediately appeared at my side, each reaching for a hand and kissing my knuckles.

"And who might this lovely creature be?" Hastings posed a diabolical grin.

Trenton scrambled over quickly, breaking us apart by placing an arm around me, then extended one hand in a barrier toward his friends. They simultaneously barked a hearty laugh in response.

"Gentlemen," Trenton smirked. "Though I can't say that title is reflective of your behavior." He cleared his throat. "Meet Kat Shelton, my fiancé."

"Kat, this raucous chap is Oliver Hastings. Though he will only respond to *Hastings*." He pointed to the first man who entered the room. His long blond bangs swept downward past his defined cheekbones as he took a low bow.

"Delighted to make your acquaintance," he said as he tilted his chin toward me and offered another cheeky smile.

"And this mate is Ethan Marlowe. Also known as . . ." Trenton nodded at me.

"Marlowe?" I alluded.

"You guessed it, *Marlowe*." Trenton pointed to the other man who unlike Hastings, sported dark, curly hair and pierced me with his poignant blue eyes.

"Charmed, Miss Shelton." He winked dramatically.

"Okay, that's enough." Trenton chuckled.

"Nice to meet you both." I smiled in return.

"I must say, Gilford," Marlowe watched us with one eyebrow raised. "I never thought I would see you so besotted."

From behind, Trenton wrapped both his arms around my waist and spoke over my shoulder. "She didn't give me a choice. She took my breath away the moment I met her."

I chuckled. "I took your breath away because I left you speechless after I railed you for wanting to sell Charlock?"

Hastings burst out laughing. "You have met your match, mate. Now where are the chits?"

"The *women*," Trenton emphasized, "have not yet arrived. Come now, I'll show you to your rooms and give you time to practice your manners before dinner."

"I'm offended." Marlowe retorted, placing his hand against his chest. "I happen to be a master of propriety, especially around the fairer sex. He shot another quick wink toward me; one that Trenton did not miss.

"If you say so, but this one," Trenton squeezed me close, "is off limits to your so-called proprieties."

"Very well, Gilford." Hastings sighed dramatically. "Lead the way."

"Cheerio, Kat," Marlowe said as they grabbed their suitcases and obediently followed Trenton down the hallway to their assigned rooms.

Lowering to the settee, I took a long breath. The amount of energy that came from those two would no doubt keep the party going at a swift speed all week. I needed to take advantage of every quiet moment possible.

Gazing upon the portrait on the mezzanine, I wondered what Merritt might think of me marrying his third great-grandson. I shook my head at the prospect of trying to explain the time-travel ordeal to him. He would likely laugh it off as an American jest of sorts.

A knock sounded from the front door. I remained still as Hennessey set forth to greet whoever stood behind it. *If it's another one of Trenton's friends, perhaps I can stay hidden for a moment longer.* I bit my lip in hesitation as a spirited feminine voice filled the air. "We made it!"

"Kelly!" I jumped to my feet once the door opened wide. She dropped her bags but found her sight distracted by the magnificent entryway, much like my own impression that first day. I flung my arms around her neck. "I'm so glad you're here!"

"Uh yeah," she mumbled. Her eyes scanned the room and widened with each astonishing discovery.

"Beautiful, isn't it?"

"It's . . ." She turned to finally meet my gaze. "Amazing." Then hugged me. "I've missed you, Kat." With only phone calls in between, our separation spanned well over a year. She released me and studied my appearance meticulously. "And you look . . . wow, girl, you look so happy!"

"I am." I reached for one of her hands. "I'm *really* happy."

She kissed my cheek.

"I put you and Maria in the room next to mine. Luckily, it's one of three rooms spacious enough for two queen size beds. Trenton's friends are down the opposite hallway."

"Why so far?" Kelly winked. "I might get lucky."

"Oh, trust me Kelly, you'll get far more attention than you'll seek." I chuckled knowing what was sure to come. Maria stomped inside past Hennessey and immediately flipped her high heels off her feet.

"You could've told me stilettos are not the right shoes for England," she snapped with sass.

"You might've asked." I laughed. "Actually, they're perfect for inside the house, just not the grounds." The scent of chili and lime wafted over me as I hugged her. For someone who paid careful attention to what she ate, *Takis* were her weakness and from what I could tell, she had a lot of them during the long plane ride over here. "You're going to love it here. I can't wait to show you around the estate."

"So, where is he?" Kelly asked with wide eyes, searching past the archways.

"Trenton?"

"Of course!" She huffed. "Where is this man who has returned my old friend to me?"

I smiled at the veiled compliment. Kelly saw me at my very worst. "He's seeing Hastings and Marlowe to their rooms. You're going to love him. He's . . ."

Kelly's eyebrow curved as she waited for me to finish.

"He's everything I could have ever wanted, Kel. He's shown me how to love again."

She smiled wide and grabbed my hands. "You're the luckiest woman I know." Squeezing my fingers, she leaned forward. "Love does not come easily *once* . . . and for you now, *twice*." Then she kissed me on the cheek. "And it's very much deserved." A warmth crept up my neck and settled into my cheeks when I noticed Hennessey waited out our reunion with patience. No doubt his ears have heard much over the years.

"Hennessey," I pointed in his direction. "I'd like you to meet Kelly and Maria, my best friends from college. This is Hennessey, our stalwart butler."

Hennessey tapped his heels with a slight bow. "It is wonderful to make your acquaintances."

"Butler, hmmm . . ." Maria lifted her chin a bit higher and flashed a bright smile. I could practically read her mind with her elitist tastes. This arrangement would suit her quite well.

Hennessey motioned to a footman standing right inside a nearby door frame. "Curtis, please assist these ladies with their luggage. Their bedchamber is in the northeast wing, next to Miss Shelton's."

Shortly after Trenton proposed, he invited me to move from my employee quarters to a family bedroom upstairs. I declined, due to my ridiculous fears and superstitions. I thought if I switched before we wed, something bad might happen. It was a silly concern, but I pacified it with the knowledge that once we're married, the next move would be to the master suite with Trenton, and nothing brought forth a bigger anticipation.

After the girls were settled into their room to recover from their flight, I headed to the kitchen. The yeasty aroma of fresh baked bread drifted from the door before I even set foot inside. My lengthy inhale momentarily transported me back to our own deli's brick oven. "Smells delicious, Helen." It didn't matter what her fists sank elbow-deep into, she always dropped it promptly and embraced me. I laughed at the flour that once again graced my blouse. Her sister, a pastry chef from London, peered up from her work and chuckled at the sight.

"Good morning, Laura."

She nodded. The woman never said more than two words in my presence. She always appeared consumed with her craft.

Helen squeezed my hand. "Doll, you're going to love dinner tonight—especially my tantalizing peach crumble." I could practically taste the tangy fruit, smothered in warm brown sugar and cinnamon, on the tip of my tongue. "Your little *hag* party, my dear, will be the bee's knees."

I chuckled at her depiction. With only our friends in attendance the first night, I hoped it would be a slow entry into the British world of tradition and celebration before the family arrived tomorrow, but after meeting the first two of Trenton's best friends, the word *slow,* hardly fit.

"You alright, dear?" Helen must've caught the dip in my chin.

"Yes, of course, I'm simply nervous that's all."

"I can assure you, doll, between Laura and myself, the delicacies are in reliable hands."

"Oh, yes, of course, that's not at all what I'm worried about."

"Then what?" Her curious stare pierced me.

"Uh, that maybe . . . maybe something might stop the wedding," I mumbled.

"Blimey, doll!" She threw her hands up into the air, and I jumped at her exuberance. "I've known that boy since he waddled around these floors in nappies, and I've never seen him jollier than he is with you." She grabbed my hands again. "I'm chuffed to bits over you two. It will be perfect; you'll see." Leading me toward the freezer she tittered, "and this should put a smile back on that dreary face." She opened the doors to showcase several portions of our wedding cake. "Take a gander at Laura's masterpiece."

I scanned the smooth iced tiers, the subsequent edible blooms, and delectable greenery with elation. The idea that this was *my* wedding cake thrilled me. I peeked back at Laura as she squeezed filling into mince pies. "Thank you, it's very beautiful."

"Pleasure." She responded without looking up.

I hugged Helen once more and departed through the back doors to the veranda. Standing at the balustrade, I inhaled the foreboding scent of rain and grimaced. Though no moisture had fallen yet, the dark clouds above hinted at its possibility. I watched the men in the gardens as they strung more lights through the bushes and tree branches. They, themselves, glared warily toward the sky, surely timing their tasks to avoid the pending downpour.

Having lived here for a year now, I'd grown used to the temperamental uncertainties of England's weather. However today, I sent a silent prayer upward to the meteorological Gods to show mercy for the week, especially a week from Saturday—my wedding day.

Another knock on the front door pulled me from my musings and another boisterous greeting led me to believe Trenton's next friend had arrived. I smiled wide. Trenton once told me his friends were more like family—more so than his *actual* family. The fact that they came to share in our happiness this week, warmed me, but a faint needling poked from within. *Will his family accept me as easily as his friends have*—an American, an employee, a woman with a complicated past?

I glanced down at my ring once more. In my heart this felt right . . . so why the baseless self-sabotage? Trenton regularly assured me of his love and devotion, it was unfair of me to doubt. I brushed the negative thoughts aside and with a genuine smile, joined him back inside.

Chapter 3

The well-known belief that women in numbers are a force to be reckoned with was about to be tested tonight at the hag dinner, marking the beginning of our ten-day house party. With my two best friends at my side, confidence surged as we readied our hair and makeup in my bedroom. Though my friendship with Gretchen grew while working together, my desire for real girlfriend-time was evident. I truly missed my roommates.

"It's great to see you smiling again, Kat." Maria finished with her final curl and sprayed half a bottle of finisher on her long dark tresses.

I smiled as Trenton's image came to mind. "Everything about this year has been amazing."

"And Trenton, he is . . . very attractive." Kelly put a glob of pomade in her hands, slapped them together, then rubbed it all over her head, spiking her hair. She cut her blond locks last year and now sported a short pixie style. She claimed she needed a drastic change, but I knew Kelly too well. She got tired of people treating her like an airhead. Her new look gave her an air of smart sophistication.

I grinned childishly at her compliment, recalling the introductions to my fiancé only an hour ago in the hallway where

Trenton appeared in a casual black blazer over a white button-up shirt and jeans. Both women were instantly taken by his striking good looks and natural charm. Though he teases often, he can be quite the polished gentleman when he wants to be.

"I don't think you'll be disappointed in his friends one bit." I added, taking my turn at the mirror, I shook my hair out to give it more volume. My natural wave bounced easily down my back. Since being in England, my normally brown locks had claimed a honey glow.

"So, which of his friends should I go after?" Maria's exotic features and spirited personality generally gave her an advantage in her pursuits, but it was her bold flirting that nearly always assured a direct hit.

"Hastings is a handsome blonde." I brushed mascara across my eyelashes. "Marlowe has breathtaking blue eyes, and Jonah reminds me of Devin Spencer from ASU—that guy we all battled over freshman year, although he seems a bit more reserved than the other two."

"And they're all single, right?"

"Yes, but sometimes there's a reason a man might be single at thirty." I laughed, trying to play the devil's advocate. I knew my friends well enough to know they sought nothing more than a fling but also knew little of the men's romantic habits or history.

"Hey, before we join the others, Maria and I have a gift for you." Kelly's wily grin surfaced as she pointed for me to sit down.

"You didn't have to do that."

"Well, I know we aren't having a traditional bachelorette party, and this type of gift isn't exactly appropriate in mixed company."

I raised one eyebrow with curiosity while Maria sat across from me on the settee. "You're going to love it!" She giggled as Kelly pulled a gift bag out from behind the desk.

"As your bridesmaids, we searched high and low for the perfect gifts."

"I'm flattered." My eyes warmed over them both as my nose stung, hinting tears weren't far behind. "Thank you both for coming; I couldn't imagine going through this week without you."

I opened the bag and removed the tissue paper. Peeking in, I laughed out loud. "You little devils!" I pulled out a small black lace negligee—a stunning and *perfect* bridal gift, yet my cheeks heated anyway. "This is really beautiful!"

"It should fit fine," Kelly added. "It's the same size as the swimsuit you left behind."

"Although, it doesn't really matter, does it?" Maria chuckled. "It's not going to stay on long anyway." Then pointed for me to keep looking. "That's not all."

I reached down and inside I found a new pair of *Jimmy Choo* stilettos, a perfume box, and a glass bottle filled with sand. I pulled them out. The silver shoes sparkled under the bright lights in the room. I ran my fingers past the long, pointed heel, across the delicate arch and back up the triple straps that elegantly intertwined upward. "These shoes are gorgeous."

"You're welcome." Maria stated with pride. "If I hadn't taken charge, you would be looking at a pair of unimpressive, blue *Converse* right now." She sneered Kelly's direction.

"I would've happily accepted either one." I winked at Kelly.

Putting the shoes down, I opened the box labeled *J'adore*. Gold overlay graced the neck of the pear-shaped bottle with an oversized pearl on top. Lifting the bubbled lid, I dabbed a small amount on my wrist and sniffed. "Oh, this is heavenly." I handed it off for them to try. "Jasmine. I'm sure of it." I searched the back of the box for the ingredients. "Turkish Damascus Rose, Indian Jasmine Sambac . . .floral and mysterious." I smiled. They knew me too well. My favorite fragrances were anything *Dior*. "Thank you."

"Last one." Kelly pointed out the final item. It was the least elegant in appearance of all the gifts. Filled nearly to the rim with sand, the rectangular bottle of clear glass sported a small red cork on top.

I glanced at my friends with intrigue. "What's this?"

"It's dirt." Kelly chuckled at her lack of explanation. Maria smiled and nudged her until she elaborated. "From Arizona. With you living here and your family in New York, you might not get back there too often. This way it will always be a part of you."

Overwhelmed with their thoughtfulness, I reached out and embraced my friends. Flashbacks of our years together, replayed effortlessly in my mind, causing a deep warmth to spread within my chest. There was no doubt without them, I would not be where I am. *They are my sisters.* "Thank you both so much, but most of all, thanks for being here."

"We wouldn't have missed this for anything."

Quickly touching up my make-up before we headed for the hall, I wound an arm through each of theirs, ready to take on the world . . . or at least the first night of my wedding week revelries.

Chapter 4

"Gentlemen," Trenton announced upon our arrival to the dining room. "Allow me to introduce Kat's best friends, Kelly and Maria." Though each of the men acknowledged the women dutifully, it only took seconds for attractions to be realized.

Once Kelly's blue eyes found Marlowe's, the magnetism that passed between them was indisputable. This didn't surprise me. Kelly, having been around fair-haired surfers most of her life, generally found herself attracted to the opposite—dark hair and olive skin. Though Kelly's blonde, tan looks often typecast her as a mindless ditz, she excelled in the college of engineering with her level-headed grit.

With no particular seating order for dinner, Trenton moved to the center of the table with me at his side. "Please, sit wherever you'd like." The inner leaves had been removed to allow for a smaller and more engaging setting.

As I watched Marlowe take the seat next to Kelly, I smiled. She was my right arm. I would not have survived ASU or the tragedy without her, and it just occurred to me now that she only left Arizona when I did. The sudden realization that she remained the extra year to be there for *me* warmed my heart.

Hastings wasted no time in holding a chair out for Maria to sit beside him. Maria, the complete opposite of Kelly in every way, sported a sassy, playful personality—with a determination to be single forever. She engaged in more "flings" our sophomore year than I racked up my entire life. Once she zoned in on Hastings, he didn't stand a chance.

Jonah Chapman, the last arrival, appeared to be as engaging and handsome as his friends with his tall form, short sandy-blonde hair, and decent build. He must surely leave women pining his absence, but unlike the other two, he didn't show a strong interest in either woman.

Trenton leaned in as the first course was being served. The mulligatawny soup nearly drew my eyes away from him. Its spicy curry aroma tempted me far more than I expected. He lightheartedly pointed to his friends. "Well, that didn't take long."

I laughed and observed the two men fighting for their chosen's attention. "I'm sorry Isabel cancelled. Then it would be even, three men and three women."

"Think nothing of it." Trenton took a sip of his drink. "Jonah is quite particular in his tastes. His weakness is for tall, dominant women. Though he's just as entertaining as the others in society, his romantic life is complicated. He's had an on and off girlfriend for nearly ten years."

"Ten years? Why hasn't he married her?"

"Well, in truth, we all vowed to *never* marry." His lip lifted in a devilish grin. "I have been thoroughly chastised to no end for breaking the pact."

"I'm sorry." I squeezed his arm.

"I'm not." He chuckled.

"Your friends must hate me."

"Hardly. After meeting you, they are surely reconsidering their own matrimonial standing."

"But we barely spoke."

"Your words were not what drew their attention." Trenton chuckled.

"You're such a rake." I teased.

"A rake? Are you attempting to use my British terminology against me?" He teased back. "Truthfully, they are all here for a dash of fun. I doubt any of my mates are looking for a long-term relationship with anyone, much less an American."

"Is that what you thought too?" I smiled coyly. Trenton told me often how surprised he was at how quickly he fell for me.

"I genuinely tried to resist you." He reached for me and nudged me closer to his lips. "It was impossible." He kissed me gently.

"Oh, no!" Hastings hollered from across the table, banging his silverware against a glass. "None of that. You'll make us all quite jealous."

Trenton kissed me once more before he leaned back. "I am at my fiancé's beck and call, mates, if she insists on kissing me wherever and whenever, I am at her mercy!" Then the corners of his lips twitched as he gestured to my friends. "And you have every right to engage in a similar practice . . . but not with my fiancé." The room erupted in laughter, and the men's eyes went straight to the women. Though my friends rarely colored, both sets of cheeks turned a light shade of pink.

As dinner progressed, a beautiful presentation of roasted duck appeared before me. Garnished with caramelized onions, lemons, and smoked bacon, I found it hard to follow the conversation in the dining room with such a delectable feast nearby. Helen warned me the dinner would not be forgotten anytime soon and she was right, rounding out the meal with cornbread stuffing and roasted potatoes dipped in sunflower and garlic oil.

When dialogue flickered from seriously engaged to light and friendly, much of the talk then turned into a competition to see which sets of friends could humiliate Trenton and I the most. *Kelly and Maria won.* Clearing my eyes from the laughing tears that sprang forth, I begged Kelly to stop before she finished the tale of my one attempt at parasailing off the beach at Rocky Point, Mexico.

"You should've seen the way she kicked the poor instructor when she landed." Kelly cried. "I'm positive he'll never walk normal again."

The others roared in laughter. "In my defense," I pouted. "He was standing directly in front of me."

A flash of green unexpectedly caught my eye near the archway that led into the hallway. My eyes blinked hard toward the fleeting image as my mind struggled to make sense of who or what I saw. I shook my head and wiped my eyes. *Did I . . . did I imagine that?* My lips pulled tight at the very thought. The hallucination appeared to be a woman with long black hair wearing a gown—a nineteenth-century style gown? My hand flew to my mouth with a light gasp.

"Kat?" Trenton inquired. "Are you alright?"

I nodded slowly but kept my eyes on the now empty doorway, expecting the delusion to suddenly reappear.

Trenton rubbed my arm. "What do you say?"

"Um," I shook my head, trying to make sense of his words without appearing crazy. "Sorry, I didn't hear the question."

His eyebrows furrowed. I quickly replaced my puzzled look with a smile. He pointed to his friends. "I believe a challenge has been issued."

"A challenge?" I glanced around. I somehow missed the gist of their newest conversation.

"Yes." Trenton's brows no longer bent, but his countenance still revealed concern. "They suggested a wager for the cricket match. Since you and I are on the same team, do you accept?"

I bit my inner cheek. I knew the traditional games planned were unlike anything I'd ever done before, but I also knew Trenton was adept at them all. "Yes, of course."

"The losing team must serve the winning team during the picnic."

"Well then," I smiled. "I guess we'd better win."

When the lively banter resumed, my mind flitted back to the image I briefly spotted in the doorway. "Excuse me for a moment."

"Are you sure you're alright?" Trenton inquired again.

"Yes, I promise. I won't be long." Stepping out into the corridor, I judiciously scanned each direction. There was no trace of the mysterious figure, I wasn't even sure I'd really seen. Moving carefully about, I only entered common rooms, but nothing seemed amiss. *Could I have imagined her?*

I shook my head. The woman could not possibly be who my mind alluded to—the vile, infuriating Margaret. The deceitful, lying schemer who made my life in 1878 a living hell. Memories emerged of the times our paths crossed—the library with Merritt, the dark hallway with her spiteful threats, and her attempts to stop me from performing CPR, to save Merritt's life.

I shuddered.

Impossible.

I must be tired.

Quickly forcing such irritating recollections aside, I made my way back to the dining room just in time for Helen's delectable peach crumble.

After dinner, we moved to the sitting room. A place, where up until now, had been nearly non-existent for me, solely because of its purpose to entertain—something I never did at Charlock.

I silently thanked Gretchen and Sara for their efforts to prepare the space for our guests. Once the sheets were removed and the dusting commenced, the intimate ambiance surpassed even my expectations. For whatever reason, neither Miss Campbell or Trenton had included this room previously in the tour and since the former curator's departure, I never questioned their reasons . . . until now.

Scanning the room, I took in the pale-green wallpaper and how it contrasted nicely against the velvet rose cushioned furniture that rested atop carved wooden bases. I'm not sure which previous Mrs. Gilford was responsible for the drawing room's decor, but whoever it was had a distinct eye for color coordination.

The crystal sconces around the perimeter created the perfect amount of light to the areas in which the sole chandelier could not reach, and the artwork displayed on the walls was just enough to entice interest but not distract from conversation. The stunning area rug appeared to have Persian ties and covered most of the tiled floor, except where both the piano and harp stood. And from the way the instruments were tucked neatly away in one corner, it led me to believe they had endured decades of neglect, though oddly enough, a man came regularly to tune all the musical instruments in the manor on the off chance they would be needed in a moment's notice.

Outside the plated glass windows with their stylishly fringed draperies, darkened skies threatened rain, so a fire was lit inside the quaint hearth, though nothing within transpired to cause a chill. The peaceful glow below the marble mantle warmed us upon entry as our guests settled down between the plush sofas and high back chairs.

Trenton sat down casually next to me on one of the sofas and linked his hands in his lap. "Tell me ladies . . ." His lips curled upward in a devious smile. "I'm curious to know what Kat was like when you met her."

"Quite severe, honestly." Kelly spoke first. "That first day when we were introduced in our college dorm, I wasn't sure if she would hug me or fight me."

"Fight you?" He chuckled. Crossing his legs at the ankles, he draped one arm over my shoulders. "That tough, huh?"

Kelly ignored my threatening stare. Though I had shared much of my personal life with Trenton, I hadn't shared *all* of it. "Have you ever sparred with her?" She questioned.

"Does wrestling count?" He squeezed my shoulder. I sighed, bracing for what was sure to come.

Kelly snickered. "No, I mean boxing."

Trenton's head whipped around first, but similar expressions of astonishment from his friends sent me cowering. "That was a long time ago," I muttered, rolling my eyes. I didn't want to have this conversation.

"Long time as in childhood or long time as in a couple of years ago?" Trenton's eyes were hard to read.

Kelly answered for me. "She's quite the fighter, lover boy. She taught self-defense classes through college." She rubbed her cheek and winked as if the one I planted on her a few years ago still stung. "There are actually a lot of women who know how to protect themselves thanks to her."

My hand covered my eyes. It wasn't that I didn't want Trenton to know this about me, my worry stemmed more from what his family might think if this somehow leaked out after their arrival. I assumed their lofty expectations already swayed negatively after they learned I grew up in Midtown as the daughter of a deli owner—far from Park Avenue.

"It wasn't a big deal, just a way to make some spending cash between classes." I shrugged. "But the more time I spent hiking the less time I trained in the gym." I actually hadn't thrown a punch in over two years; unless I counted the one against Margaret in 1878. *Margaret.* Why was her memory resurfacing all of a sudden?

"Why didn't you tell me, love?" Trenton's expression turned surprisingly pleased.

"Really?" I threw him an exhausted look.

"Certainly! We could've added it to the games. I would've thoroughly enjoyed seeing you spar."

"And exactly how do you think your parents would have reacted to such a sport?" My expression remained firm. "I can see it now . . . the whispers and talk of the lunatic pugilist from New York who somehow weaseled her way into the prim and proper Gilford family."

He chuckled and wrapped his arms around me tighter. "Hardly weaseled."

Jonah leaned forward and rubbed his chin. "Well, it's not a bad idea, Kat. His parents could certainly use a good dose of pragmatism." He shot Trenton a knowing look. "It would keep his mum from turning the games into politesse for gentility, that's for sure."

"I, myself, would not mind seeing a boxing row." Marlowe laughed out loud. "I could place another wager." Then winked at Kelly.

"I wouldn't tempt her, Marlowe." Kelly snorted. "She has a serious right hook."

His eyebrows furrowed. "And you would know this . . . how?"

Kelly laughed. "I was her sparring partner."

His eyes lit up with admiration as if his attraction to her grew ten times stronger with this knowledge. "Now this I *must* see!"

"No," I countered, surprised at how quickly this conversation spiraled out of control. "I'm getting married, I hardly want a black eye on my wedding day."

"When have you ever had a black eye?" Maria quipped. "You were rarely on the receiving end."

I frowned. My friends were not helping. "Besides," I glanced at Trenton. "I left that life behind in Arizona."

Trenton's eyes met mine. He must've felt my body stiffen under his touch for he quickly changed the subject. "Kelly, Maria, have either one of you been on a horse before?"

Maria shook her head. I knew her to be against any animal larger than herself. Kelly was the only one who responded, "Yes, twice."

Marlowe swiftly interjected. "Well, allow me to add a third, Kelly." He beamed. "Would you join me for a ride tomorrow?"

"I'd love to." She answered with a wide grin.

Trenton affirmed. "Sound plan, mate. Once the additional guests arrive, they might monopolize the stables." Then he turned to me. "What about you? Would you like to go out in the morning before things get chaotic?"

I smiled. "Absolutely."

Not to be outdone by his friends, Hastings spoke up next. "Maria, love, would you do me the honor as well?"

She shook her head with more force this time. "Nope, I don't think so." Lifting one finger, she waved it vigorously side to side. "Sorry, *love,* I'm staying on the ground."

Hastings' mouth flew open. He had likely never been turned down for anything with those golden-brown eyes. I chuckled, but the men in the room roared in laughter as Hastings' sensationalized the dismissal. "I have been thoroughly rejected." He pounded his tightly balled fist against his heart, then winked Maria's direction. She tried to stifle her growing smile but failed.

Before England, I'd never been on a horse before. However, during the months of our engagement, Trenton met the challenge of teaching me with absolute gentleness, considering my only previous interaction with the animal came in the memory of Merritt falling off Captain.

I instantly fell in love with the sport, but more specifically, with his docile mare, Darby. Mild and obedient, she quickly grew familiar with my needs, and even though I could've graduated to a faster steed over time, I stuck with Darby.

With the families arriving in the early afternoon, riding would be a wonderful distraction to the lump that somehow took residence in my throat. Every time I allowed myself to think of the pending introduction to Trenton's parent's, his grandfather, and other extended family, I felt overwhelmed and inadequate. Surely they would not understand why Trenton, their handsome, rich, and desired son would choose *me*. I barely understood why myself.

As Trenton walked me to my room later that night, he walked slower than normal. I loved that our goodbyes were as dreaded for him as they were for me.

"I have to say I'm quite impressed that you box." The way his smile curved on his lips disarmed me from becoming defensive. There was still much about my past that felt like another life, and a portion of that I wanted to bury with Jeff.

"Not exactly boxing like you imagine . . . you know, no Tyson Fury."

"You know Tyson Fury?" His lower lip dropped. "He's British."

"Well, if you're in the sport, you watch the champions, specifically their moves and strategy, but it wasn't like that. I wasn't in the ring for money or anything. I just wanted to help other women." I bit my lip. "My brothers and cousins were protective of me but insisted on teaching me how to defend myself. Growing up in the city, I would get into small neighborhood scraps but once I understood the art of using your mind to direct your fists, I wasn't messed with much after that."

"Why did you stop?"

"I . . . found other interests."

Though Trenton never stopped me from talking about Jeff, it wasn't something I always felt I needed to bring up. I had stopped fighting because Jeff helped me channel some of that raw energy into outdoor activities. After his death, however, when anger consumed me, my desire to release that energy through my fists emerged more than ever, but I feared my irrepressible rage wouldn't allow me to stop. I didn't dare spar at that point . . . especially with Kelly.

"Self-defense, huh?"

"Yeah. ASU experienced a rash of date rapes when I first got there, and even though karate shops could be found at every strip mall, they didn't necessarily meet the needs of college girls. I made arrangements with the school to teach classes in one of the training rooms at the stadium."

"So, did it help? Did the attacks stop?"

"The numbers went down significantly. I don't know if it had anything to do with me, but I must've taught a couple hundred girls." My lips lifted into a contented smile on their own. "I really hope it did."

"That's truly amazing, love. You should be proud."

"I was proud back then. I'm simply different now."

Trenton stopped me before we reached my room. Pulling me directly in front of him, he rested his hands tenderly on my hips. "I want to know everything about you. I don't want you to ever be afraid of losing me if I learn something about your past that, in your mind, might not be civilized."

My hands rested atop his arms while my fingers fidgeted against the soft, luxurious fabric of his suit coat. Glancing downward and away from all the signs of his affluent image, I sighed. "But you are part of this world that has expectations, Trenton. I'm afraid of disappointing you or your family."

"Kat." He let go of my waist and pulled my hands up to his lips. "You could never disappoint me. It's your unwavering spirit that drew me in from the beginning. I love that you are different than all the women I have ever been acquainted with. I love that you don't mind getting dirty, or roughhousing, and I don't mind that you have strange talents." He chuckled on that last one. "Don't ever feel that you can't be honest with me—your honesty is what made me fall in love with you to begin with. You risked everything when you told me about your time spent in 1878." He took a shallow breath. "I realize I've given you a reason to doubt me because of that, but I hope I have proven my devotion to you since."

My heart quickened under his words. How could I ever question him? He was as hopelessly in love with me as I was with him. Releasing my hands, he drew me toward him and kissed me goodnight.

Nine days . . . I repeated in my head . . . only nine days before we never have to say goodnight outside of a bedroom again.

Chapter 5

Friday, 13 May 2011

I should have slept well.

My elaborately cushioned bed never failed to provide a comfortable night's sleep and with the way Trenton's parting kiss lingered on my lips, it should've easily carried me through the night—only I jarred awake before dawn. The thought of meeting his family today invaded my dreams and pilfered a restful night.

I arose early and paced my room. Settling my thoughts on the upcoming ride, I trusted it would bring me the desired peace before the pandemonium hit.

Trenton's parents, Trenton Gilford II and Juliana, his grandfather Trenton the first, two aunts, and an uncle were coming sometime around ten o'clock this morning. A half dozen Gilford cousins and my parents were due to arrive by early afternoon.

Unfortunately, neither one of my brothers could make it to my wedding. Mike's wife is due with their second child in less than a month and Kent, though he tried, could not miss more than a couple days of his medical residency, not long enough for a flight over seas. My uncles stayed back in New York to run the deli so my parents could travel, and though my *allies* were small, they were strong. I chuckled lightly at my reference to the military term. Though I had no reason to believe they were coming to *war*, just the mere thought of people nearby who genuinely knew and loved me brought forth a great deal of comfort.

Arriving at the side window, I glanced out. With the climate so sporadic, I feared the ominous skies from the day before had finally unleashed. A slow pattering of rain rapped steadily against the blurred pane. Disappointment cultivated in my chest, knowing the miserable weather could alter some of the week's events since most were planned to be outside in the elements.

Mesmerized by the simple glide of each raindrop as it hit the glass, I rested my head against the wooden frame, then stilled. Movement outside caught my eye. The figure of a person appeared, racing from the house and through the gardens. I wiped the remnants of sleep from my eyes and leaned inward for a better look, but the person had vanished. *Who in the world would be outside running in the rain at this hour?*

I had not met any of Trenton's extended family yet, nor had I been notified of any late-night arrivals. Though I wouldn't have put it past Hastings or Marlow to be up and about causing mischief, this person undoubtedly wore . . . *a gown.*

I hustled down the hall and into the boot room to find my rain jacket and a pair of rubber boots I often used in wet weather. Why I felt the sudden need to go dashing into the rain was beyond me, but an irritating pinch twinged somewhere deep inside my chest. Something felt off about what I'd seen.

Tucking my hair under the hood, I shot out the back door, down the veranda steps, and ran the same direction as the stranger.

The rain fell harder and pelted ruthlessly against the only exposed part of my body—my face.

I studied the grounds. With no one in sight, I could only assume the person bolted for the closest refuge—the stables. Regardless of our scheduled ride in an hour, I doubted anyone from our party would willingly come out this early in such a barrage.

Once past the heavy wooden doors of the stable, I pushed my hood back for better sight. Droplets fell to the ground all around me as I shook the excess water off me. The overpowering scent of horsehide and manure swirled about, but my focus remained. After wiping my eyes of the extra moisture, I tiptoed cautiously and scanned the stalls stealthily through the dimness. The gloomy clouds prevented any natural light to stream in or aid in my search. Little sound surfaced aside from an occasional whinny from a horse; even the grooms hadn't yet budged from their quarters above, but to their defense, they weren't needed for another thirty minutes.

"Hello?" I called aloud, tamping down any hesitation that wanted to surface. "Is somebody out here?" I continued moving forward, but the squeaky sloshing of my rubber boots hardly concealed my approach.

I peered past each separation, beyond the horses, the gear, and the odorous bales of hay. When I reached the last stall, I stiffened in place. Gripping a pitchfork with both hands, the person in question, thrust it perilously in my direction. I jumped backward and gasped. "No! No, no, no!" The words slipped through my stuttering lips. *This cannot be!* Pulling my wet hair out of my face, I rubbed my eyes for further clarification while my heart pounded wildly through my chest. Long black hair clung to the woman's face and against her wet garments. An all too familiar scowl formed on her mouth as she shoved the pitchfork forward, once more, toward me. I hastily dodged out of range and threw my hands up in defense. Growling, she bared her teeth like a feral animal.

"Margaret!" I yelled. "Stop!"

Her cheeks paled and her jaw dropped as she fumbled with the weapon. Grappling for a tighter grasp, she shrieked. "H—how are you acquainted with me?"

"Margaret." My jaw tightened. "Put the pitchfork down."

"Who are you?" Her voice squeaked weaker than the *Maggot* I remembered. I focused on her eyes. The smoky gray pupils from my memory were tinted with a hint of red. Unsightly lines sagged beneath her lower lashes, appearing as though she had aged a decade since I had last seen her. *Maybe it's not her and only a distant relative.*

"Take your leave, miscreant!" She screeched in a tone only appropriate for hunting fowl.

Nope, it's her.

I tried to sound calm under my chattering teeth. The rain that had pooled on my hood slid down my collar and dripped down my back, causing a chill. "Margaret, it's me, Kat." I took one step forward. "I mean Katharine, remember? Miss Katharine."

Her eyes narrowed, and a nasty grimace covered her face. "Katharine? Th—the governess?"

I waited for her forked tongue to hiss when she spoke my name. "Yes, the governess for Lizzy and Abby."

"What devilry has transpired?" She wailed. "Where are my father and brother?" She gritted her teeth tightly and frowned as if

I were to blame for her current circumstance. "And why are you clad in breeches . . . like—like a man?"

I shook my head, yet kept an eye on her. I hardly trusted her without a weapon, much less with one. For a brief moment, panic seized my chest and I shuddered at the alarming thought that crossed my mind. What if *I* somehow fell down the stairs again? *What if I am the one who is in the wrong time?*

"Wait here," I cried. Blood rushed to my head as I sprinted toward the entrance of the stables. Tears teetered at the corners of my eyes at the very possibility of being separated from Trenton. Though there was much I discovered about myself during my jaunt back in time, I had little desire to relive it.

Peering out, I scanned for anything that assured me of my whereabouts. "Cars! I see cars!" I exhaled with relief. My fingers wiped the growing moisture from my eyes, then the sobering thought emerged, if I was in *my* present day, Margaret couldn't possibly be.

I peeked back inside, placing my hand over my forehead and groaned. "This cannot be happening . . . not today! Not ever, but especially not today!" I sluggishly turned around, and when I walked toward Margaret once more, I did so with lead in my feet. "Why now?" Of all the days, weeks, or years she could show up, it just *happens* to be the week of my wedding? *I can't deal with this.* I can barely process the notion of Trenton's family arriving shortly, much less a nemesis from my past.

By the time I made my way back to the last stall once more, I had chewed through one fingernail and was close to tearing a second, but no closer to a solution over the pitchfork-wielding fiend. Facing her, I kept a safe distance and sighed. "We need to talk."

"Where is my father?" She ignored my attempt to speak rationally and prodded the weapon toward me again. "Where are Merritt's guests?"

"What are you talking about?"

"For heaven's sake . . ." She cried aloud. "What impiety is occurring here?" Her neck muscles strained as she took another step forward, but her drenched hem caught beneath her shoe and she tumbled face first to the ground. Swiftly, she clamored to her feet. "I demand answers!"

"Demand?" Both my hands rested on my hips as I fought the desire to grin at the pitiful sight before me. Mud splotched across her nose and cheeks and broken pieces of hay grass poked out from her hair. She resembled more of a wet sheep dog that had rolled in the dirt than the entitled priss from my memory. "You have no demands here, missy. This is *my* house, *my* stables."

"This is the Gilford estate, you little wretch. Merritt's house, grounds, and stables."

"Yes." My eyes fired up. "It was! A hundred years ago!"

A brief flash of terror rose in her eyes, then melted into anger once more. "You lying *cyprian*. Cease this debauchery at once!"

All the buried irritation I felt for this woman rose with record haste. The fire in my chest radiated up my neck and heated my cheeks. I had just told Trenton that my fighting days were past me, yet my fingers slowly curled into fists. "You're a piece of work, Margaret." I thrust a finger in her direction. "Something has happened to you, and I . . ." pointing back to myself, I continued. "I am the only one that can help you."

Her skin grew pale, paler than when I first arrived. She leapt forward with the pitchfork, a look of hatred clearly evident as she tried to stab me. I batted it down forcefully and pulled it out of her hands. Throwing it over into the next stall, I hollered. "Stop acting like a child."

She buried her face in her trembling hands and muttered nonsense for several seconds. Somehow, seeing her here in this state made a part of me feel sorry for her. She was lost in a different time. She appeared confused, vulnerable, and terrified—something I knew all too well. I reached forward and tapped her arm, but just as quickly as my sympathy arose, it dissipated the moment she spun around and lunged at me with her claw-like fingernails. Glimpsing the faded scars on the back of my hands, I was reminded of her success the first time she attacked.

I dodged to the side and swiftly debated my next move. I really didn't want to hit her again, but the moment she grabbed a chunk of my hair and pulled, all bets were off. I squeezed her tightly clenched hand between both of mine, long enough to force her to release, then restraining her wrists to prevent further damage, I rotated and shoved my hip into her stomach, forcing her down to the ground. She fell to her back with a thud, bringing her screams to a sudden halt. The toss had left her winded and silent.

Fuming, I stood over her and pointed my finger at her chest. "Forget it. I am *not* going to help you, you selfish piece of ancient trash." I turned away, struggling to catch my breath. As I stormed out of the stables, I could feel the heat rising in my throat. I couldn't quite identify if I was angrier over the fact that she was here, or the fact that she attacked me.

The sloshing of my boots against the wet grass, did little to distract my mind. My frustration grew with each passing minute. I didn't even bother to cover my head as I stomped back into the house, and slammed the door, sure that the smoke that rose steadily from my ears left a trail. Everything I felt toward that woman from before, flooded back in a heartbeat.

Inside the boot room once again, I paced heatedly. "Who does she think she is?" I muttered partially to myself and partially to an imaginary audience. "There is no way I will help such a person." Stopping and peeking through the window, my irritation festered. "But what if she shows up inside the house when our guests are here?" Fury clouded my logic. "What if she somehow reveals she's from the past and I know her?" I grabbed a towel and wiped the moisture from my face. "Trenton's family will think I'm nuts. Then what if they do everything in their power to stop him from marrying me?" My fists clenched. *Is it possible to have her committed? Maybe I could drag her off to a mental hospital.*

I wiped my nose. Tears brimmed at the edges of my eyes as a raw agonizing ache settled in the pit of my stomach. Memories of the morning I woke up at Charlock Manor after my fall, materialized. Scared and alone, I had to put my faith and trust in others. Everything about this situation has blurred my judgement . . . could I really turn my back on her?

I am not that cruel.

What if the Gilford's had thought the same thing about me—or Joanne? What if they sent me to be locked up somewhere? *Aghhh.* I groaned. I must control this somehow. Shaking my head, I pulled my jacket tight across my torso. I can't leave her alone. I stepped back out and onto the path, the very same time a horse bolted from the stable in a frenzy. Margaret sat on top and a confused groom came running out the doors holding his head. I rushed over to him.

"Miss Shelton," he gasped, leaning over, and braced his hands on his knees. "I don't know what happened." The man fought for breath. "Th—this woman came out of nowhere, hit me on the head with a pitchfork and took Mr. Gilford's horse." He rubbed the side of his skull. "I only prepared him moments ago for your ride."

"Are you okay?"

"Yes," he said, straightening to his full height. "I'm fine. It just stunned me is all."

"Are you well enough to help me get Darby saddled?"

"Certainly, but what should we do about the woman?"

"I'll take care of it."

After my personal saddle was strapped on my favorite horse, I led her outside and in the direction I had seen Margaret ride. Though the rain had now settled to a mere trickle, the saturated ground revealed fresh shoe impressions from Achilles and a clear path to find him.

Where does she think she's going? I wondered. It's not like she could go home. I knew her family owned an estate in the county, but it wasn't close by. She couldn't possibly think to go there, would she? I increased my speed to make up the distance. I was no expert rider but I had steered Darby to a full run more than once.

I only slowed when Achilles appeared riderless near the far end of the property and close to the Hampstead ruins. I had only ventured out this far twice and both times were with Trenton.

I remembered this to be the site of Merritt's accident with his father's horse at the young age of eleven. Though Merritt walked away unharmed, Ivan was put down from his injuries. It was the sad story he shared with me on the boat. When I didn't see Margaret with Achilles, I couldn't help but fear the worst.

"Whoa." I slowed Darby down. Once she arrived next to Achilles, I jumped off and patted her neck. "Stay here, girl."

Glancing around, my sight was restricted from the heavily vined enclosure and thick vegetation. Hardly the place to take shelter with its lack of a roof overhead. *Why did she choose to come here?*

I meandered the terrain carefully. The uneven landscape was heavily dotted with patches of shrubbery and wild grass, both of which shrouded boulders the size of small children. A lone path wound jaggedly past the dilapidated wall that bordered the old stone stronghold, known to be the remnants of a thirteenth-century medieval castle. A handful of fragmented chambers stretched into various wings from the imposing central tower. Though the charcoal-covered vestiges were hauntingly romantic when I explored the grounds with Trenton, without him, it was just haunting.

I stepped forward with vast awareness that a crazy woman from the nineteenth century could be wielding a weapon and ready to strike at any moment. I doubted she brought the pitchfork with her, but as vengeful as she was, her weapon of choice could be anything she laid her hands upon.

I stopped when I reached the outermost stone fortification. She crouched weakly against the crumbling barrier. I sucked in my breath. Whenever I had interacted with Margaret in the past, her tall, shapely frame intimidated me. Between her long black hair and deep-set eyes, she had the ability to unnerve even the strongest of opponents, but here at this moment, she huddled in a corner like that of a frightened child. Her legs were pulled tight underneath her dress, and her arms shielded her chest protectively.

I approached with caution. Her reactions thus far spoke clearly of her unpredictability. "Margaret," I whispered softly. The kindness in my voice took me by surprise, though she didn't raise her head. I stepped closer. Her vulnerability laid bare.

It reminded me of the night of my release from the Gilford's and my ensuing homelessness. Of course, the reason for my turn-out sat right in front of me. My mind flitted over the idea of sweet revenge. If I wanted to, I could exact a severe retaliation for the pain she had caused, but the thought only lasted a brief second. I could never live with myself knowing the harm I could inflict and especially never find joy in her misery. We now shared an unlikely bond.

"Margaret?" I moved within a foot of her now. "Please let me help you."

She finally glanced up but sniffled hard. The way her mud-caked hair strung wildly across her face reminded me of a horror movie I'd seen years ago. "Let's get inside where it's warm, and I will explain what's happened to you." I extended my hand and tried to meet her eyes. "I'm warning you though . . ." I sighed. "What I have to say won't be easy to hear." As if she didn't hear me, she remained completely still. I shifted anxiously in place. Though my patience wore thin, I kept Merritt and Lizzy's admirable examples of tolerance foremost in my mind. If they could endure *my* peculiar behavior, I could at the very least try harder for their sake.

"Margaret, come on. Let me get you back to the house."

Refusing my outstretched hand, she maneuvered awkwardly to her knees. I bit my lip to keep from smiling and quickly smoothed my face as she attempted, quite clumsily, to get to her feet. Once she managed, she brushed her hands over her skirt like a gently bred lady, despite the reality she faced. Pulling her hair back, she twisted it into a loose braid and through tight lips snapped in my direction. "Fine, I'll go!"

I wrinkled my nose and fought the desire to change my mind and push her back down. I watched as she angled her head upward and walked as if she held a board tightly between her knees. Only the sound of her wet skirts swishing filled the space. I stared at her empty spot for several seconds before I turned around to join her. Mumbling low, I cursed my fate. "I can't believe this is happening."

Back on the horses and only a short trot away from the manor, a new challenge emerged—to get Margaret into the house unseen. A nearly impossible feat now that Trenton and his friends were walking from the house toward the stables. I watched as Marlowe slapped a hand on Trenton's back and somewhere in the exchange, Trenton's laugh could be faintly heard, even from our distance.

"Whoa." I slowed our horses to a walk and kept them out of sight behind a row of trees. "We can't go back to the stables."

"Whyever not?"

"Because you can't be seen."

"I may appear untidy now, but as you're well aware, I'm capable of absolute elegance." She lifted her chin high into the air. "I have no cause to hide."

"*I* have reason to hide you." I brought Darby to a stop. "Margaret, look at me." I shot her a stern gaze.

She rolled her eyes and only faced me after I repeated myself. "You need to listen to me." I pleaded. "It doesn't matter if you hate me and I hate you, it's imperative you do as I say." I pointed to the path. "We need to stay behind this tree line and go to the opposite side of the house."

Margaret protruded her bottom lip in defiance but followed me anyway. I led the horses forward and made sure we stayed hidden until after the men were in the stables, then tore off in a gallop toward the rear gardens. Once we arrived at the edge, I hopped off Darby in a swift descent and motioned for Margaret to do the same. Glancing around for privacy, I clasped her wrist and ran ineptly toward the veranda.

"Pray tell, why must we run? My feet ache dreadfully." She yanked her arm from my grasp and headed toward a bench. "I must sit." Catching a glimpse of her feet, I noticed her slippers were nearly worn through. Despite my commiseration, we could not remain still.

"You can't sit now, Margaret, we need to go inside." Peering around anxiously, I feared being seen. Then tried a different approach. "Look, you're shaking. Come inside and get warm. I'll get a bath ready for you."

"A bath?" Her eyes lit up.

"Yes." I reached for her again and sluggishly hauled her damp form up the veranda steps.

Inching my way indoors, I waited until we could move unseen and continued the rapid pace down the hallway. Though her feet moved forward, it wasn't without a struggle. Her height gave her an advantage, but my determination prevailed.

The moment we were both inside my bedroom, I closed the door and leaned heavily against it. Finally taking a breath, I stared at the woman who stood disoriented before me. *Why can't this be a dream?* I would even be okay if it were a nightmare, one that I only needed to wake up from for it to disappear. I rubbed my eyes. Margaret steeled her face as if preparing for battle.

What am I going to do with her now?

A loud knock vibrated against my head and shuddered me from my stupor.

Chapter 6

"Knock, knock." Kelly's voice rang through the door. My eyes flashed to Margaret whose expression remained impassive.

"Don't say a word," I whispered through gritted teeth.

I cracked the door open only a smidgeon.

"Hey, looks like the weather is getting better. Aren't we going riding this morning?" She maneuvered her head to see me more clearly. I kept a solid grasp on the door handle with one hand and the frame with the other.

"Oh, actually," I attempted confidence, yet my voice squeaked. "I went walking earlier and think I might've caught a cold." I fake sneezed.

As expected, Kelly eyed me warily. "Why were you out walking in the rain?"

"Oh, uh, I had trouble sleeping. I thought it was a good idea at the time, but now I'm really exhausted . . ." My eyes dipped to my thumb as it rubbed against the door handle. It was much easier looking anywhere but at her. "Would you let Trenton know I'm sorry?" *Dang I forgot. The horses are next to the garden.* I glanced back up but focused on the tiny mole on her left cheekbone. "Um, actually, if you don't mind . . . would you also let him know that his horse is near the garden behind the house?"

"What's going on with you?" *Shoot.* Kelly knew me too well.

"I'm not feeling too good right now. Sorry, love you." I quickly shut the door knowing a more credible excuse would need to come later, but at the same time, I was fully aware I had no idea what that excuse would be. I never told anyone, other than Trenton, about my time travel experience and despite the bizarre situation I currently found myself in . . . that conclusion could never change. I just needed to figure this out on my own.

Circling back around, I found one of my wardrobe closets wide open and an oblivious Margaret buried in half of my clothes. I blinked rapidly in response. Pulling my lips tight, it took every effort to restrain a response.

"Deplorable," she grumbled. A handful of blouses were gripped in one hand with a scarf looped around her neck, and her other arm shoved up a pantleg. When she peered over to me, her face revealed sheer mortification. She dropped the blouses and held up my black bra. "And what the devil is this?"

I pounded my forehead lightly with my fist. "Heaven help me."

"Heaven help you?" She droned. "It is I who cannot comprehend this madness."

"Listen, let's just start with a bath, then I'll figure out what to do with you."

"What to do with me?"

"Yes, Margaret." My chest tightened under the additional pressure. "You *can't* stay here." I pointed to the floor. "You don't belong here."

She heatedly threw the clothes onto the bed. "I would've belonged here!" She cried. "If you weren't so meddlesome and intrusive."

"Me?" My fingers pinched the bridge of my nose. "Just how do you figure that?"

"*You* persuaded Merritt to break the engagement. *You* are the reason I'm ruined."

"Ruined? What are you talking about?" I struggled to follow her accusations.

Her babbling continued as she paced the room. Her arms flailing wildly as she spoke. "Within a week of Merritt's visit to my Aunt's townhouse in London, I didn't receive Lady Avondale's promised invitation to tea, the Chapman's rescinded their offer to share their box at the opera, Mrs. Hughes told Lady Bell I was unfit to be seen at Amelia Watson's coming out, and now I have been informed I am to be the footrest to a pompous old fool because of his wretched 10,000 a year—"

"Margaret, stop." I held up my hands. "I have no idea what you are talking about. All I know is that Merritt didn't want to marry you."

Her cheeks flared bright red, but when she glanced away, a slight sheen glossed her eyes.

I cringed. *I could have said that differently.*

"Summon a carriage promptly," her voice cracked. "I wish to return home." She stomped toward the door, but I blocked her way.

"I *wish* you could, but you can't." I bit my inner cheek and seized an additional breath before I spoke. "I didn't mean for it to come out like that, I'm sorry."

She didn't respond.

I sighed, recognizing my need to be the rational one here. Arguing over Merritt's intentions were clearly the least important concern at the moment. Somehow, I needed to explain what has happened to her. Despite my good intentions, any explanation would be difficult to hear. "Please, just have a seat." I pointed to the settee. "Let me get a bath ready for you."

She glanced down at her wet clothes and nodded.

Once she settled down, I stepped into the lavvy and turned the faucet handles. At the sound of rushing water, Margaret flew in and joined me. She stopped abruptly when she caught sight of the water gushing out from the spout.

"Curse me to Hades," she whispered and ran her hand underneath the running water. Screaming, she yanked her hand back so swiftly that she tumbled to the floor.

"What happened?" I cried, fearing she burned her hand, but once I touched the water myself, I knew that to be impossible. It was only mildly hot.

"It—it's warm water?" Her wide eyes glanced between me and the tub.

"Yes. It's a bath." Irritation trickled in. "I do know you are familiar with that word because I took a few in this very house in 1878." She missed my sarcasm. I cupped her elbow and helped her to her feet. "A lot of things have changed over time." I hesitated and took a moment to realize how profound that statement was—even from the time I spent in the past to now, the world was nearly a different place.

She touched the water again. A slow smile formed on her lips.

I rummaged through a small wicker basket on the side and dropped a pineapple scented bath bomb in.

She reached for it, soaking her sleeve all over again. When her hand returned to the surface, only crumbles of the bomb remained in between her fingers. "What is this?" She lifted it toward her lips right before I stopped her from sticking her tongue out and tasting it.

"Don't do that." It felt like the time I prevented my nephew from eating Play Doh. "It's soap. It's like when you put rose petals in the water to scent it. It's basically the same thing."

She lifted it to her nose and squealed in delight. "It smells like a fluff salad."

Whatever fluff salad is . . . hopefully that's a good thing. "Oh, and if you have to . . . you know, pee or what you might call *relieve yourself . . .*" I pointed behind us and lifted the lid of the toilet. "This is our *bedpan.* Push this lever when you're done." I stepped back to the bathtub and checked the temperature once more.

Flush!

Seriously? I spun around, worried that she had actually used the commode with me in the same room. *She hadn't.* I watched as she flushed again. Her eyes radiated fascination.

I groaned. *At this rate, it will take hours just to get ready for the day.*

With the tub filled, I turned off the water. "And these . . ." I pointed to the plastic bottles clustered on a nearby bench. "Are the shampoo, conditioner, body wash . . ." Subtle lines formed between her eyes. "Uh, shampoo is soap for your hair. Put a small amount in your hand and lather it up, then rinse it out."

Not only did the lines continue to deepen from her expression, but her eyes narrowed as well. "Why must you relay these directives to me?"

"What do you mean?"

"Aren't you bidding a lady's maid to attend me?"

I choked. "Uh, no, Margaret. We don't do that."

Her cheeks paled. "Surely, you're jesting."

"No, I'm not *jesting.* You're an adult. You can bathe yourself." I retrieved a fresh towel and a robe from a shelf and hung them on a nearby hook. "When you're finished, dry off with the towel, then put the robe on." I paused and pointed to the robe. "This is similar to what you call a dressing gown, it's worn the same way. I'll be in the bedroom when you're done."

Margaret stood frozen in place.

"It's only a bath." I faced her. "Wash and dry yourself and I will be back." I closed the door and pressed my fingers to my temples where a slight headache formed. Running to the door, I ignored the fact that I, too, needed to change into something drier and rushed out. Barely into the hallway, I ran directly into Trenton.

"Kat!" He held me up as I lost my footing. My damp hair stuck to my face.

"Kelly said you weren't feeling well." His curious eyes washed over me as he kept one arm securely around my waist. "What's happened?"

"I'm alright, I promise." I couldn't help my eyes from drifting back to my closed bedroom door. "I'm going to take a bath and rest a bit before the guests arrive."

Trenton watched me carefully. Another person who knew I failed at lying. "Why did you go out in the rain?"

I rolled my eyes with as much subtlety as I could muster. *Why did I?* I asked myself this very question several times already. Only I knew from my own time travel event, I couldn't leave Margaret out there. "Just a quick ride. I'm sorry the horses weren't returned."

"About that . . . Devon said something about a woman stealing my horse and you rushing off to go after her? What's going on?"

"Um, I can explain, but—" I glanced past Trenton as Hennessey appeared down the corridor. "I'm sorry, Trenton, I really need to speak with Hennessey. I'll come find you after your ride." I kissed him on the cheek and ran down the hall. I made sure Trenton disappeared out of earshot before I spoke. "Hennessey!" I gasped for air. "What bedrooms are available?"

"None, Miss Shelton."

"None?" My nose wrinkled to the news. "We have seventeen bedchambers."

"Yes, and all are due to be occupied."

"I thought we had a spare one."

"We did, but Mrs. Gilford rang last night and informed me of an additional guest."

"She did? Who is it?" I tried to hide my surprise. *Shouldn't she have asked me first? Or at the very least, asked Trenton?*

"She didn't say." Hennessey paused and clasped his hands behind his back. "You seem a bit out of sorts, Miss Shelton."

"I'm fine." I tapped my finger to my lips as my mind whirled with possibilities. We have other rooms, even the schoolroom could be made into a makeshift bedroom. "Do we have a rollaway bed?"

"A rollaway what?" Hennessey's forehead wrinkled.

"Maybe an air mattress?" There must be some place to put Margaret other than my own room.

"I'm afraid I don't understand."

"Yes, I don't imagine we would have one." I doubted any grand mansions were found to have accommodations similar to that of a cheap hotel. I chuckled, more out of frustration than humor.

Hennessey's eyes narrowed. "May I get you a drink?" He prompted. "Tea perhaps? Or something . . . stronger?"

"No, I mean yes, two cups of tea please."

"Two?"

"Send them to my room."

"Very well."

"Thank you, Hennessey."

I ran back to my room, thankful that the traces of Trenton's cologne that lingered in the air were not from the man himself. Though I longed to be with him as often as time allowed, I had much to sort through and fibbing my way around it all, didn't help. I entered cautiously, hoping the *primadonna* remained preoccupied.

Thankfully, she was still in the lavvy. This gave me a few minutes alone to contemplate my next move, though I found myself completely stumped. Sitting on the edge of the bed, I let my head fall into my hands. How did I get myself into this situation? But most importantly, how am I going to get myself out of it?

Out of the blue, that famous quote from *Casablanca* materialized— "Of all the gin joints in all the towns in all the world, she walks into mine." My mom had a thing for old movies, and *Casablanca* was one we watched regularly. But just like those words—in all the places Margaret could appear, it happened to be here, and it happened to be now.

Just my luck.

Chapter 7

"Katharrriiinnne?" The high-pitched whine made its way through my ears, pinged around like a pinball game in my brain, and shot to my toes. I launched to my feet, afraid Margaret had done something perilous and ran to the lavvy. It could be something as small as soap in her eyes or she could've attempted to investigate the purpose of my razor. Truly it could be anything with her.

I cracked the door open. "Are you okay? What's happened?"

"Gads, Katherine, this has been the most delightful bath I have ever partaken of."

I tilted my head. "That's it?"

"What is *it*?"

"That's what you shrieked about?" I rubbed the back of my neck. It was barely past nine in the morning and every muscle in my body screamed at me.

Her voice lowered sheepishly. "Yes, that . . . and I suppose how astonished I am that . . . well, that it didn't necessitate a dozen buckets to prepare such an indulgence."

I exhaled in relief that she wasn't bruised or bleeding, but her method in getting my attention would need to stop. "Yes, it's quite the miracle. Just wait until I show you the shower."

"Pardon?"

"Never mind, come out when you're done." I turned away, then added one more thing. "And please, if you have something to say, just lower your voice a tad, if you don't mind."

I went back to my bed which was shrouded with nearly every piece of clothing I owned. I glanced between the closed bathroom door and the options before me, then moaned. How am I going to get her to wear underwear and a bra? *And why in the world is this something I must figure out anyway?* I grumbled silently, while hanging my blouses and refolding my jeans. I reached for a couple of dresses and maxi skirts, knowing it would be impossible to get her to wear a pair of pants. I laid out the choices and retrieved a towel for my own head.

Drying my hair, I contemplated a plan. I can't let her out of my room. She needs to stay in here until I figure out what to do with her. If she arrived the same way I did—falling down the stairs—the outlook might be promising. A slight smile reached my lips as I imagined her falling down the stairs. I hastily recanted my dark thoughts, realizing what a mess it would be if she actually got hurt. If something more serious happened, like broken bones or other injuries, I would feel bad. Even though I personally lived through it twice, luckily with only concussions, there wasn't any guarantee that she could return to 1878 unharmed.

The lavvy door opened and she stepped forward. Though her damp hair tangled wildly, the absence of dirt proved her striking features were as memorable as ever.

I pointed to a nearby chair. "I need you to sit down and promise me you won't scream or be hysterical." When Margaret silently obeyed, I nearly fell over. Could this be progress or just a ploy?

A knock came. I immediately stiffened. *Could it be Trenton or Kelly again?*

"Miss, I have your tea." A timid voice called through the door.

Oh yes, I almost forgot. Opening the door, I only cracked it wide enough for me to stick my hands out to retrieve the tray. The maid, a new one, appeared bewildered.

"Thank you, uh, what is your name again?"

"Kimberly, miss."

"Thank you, Kimberly, I'll take it." I pushed the door closed with my foot. Offering a cup of tea to Margaret, I exhaled as she accepted it with obvious pleasure, then her nose wrinkled.

"What do you intend by saying . . . do not go into hysterics? I'm a sensible lady, Katharine. I don't swoon at the first sign of discord."

"Oh, just wait." I set the tray down on the dressing table and rubbed my forehead. I was not entirely ready to have this conversation, yet it needed to happen and the sooner, the better. "Okay, what year do you think it is?"

She scoffed. "What a trivial inquiry. 1878, of course." Her brows pinched together. "Why do you ask?"

"Because . . ." I bit my bottom lip. "Well, because the calendar year is actually 2011. Not 1878."

Her mouth pulled into a flat line as she replaced the cup to its saucer. I waited for her to scream or wail but she didn't, she just stared so I continued.

"It's 133 years after we met." I watched carefully for signs of distress, but she sat still. "When you met me before, Margaret, I fell down some stairs and magically appeared in 1878, but I'm from now, today, 2011. I don't know why or how it truly happened, but I assume something similar happened to you, only you came to the future. Can you tell me the last thing you remember?"

Margaret's lips now formed an odd frown and the muscles in her throat strained. I reached for a nearby wastebasket in case she barfed instead of spoke.

"I—I was attending Merritt's wedding."

My mouth dropped open. "Why?"

Apparently offended, she jutted her chin out and a blush rose across her cheeks. "Whyever not? I'm not a common simpleton, I have every right to attend amongst the privileged."

"No, Margaret, that's not what I meant. Why would you go to the wedding of your former fiancé and his new bride?"

The color now bled to a ravenous red. "That is none of your affair!" she cried louder than expected. I glanced at the door afraid anyone nearby might've heard her.

"Shhh, please! Okay, so you were here at Charlock Manor for Merritt's wedding. Then what happened?"

"I—I sought solitude from the crushing demands of society." She shifted awkwardly in her seat. "Since the engagement ended a little over a month ago, I have been pursued by an endless procession of suitors."

I eyed her warily. Didn't she just say thirty minutes ago that she was ruined from the engagement being cancelled? "Fine. You were sought after . . . then what happened?"

"I fancied a moment of respite from all the tremendous attention and found refuge."

I rolled my eyes to her dramatics. "And?"

"Somehow, I fell."

"Were you in the library?"

"Yes."

"Did you fall down the cellar steps?"

She nodded slowly. Her eyes lit up like a burning flame. "What ungodliness brought me here?"

I ignored her and stood up, processing all the information. "It must've been the same way," I mumbled. It must also be the way she goes back. She *must* go back. My eyes flashed in her direction. "But Merritt's wedding was in December. It's May. Did you get hurt, were you unconscious?" I scrambled to unravel the missing months, then smacked my head again remembering how trivial that was, like before, compared to the years. "Did you get hurt, Margaret?"

She nodded again. "I'm unsure how long I remained unaware, but when I awoke, my head suffered tremendously." She touched the back of her head. "I sought reasoning, but the house appeared out of sorts—an empty ballroom, varied amendments, and when I peered into the dining room, I failed to recognize the occupants and fled."

That must've been when I saw her in the doorway last night. I pointed to her head. "May I see?"

She turned around as I carefully separated her black strands. They were wet and easy to move, consequently, it didn't take long for me to find a rather large goose egg. The cut seemed minimal or cleansed by the rain or bathwater, but without a doubt this bump caused her pain. "Does it hurt now?"

"Indeed, I dare say there is quite a severe throbbing. Might I have a sip of Laudanum?"

"I honestly don't know what that is," I said, shaking my head. "I can get you some Ibuprofen, you probably have a concussion." I tried to peek at the size of her pupils simply to confirm, but she gave me a snarling look in the process.

"This is utter madness," she whined.

"I could not agree more."

Margaret crossed her arms defiantly across her chest. "Since you are quite aware of how I arrived and apparently how I must return, I demand you remedy this conundrum."

"Demand?" My lips pulled into a tight line. "Once again, *my liege . . ."* My words were ripe with sarcasm. "You're not in any position to *demand* anything. *I* am the mistress of this house; you are but a guest." *An unwanted guest.* I whispered hotly under my breath.

Her lips separated in a scoff. "You are hardly fit to be a mistress. Your social status is beneath the Gilford's; you are unrefined, ill-mannered, and your attire is that of an uncivilized man."

I rolled my eyes. "As I said before, things have changed drastically in the last century. Women wear what they want, say what they want, and do what they want."

I expected her to sass me back. Her eyes fluttered down to her hands as she folded them in her lap, but not before I saw them shaking.

"Now I believe you have what is called a concussion, a head injury that takes time to heal." I took another breath, recalling the bedroom conversation with Hennessey. "You must remain here, in this room, until you are well enough to—"

"—To what?" She cut me off. Her eyes darkened in a scathing glower.

"Well," my patience stretched thin. "It's possible the only way you will get back to *your* time, is if you fall down the stairs again."

A look of terror replaced her glare. I jumped to her side the moment the scream began to slip from her lips and placed my hand tightly over her mouth . . . until she clamped down on my fingers with her teeth.

"Ouch!" I howled, removing my hand then quickly replacing it with the other. "Be quiet! Nobody can know you're here!"

"Whyever not?" She didn't scream this time, but her voice elevated to that abnormal pitch she loved so much.

"Because you're not from this time. It will shock people. Then it could lead to more serious things like being put in a mental hospital."

"Mental hospital?"

"Um, an asylum . . . like a looney person clinic."

"In bedlam?" Her eyes widened again.

"Yes, I guess. The point is . . . you can't leave this room! I will have meals brought in and here . . ." I pointed to my dresses. "I know these are different than yours, but the dress you arrived in is ruined. At least you'll have something to wear besides a robe."

She stared at the options I laid out and pinched her mouth tight.

"I'm fully aware these are much simpler than what you're used to." I walked to the wardrobe and opened my underwear drawer. "But you can't be wearing gowns like yours around." Sifting through my underclothes, I retrieved a white bra. "Now don't freak out again, okay?"

Her body stiffened.

"Okay?" I said, a touch louder.

"Very well." She scoffed again.

I held up the bra. "We don't wear *stays* anymore. This is the only thing we wear up top, unless you want to wear this too, and I held up a camisole, then a slip. "Instead of *knickers* . . ." Taking another long exhale, I dangled a pair of my underwear from my fingertips. They were bikini style and quite small. "We wear these."

She gasped. I watched her carefully for signs of a faint. She didn't, but the white in her eyes expanded and nearly overpowered her misty gray pupils. I reached for my newest unused pairs, the ones I bought a couple of weeks ago in London. I ripped off the tags hoping they would fit her. I tried not to linger on the logistics. The thought of having her here mortified me as it was—but having to explain how to wear underwear had to be the worst—

well not the very worst . . . I conceded as I spied my box of tampons.

"That is entirely indecent." She stood up and rifled through the drawer. With all different colors, and all much less fabric than she was accustomed too, she balked. "I am not a woman of easy virtue, Katharine."

Despite my frustration, I felt I had a responsibility to look out for her. If the only way she can truly return is to fall down the stairs, she needed to heal first. Her injury was too fresh. If she hit her head again, she might never recover. I wasn't entirely sure why that bothered me, but I wasn't heartless and cruel either—even to Margaret.

I sighed. "Look, if you only want to wear a slip and then the dress that's fine, you aren't going out anyway."

She lifted the lacy négligé Kelly and Maria had given me the night before. She pinched it between two fingers. "Well, aren't you a brazen tart."

I reached for it and stuffed it back in the drawer. "That is for my wedding night, hands off." I glared at her.

"Wedding night?" She laughed aloud. "So, you truly aren't the mistress of Charlock Manor. I should have known."

"I'm getting married in nine days, Margaret, and you will not ruin it for me, or so help me, I will drag your sorry butt out to the road and leave you there."

"You wouldn't." She provoked.

"Try me." I stared hard. "And by the way, we don't use carriages for transportation anymore." I led her to the front window. "Do you see those?" I pointed to the cars. "Those vehicles are a much faster and more dangerous way to come to a quick death."

She yanked her arm away and pouted. I retrieved my teacup off the small silver tray. My cucumber mint tea was lukewarm now, but I sipped it anyway, hoping for a miracle to calm my frazzled nerves. Margaret remained frozen at the window.

A knock came to the door.

She swung around and I held my finger to my lips. "Shhh," I demanded. Much like before, I cracked the door barely an inch. "Yes?"

Hennessey stood before me. "Forgive me, Miss Shelton, but you asked to be informed when Mr. and Mrs. Gilford arrived."

"Yes, yes, of course. Thank you, I will be right there. Is Trenton back from his ride?"

"Yes, miss, he's on his way to the foyer."

"Thank you, I'll be right there." I flipped around to Margaret once more. No doubt my shaky hands revealed more than I intended.

"I should be obliged to greet Mr. and Mrs. Gilford." Margaret blinked in my direction.

"No!" I snapped. Replacing the teacup, I quickly twisted my hair into a loose bun and threw a hoodie over my damp shirt. This is not what I envisioned wearing for a first impression, but time didn't allow for anything else. "You don't know these people, Margaret. They are not the Mr. and Mrs. Gilford from your time, they are many generations later."

Her eyes narrowed. "You are nervous, why?"

"I haven't met them yet. They're Trenton's parents."

"Trenton, your beloved?"

"Yes," I said, unsure why I shared anything with her. I dotted some lip gloss on, checked my appearance in the mirror and rushed to the door, then swiftly turned back around. "One more thing . . . in this house you dress yourself. And stay put!"

I closed the door behind me and leaned against it long enough to take a steadying breath. Squaring my shoulders, I stepped forward ready to face the next daunting part of the day. "I can do this," I whispered. "Trenton loves me, his parents will love me too."

Forcing confidence into my feet, I walked to the front entrance to meet my future in-laws for the very first time.

Chapter 8

As I drew near the entryway, my heart pounded riotously. Trenton met me on approach and draped his arm around my shoulders.

"You look refreshed," he whispered in my ear. "How do you feel?" He led me toward the couple that now graced the front door.

"Much better, thank you." Seeing Trenton always brought a smile to my face, but this particular grin emulated a false enthusiasm—both from the woman in my bedroom and the couple I now faced.

Keeping me next to him, Trenton stepped forward. "Good morning, sir, Mother." He cleared his throat. "This is Kat Shelton. Kat, this is my mother, Mrs. Juliana Gilford and my father, Mr. Trenton Gilford II."

I extended my hand. Dressed in an expertly tailored suit accentuated by a deep burgundy tie, Mr. Gilford portrayed an air of professionalism through his commanding appearance. His dark hair was much like Trenton's, though shorter with graying streaks barely above his ears. He was clean shaven with a square jaw and broad shoulders. When our hands met in a sturdy grip, he nodded curtly. "Pleased to meet you, Miss Shelton." Then he swiftly turned away and eyed the walls and ceiling judiciously.

Mrs. Gilford remained in the doorway. Her lips pinched tight and, unlike her husband, she scanned every inch of *me* as opposed to the house. Her eyes blinked rapidly past my clothes and paused when they settled on my face. Reaching into her purse, she retrieved a satin handkerchief, held it to her nose, and sniffed as if the air had suddenly turned musty.

I smiled tightly under her scrutiny. The woman carried herself with regal poise. Dressed in a dark blue travel suit, she too appeared to be the epitome of class with her auburn hair coiffed perfectly into a tight bun at the base of her neck. Her cheeks were a bit hollow and her eyebrows thin, but no doubt, she claimed the features of a striking beauty in her youth. My smile started to fall under her gaze, so I quickly tipped it up again. I extended my hand to shake, but by the time her hand reached mine, it drooped as limp as a noodle.

"You're the curator, correct?"

"Uh, y—yes." I stuttered. *I'm also your son's fiancé.* I wanted to say aloud but remained polite. "It's a pleasure to finally meet you."

Her pasted smile appeared oddly identical to mine. "Charmed," she murmured.

Trenton shot an uneasy glance in my direction and turned to his parents. "You must be fatigued from your travels. We'll assist you to the master suite and you can rest before dinner."

"Yes, and please have tea brought up." His mother droned. "The turbulence on the flight from Florence simply exhausted me."

"You came from Florence, Italy?" My face lit up. I'd never been there but knew it to be an art haven.

Mrs. Gilford peered at me as though I was foolish to ask or even speak. "Of course, Italy, where else would we travel from other than our estate?"

"I apologize," I whispered. "I didn't know." How could I? They have three estates in three different countries!

Trenton picked up two suitcases, and Curtis carried an oversized trunk. I glanced around at the amount of baggage and winced. Its size was hardly reflective of a *short* visit unless she planned to change clothes three or four times a day.

"There's an additional valise in the car, Trenton." His mother called out as we headed upstairs.

I jumped at the chance to be of service to her. "I would be happy to retrieve it for you, Mrs. Gilford."

She stopped on the mezzanine with one eyebrow raised. "I don't recall asking *you* to do so."

My shoulders sagged. "Yes, ma'am." I followed behind the group like a discarded puppy.

"Thank you for offering, Kat." Trenton peeked back at me. "That was kind of you."

I smiled for him. *How did someone so wonderful spawn from this woman?*

"I'll retrieve it after you are shown to your rooms, Mother."

Mrs. Gilford swept into the first suite with a frown. "Oh son, why have you not refurbished this bedchamber? It is such an eyesore."

I froze in the doorway and watched her swipe her finger along the expansive dressing table as if she expected to find dust . . . which she wouldn't. I personally oversaw the meticulous cleaning by Gretchen and Lara.

"The room's antique design accentuates the authenticity for the tours, Mum." Trenton placed the luggage down.

"Humph." She sneered. "It's due for a restyle. If I find the time, I might manage the undertaking myself while in residence."

I found my feet cemented to the threshold. *Did I hear her correctly?* She certainly has forgotten quite quickly who the current owner is.

"Excuse me, miss." A gentle voice reached my ears from behind. I forced myself to step aside while Trenton waved the staff members in.

"Mother, this is Lani, your lady's maid, and Jonathan . . ." Trenton encouraged the tall, thin man behind her to step forward. He pointed to his father. "Your services will be to Mr. Gilford as his valet. Rachel will be arriving soon and see to all the other needs of the suite."

"Very well." His mother continued her inspection.

I entered and faced his parents. "I'm really glad you're here. We missed you at Christmas, but I'm grateful all worked out for you to come to the wedding."

His mother scoffed in my direction. "I would hardly miss the wedding of my only son."

"Well, I'm pleased you're both here."

"Jonathan," Mr. Gilford waved his valet over. "Place my attaché on the desk in the next room, I have papers to address." Then his father disappeared into the connecting chamber without as much as a goodbye.

Mrs. Gilford pressed the same handkerchief to her nose once more. "Close the door, Trenton, I feel a headache coming on."

"Yes, Mum, rest well."

"And don't forget my valise," she said through the door.

As we stepped away, I tried not to show the discouragement I felt, but Trenton seemed to notice. He led me down the hall and stopped before his own bedchamber. Without a word, he opened the door and drew me inside. In a flash, his arms pulled me against his chest.

"They will warm up to you, I have no doubt." His whisper sent tingles along my skin, and I allowed myself to savor in the moment.

"What if they don't?" I didn't want to bring my fears to the surface but needed to ask. "What if she despises me?"

"Then it's her loss, love." Trenton brushed my hair aside and kissed my neck. When he spoke, the heat of his breath tingled my skin. "I have made my choice and nothing at all can change my mind."

I leaned back far enough to let my hands cup his jaw. Trenton's face remained smooth and confident, no hint of humor or dishonesty present. I slid one finger up his cheek and tucked a wayward strand of hair back into its perfect position. His eyes fixated on mine. Their uncanny ability to read me often left me exposed and vulnerable.

"I was worried about you this morning," he said somberly.

As my hands slipped back to his chest, I calculated my words. They were guarded. Of course, he worried—our horses were not in the stable when he arrived, I abandoned him for our scheduled ride, and when he came to me, I behaved like a lunatic.

"I'm sorry, I really wanted to be with you this morning." My eyes lowered. "I needed to help a friend. It turned out to be much harder than I anticipated."

"That doesn't surprise me. You're a kind person, Kat." He lifted my chin upward. "Please don't worry about my parents, they are snobs to everyone, even me."

"Are you sure they are leaving after the wedding?"

"I'm certain I made our intentions clear. Although, they do know that we will be gone for a month on the boat, maybe they thought to stay in our absence." He chuckled low. "Forgetting, of course, that they should ask first. They often forget I now own Charlock."

"It would be hard for anyone to leave this place." I smiled up at him.

"Which is why I'm glad you didn't." He brushed his thumb across my lips. "They did have a lot of baggage, didn't they?"

I chuckled. "Quite a lot."

"No matter. They may stay while we are on our honeymoon, but I will make it clear they are to be gone when we return. It's *our* house now." With that, he placed a slow and deliberate kiss on my lips that strengthened with each passing second. His hands wound around my back, up my spine and caressed my neck beneath my hair. Each riveting motion magnified my senses a thousand times over and drew me further into his immersive embrace.

I reluctantly pulled away, fully recognizing the temptation that laid before us—kissing passionately in his bedroom could no doubt lead to trouble.

Regaining normal breath, I licked my lips. "Though I could kiss you all day . . ." I sighed. "I have work to do."

"Fine." Trenton kissed my nose. "Just remember there is no work after today."

I laughed at the command. When I first met Trenton, *Mr. Chill*, he was all business and little play. Now it has reversed, and I loved it.

"Agreed."

I reached for the handle, but he whipped me back into his arms one last time. His final kiss left me winded with my nerves humming wildly. Sporting a sly smile—knowing full well what he'd done—he nodded and disappeared out the door. I shook my head to clear my scrambled thoughts. "Curse that man," I whispered. Straightening my shirt and patting my cheeks, I hoped the heat that repeatedly arose around Trenton had disappeared by the time I stepped into the hall.

Searching the house, I needed to confirm with Hennessey any arrivals I might've missed. As I descended the stairs, a figure flew into the ballroom. It could be any number of guests exploring the house, including my own two friends, but an irritating forewarning gnawed beneath my skin.

Whoever it was, their dress looked awfully similar to my forest green maxi skirt. I hustled faster down the stairs, gripping the handrail to avoid an embarrassing fall and ran inside the ballroom which I found to be dark and eerily quiet.

I flicked on all the lights. The chandelier buzzed to life. Each individual electrifying flame lit up in descending order and it never failed to capture my full attention. Scanning the room, I spied Margaret's form motionless before the expansive front window.

"Margaret." I frowned and hurried in her direction. "You weren't supposed to leave the bedroom."

She tossed her frayed, messy locks behind her with a flick of her wrist. "I daresay, this day has been most vexing." She ignored my directive and fixed a nasty glare in my direction. "Consider my torment, Katharine, you *must* compel a servant to attend to my privations . . . and this dress—" She tugged at the skirt. "—it's atrocious." Despite its simplicity, Margaret somehow managed to have it distorted in an awkward twist and the buttons on the blouse were mismatched. "Simply unadorned and utterly distasteful."

I folded my arms across my chest and huffed. "That is the style of today. I can't have you traipsing around in the gown you came here in. Actually, I can't have you traipsing at all." I grabbed her arm, but she wrestled it free. "Margaret, please, I can't tell you how important it is for you to stay out of sight."

Voices entered the ballroom and thwarted my attempt for an easy escape. I quickly turned in a faint effort to block Margaret but shrank the moment I recognized them.

Chapter 9

"There you are." Kelly said as she and Maria entered the ballroom.

Shoot!

"Where have you been?" She tilted her head. "I thought you weren't feeling well, but you weren't in your room."

"Yeah, I'm doing much better."

"We've gotten lost twice." Maria placed her hands on her hips. "You said you would give us a tour."

"Yes." I faced my friends directly. "I did offer to show you around, I'm sorry. How did the ride go this morning?"

"Oh, Marlowe is a hoot and quite a gentleman. I only fell off once." Kelly's expression was unreadable.

"You fell off the horse?" My mind owned only one recollection of someone falling off a horse—Merritt.

"I'm joking!" Kelly chuckled after catching sight of my face. "We only trotted. I promise I didn't fall."

"Okay, good."

"Ahem." A self-righteous cough arose from behind me. My mouth went slack. My friends stretched playfully past me to see the woman who demanded their attention.

"Who's this?"

I winced and stepped aside trying hard to establish a logical reason for this person to be here. She could be passed off as one of Trenton's friends, but if Margaret somehow crossed paths with him, they would know I lied.

"Kelly, Maria, this is Margaret, a friend of mine from here in England. Her family has an estate a short distance away."

"Hardly." Margaret sighed beside me. "By carriage, it's no less than a half day's ride."

I laughed nervously, though irritation stifled the humor. "Margaret is . . . an actress." I blurted out shortly before she threw me a nasty scowl. "She loves to imagine herself in a different time when she visits. It's a game."

I cowered under their odd expressions and wiped my forehead from the small beads of sweat that surfaced.

Kelly stepped forward to shake her hand. "Nice to meet you, Margaret. I'm Kelly."

Margaret gawked at her hand with narrow eyes. I quickly grabbed Margaret's wrist. "We have to go. Give me about five minutes and I'll show you around."

"I would fancy a tour." Margaret released my hold and rooted in place.

"I don't think that's a good idea." I tried to discipline her with my eyes but failed since she didn't return my stare.

"We should go." I reached for her again but missed as she sashayed to the center of the ballroom.

Raising her arms, Margaret twirled with an imaginary dance partner. "Oh, it's been ages since I waltzed in here. Remember the Gilford's glorious autumnal ball—the night we were introduced?"

I choked. "Uh, yes." My eyes blinked as I rapidly conjured up a logical explanation. "Oh, you're referring to your performance in *Phantom of the Opera* and the masquerade ball." Thank goodness I'd seen my fair share of Broadway musicals. Covering up her outlandish comments will take every effort. "We met in the foyer afterward."

She stopped, stunned. "Phantom of—"

"—It's time to go." I insisted.

"Please, Katharine, permit me to stay."

"Katharine?" Maria's lip curled. "I thought you hated that name."

"Yes, well . . ." I lowered my voice. "It's all part of the act. She is quite the method actor and I hate to embarrass her. I just play along."

They both nodded but eyed me from beneath crumpled brows.

"Please?" Margaret whined and spun again.

I stepped over to the twirling ballerina and pulled her close. "Fine, but don't say a word."

She scrunched her nose. "I'm perfectly capable of behaving like the lady I am."

I pasted a smile on my face and turned back to my friends. Initially, I intended on giving them the full tour, but considering Margaret's unpredictability, I couldn't risk the *actress* interjecting offbeat comments with her unbridled tongue.

Waving my hand upward, I announced. "Okay! This is the ballroom." I stepped around the space with awkward urgency as I pointed out some of the main features—the chandelier, of course, the tiles with the family coat of arms, and the angels etched into the ceiling.

I normally would have the guests close their eyes and envision the night of a ball as I described the placement of the string quartet, the bountiful delicacies, the smells, the dances, and the superior dress, but I feared Margaret's mouth more than anything and cut the experience short, knowing the sooner we moved on, the better.

Through the school room, the music room, billiard room, fine art hall, and many other random places around the house, Margaret surprisingly behaved better than expected. Each time she looked as though she might speak up, I silenced her quickly. It didn't matter much what she said when we were alone, but I feared her language and comments would expose my secret, or at least give rise to questions I wasn't prepared to answer.

Though listening clearly stifled her, she obeyed, albeit with a puckered pout on her lips, and a furrowed brow. Once we reached the mezzanine and the stunning family portrait, I elaborated generously on the Gilfords. It would not do them justice if I passed by and didn't explain their importance and their connection to Trenton and his parents.

Out of habit, I described the process of sitting for a painting, from the hours sustaining one pose, to the elegant gowns and handsome gentlemanly apparel including waistcoats, cravats, and Hessian boots.

"This particular work," I brushed the bottom edge of the gilded frame, "is over a hundred and thirty years old, commissioned in 1878 shortly after their annual ball and before the devastating death of Mrs. Martha Gilford."

Margaret stepped forward. I held my breath and readied myself to intervene, but her eyes only lovingly appraised the woman who sat in the center of her family. "Such a lovely woman." She spoke without directing it to anyone. Her hand went to the painting and brushed softly across the matron's fair features. "Martha was the most decent and proper lady I knew."

I coughed.

"Knew?" Maria spit out.

I stumbled to fix her words. "Margaret has heard me talk of the Gilford's journals for months. I have spoken of Mrs. Gilford's charities and the love for her family so often that we both feel we know her that much more."

Margaret blinked in my direction but didn't respond.

"The girls are beautiful, and the son is really handsome." Maria stared.

I quickly flashed my eyes toward Margaret and willed her to remain silent. "Yes, the girls went on to marry well in influential families . . ." My voice softened in reverence. "And Merritt was . . . uh, his kindness and character influenced many people."

"Was he a member of parliament?" Kelly asked.

"No, but his father was." Then forgetting my audience, I added. "Merritt actually saved the lives of many slaves."

"Slaves? In the late 1800s?" Kelly knew her history. She had the same reaction I did when I entered the cave and learned that the deplorable practice still existed.

"I daresay," Margaret spit out fiercely, "that's an embellished falsehood."

"What is?" Maria's attention bounced curiously between us.

Margaret's eyes flickered like a newly lit flame. "I can assure you Merritt never partook in anything so illicit. I would have been informed."

"How?" Maria chuckled.

I struggled to swallow the lump that built in my throat. "He did, Margaret." I peered nervously toward my friends. "He wrote about it in his journal." *I lied.* He never disclosed the full details of his involvement for fear of the reaction of others . . . and for good reason based on Margaret's response. It seemed a gentleman of his standing should likely have ignored the practice than take action to stop it. "There were very few people who knew of his involvement."

Margaret's cheeks cooled, but she didn't meet my eyes. I led the party back downstairs to the entry. "Well, outside of the private bedrooms, you've seen mostly everything."

"I heard someone mention a library," Kelly said. Her love for books rivaled her love for surfing.

"Yes." Though the room could very well be my favorite in the house, I found myself feeling strangely reluctant. Not because of Kelly and Maria, but maybe having Margaret present in a place that held some of my own significant memories unsettled me. My dances with Lizzy and Merritt happened there, I watched newly married couples embrace from the main window, Trenton and I connected over Merritt's journals in that room, and only a few steps away were the very stairs that led to my time travel journey.

I glanced over to my friends and quickly smiled to appease them past my awkward silence. "Follow me."

Entering the library, the instant serenity hovered like the quiet before the storm. With a couple dozen guests in the house, this place will hardly remain this silent. The musky, vanilla scent, from the oils used on the cherry wood drifted around us the deeper we went.

Pointing out the intricately carved desk with its harp shaped legs, I moved about the room in quiet reverence. Everything here held a story, from the Shakespeare bust and antique humidor to the baroquely fashioned bookshelves, intricate tapestries, grand fireplace, and Martha's bridal portrait.

"I have never seen anything like this." Maria's mouth parted as she walked past the ornate furniture seemingly drawn to the enormous fireplace. Brushing her fingers over the mantle, her eyes marveled at the elaborate gold dipped candlesticks and matching vases but stopped at a carved bronze chest.

Trenton had explained to me that his grandfather procured it on a trip to Wadi Musa, the town next to Petra, the *Lost City* in the country of Jordan. Picking it up, she gasped at its detail. Each etched geometric symbol suggested a cryptic, archaic message. "I feel like I've stepped onto a movie set for *The Mummy.*"

My laughter came easily. She wasn't far off with her assessment since she held in her hands only one of the many mystical treasures found in this room.

Kelly hadn't wasted any time perusing the bookshelves. "How many books are in here?" She cocked her head in mental calculation.

"How many do you think?" I grinned. "There are fifteen shelves on each bookcase, and we have twenty bookcases."

"There must be fifty books on each shelf, like 15,000?" Her eyes danced.

"Good guess. I actually don't have an exact number, but it's well over 20,000 titles."

"How many have you read?" She teased, unaware my love for reading only accelerated after we parted ways in Arizona.

"Maybe forty." I laughed.

"Forty? Well, that's more than I would've guessed." She snorted.

"I had a lot of time on my hands when I first arrived. It's become a favorite pastime now." I circled back around to face Margaret, only she had disappeared. Panic rose immediately. Despite the nature of her adulthood, I worried over her every move.

"Wait." Kelly grabbed my wrist, seemingly unaware of my sudden alarm. "Where is that awful storage room that you sent a picture of?" She chuckled. "Remember back when you were fuming about *Mr. Chill's* ridiculous task, and the previous curator's lack of organization?"

"Oh, yes, that's over here." Moving toward the alcove, Margaret's silhouette materialized. She stood frozen before the opening of the cellar, her hands clenching her skirt in apparent distress. I rushed over and opened the opposite door—the storage. "It's here, Kelly, if you guys want to take a look. It's not as bad as before. I spent an entire month fixing it." I pointed inward and they followed. Quickly turning back to Margaret, I rushed to her side as if thwarting a suicide attempt.

"What are you doing?" I whispered.

"Is this where you likewise tumbled?" Margaret asked, her voice much calmer than before.

"Yes." I stared at the steps we both seemed to have an odd connection with.

"Maybe I should endeavor . . ." She lifted the fabric of the skirt to expose her borrowed shoes.

"No, Margaret." I kept my voice low and checked to make sure we were still alone. "If you hit the bump on your head again, you could sustain a serious injury . . . possibly even death."

When she faced me, tears bubbled on her lashes. "Death might not be so dreadful."

My head tilted to her strange remark.

"What does this lead to?" Maria appeared behind us.

I pointed down the steps. It's only a cellar, not really used for anything." I reached around Margaret and closed the door.

"Miss Shelton?" Hennessey called from the door of the library. "Your parents have arrived."

My smile lit up genuinely. "Thank you, Hennessey. I'll be right there." Then turned to Margaret and tugged her arm. "Why don't you go back to the room and rest?"

"Perhaps," she said with quiet anguish—one of her more unfamiliar traits. "The day has rendered me weary."

"Go, we'll walk back with her. What room is she staying in?" Kelly placed an arm through Margaret's.

I frowned. "We had a mix-up in the rooms. She's in mine for now."

"Great, we know the way."

I smiled weakly. I didn't want her to be in anyone's company without me. Who knows what bizarre remarks might be said? *At least I laid the foundation for her dramatics.*

"Go, Kat. It's your parents."

Chapter 10

Running toward the front entry, I caught myself and slowed. I had broken every single act of professionalism today, and though I didn't need to put on airs for my family or friends, I wasn't naïve enough to believe they were the only ones watching me.

"Mom, Dad!" I rushed into open arms. The familiar mixture of *Old Spice* and *Olay* comforted me. *Finally, people who actually want to see me.*

"Kat," My dad's scruff tickled my skin as he spoke. "Missed you, Peanut."

"I've missed you both a lot. How was your flight?"

"Good, good." Mom wiped her forehead and let her bag fall off her shoulder to the ground.

"Curtis." I called to the footman. "Will you please assist with their bags? They're in the green room, the same one they stayed in over Christmas." Mom loved the flora and fauna designs that overflowed in there. The man swiftly carried the bags and disappeared down the hallway.

"Are you hungry? Helen would love to see you."

"Sure, maybe a sandwich."

"Dad," I rolled my eyes. "You can eat something other than a sandwich when you're away from the deli." I chuckled.

We entered the kitchen and from across the room, Helen hollered and ambled toward us. The moment she met my parents in December, they became fast friends. I attributed part of that to her resemblance to my grandma Jo, but Mom and Helen found to have a lot more in common than that.

"You must be famished!" Helen cried after she released my mom from a gregarious embrace. "Come, come you must eat, and I'll get you all a cuppa as well."

Within minutes she had laid out an assortment of appetizers including a selection of British delicacies I had only been introduced to in the last year.

"Do you just keep these on hand?" Astonished at her variety, I admired Helen's skills in the kitchen like no other.

"Oh, doll, you'll find with fancy do's like this one, we must always be on our toes." She winked and handed us some plates. "Try some of these." She grated cheese liberally over the dish. "I daresay, my 'angels on horseback' are absolutely scrummy, but if you be wanting hair on your chest, eat my 'devils on horseback'.

I reached for a couple of each. The main difference I found within the crispy bacon-wrapped shell was either a lemon-juiced oyster or a chutney-dipped prune, and though I couldn't say which was considered the *angel* or the *devil*, they both burst with mouth-watering flavor.

Topping off the board with some fruit and sausage, Helen left my parents and I to catch up in private at a side table in the kitchen. As the hour passed effortlessly, I fell into such a relaxed state I nearly forgot my *other* problem.

"Oh Mom, Dad, sorry, I have to go, but your stuff is in your room and you remember where it's at, right? Dinner is um, Helen what time is dinner again?"

"Seven o'clock, doll."

"Yes, of course, honey." Mom patted my arm. "Go do your thing. We'll see you at dinner."

"Thanks, Mom." I hugged them both once more and again ran down the hall headed for my bedroom. When I entered, my *living nightmare* was nowhere to be found. I checked the lavvy and peered out the windows. Maybe she ventured to the garden or explored the grounds. Then I heard Kelly's outlandish laugh coming from the next room. *Great.* I stepped out and knocked on their door petrified of what I might find.

Kelly opened the door. "Hey Kat, come on in."

I stepped forward apprehensively to see Maria doubled over on her bed, and Margaret sitting stiffly on a settee. When Maria's face met mine, tears clouded her eyes.

"What's happened? What's going on?" I asked, stepping forward apprehensively.

"Your friend is a crack-up." Kelly answered as she closed the door and joined Maria on the bed. My brows furrowed as I looked between my friends and Margaret.

"Wh—what has she been saying?" I sent a fierce look at Margaret. "I thought you were tired? You look tired. You should go lay down."

"No, Katharine, I believe it is *you* who could benefit from a kip." She brushed something off her sleeve and angled her chin haughtily in my direction. This woman's mood swings were like a netherworld pendulum, one moment she appeared innocent and repentant and the next she's back to being bold and shameless.

I fumed. The reality of her words hit close to home. *I am exhausted.* All this mental and physical run around wore me down, especially since my body had little sleep to begin with.

"She told us this outrageous story." Kelly kept chuckling.

"Oh really, what story?" My eyes pierced Margaret again. She glanced away and shifted condescendingly in her seat.

"There was this guy that, wait . . . how did she put it?" Kelly struggled to keep a straight face. "Oh yeah, this gentleman who *fancied* her. They were the *crème de la crème* of society and engaged to be married when this absurd governess tried to intervene."

Maria wiped the tears from her eyes. "I haven't laughed this hard in quite some time. The way she tells it . . . it's got this melodramatic flair."

I growled lightly knowing her version of *our* story was sure to be tainted with lies. "I bet it was hilarious."

"What's wrong?" Maria scrutinized my frown. "Haven't you heard this?"

"Oh, I've heard it. I just didn't find it that funny."

"Not funny? It's hysterical." Kelly added. "Margaret describes this woman as a plain and prosaic fool who thought she could win the favor of her wealthy fiancé. It's totally out of the storybooks. The best part came when the wicked woman tried to kiss him. Can you believe it . . . kiss her man? Margaret punched her in the eye."

"Oh?" My eyes popped open. "She did, did she?" I squared my body toward Margaret and set my jaw, ready to show a demonstration of who really hit who.

Margaret must've noticed my stance and jumped to her feet. "I must take my leave." She shrilled. "A moment of reprieve will do wonders for my complexion before we reconvene for dinner. Thank you for this most diverting conversation, ladies."

My hand shot forward. "You're taking dinner in your room, remember Margaret?"

"Oh, come on, Margaret, join us for dinner." Maria pleaded. "It'll be fun."

"Well—" That same serpent smile from before took shape.

"No." I snapped. In my peripheral vision I saw the confusion that blanketed my friends' faces. "I believe it's best that you remain in the room." I attempted to smooth my features. "The evening is sure to be exhausting, especially considering your recent injury."

"She looks perfectly fine." Maria hopped down from the bed. "Join us, Margaret, I'm sure the men would love to meet you."

"The men?" Her eyes lit up. "There are eligible gentlemen present? Anyone titled?"

"Titled? Uh, not sure, but they're pretty hot." Maria added.

"Hot?" Margaret couldn't hide the uneasiness in her voice. She most likely pictured flames rising from their skin.

"Gorgeous and fun. So, you must come."

"Very well . . ." She didn't look in my direction. "If you insist." She tilted her head and eyed my friends with feigned innocence.

A spontaneous throbbing pounded between my ears. I turned away from the group before they noticed my irritated expression. Moving quickly to exit the room, I groaned at the childlike emotions rising within. I felt like a jealous teenager who recently lost her best friends to her enemy.

Once inside my room, I paced with agitation, clenching and unclenching my fists a half dozen times before Margaret opened the door. She gracefully swept past me as she set herself down at my dressing table and began to examine her unruly hair in the mirror.

Overlooking the heavy loathing that surely seeped from my every pore, she viewed herself from different angles. "Katharine, beckon a servant to arrange my hair," she charged. Then pinched the collar of her blouse and pouted, "and procure a new gown. These threads are confounding."

"Ahhhh." I threw my hands to my head.

She ignored me. "And I must rectify the folly you created when you declared me an actress. Surely, you're aware they are light skirts and mistresses, I am not a totty."

I blew out a puff of air and walked toward the lavvy. "Whatever, Mags." She exhausted me. "Please don't leave this room. I'm taking a shower." Then closed and locked the door. Turning the knob on the shower to spray ice cold water, I let the flow numb my hand. My need to calm my heated temper surged. *What am I going to do with her?* My pounding headache continued. *How am I going to get through the next eight days when I can't even get through one?*

Adding in the hot water, I undressed and stepped in to let the warmth of the shower relax my muscles and calm my nerves. If Trenton's parents planned on staying here at the house while we are on our honeymoon, I would need to figure out what to do with Margaret. They cannot be here together without my presence.

Though my contemplations were crucial, they were laughable considering my current state. This week was sure to be a trial to my sanity. Margaret won't listen to me. She won't stay inside this room, and I can hardly control what outlandish comment she'll say next. I couldn't very well tie her up, although truthfully, no one would miss her. Chuckling, I tried to mentally recall where I kept the duct tape in the house.

Stepping from the shower to the mirror, I wiped the steam off the glass and held still while my eyes followed the angles of my face then settled in to what appeared to be a staring contest . . . with myself. I probed deeper. "This isn't like you, Kat." I groaned. Snippets of my life whizzed before me though I never blinked. Memories of all the good I had been a recipient of weighed on me like drops of water falling into a bucket. Each momentous drop was one more reason I needed to try harder. Closing my eyes, I blew out an exhaustive breath and whispered, "you're better than this."

Wrapped in a fresh robe, I stepped out to face my *infernal torment* once more.

Chapter 11

"I summoned a servant." Margaret announced and pointed to the bell pull. "She is going to fetch me a maid for my hair."

"Margaret . . ." The tranquility of my shower quickly dissipated. "I don't know how to get it through your thick skull. Things. Are. Different. Here." I enunciated each word slowly.

"Hmph." She grunted and crossed both arms over her chest.

"And while I have your attention," I ignored her childish stance. "Why did you tell *my* friends lies about Merritt and I? I popped *you* in the eye . . . which I'm sure you haven't forgotten." My newly transformed resolve to try harder hit a solid brick wall. Walking to my armoire, I turned around and bellowed. "And above all Margaret, Merritt never loved you! He never *wanted* to marry you."

"Well, he would have if you hadn't interfered," she retorted nearly as loud.

"You keep saying that. What makes you think that I was involved?"

"Josiah claimed you meddled."

"Josiah, your brother? That weasel can't be trusted for anything. He's a slimy excuse of a man."

She went motionless. When I glanced over, her hands covered her face and her shoulders trembled. *Could she be crying?* In the eight or so hours since I came upon her in the stables, her turbulent temperament fluctuated in competition to the weather outside. My eyes flitted past her to the afternoon sunshine that now beamed through the curtains after such a miserable morning.

I sat on the bed across from her and wiped my brow from the drops of water still leaking from my hair. "Margaret," I exhaled and proceeded with both caution and a softer tone. "Merritt only loved Joanne. She was his one true love."

"Perhaps," she whispered.

"All I did was remind him of it." My voice sympathized. Nobody wants to hear that you were a second choice. To see Margaret here, so vulnerable, made me believe we might get through this situation in one piece.

The room swelled with an awkward silence. Even the birds that had reappeared on the branch next to the windowsill seemed to hold their chirps with bated breath.

"Look," I peered over to her slouched form. "I realize I can't keep you in here, but you can't slip up and tell someone you're from the past." I touched her arm. "Do you think you can keep your fall a secret?"

Her head lifted curiously, while her eyes searched mine for something—honesty, maybe. "Might I join you for dinner?"

I studied her carefully. Her expression carried that of a child anticipating a scrumptious dessert. I nodded, full on regretting it the entire time. She could easily be my undoing this week.

Her eyes brightened.

"But wait . . ." I held up one hand. "Only if you agree to stick to the story about you being an actress. I promise you they are not thought of the same way in my time. They are actually celebrated and popular, invited to all the biggest social events and people are eager to meet them."

"Truly?"

"Yes."

"Astonishing," she murmured, then arched one of her eyebrows in cloaked innocence. "And might these actresses find themselves attired in extravagant dress and have their hair styled in the latest fashion?"

My mouth tipped up in a shallow grin. *Oh, this woman is good.* I chuckled. "I suppose we could have your hair arranged, if there is someone here who can see to it."

Margaret sat up straighter and clasped her hands eagerly in her lap.

"We do have a lady's maid for Trenton's mom after all." I twisted a wet strand of my hair around my finger. "I could probably use the help myself . . . but please, please don't talk about your past and *our* past. Nobody but Trenton knows I went back in time. They will think we're nuts, and I can't have my new in-laws think that about me when they already don't like me."

"They're cross with you?"

"I don't think so, but I'm not sure."

A knock came to the door. Naturally, I stiffened and answered cautiously. A woman bobbed her head. "Pardon me, miss, but Gretchen asked me to come and help style someone's hair."

"Yes, please, come in. What's your name?"

"Anabelle."

"Anabelle, please help Margaret with her hair first and then if you are okay with it, I could use a miracle myself."

She nodded and walked over to Margaret.

I pointed to the curling iron on the table. "Once that's plugged in, Margaret, don't touch it."

"Plugged in?" Wrinkles formed across her forehead.

"Once it's hot, don't touch the silver part." Her chin tilted sideways. "Never mind, just let Anabelle do the work and sit still."

I went to the armoire Margaret hadn't raided yet, the one where I kept my nicer clothes, including evening wear. Nothing remotely close to a formal ball gown, but elegant enough for our dinner parties. I retrieved two dresses. The cerulean satin would go perfectly with Margaret's complexion. I appeared behind her with the dress. She whipped around so quickly; poor Anabelle still had her fingers attached.

"Oh, that is most improved." Margaret's eyes sparkled as she examined the delicate embossing along the collar and hem. "I'm certain to be the belle of the ball."

I laid the dress down on the bed and grumbled to myself. "I'm supposed to be the *belle of the ball*."

Green never looked good on me, but twice now, Margaret managed to rouse innate jealousy inside me with very little effort.

I took my dress into the lavvy with my underclothes and dressed quietly. I didn't really need to be worried about anyone's attention but Trenton's. I glanced in the mirror. *He's the only one that matters.*

The dress I selected revealed a silver lace applique across the bodice where two straps crossed at the neckline, creating a keyhole, then draped over my shoulders and down the back. Once pulled over head, the skirt's thin black fabric flowed easily over my hips and down to the floor. My new silver heels from Kelly and Maria would match it perfectly.

I dried my hair then applied my mascara and lipstick. Surely by now, Anabelle had finished and was ready for me. I opened the door. Margaret had, somehow, encouraged the woman to pile her hair up in an extravagant bun with tendrils framing her face. *Of course, she would.* I chuckled. I can't change her in a day. Although it was a bit excessive for this first night, I relented. To argue everything, only made things more difficult.

Margaret traded places with me to dress but called back to me and whispered, "are you certain you don't have any knickers or pantaloons I might wear?"

"I don't, and the ones you came in are muddy and torn."

"What shall I do?"

"All I can offer is what I have—the underwear, a bra, and a slip."

"No corset?"

"No corset." I confirmed.

"How do you constrict your waist?"

"I eat less sugar."

Margaret bit her lip. I glanced over to Anabelle as she cleaned Margaret's hair from the brush, hoping she couldn't hear us. "You might find it relieving to not have to wear all that extra stuff, the corsets, stockings, and garters."

She exhaled noisily. "Fine. Retrieve the underthings."

"Please?" I stipulated, then waited with a flat smile.

"Very well, *please* retrieve them for me."

Though her request lacked any sincerity, I went to the drawer and pulled out the necessary items. Walking into the lavvy, I groaned at the need to verbally advise their use.

My mind unintentionally flitted back to the first time Ana, Abagale's lady's maid, brought me a dress and all the necessary contraptions required underneath. I refused her help and stuffed them in a drawer reverting to my own *underthings.* Margaret's reaction paralleled mine, only Ana treated me with kindness regardless of my frustration. I wiped the perspiration from my nose and resolved once more to appear less annoyed.

Laying all the stuff on the vanity, I pointed out each item. My help would certainly not extend to dressing her, so I attempted to be as thorough as possible in the instruction.

"Wait!" Margaret cried with the new undies in her hands. "I—I can't wear these."

"Why not?"

"They belong to someone else?"

"They're brand new," I argued.

She pointed to a delicate imprint of ***VS*** on the waistband. "Whose initials are these? They're certainly not yours, Katharine."

I couldn't fight the grin that formed. "That, Margaret, is simply the name of the company that made this underwear . . . *Victoria's Secret.*"

Though she didn't appear completely convinced, her face relaxed.

"I promise nobody owns them. They really are new."

She stammered, "I—I won't attempt to deny my trepidation."

"You'll be fine."

She nodded as I closed the door behind me. Taking a seat before the dressing table I slumped, secretly wishing this day had already come to a close.

"Are you well, Miss Shelton?" Anabelle's smile reflected through the mirror.

"Yes, I'm fine, thank you."

"Do you want a similar fashion to Miss Margaret's?"

"Oh, no. No, thank you. I would be happy with a simple chignon, relaxed at the base of my neck. And no curls, just a few loose strands framing my face."

She smiled and went to work.

When she finished, she excused herself and left. I remained frozen to the seat. My mind flooded with erratic thoughts, almost to the point that it deprived my limbs of energy. Barely twelve hours ago, my life seemed somewhat normal, and now, well now I couldn't even put it to words if my life depended on it.

When Margaret stepped out, I couldn't pull my eyes away. Her goddess-like appearance from before had been reborn with her tall thin frame, perfect complexion, and high cheekbones.

"Why do you appear grievous?" She froze in her stance.

My mouth hung agape. I quickly closed it. "No reason. You're um . . . as beautiful as I remember."

Her eyelashes flickered in surprise. "You consider me to be beautiful?"

"Yes, just nasty mean." The words slipped out. "Sorry." I quickly followed up with a curt apology, not sure that I truly felt repentant.

"It matters not. I'm accustomed to such misplaced distinction."

My eyes narrowed. *Misplaced distinction?* Does she really *not* hear her own voice?

She wiped all unease from her face and ran her hands down the bodice of her dress. "On the ready?" she quipped with her chin held high.

Though she despised the notion of being called an actress, her skill in theatrics teetered beyond reproach.

Chapter 12

As we stepped out from the bedroom, I hesitated, praying heartily that she would not humiliate me tonight. I spun around and faced her squarely. "Remember, no talk of 1878, at all."

She nodded and followed me down the corridor but wandered to the nearest mirror and examined herself meticulously. I rolled my eyes. "Some things never change."

As I glanced down toward the end of the hall, a handsome man approached. Trenton's smile broadened, and his eyes glowed with adoration. He wore a black dress suit, white shirt, and black tie. We matched as perfectly as two people could, having not planned it that way.

When he reached me, his eyes soaked me in and warmed me from head to toe. The very sight of him brought a much-needed comfort to my hectic day. His hands went to mine and drew them up to his lips. "You're breathtaking." His kiss lingered on my skin. "And making it increasingly difficult to wait out these next eight days."

I smiled under his expressive attention and stole a shallow breath. He had a keen way of making me feel wanted.

"Surely I can locate a pastor within the hour." His lips curved in his spirited half-smile.

I chuckled. Though the suggestion came lightheartedly, it gave me reason to pause.

"And who might this gallant gentleman be?" Margaret shuffled up next to me. Trenton's eyes widened as he took a half step backward.

"This fine-looking gent . . ." I shot Margaret a clear warning. "Is Trenton Gilford, *my* fiancé."

Her lips curled into a sly smile as she demurely lifted her hand to be kissed. I slapped it down to her frown. "Trenton, this is my friend, Margaret."

He bowed his head fighting a smile and kept one hand clenched to mine. "Pleased to meet you, Margaret."

"A pleasure, Mr. Gilford." Margaret batted her eyelashes coyly. I bumped her with my hip and jarred her out of her dreamy state.

"He does have a similar likeness to Merritt, does he not?"

He cleared his throat. "M—Merritt Gilford?"

She rested one finger against her lips and tapped. "Yes, I believe it's the jaw."

"From the portrait." I scrambled.

If anyone could understand and believe Margaret's visit through time, it would be Trenton, but this was not the time to enlighten him. If I could somehow contain the problem and get her back before anyone knew, then that would truly be the best-case scenario.

"Yes, the portrait." Margaret lamented as if amenability required effort.

"When did you arrive, Margaret?"

"She is . . . a late addition." I interrupted. "She's rooming with me for the time being."

"Smashing." Trenton chuckled. "I'm sure Chapman will be more than pleased. With your friend from New York cancelling, I would say this is quite advantageous." Trenton turned and lifted his arm for me and like a true gentleman, he lifted his opposite arm for Margaret. I took another deep breath. *Nothing to worry about*, I repeated in my head. *Nothing at all.*

As we rounded the corner toward the entry on our way to the parlor, Hennessey held the front door ajar. A tall, leggy woman appeared. One hand rested on her curvy hip. The other pushed her long flaxen bangs behind one ear, revealing her striking blue eyes.

"Justine?" Trenton choked out.

My feet froze to the ground and my hand went limp.

Trenton struggled for words. "What are—"

"Justine, darling." Mrs. Gilford flew down the stairs and with open arms reached for the woman who stood before us all.

Justine? Was my sight deceiving me?

"I'm so pleased you could make it." Mrs. Gilford gushed over her.

"Mother—" Trenton's voice rumbled low and stern. I slipped my arm out of his and pulled Margaret to the side.

Why is she here? I bit the inside of my cheek and watched the exchange with growing angst while my heart pounded wildly in my chest.

"Trenton," Mrs. Gilford's jaw stiffened. Her eyes flamed bright and intense. "Is this how you greet an old friend, a *very close* friend?" She physically nudged him toward the door. Justine stepped away from her luggage and smiled with her full enviable lips—a small grin aimed at me and a much larger one at Trenton. He nodded. "Good evening, Justine."

"Oh, come now, it is entirely proper to embrace someone who is quite central in your life. Isn't that correct, Katharine?" The use of my full name grated on me, but I hid my ire as she turned my direction and lifted one eyebrow while she awaited my answer.

"Of course." I regarded Trenton in an effort to ease the awkwardness. Justine swiftly opened her arms to receive him and then, without shame, clutched him tightly, ending with a kiss on his cheek. Her blood red lipstick marked my fiancé's skin. My teeth clenched, and I quickly linked my tightened fists behind my back.

"Oh, I have interrupted dinner." Justine gazed around the group dressed in evening attire.

"Nonsense, love." Mrs. Gilford reached for both her hands affectionately. "Hennessey, please show Justine to her room. The one I arranged. And Justine," she winked, "if you happen to have that saucy little number you wore with us in Athens, put that on. We will wait for you to join us."

Margaret glanced at me and whispered, "Your mouth is open."

I slammed it shut. Then my eyes narrowed as Hennessey started up the main stairs with Justine's bags. *She's being placed in the family rooms*? I choked. *Near Trenton?*

My gasp brought Margaret's eyes upon me once more. I quickly turned my head knowing the heat that surfaced in my neck surely appeared on my cheeks.

Trenton stepped over to me and wound his arms around me. Leaning in, he whispered, "I did not invite her here. You must believe me, Kat. I'll request that she leave at once. This is unacceptable behavior of my mother, and I will not stand for it."

"Wait." I placed my hand on his chest. His heart beat as nearly as fast as my own. "Can we talk first?"

He nodded and turned to face the others. "Margaret, will you proceed to the sitting room with my mother? We will join you shortly."

"Mother, Margaret is a friend of *Kat's*." He emphasized my nickname. "Do show her the kindness she deserves."

He took my hand and led me into the library. I moved toward the back window. For almost a year, I had stared out this window and watched the brides and grooms embrace in their first dance. In a little over a week, it would be me . . . *or so I hoped.*

Trenton stood in front of me. I quickly wiped my tears off my cheeks, but he'd already seen them. His hands went to my face, his thumbs rubbed their remnants.

"Kat." He leaned forward. His eyes conveyed the familiar warmth I found to be home. "I'm sorry," he whispered.

His arms curled around me, and he pulled me close. I fit easily into the curve of his chest and shoulder. I inhaled his tantalizing, spicy scent and allowed it to soothe me.

As I rested my head against him and reflected on the day, I realized in my frenzy that I believed it couldn't get any worse. *I was wrong.*

"She will be gone tomorrow, I promise you."

"Do you have any feelings for her, Trenton?" I spoke with a small gust of confidence. "Is there anything unresolved or not clear in respect to Justine?"

"Nothing." He drew back and attempted to catch my eyes. We never really spoke much about his past relationships before. The only thing I knew about Justine came from the night of his dinner party when she draped herself over him. Shortly after, he tried to explain, but it hardly made sense with our new friendship. "Look at me, please." His fingers tenderly lifted my chin upward. His gaze nearly melted me on the spot and confirmed the sincerity of both his touch and his words. "Our families are quite close. My parents always assumed we would marry. I never once felt that way. Yes, we traveled and spent time together, but I never even kissed her." Glancing at his cheek with her lipstick staining his skin, it was hard to believe.

I moved my hand to his face and gently rubbed the mark off with my thumb. "She has an interesting way of showing friendship." Once the red makeup transferred to me, I left my hand there against his warm cheek.

"You're the only woman who has my heart and nothing, nothing at all could prevent me from making you my bride next week. Please don't lose faith in me." His eyes pleaded for me to believe him. I wanted to, I just struggled with all these bizarre distractions. They muddled my thoughts and weakened my bearing. "Kat, you are my future." He breathed softly. "I love you."

The assurance that radiated from him overpowered everything else. I met his gaze. "I love you too, Trenton."

"I will have Justine gone by tomorrow."

"No."

Trenton's forehead creased. "No?"

"I don't want to do anything that would make your mother dislike me. If having Justine here makes her happy, then so be it." I bit my bottom lip. "As long as I'm the only woman who claims your attention."

His smile grew. "You have such a kind heart, Kat. Though my mother does not deserve your compassion, I respect your decision and no need to fear, my heart is thoroughly taken." He tilted his head forward and kissed me tenderly. "Now I think you can see why I haven't been close to my parents for years."

"I really do hope that changes. I *want* to have a relationship with them."

"Well, we can worry about that after the wedding. This week is meant to be fun. Let's enjoy the games and events and not stress about who is here. The only two that really matter are you and me."

When I walked into the parlor on Trenton's arm, all eyes fell to me. From their expressions, they might have been expecting a scene, but my smile only grew. Especially when I caught sight of my own parents and friends. Regardless of what had just transpired, my determination to make the best of it surpassed my inadequacy.

I browsed the room as hasty introductions were made. In the rush of the day, I had either missed or only briefly met the other members of the party—Mrs. Gilford's sister, Beatrice Wright, her husband, Clarence and their twenty-year-old twin daughters, Ashtyn and Adele, Grandfather Gilford—the original Trenton Gilford, and his youngest son, Charles, who arrived with his wife Tabitha and their sons Henry, Leo and Roger, ages twenty-two, nineteen, and seventeen, respectively. Trenton's oldest cousin William, at thirty-two, is the only son of his Uncle Frederick, who could not make the wedding.

I glanced momentarily toward Mr. and Mrs. Gilford—and Justine, who apparently dressed expeditiously and, of course, appeared in flattering attire. When I peered back up to Trenton, his eyes remained firmly on me.

Hennessey promptly stepped forward. "Dinner is served."

As we filed into the dining room, Trenton led me to the center of the long table and pulled out my chair. Mrs. Gilford called to him from the far end. "Trenton, darling, come here. You are the host. It is your responsibility to be seated at the head of the table." She pointed to the dining arrangement's most significant chair and, without fail, swiftly seated Justine in the seat to his intended right side.

He glanced up and smiled, "Thank you, Mother, but we are all friends and family here, and since we will be spending the next week together, I prefer we keep all of our seating arrangements casual." He leaned down and kissed me on the cheek before he pushed in my chair and took the seat to my left. "Please," he waved his hand to the rest of the guests, "sit wherever you would like."

I forced myself not to peek in his mother's direction. I could only imagine the fiery darts aimed at me.

"May I sit here?"

I peered up to see a handsome older gentleman. His features were as similar to a Gilford as I had ever seen before. Though his posture curved slightly, he looked dashing in a dark brown double-breasted suit. His hair, peppered black and silver, brushed neatly across his forehead and bordered a gentle face.

"Kat," Trenton swiftly stood up. "This is my grandfather, Trenton Gilford, the first."

Though he had been briefly introduced with the assembly in the sitting room, this would be the first time we talked. I could barely conceal my excitement. *Another Gilford man! Another Trenton!*

"I'm so pleased to finally meet you," I said.

"The pleasure is most assuredly all mine, Miss Kat." He reached for my hand and squeezed. "I am delighted to finally meet the woman who has turned my grandson's life upside down or if you will . . . right side up."

I laughed. *He is kind too.*

He leaned forward and winked at Trenton. "You don't mind if I steal her attention for dinner, do you? You will, in the end, have her for the rest of your life." He chuckled.

Trenton laughed and tilted closer to me. "My grandfather is nothing like my father. You are entirely safe in his hands."

I smiled in relief and faced the older gentleman again.

"Tell me lovely Kat, how did you manage to convince my grandson to find joy in life?"

I watched him carefully for any underlying pretext. His question rang true. Since we started dating, Trenton's actions and conduct emerged less stuffy and more carefree. I hoped the family business didn't see me as a threat, but nothing in his eyes or voice indicated anything other than delight. "I doubt I had anything to do with it. I believe he found he could be effective in business and still enjoy the great things life has to offer."

"Oh, you are selling yourself short, dear. I know this man, and to see how he is now, is nothing short of a mighty change of heart. He has transformed, and I'm certain I have you to thank."

"Me?"

He nodded his head. "I learned much too late in life that there was more to living than simply *earning a living*. I'm afraid by the time I understood the value of joy, my beloved wife, Louise, departed soon after."

"I'm sorry to hear that. I would've liked to have met her."

"She would've loved you, she was a real spitfire, too."

I laughed, wondering how much Trenton had told him about me.

"I'm afraid all my attempts to convince these two . . ." he pointed to Trenton and his father, "fell on deaf ears. Then out of the blue a little over nine months ago, I noticed a change in Trenton—a momentous change. Each time we met, he proved to be less and less driven by numbers and bottom lines. We spent more time talking, golfing, fishing, and socializing. He asked me all about my childhood here and my parent's as well. He took this sudden interest in our family history and I wondered why until he confessed that he had met someone." He winked. "Someone who taught him how to see life differently."

I grinned shyly. To hear Trenton's thoughts after our initial battles, humbled me.

Grandfather Trenton patted my hand and pointed down to the other end of the table. "Don't trifle with that." He shook his head toward Mrs. Gilford in disgust. "Juliana and I never saw eye to eye on much, so her little stunt here, inviting Justine, does not surprise me, but please don't let it trouble you. I know who holds my grandson's heart."

I leaned over and kissed his cheek. "Thank you, thank you so much."

Trenton tilted his head and grinned, whispering only to me, "How many Gilford men do you plan on kissing?" He held out a finger with each name. "Merritt, Grandfather, and me? Who's next?"

I laughed out loud. "I will kiss you the most."

With the wonderful conversation at dinner, I nearly forgot about Margaret. Halfway through my buttered smoked haddock, I whipped my head around the large number of guests to locate her. I should've insisted she be seated near me, but being both distracted and pleased by Trenton's grandfather, I let my guard down. Biting my lip nervously, I watched her openly flirt with Trenton's friend, Jonah.

What could she be saying? Please, let her not embarrass me. I glanced over to Kelly nearby. She caught my eye and mouthed the word, "Wow". My face fell into my hand, then two fingers split for better sight of her.

"It appears Chapman will not be solo this week after all." Trenton noticed the direction of my stare.

I pulled my hand to my lap and nodded.

"If she's from here, why haven't we been introduced before?"

"She lives closer to L—London, and she's been b—busy," I stuttered.

"Well, he appears quite taken with her."

I tensed, watching Jonah's eyes fully engaged, then he broke out into a hearty laugh. *What could possibly be that funny?* Not the tale of the uninspiring governess, I hoped.

"It's quite fortunate Margaret arrived when she did." Trenton leaned in close. "Now there will be an even number in the wedding party once again."

My eyes grew wide at the thought.

"She is one of your bridesmaids, is she not?"

"Uh . . ." I tried to wrap my head around all of this. "She uh, has never been measured. I'm not sure she'll fit into Isabel's gown."

"I'm certain it will all work out. I imagine she would be a better option than Justine." Trenton chuckled. "If my mother had her way, she would insist Justine fill the gap."

"Oh no, Margaret will do quite nicely." I peeked once more to the opposite end of the table where Mrs. Gilford and Justine huddled in quiet conversation. I could only imagine what conniving plans were being constructed. Maybe Trenton should've removed her after all, but if I didn't trust him now when he swears his loyalty, when would I? I met his eyes once more as his lips curved into a rousing grin. He would not do anything to hurt me, of that, I was certain.

Chapter 13

Though conversation with over twenty people at a grand table proved to be difficult, I focused my attention on Margaret once more. I couldn't hear the details of her remarks, but between her fluttering eyelashes, occasional touch, and alluring smile, she more than fit the title of being an expert flirt. Jonah was nearly wrapped around her finger by the time the treacle tart topped with clotted cream arrived.

After dinner, Trenton announced that we would meet back in the sitting room to go over the events of the week, and afterward, the guests were free to do as they pleased.

When we moved to the parlor, I rushed to Margaret's side. "Excuse me, Jonah. I need a word with Margaret, please."

She turned to me and her smile waned. "I am otherwise engaged, Katharine."

"Engaged?" I choked and Jonah chuckled nervously, but his eyes betrayed him. He appeared entirely smitten.

Margaret's eyes flitted between us both. "Occupied, Katharine, I'm rather occupied at the moment." She turned to Jonah. "Let us secure another couple for a game of whist."

I exhaled and Jonah laughed a bit louder. "Whist?" He shook his head. "I've never played."

Her lips parted slightly. "Never played?"

Jonah's smile widened as if he saw her as a perplexing puzzle. "You're something else, Margaret."

"Pardon me, sir—" Her eyebrows dipped together. "—I have not acquiesced use of my Christian name."

I grabbed her wrist. It must've been tighter than I anticipated because she let out a small squeak. "Excuse us, Jonah. She'll return shortly, I promise." Then pulled her into a corner.

"I refuse to be waylaid like chattel." She grumbled.

"Chattle? Oh please, Miss Melodramatic, I just need a word."

Margaret squared her jaw and brushed out her skirt. Then as if she forgot her irritation, she tittered like a schoolgirl. "What a most extraordinary feast tonight, Katharine. I simply adored the Yorkshire Pudding, and the crème fraîche on the fish was divine, but I failed to identify a spice on the aubergines. Nutmeg perhaps?" She hardly noticed my arms crossed over my chest in impatience. "And why on earth did the men accompany us in here?" She stepped away from me and went to the nearest mirror. She examined her appearance again, then brushed a curl off her forehead. "Do they not engage in their traditional after dinner port?"

"No." I moved next to her in my attempt to not draw unwanted attention. "Nothing like that happens here."

"Come now, Katharine, I'm sure men have not altered that severely. Drink, women, and wealth is all they ruminate over. I'm certain your affianced is no different."

I groaned. "What are you doing?"

"Whatever do you imply?"

"Can't you just be normal?"

"Normal?"

"Look, everything you say speaks nineteenth century."

Her chin jutted outward. "I *am* from the nineteenth century."

I pointed to the other guests and muttered hotly. "But they don't know that, and I need to keep it that way."

"Humph." Her eyes flew upward precariously close to an eyeroll.

"Limit your conversation please . . . and don't flirt."

Her eyes steeled in my direction again. "It's in my nature to be enticing. I cannot help it if men find me irresistible."

"You're a tease," I whispered. A fire blazed beneath my skin. "What's going to happen when you make this guy fall for you and then you vanish? I will have to lie about your disappearance."

"Oh gads, Katharine. I am simply indulging in the moment. I have no intention of securing an attachment to Mr. Chapman." She glanced past me. "Oh . . .a pianoforte. I should play."

"No! No, no, no!"

Her mouth pulled into a thin line. "You hardly have the right to tell me what to do." A few faces turned our direction when her tone increased.

I lowered my voice. "Margaret, please . . ."

"Everything okay, honey?" My mom stepped up next to me, then extended her hand. "Hi, I'm Kat's mom, Emily. Who are you?"

Margaret looked at her hand and crinkled her nose. I knew that whole handshaking thing threw her off.

"Mom, this is my friend Margaret. We met here . . . in England."

"Oh," Mom grabbed her hand in both of hers and shook gently. "I'm happy to meet you."

"Pleased to make your acquaintance as well." Margaret dipped into a shallow curtsy.

Mom's mouth formed an "o".

"Uh, Mom, Margaret is an actress in London."

"Oh?" My mom's smile grew. She, alone, fostered my love for Broadway shows. "What performances have you done?"

"Uh, the usual." I cut her off. "She tends to be a bit dramatic off the stage as well." I chuckled, but it surfaced more like a nervous laugh. "Um, Margaret. I need to speak with my mom. Remember what I suggested, okay?"

Margaret smiled curtly and turned away without another word.

"Your friend is interesting. How did you meet?" Mom's right eyebrow lifted. I knew she suspected something.

"A friend of a friend." I grinned.

"Kat?" Now both of her eyebrows curved in. "You seem . . . troubled. Is everything okay?"

I huffed, knowing she of all people could read me thoroughly. "I've been a little stressed."

"I suspected so." She pulled my arm through hers and patted my hand. "Because of the upcoming wedding?"

"No, no Mom. Honestly, that's the only part of my life that's actually sane right now."

"Are you sure you aren't nervous about . . . you know marrying someone other than Jeff?"

"No, believe me. I know we haven't spent much time talking about this, but I want you and Dad to know I have no doubts about Trenton. He's the man I'm meant to marry."

She beamed and tugged me closer. "The way he looks at you, Kat, *I* get chills." She giggled. "And he's such a gentleman, so considerate of us all."

I spotted Trenton near the hearth. He laughed enthusiastically as he and his Uncle Clarence conversed. "Yes, he really is a remarkable man."

She embraced me tenderly, then kissed my cheek. "I guess I worried for nothing, sweetheart."

I swallowed against the small lump in my throat. "Yeah, Mom, I promise, nothing to worry about."

"May I have your attention, please?" Trenton tapped a glass tumbler with a spoon. When his eyes met mine, he smiled broadly. "And might my beautiful fiancé join me over here?"

I smiled back and walked to his side.

He put the glass down and wrapped one arm around me.

"Kat and I are most obliged to you, our family and friends, for joining us this week as the hour draws closer to our wedding day. I know many of you have not met one another before tonight, but I hope at the end of the event you will have become lifelong friends."

"Here, here." Hastings lifted his glass in a solo cheer. Laughter erupted around him.

Trenton gazed down upon me. "Many of you who know me probably believed I would never marry."

Marlowe took his turn to lift his glass. "To bachelorhood." This time, Jonah and Hastings, both stood to their feet in rowdy agreement.

Trenton cleared his throat then smiled. "Happily, a bachelor no more. This woman showed me how to argue," he chuckled, "laugh and love with a zeal unlike anything I've ever known. She showed me how to respect my family name and legacy and has forever changed my life." He tipped his head and kissed me lightly to a thundering applause. My heart burst beneath his touch, grinning as he continued, "Thank you for taking the time out of your busy lives and schedules to celebrate this most amazing week with us."

"To Trenton and Kat." Grandfather raised a glass in our direction. When my eyes met his, he winked. Everyone raised their glasses to that toast. Or at least I believed everyone did.

"Now we are quite excited about the events this week, but please do not feel required to participate in any or even at all if you prefer. The events are completely at will and are assured to be as entertaining for the spectator as well as the partaker." He squeezed my shoulder. "Kat, would you do us the honor?" Then took a step backward but stayed nearby.

"Yes, well, as I have learned," I grinned genuinely. "The Gilford family holds a traditional house party the week before the nuptials. This includes a cricket game, which will be played tomorrow, weather permitting, and a picnic. There will be an archery tournament on Sunday. Monday, we have the final dress fitting for the bridal party in London, and the men have a hunting trip planned that same day. Those who are not involved in either may do as they please. Tuesday is the boat ride down the Thames and another picnic. Wednesday is the horse races or rides. Thursday is the charity event. Friday is the talent show. And, of course, Saturday is the big event . . . the wedding, followed by the wedding dinner." I smiled at Trenton and stole a subtle breath. "An in-depth copy of these events has been printed and posted on your bedroom doors, but of course, if you have any questions, please ask. I look forward to getting to know you all better and especially becoming the newest member of the Gilford Family. Thank you again for spending this special time with us."

A final applause confirmed to us the excitement and eagerness this week would bring. I scanned the room carefully, not letting my eyes fall on anyone too long, yet as they passed Mrs. Gilford, discontent seeped from every line in her face. I forced a smile once more as she tipped her head toward Justine who glanced up at me and chuckled. I faced Trenton, hoping their eyes were still upon me as I reached for his lapels and brought him to me in a loving kiss.

"Mmmm," Trenton whispered as we released. "To what reason do I deserve such a display of gratitude? Not that I'm complaining, mind you." He grinned.

"No reason." I fibbed. My motive clearly aimed at showing my hand. "I am the luckiest woman in all of England."

"Only England?" Trenton's lips twitched, fighting a smile.

"No," I teased. "Maybe just Bedfordshire County."

His laugh broke through. His hands went for my waist. I pushed them off knowing his intent meant to tickle and though I wanted his mother and Justine to witness our closeness, I didn't want them to see me squeal like a pig. "Not in front of everyone." I clasped his hands.

"Very well, I will resume your penance in private." He grinned mischievously and kissed my hand. "Now let me introduce you personally to my uncles and cousins, they have been eagerly awaiting this day since I shared the good news with them."

I gladly complied, but not before I stole a peek at Justine in passing. With my arm tucked cozily through Trenton's, I smiled deliberately in response to her distinct glare. *This just might be the best part of my entire day . . . truthfully, it was the kiss, but this is definitely a close second.*

Later that night, after making the rounds amongst family and friends, the exhaustion from today's events and lack of sleep finally caught up with me. I returned to where Trenton sat on a sofa visiting with his cousin William, who he hadn't seen for over a year.

With a simple kiss on his cheek, I said goodnight and excused myself, then turned around and caught Margaret's eye. When I motioned to the door, she frowned, though her eyes appeared as heavy as mine. In the end, she joined me down the hall.

Once inside the bedroom, I located a nightgown for her—a wedding gift from my Aunt Carol. The nightdress' length fell significantly shorter than what Margaret would find appropriate, but much longer than anything I wore, so when I presented it next to my normal one, she accepted it with little complaint.

"Here's a toothbrush, toothpaste, deodorant, and lotion." Earlier I had the foresight to raid our supply closet. "And I suspect you will find this method of brushing your teeth more comfortable than a birch twig."

She studied the items with curiosity as I demonstrated each one.

"I position that where?" Her voice cracked after I pointed out the deodorant.

"Under your arms to avoid sweating."

"A lady doesn't sweat."

"Fine." My tolerance for the day had hit its limit. "Stink for all I care." I sighed. "Maybe it will help Jonah keep his distance."

"You're rather starched up in piety." She snapped.

"Me?" My mouth gaped open. "I'm the one trying to help you."

Her nostrils flared. "The particulars of this time are mortifying. And I daresay, women have become a dreary lot."

"It's simple hygiene, Margaret. We like to smell good just like you, but if you prefer perfume instead, I have that as well."

"Very well, I will pacify you."

I groaned and rubbed my eyes. "I appreciate your inclination to mollify the lower class, Miss Abbott." Oblivious to whether she caught my sarcasm or not, I slipped into the lavvy to get ready for bed. Finally, the longest day of my life was coming to a close.

Although the enormous king size bed offered more than adequate space for us to share . . . it simply felt odd. My body settled in and tried to relax, but my mind didn't follow suit. It struggled to accept the idea that Margaret was *here*, not only here, but sharing a room with me, wearing my clothes . . . wearing my underwear! The one woman I would've happily strangled back in 1878 without a hint of remorse, the very person I detested above all else now slept beside me. Her mannerisms were still aggravating and obnoxious, but to Margaret's defense, *her only defense*, she remained stuck in another time and another world—something I understood all too well.

Chapter 14

Saturday 14 May 2011

The next morning, warm sunshine radiated through the window that faced the gardens, bringing peace and tranquility with it. That is, until I turned to my side and found Margaret lying still next to me. Her mouth gaped open, and her drawn-out breaths signaled her exhaustion. I remembered those first few mornings in the past when I awoke wishing with all my might that I had returned to my time but hadn't.

The arrogance and callousness Margaret spewed may very well be amplified from her fears regarding the time travel experience. I didn't know her well enough to know how she handled stress, but having crossed her temper back in her own time, I wasn't entirely sure.

Watching her now, I wondered if she handled the change better than me. I believed she understood the significance of what she faced, but she didn't appear as distressed with the time-travel—at least not when she socialized. Maybe she assumes, much like I did, that it isn't real . . . that it's just an elaborate dream. She snorted awake.

"Oh," she cried.

I swiftly turned my head away. I didn't need her to think I watched her sleep. Stretching my legs, I pushed the covers aside. "Did you sleep well?" I feigned interest in her answer. It wouldn't matter if she had a lousy night or not, since Justine arrived and took the last available bedroom, she was stuck with me.

"I believe so." She yawned. Then sat up abruptly and wiped her eyes. "Oh no!" She jumped from the bed and ran to the window. "It—it's true?"

"What's true?"

Her shoulders sagged. "We are still in your time, are we not?"

A fleeting moment of sympathy surged in remembrance of my first frightening morning . . .fleeting because the second she turned back toward me, she scowled. "If I am to remain here, you must attain more suitable attire for me to don. These scraps will, unequivocally, *not* do."

My face scrunched, but I ignored her denigration and spoke on something entirely unrelated to her wardrobe. "Since the main events today are a cricket game and a picnic shortly afterward, I suspect it will be another long day." I reached for my cell phone and glanced at the time. "It all starts in a few hours, but until then, I think you should relax in here."

"I most certainly will not." Margaret's arms folded at her waist. "I'm riding this morning with Mr. Chapman."

"You agreed to go riding?"

"He insisted on it."

"What exactly did you two talk about last night?"

She flicked her hair and moved toward the lavvy. "You are not privy to my personal conversations, Katharine."

"Your personal conversations affect me. What did you talk about?" All niceties aside, her stubbornness infuriated me.

"We spoke of London—"

"You do realize the London *you* know isn't the London of today."

"We discussed the Royal Opera House, Regent's Park, and Belgrave Square. He seemed to be quite aware of all three."

"Only because they're centuries old!" I snapped. "You agreed to ride with him this morning?"

"After I borrow a suitable riding habit and secure a chaperone. Possibly one of the groomsmen, if a lady cannot be arranged. Heaven knows you'd make an abysmal chaperone."

"I would not!" I countered, then shook my head at the madness of our argument. "Look, I can lend you my habit, but I'm afraid it will be short on you."

"Short? Are you suggesting the skirt will show my ankles?"

"My riding habit is not a dress." I stood and crossed my arms over my chest. This conversation echoed in repetition. "You also don't need a chaperone."

"No chaperone?" She shrieked. "But my reputation . . ."

"Will hardly be affected by a man of this century. You don't need to worry about Jonah taking advantage of you."

"Mr. Chapman is quite enamored with me. I'm sure taking liberties has crossed his mind."

"Women today don't require chaperones."

"Humph." Margaret grunted and slammed the lavvy door shut.

I moaned and ran my hand through my hair. "This is going to be the longest week *ever*."

I went to my wardrobe and retrieved the riding habit that Trenton had custom-made for me. Sure to be quite different than what Margaret identified with, I laid it on the bed. The sleek, beige riding coat was tailored to my form and accentuated my figure nicely, while the tail portion flared slightly above a pair of black, skin-tight pants. Though Margaret and I had similarities in the waist and chest, her hips were wider and her legs longer.

When she came out, I held it up.

"Breeches?" Her cheeks grew pale. "Have you gone mad? I cannot wear this!"

"Fine," I said with little sympathy. "You can wear anything you want but also keep in mind, we don't have side saddles. You'll have to ride astride."

I might as well have told her she had a horn growing out of her head. Her hands flew to her face aghast. "You cannot be serious!" She screeched. "What kind of uncivilized delirium have I awoken to?"

I fought my smile, enjoying this way too much. "It's called the future, Margaret."

Seeing her terror, I stopped myself. The memory of my time travel experience still lingered raw and unnerving, reminding me of how my words and actions affected my consequences. Especially the chilling notion of being stuck in the past forever. Then I grew frustrated. I didn't have someone like Margaret does, one who knew what happened and offered to help—*I* was entirely alone.

"Look," I softened my tone. "Much of what was familiar to you has changed greatly, and until we can get you back to your time, you have to make adjustments."

With choppy breaths, she stepped to the window and peered out. The silence that followed lasted several minutes until she spoke. "This grieves me to the soul."

I approached her cautiously. When the vulnerable side of Margaret surfaced, like now, it made it almost feasible to speak like normal people. I placed a hand on her shoulder. "When I fell down the stairs and appeared in your time in 1878, I had no one. No one to help me navigate your time and the differences, but here, now, *I* can help you. All I'm asking is that you listen to me and not make things difficult." She faced me expressionless. "I already have a mother-in-law who can't stand me, and a woman who is most certainly trying to sway Trenton's affections, I don't need you to add to that stressful list the week before I'm to be married. Can we please just agree to work together?"

She nodded her head subtly. "I will try."

"That's all I'm asking."

Her lips pulled into a frown as she peered over to the riding habit.

"Now what do you want to wear for your ride this morning?"

She sighed loudly. "I should decline, I can't possibly ride astride with a gentleman present."

"You could if you wore pants."

"Certainly not."

"Okay, well, I can tell him you're not feeling well and are resting. He'll understand. Then he will be that much more excited to see you at the cricket match."

"I'm terrified to inquire, but are the women participating?" Margaret's iridescent complexion hinted a bit greener this morning.

"Only if they want to."

"Are you?"

"Yes. Trenton has shown me the basics. I can hit a ball pretty well from when I played softball in Arizona, but I still don't entirely understand the rules."

Margaret sat down at the dressing table. "I feel so . . ." She mumbled. "I feel . . ."

"Lost?"

She bobbed her head.

That very word summed up my own sentiments when I time traveled. "Believe me, Margaret, I understand completely."

She took a deep breath and fiddled with her messy hair. "I suppose I must manage this on my own?"

"No, I'll send for Anabelle again. She didn't seem to mind doing it yesterday."

"You will?"

"Of course." I chuckled. "I'm not as spiteful as you might think."

Her lips curled into a subtle smile, probably the most genuine I'd seen from her.

"I'll be back. And I'll send a breakfast tray in for you as well."

"Thank you," Margaret whispered.

I froze at the door with my back to her. *Did she really just thank me?* I glanced subtly over my shoulder and spied her through the mirror. The solemnity in her face tempered my frustration. If only she could be this humble all the time, she might actually be pleasant to be around.

I stepped quietly out of the room. With the sun shining fully today, the party unquestionably gathered for breakfast on the veranda. I entered the kitchen first and waved at Helen, who just happened to have my mom by her side, apron on and everything.

"Mom, you're a guest." I laughed.

"Good morning, Kat." She bent over a frying pan filled with tomatoes, mushrooms, and sliced bangers. "Now, how could I possibly pass up the chance to learn from the best? Besides, I could bring some of these ideas back to the deli."

I hugged her from behind and the scented smoke that settled in her hair made my mouth water. "Great plan, this smells yummy."

Mom winked as I pulled away. "They took a tray outside with some bacon, eggs, and beans but you must be quick, or it will be gone before you get there."

"Sounds good."

Helen shot me a curious look. Thankfully, she hadn't mentioned to my mom that my morning eating habits had recently waned. My positive attitude didn't need a blighting lecture.

I smiled her way. "Helen, could I get a breakfast tray delivered to my friend Margaret? She's staying in my room."

"Certainly!" She called a staff member over quickly.

I hugged them both once more and, with a light step, walked through the doors to the veranda. The sunshine dazzled and the warmth flooded my soul. I could not resist stopping in place to let the sweet scent of the vibrant Westerland roses with their copper-colored petals fill my lungs. "What a fantastic day," I said with my eyes closed, that is until I was jarred out of my serenity by a loud giggle from the table. Unfortunately, I heard enough of that sound last night to know exactly who it belonged to.

I glanced toward the large dining table with several shades overhead to locate the source, then froze. Justine leaned tightly across Trenton's chest to speak to his mother, who just happened to be seated on his other side. My brows furrowed. She could've easily sat next to Mrs. Gilford, but as it appeared, they sandwiched him . . .or ambushed him more likely.

I held my tongue as the women looked over to me. Justine's lips curved into a smug smile. A smile vaguely familiar to Margaret's. "Good morning, Katharine."

I stiffened. Trenton's eyes met mine and he jumped to his feet. I waited until he arrived at my side to speak. I took an additional breath to calm my voice, though my words still came out shaky. "I see you're enjoying breakfast?"

Trenton faced me and pulled both my hands into his. "I waited for you. They just arrived and sat down. What am I to do? I can't very well cast-off my mum. I'm a gentleman."

"Yes, I know." My eyes searched his. His honesty displayed in every line, but somehow, my own betraying thoughts clouded mine. "How far is a gentleman willing to go to make a guest happy?"

"Kat . . ." His eyes pleaded. "I don't want to have this conversation here, please come and sit with me. Let's have breakfast together."

"It appears the seats are taken."

"I will move."

Squeezing his hand, I shook my head. "I don't want to control you, Trenton. Honestly, you may sit wherever you like."

"I want to sit next to my fiancé." His voice grew husky. "I want to sit with you, Kat."

The ice slowly melted around my heart. Trenton radiated sincerity. "Thank you for inviting me, but I'm not really hungry."

Faint lines appeared between his eyes. "You need to eat if you're going to play today. You need strength, it's a pretty fast-paced game."

"I'll grab a scone. I need to find Jonah. Do you know where he is?"

"Jonah?"

I nodded.

"He's headed to the stables for a ride this morning. I believe he's taking Margaret out."

"She's not feeling well and won't be able to make it. I just wanted to let him know."

"Well, please allow me to do it while you sit down and eat."

Looking back at the table, I snickered. "I'm not sitting between Justine and your mom."

"No, of course not." He chuckled nervously. "There are open seats across from them, but please eat. You'll need all of your energy for this week . . ." Then he bent forward so only I would hear, "I would be sorely dismayed if you were exhausted for the honeymoon." He kissed my cheek then hustled toward the stables.

I turned to the sideboard and selected a few strawberries and a scone. Meandering slowly toward the table, I sat in the seat

Trenton suggested across from the women. Relief flooded my mind, seeing Grandfather Gilford nearby. "Good morning," I said to the group as I sat down.

"Where is Trenton off to?" Mrs. Gilford must've just become aware of his disappearance.

"He went to see Jonah in the stables." I smiled, though nothing was reciprocated.

Justine's lips protruded. "He promised to take me for a ride, why would he leave without me?" She blinked in my direction.

"Actually, my dear," Grandfather cleared his throat. "He promised you a chance to ride during the events, but never offered to personally accompany you. In fact, I do believe he suggested making it a group event."

I smiled behind my scone and peeked over to see him wink at me.

Justine scowled. "Well, he and I have ridden together for so long I presume to carry on as before." I studied her. The stare that transpired revealed a woman who would not easily give up. "There is much we've done in the past, and *nothing* will change that."

"Just short of a wedding I assume." I added after I finished chewing. "Trenton is sure to be quite occupied with his bride." I picked up my plate, barely touched, and stood to leave.

"Good to see you again, Grandfather." I smiled in his direction, with nothing short of a curt nod at the women.

Being unfriendly would not win me points, but they were solely responsible for souring my good mood.

As I turned down the corridor to rejoin Margaret, I heard a noise stir behind me.

"You know you're not good enough for him, right?"

I circled around to see Justine's shapely outline behind me. She must've followed me inside. The sunlight from the nearest window incalculably highlighted her feminine features.

"Good enough for who?" I questioned, knowing exactly who she inferred.

Her lips twisted slightly to the rise in my voice.

"He will get bored with you. Just like all the other women who have thrown themselves in front of him over the years." Her nostrils flared. "And even if he doesn't see it now, I will endeavor to make sure he knows he is making a big mistake."

My right eye twitched irritatingly while I watched her inch closer. The faint memory of Margaret cornering me back in 1878, transpired. She assumed I had designs on Merritt and spewed similar threats and, much like the past, I had no intention of backing down.

"Let me be perfectly clear, Justine." We stood a mere meter apart. "I didn't throw myself in front of anyone. I didn't need to, Trenton pursued me. And as far as being bored in the past, it most likely happened because Trenton grew tired of high-maintenance British women who didn't know how to take *no* for an answer."

She gasped. "You little—"

"—Enjoy your week, Justine." I cut her off and spun on my heel. "It's bound to be your last here at Charlock." Then opened my bedroom door and slammed it shut behind me.

Chapter 15

After I double tied my sneakers and tightened my ponytail, I stood slightly hunched holding the "bat," which resembled more of a paddle, firmly within my hands. The sticks driven into the ground just below my stance were referred to as *wickets*, the object to defend at all costs. I licked my lips as the opposite team readied, though a hand quickly raised nearby and halted the game to a series of moans from the other players.

"A moment, gentlemen, and ladies." Trenton nodded and approached me. Reaching for my waist, he tugged me toward him. When his lips hit my ear, he whispered, "Now remember love, this isn't baseball." He gently pushed the bat down near my feet. "You're defending the wicket. Strike to the right side, it's weak." He inched back only enough to kiss me. As the cat calls and hollers grew louder his kiss lengthened. Once he pulled away, I grinned madly at his deception. "Forgive me." He hollered and waved a hand to the rival team. "I couldn't resist." Then he winked at me before he walked away.

I steadied myself back into position and scanned the field carefully. He was right. The strongest team members, including Hastings and Jonah, staggered weightily to the left, most likely assuming a righty would angle that direction.

In a traditional cricket match, there are eleven players on each side, however with our participant numbers significantly less, we opted for a less customary structure of seven on each team. This modified a few other rules as well, but since I claimed no prior knowledge of the game before today, it mattered little.

I pivoted my toes slightly to the right and angled my hips shortly after the "bowler" took a few steps and released the ball. *Smack!* Solid hit! The ball flew a good ten feet past his cousin Roger who scrambled backward to retrieve it. Gifted with more ambition than athleticism, Roger fumbled the ball several times before he grasped it tightly in his fist. By the time he threw the ball to his brother Henry, Marlowe and I had passed each other several times, scoring four additional points for our team.

Marlowe's wide smile and thumbs up bolstered me before Leo's turn came to stand before the wicket. With his firm grounder out past the bowler, he became my new running mate. Ashtyn was next and, like all the previous batsmen, she scored with an in-boundary strike, adding another two points and launching our team easily into a six-point lead only ten minutes into the game.

Trenton met me off the field and lifted me up with pride. "Brilliant, love!"

"Thank you, babe. But I do believe my coach gets all the credit."

He chuckled and whispered close as he put me down. "I only pointed you in the right direction. You did all the work."

I smiled and glanced over to the opposing team where some serious heckling had begun. Hastings, my formidable rival, shook his finger quite animatedly in my direction, but smiled approvingly. Trenton's cousin, William, ran over and gave me a high-five—a move most Brits don't normally do, so when he awkwardly held his hand up, I laughed aloud and smacked it back to his satisfaction.

"You're up Gilford!" Marlowe shouted in our direction.

"Yes, Gilford, do get on with it." Jonah taunted from the pitch. "Leave the lass alone to bask in her triumph. It's entirely possible she will outshine you today."

Hastings joined the fray. "Not to worry, Chapman, he most certainly lost his edge when he relinquished his man card."

Trenton's lips lifted in his infamous half smile and glanced between me and the men who he called friends. I chuckled and kissed his cheek. "Just go shut them up."

He wiggled one brow and headed over for his own turn.

Instead of directing it toward Roger, as he suggested to me, Trenton squared his shoulders and sent taunting looks to both Jonah and Hastings. When he strategically hit it between both men, his provocation only showed this competition would only get more rambunctious. Now, knowing how much fun cricket is, I will insist we do it more often, and include the staff.

Taking a seat on the ground next to Maria, I opted to relax until I was needed on the pitch again. Within seconds, a maid appeared beside me with a cool drink. "From Mr. Gilford, miss." I glanced behind me to see Grandfather seated comfortably underneath a shade tent. He raised his glass and smiled. I waved my thanks. Now, he was one relative I would love to have around more often.

"You definitely haven't lost your strength." Maria commented on my hit.

"Just a lucky shot, besides, Trenton gave me tips."

"Oh, is that what you call it?" She chuckled. "Maybe I should've played after all, perhaps Hastings would have given me *tips*."

I barked a laugh. "I'm sure Hastings would be more than willing to give you *tips*—that's if he hasn't already." I turned to catch her evading my look. A broad smile filled her cheeks. "He has, hasn't he?" I playfully pushed her over as she burst out laughing.

After William's solid four points for his ground-hitting boundary mark, the next two batsmen were stumped and caught, rounding out the four outs we had agreed upon versus the normal ten.

When we took the field, the same playful taunting continued. Trenton took his place as the bowler and I went out to the right side to be a fielder.

"I'm aiming for you, Kat!" Hastings hollered as he stepped up to bat.

"Bring it!" I hunched into a ready stance and, with my two fingers rotating from my eyes to his, I sent the clear message I was ready and waiting.

He snickered and Trenton nodded in my direction right before he wound up for a fast bowl when in fact, he slowed it to a crawl. Thankfully, the ball didn't hit the ground more than once and was still considered a fair ball. Hastings was caught completely unaware and missed it entirely.

"You're out!" Trenton shouted as the ball waylaid one of the bails of the wicket.

"You cheated!" Hastings refuted.

"And exactly how did I do such a thing?"

"A lousy bowl."

"Was it illegal?"

Hastings' face pinched in frustration, but he didn't disagree with the legality of the move, instead, he threw his fingers up mimicking my earlier movement and pointed at both me and Trenton. "This isn't over."

I laughed out loud. "I'll be waiting . . . that is if you can actually get a hit."

He stopped mid-stride after that last banter, pivoted in my direction, and smiled wide. "Oh, I am coming after you next time, little miss sassy pants. Mark my words!"

It took another two rounds at bat before Hastings' threats rang true. He didn't hide his intent on aiming my way, and this time came prepared for anything Trenton threw at him. Though I remained focused, his admirable hit caught air. Leaping for the ball, I barely missed the catch as it brushed the tips of my leather riding gloves and hit the ground right behind me. My swift moves to retrieve it and pass it on not only stole his out-of-boundary points, but also prevented him and Henry from scoring more than one point. "Bollocks!" He shouted when he reached the second wicket and realized he would get no further. Shaking his head dramatically, he pointed my way. "This has only just begun."

I grinned. Trenton's friends had quickly become my own. I relished the thought of all the years to come and all the memories we would make.

After another two hours of similar play, and a close game, our team celebrated a hard-earned victory and the subsequent collection on the wager made the night of the hag party. Unfortunately, not all the players had been present to agree to the terms of the bet, but still willingly participated.

Above the grassy playing field, a short walk took us to a lush hill that resembled more of a bump in the earth than a steep mound. This was a perfect site for the picnic. Though the sky was scattered with clouds, the white ones outnumbered the gray, and a slight breeze offered instant relief from a brash sun when its rays found a window.

A handful of colorful blankets were spread all over the lawn and as people meandered over to different groupings, somehow, Mrs. Gilford and Justine arrived at Trenton's and mine.

"Is there room for your dear mother, son?"

"Of course, please join us." He moved closer to me which could never be faulted, and we watched as the prim and proper Mrs. Gilford awkwardly lowered herself to the ground.

Once settled, she sighed dramatically. "At our wedding festivities, we provided comfortable seating for our elder generations at the picnic." She cleared her throat. "We did not require them to stoop like farm animals on the grass."

"I would be happy to arrange a chair for you, Mother. I apologize for overlooking your needs."

"It is clearly not your fault, Trenton. An adequate house manager would have seen to it properly, but seeing yours is preoccupied, it is merely a misunderstanding."

I stared at the woman. *Did she just take a shot at me?* I wasn't entirely sure since I'm not technically the house manager, but then again, I do fill the responsibilities of that role.

"An innocent oversight, Mum. I will see that the next picnic will have tables and chairs available." Although his answer seemed cordial enough, I wondered if he recognized her underlying jab.

A graceful Justine maneuvered down beside her, reaching for Mrs. Gilford's hand and patting it as if she required comfort from the injustice I had somehow imposed. Biting the inside of my cheek, I forced myself to be careful and not allow the words that formed in my mind to reach my lips.

I shifted my gaze to my parents as they filled their plates on the far end of our blanket and happily chatted with Trenton's Uncle Charles nearby—the youngest of the three sons from Grandfather Trenton. And while he possessed a kind face, his features showed nothing similar to the older Trenton's—his brother *or* his father. In fact, if I hadn't known he bore the Gilford name, I might've assumed him to be from Mrs. Gilford's side of the family.

"Mr. and Mrs. Shelton?" Mrs. Gilford called over to them. "I understand that you own a business?"

I braced myself.

"Yes," my father spoke first. "We own a deli in New York."

"A deli?"

"Yep! Delicatessen. Sandwiches, drinks, snacks, you know, carbs."

"Y—yes, of course . . . how charming." Her painted smile dwindled.

"If you ever come to the city, ma'am, be sure to stop by, we'll set you up just right."

"Set me up?" Her tone shuddered.

"Sure, anything you want on the house." Dad enthusiastically smiled.

Mrs. Gilford dipped her chin and sent Justine a pointed look, one that was not missed. When it came to her barbs against me, I expected it, but I won't tolerate her slinging mud at my parents. They were only being friendly.

I inhaled deeply and forced the pressure in my chest to subside. What little I knew of Trenton's mother, assured me that she loved being the center of attention, so I turned the focus back onto her. "Mrs. Gilford?"

She raised one eyebrow in my direction.

"Do you mind telling us about your home in Italy? I would love to hear what it's like there."

The crease on her forehead disappeared. "Oh, yes." She cooled herself with a cobalt-colored fan depicting a vibrant sunset on the front. "It's utterly divine . . . Tuscan stone, hand-painted tiles, and a half-dozen olive trees. A slice of heaven, wouldn't you say so, Justine?"

My smile faltered. *She's been to their estate in Italy?*

Justine sat up straighter, and her countenance brightened. "Simply wonderful. They have these arched doorways with spiral staircases and two lush patios, but my favorite part is the charming courtyard covered in hanging vines, bougainvillea I believe, and an exquisite fountain of the Goddess Vesta."

"Interesting." Trenton peered toward his mother. "You only acquired the property six months ago. I haven't even been there, yet."

His mother flicked her hand dismissively in his direction. "An invitation was issued, son, you merely refused to come."

Trenton's lips pulled tight. "The timing . . ."

I held my breath. I remembered when Trenton received the formal request. It arrived a mere week after he proposed, yet the missive was only addressed to him. We didn't speak of it afterward. *I wonder if that's when Justine received her invitation as well.*

"The timing was unsuitable." He finished.

"For whom?" Her eyes flickered over to me then back to Trenton.

"Lemonade, Miss Shelton?" A droll voice with a hint of mischief pulled for my attention. I gazed up to see a prim and proper Hastings in a serving apron, fulfilling his duty bound by the wager and holding a pitcher of juice.*Perfect timing.*

His wide smile and arched brows brought a nice relief to the stuffy atmosphere. He leaned down to where only I could hear him, "I do believe Mrs. Gilford has devoured her fair share of lemons already, would you care for a taste?" I covered my mouth to prevent my laugh.

"Absolutely." Smiling back, I lifted my glass. "Thank you, Hastings." He winked before he moved on. Trenton's friends really were more like family.

"Mrs. Shelton?" Trenton turned to the other end.

"Oh, please call me Emily. We're family."

I smiled. Mom never left a room without making new friends.

"Very well, Emily. Where does Kat get her skills from? She's quite the athlete."

"Oh, definitely not from me."

She looked to Dad as he shook his head. "Not me, either."

"I think it came from having to defend herself from her older brothers all those years." Mom laughed. "They teased her mercilessly."

"I can't wait to meet these tormentors." Trenton chuckled. "I must thank them."

I smacked his arm. "You mock my suffering?"

"Quite the opposite." His ardent eyes entranced me "I admire your determination and strength to overcome."

Gazing back at him, I lost myself. The kindness in his countenance brought my heart to a solid stop and compelled me to forget there were others present.

"I, for one, couldn't tolerate doing anything significantly masculine." Justine shattered our moment. "Women that sweat are so . . ." She wrinkled her nose and brushed grass off her linen dress pants. "Unpleasant."

Mrs. Gilford shook her head. "Oh, I must agree with you, Justine." *Of course, she must.* "I cannot see how any man would find assertive behavior attractive."

"Well, it certainly is a good thing you are not a man, Mother." Trenton popped a grape into his mouth. "I for one find it quite desirable in a mate." He jiggled his eyebrow in my direction as his mother huffed loudly.

"Mrs. Gilford?" My mother called to her in such a friendly tone. I doubt that Mom noticed the underlying insults coming from our end of the blanket.

Mrs. Gilford peered in her direction under the wide brim of her sun hat.

"Tell me about the Gilford wedding traditions. When Kat called to give me the details, I have to say, I was thrilled to take part. How long has this custom been going on? Has every Gilford participated?"

All eyes turned to Mrs. Gilford for the answer to a question I would love to know myself, but without the cynical quip that would surely come if the inquiry came from me.

"It's a lovely tradition. Started I believe with . . ." She turned her head sideways as if she tried to remember the names. "Oh goodness, I can't recall, but sometime in the 1700s."

"That's fantastic!" Mom looked at me, her eyes smiling with her massive grin. "Just think, Kat, what a wonderful story you'll get to tell your kids one day."

I smiled back. It was impossible not to. Of course, Trenton and I spoke of raising a family a few years from now.

Mrs. Gilford considered us. "Well," she shifted in place. "Traditions have been broken before." My nose wrinkled at her inference. Did she mean the wedding or the children?

She continued, "One couple relinquished due to mourning the death of his mother."

I gasped subtly. *Merritt and Joanne.* From his journals I learned his mother had passed only a month before they wed. After all they had been through, it made sense he refused to wait any longer than the time required for the banns to be read. He and Joanne belonged together. Then on top of that, it was strange to think Margaret's presence came about because she fell on the night of their wedding. If I hadn't known such wild possibilities existed from my own experience, I would be completely undone.

Mrs. Gilford then added, "And my husband insists there is a family tale where one of the couples negated the customary festivities, against the wishes of the family, and they lost a child. Sure to be the result of such thoughtless behavior."

"Lost a child?" I cried. "From the choices surrounding their wedding? That doesn't make any sense."

She snapped back to me. "It makes perfect sense. In fact, you of all people should know the history. The child's handprint is framed in our suite. Although I must say every time I visit, it's the first item removed. I cannot tolerate the dismal sight."

She spoke of Peter, Merritt's younger brother. A spark of anger triggered from within. I knew the history—*I lived the history.* I heard the very truth of the tragedy from Merritt's own mouth. It had nothing to do with superstitions or unkept traditions, only a devastatingly painful lesson learned by an older brother. When Merritt told me the story of his role in Peter's drowning and the unbearable heartache and guilt he still carried, my own heart ached agonizingly for him.

Trenton's eyes fell upon me. His hand reached for mine and squeezed. Fighting back an assault of disobedient tears, I picked up my drink and kept my cup close to my face to hide my distress.

"What a t—terrible ordeal." Mom stuttered. She must've seen my reaction and attempted to change the subject. "Your home and gardens are quite magnificent, Mrs. Gilford. When did you decide to turn the home over for tours and weddings?"

"Over twenty years ago. Right before Trenton turned nine."

"How sad to leave such a beautiful place."

"It no longer met our needs." Mrs. Gilford reached for a biscuit, but before she took a bite, a hint of what might've been remorse flickered in her eyes.

"Well, the wedding will be enchanting here." Mom's eyes radiated. "I can't wait."

Mrs. Gilford glanced away and flicked her fan wide open once more. When I caught sight of her face between wafts, she frowned profoundly.

"Trenton, you should tell my parents about your childhood here." I turned my attention back to him but was swiftly interrupted.

"You were a horribly mischievous child, wouldn't you agree, Son?" Mrs. Gilford once again wielded the conversation. "You and Justine romped all over this place. Remember dear, that time you both got stuck in that tree?" She pointed to a nearby row of trees, one trunk larger than the rest. I narrowed my eyes and a certain familiarity hit me—the tree I took refuge under when Merritt came looking for me. The one with his and Joanne's carved initials. I grinned at the memory.

Trenton filled his plate with more Artisan cheese and Jaffa cakes. "I remember."

"A most foolish ordeal." She continued, "Justine climbed up there to save a kitten, but her dress got caught on a sharp branch, hence Trenton took on the role of the chivalrous gentleman and attempted to rescue her."

Justine giggled. "Only you ended up getting caught on a similar branch and we were stuck up there for nearly an hour until Hennessey found us."

My mother chuckled in response. "Oh, that must've been quite the adventure. How old were you?"

"Six." Justine answered. "And Trenton was eight. We were inseparable, weren't we Trenton?" Her smile broadened as the attention fell to her. I bit harshly into a sausage roll. The overpowering surge of garlic and sage caught in my throat.

"If you remember correctly," Trenton emphatically addressed Justine. "I told you *not* to go up there and retrieve that wicked feline, that he would come down when he was good and ready."

"I did have a tendency to disobey," Justine snickered, "but you were always there to rescue me." Her eyes sparked his way.

I coughed and reached for my lemonade again. Once I got a hold of myself, I smiled playfully at Justine. "It sounds like you were a handful." Then directed my next comment to Trenton.

"Thank goodness that is no longer your concern." I chuckled as he placed his arm around my shoulders.

Leaning in, he added, "No doubt."

The group went silent once again. I dared not look toward Mrs. Gilford or her trusty sidekick and kept my eyes solely on Trenton. Then as if the world evaporated before us, he nuzzled his lips against my neck and whispered, "Eight days, love." When he drew back, he mouthed. "We will be entirely alone."

"Miss Shelton." Hennessey appeared before me and cleared his throat. "Your presence is being requested inside."

"Is there a problem?" Trenton stood to his feet. I quickly joined him.

"No, sir." Hennessey bowed. "I—er was beckoned to retrieve Miss Shelton." I eyed him suspiciously. Hennessey was never at a loss for words.

"I'll come with you." Trenton offered.

"No, no it's fine." I placed a hand on his arm. "Please stay with the party. I'm sure it's nothing and will return shortly." I glanced around at the inquisitive expressions and smiled. "Excuse me."

As I fell into step next to Hennessey, he whispered, "Your guest is quite distraught."

"My guest?"

"I believe you have referred to her as Margaret."

My stomach churned. "W—what happened?"

"It is a rather delicate situation, miss. One I presumed to best be handled by you alone."

My heart thudded in my chest, conjuring up varying scenarios. I wanted to ask him more details but found my throat dry and my lips unable to move.

"Follow me," he directed. "She's in the house."

Chapter 16

Hennessey led me up the veranda steps and through the back doors. The screams coming from the kitchen were more than enough to alert me to her whereabouts.

When I entered the kitchen, Margaret was in a full rage, throwing a pot across the room. It crashed against the wall and clattered to the floor. Helen, bless her heart, stood boldly in front of one of the household maids with both hands lifted, a wooden spoon as her only defense. Although from her outraged expression, if Helen knew she could reach a suitable weapon without leaving the maid exposed, she would have.

"Of all the dreadful things to occur!" Margaret screeched. "Do you not possess the wits to do an elementary task without a clanger?"

I raised my hands as I slowly approached Margaret, another pot gripped tightly in her other hand positioned to fly at a moment's notice. "Margaret! Stop! What is this all about?"

"This useless servant had the audacity to spill tea on me and in the presence of Mr. Chapman!"

"I'm truly sorry." A weak voice cried from the corner.

"Tea?" I gaped. "You are seriously acting like a three-year-old over spilled tea?" I shouted.

She glared at me with wide eyes. "Do you not see the damage she's done? The dress is ruined, and I am humiliated. If this were my house, she would have been removed immediately."

The poor girl huddled behind my fuming cook. Helen's face flared a bright shade of red and from her stance, appeared only seconds from pouncing. I reached for Margaret's wrist, the one with the weapon, and with the other hand unclasped her grip. Keeping her hand detained in mine, I turned to Helen. "I'm sorry, Helen. She won't bother you again."

"You're in agreement with this nonsensical tosh?" Margaret lashed out.

I pointed one stern finger in her direction. "Not another word." Then squeezed her hand and led her out and down the hall at a swift pace. She nearly ran to keep up with me.

"Are you daft, Katharine? The tosser behaved recklessly. I am sopped in hot tea and disgraced."

I entered our bedroom and forcefully pushed her forward. "Sit!"

She crossed her arms defiantly. I approached with as much restraint as I could muster and pointed my finger in her face. "Sit down now!"

Fear flashed momentarily until she smoothed her expression and sauntered slowly to the settee. I turned and wiped the sweat from my forehead.

"You are being foolish." Margaret ranted. "You should be as mortified as I am over the utter incompetence."

"Stop!" I yelled. Her body stilled. "You can't behave this way here." I continued to shout. "We don't live in the nineteenth century where it may have been acceptable to treat the domestic servants as lower class. Here, they are paid employees and treated with dignity and respect!"

Her lips separated, and a light gasp escaped. When she closed them, they quivered lightly.

"Yes, she made a mistake, but that's all. She accidentally spilled tea on *my* dress by the way, not yours—mine, and she apologized."

"She—"

"No! You don't get to speak. You listen. Might I remind you whose house this is and how your conduct affects me more than it does you. If you ever behave this way again to any member of this household, guest, or staff alike, I will march you to that bloody set of stairs and push you down myself, without a second thought. Do you understand me?"

She jutted her chin out. Annoyance settled into the lines around her mouth and the corners of her eyes.

"Answer me, Margaret! Do you understand?"

"Yes." She spit out sharply, then marched into the lavvy and slammed the door.

My head pounded. I'd never experienced this many headaches back-to-back before. Sitting down on the edge of the bed, I realized I had lowered my guard with Margaret and allowed her too much freedom. Yes, she's an adult, but if I weren't more careful, her actions could produce severe consequences. The risk no longer only affected me, as evidenced in the kitchen, it had the potential to harm others.

Retrieving some clean clothes and underclothes from the wardrobe, I knocked on the lavvy door.

Margaret cracked it open but said nothing. I handed her the new apparel. "Hand me the dress." She did and slammed the door once more as if I were the one, she had a right to be angry with. I glanced over the garment. It revealed one decent sized stain and a small trickle, something that could easily be removed with spot cleaner. I gritted my teeth. She behaved like a spoiled, rotten heiress.

I mulled over the mess she created, noting that timing was paramount. If word got around to all the staff over what had occurred, I feared its spread could easily reach the ears of Mr. and Mrs. Gilford.

I went to the lavvy door and spoke through it. "Do not leave this room. I will be back."

As I set forth down the hall once more, an annoying ache throbbed across my shoulders and settled into my neck. I should not be here trying to manage her; I should be out there enjoying the picnic with my fiancé and the wedding week festivities . . . *my* wedding week festivities.

The thought of Trenton out there with his mother and Justine brought a frown to my face. After the conversation that occurred in front of me, there was no doubt it would be even more comical in my absence. Then I chastised myself. Trenton is a grown man and has shown more fortitude in their onslaught than I gave him credit for. There should be no doubt whatsoever where his loyalties lie.

"Helen?" I entered the kitchen once more. She patted the hand of the poor girl who now sat pale and trembling on a stool and for the first time ever, my cook acknowledged me without her typical exuberant greeting. "I'm profoundly sorry." I walked toward them. "I can't tell you how horrified I am at my guest's behavior."

"Blimey, Kat. She lost the plot!" Helen's cheeks still steamed. It's possible if I hadn't arrived when I did, she would've flattened Margaret in a hot minute. "What a piece of work, throwing a wobbly like that! Is she your chum?"

"Um, not exactly."

"Why is she in-company?"

I shifted weight to my other foot. Helen was one of the staff I adored above all others, but her anger was justified. "That's a fair question. I can't explain much in detail, but she needs to be here for now. I assure you; she won't get anywhere near the kitchen again, and I'll personally see that no other staff member is threatened." I peered around Helen to the girl and knelt to her side. "Please accept my apology." I reached for her hand. "Take the rest of the day off, and if you choose not to return, I understand. Your wages are covered for the week, regardless." The young woman who couldn't have been older than seventeen, smiled weakly. "Helen, will you see that she is escorted downstairs? I want to make sure she arrives safely to her room."

"Of course." Helen nodded her head, her jowls flapped in dramatic vindication.

"And please," once again I begged for her forgiveness, "please know how truly sorry I am."

Helen placed her hand over mine. "I know, doll."

I stole a hefty breath and stepped back into the entryway. Sitting down at the closest bench, I relished in the momentary quietness of the space. Not only was I missing out on the full enjoyment of the events, time with my parents, friends, and most of all Trenton, I'm tethered to a shrew.

As sounds of the party entered the house once more, I slipped quietly back to my bedroom unseen. When I entered the room, Margaret sat at the dressing table. Her eyes reflected the anger that simmered within me. She didn't seem to recognize her wrongdoings.

I bit my lip and sat on the edge of the bed. Glancing at her, I debated over what I wanted to say. She's already proven she disregards my requests, but they were needed now more than ever.

"Do not . . ." I stared at her reflection in the mirror. "Do not ever go into the kitchen again." My voice commanded through a whisper while my fingers trembled against my thighs. "Do not ever treat one of my staff the way you did today, or I'll find a way to lock you in this room and you will not set one foot out of it again until your head is healed."

Her eyes rounded, and her lips parted as if she intended to speak, but I didn't allow for it.

"You will stay here until dinner." My nostrils flared under the incalculable control needed to keep my tone even. "If you comply, you may join us for dinner, if you do not, you stay here for the night."

"I am not a child!" Margaret hissed.

"Yet, you're acting like one."

She lowered her eyes.

"Now I will be back to dress for dinner in a bit. I hope your attitude has changed by then because I can't stress enough how important this week is to me and so far, you've shown little regard for that." Then I shut the door tightly behind me.

Chapter 17

As I entered the dim corridor outside of my bedroom, I tried to erase any signs of discouragement before anyone saw it.

Too late.

"Hi, Kat." Kelly approached from the foyer. "Hey, what's wrong?"

"Nothing." I forced a smile.

"No seriously, what's happened?" Her own smile waned. "You know I lived with you for five years. I can tell when you're lying."

I pressed my lips together.

She wound her arm through mine. "Why don't we take a walk in that beautiful garden of yours, and you can divulge your little secret before I strategically pry it out of you." She chuckled, but I knew her humor only masked her seriousness.

"It's no secret." Although I knew very well the woman who occupied my mind in the other room was very much a secret.

"Come on." She led me out the doors to the garden facing east. Though not the main garden, it offered comparable charm through a sea of French rose bushes. The perfumed scent alone induced a soothing calm the moment we stepped foot onto the dirt path, but my shoulders didn't relax until we located the lone bench hidden underneath a fully covered pergola and sat down.

"Now, we're completely alone," she said. "Tell me the truth." She eyed me with a compelling stare.

"I'm just stressed."

"Really?" she quipped. "I hadn't noticed."

I chuckled lightly. "I—I can't seem to handle what is being thrown at me this week. It's too overwhelming."

Kelly's eyes never left mine as she reached for my hand. "I'm guessing your anxiety is coming from a menacing blond by the name of Justine, and a patronizing soon to be mother-in-law?"

I chuckled again. "Yes, that's part of it."

"Only part? I believe that would be enough to put anyone over the edge."

"Yes, but Trenton has assured me there are no feelings there on his end, so I must trust him."

"Trenton is no doubt loyal to you. Even on the walk back to the house after the picnic, I noticed Justine attempt to take his arm, though he didn't offer it, and in a swift move, he transferred her to Marlowe and escorted his mom instead."

I smiled at this news and felt slightly ashamed of my earlier thoughts of leaving him alone in their presence. "He's good to me, Kelly." My heart raced as his image came to mind. "He's the best of men."

"Oh, there's no question in that regard. The way he looks at you is every woman's fantasy. You're definitely adored."

"So why do I let them get under my skin?" With one deep exhale, my body finally loosened up. "Their conniving ways and negative demeanor constantly test my resolve. I mean, we're about to be married and these women are on the war path, determined to cause havoc."

"Remember Paige Callahan?" One corner of Kelly's lips curled.

I nodded. She was the very person I compared Margaret to when I first met her in 1878. A devious and cunning woman, Paige had Jeff fooled. Like Trenton, Jeff was kind regardless of her underhanded attempts to snare him.

"Do you remember why she stopped hanging around us?"

"I thought she gave up because Jeff and I grew serious, then exclusive."

Kelly smirked. "Yeah, that may have only been part of it."

"What did you do?"

"What any good friend would do."

I glowered until she relented. "I encouraged a guy to hit on her and then had someone take pictures of her making out with him."

"You did that?" I laughed aloud.

"Yep, and I was all too happy to show her those pictures with the threat they would go viral by nightfall if she didn't leave you two alone."

"You are . . ." I tried to find the right word. When I glanced at her, only the best of feelings evolved. She has always been my truest confidant, never abandoning me for a moment. "You're incredible." I hugged her tightly. "I could never ask for a better friend."

When we let go, she grabbed my hand once more. "So simply say the word, and I can very well arrange another Operation Paige . . . though we would call it Operation Justine." We laughed.

I didn't want to stoop to that level. I hoped we wouldn't have to. "I'll keep that in mind."

"So, what else is bothering you because I know there's more."

"Nerves, I suppose." I didn't entirely lie. My real concerns over Margaret must be kept private, regardless of our closeness.

Kelly wrapped her arm around my shoulders. "It's completely understandable. Many brides have pre-wedding jitters, but you have emotional scars on top of that. You're allowed to be scared, Kat." She squeezed. "You have faced seemingly unconquerable heartache and survived, but what you need to truly focus on now is your future. The one where an amazing man is joining his life with yours, and you no longer need to face your fears alone."

I smiled. She was right. *She was always right.* Her strength bolstered me in the darker moments of my life, her humor drove me to apply for this position at Charlock Manor, and ultimately her advice encouraged me to accept it. Kelly was a big part of the reason I knew happiness again.

"And I'm quite jealous, might I add." Kelly smirked and intertwined her arm through mine again.

"Oh, right! You could have any man you choose." This rang true, she dated many men but always broke things off first. "I believe you need to take your own advice and let down your defenses. I know for a fact a certain Jake Hallihan would be more than willing to take that plunge with you." She dated Jake in high school and reconnected often when she went home for the holidays. I met him once in Arizona.

Kelly giggled. "He *is* smart, good-looking . . . and interested, isn't he?"

"See where it goes when you get back to California." I chuckled. "If I can do it, anyone can."

She nodded. "I suppose you're right. I have tried to be the last one standing for quite some time, but I think I'll relinquish that title to Maria." Laughter came easily as we continued to speak of our past and our futures. To have someone like Kelly as a best friend was truly one of my greatest blessings in life.

Once I returned to the bedroom, a surprisingly calm and fully dressed Margaret met me at the door. "May I be obliged to speak?" Anger no longer flushed her cheeks.

"Yes, you may," I said. Kelly's talk renewed my strength. I could possibly face anything at this point and still come out unscathed . . . *maybe.*

"As you are aware, I'm not accustomed to this time." The muscles in her jaw tensed and released as she spoke. "One moment I'm attending a wedding, the next, I'm plummeting down a set of stairs and waking up to a peculiar world. Everything is confusing and uncertain." She fidgeted with her sleeves. If I didn't know any better, Margaret showed signs of being nervous. "Nonetheless . . ." She seized a lengthy breath. "I am most obliged for your guidance."

"Wait." I stared hard. "Did you just thank me again?"

Her lips pulled into a thin line. "It may appear to you that I'm not beholden to your efforts, but it is my upbringing that has taught me to withhold sentiment."

"I think you showed a great deal of *sentiment* in the kitchen earlier."

Margaret winced. "I refer to benevolence. My tutors taught me to only consort with my equals or those who could elevate my status. Those below my station were not worthy of my time, and servants especially were to be handled as though they were undeserving and contemptible."

I held my tongue and let her finish.

"I see now, that over time, that is no longer the case. Please do not fault me for my learned behavior when it is all I have ever known."

I contemplated the truth to her words. I, too, needed compassion back in her time and without the kindness Merritt, Lizzy, and Abby bestowed upon me, I would've been seen as an enigma. One they had every right to turn their backs upon but didn't.

"You're right."

Her forehead wrinkled.

"I understand how difficult change can be, and you have been thrown into this foreign world and expected to behave naturally."

She shifted in place.

I sighed. "I will try harder to be mindful of this, if you will try harder to heed my advice." Her eyes met mine, a hint of red within suggested she may have been crying. "Agreed?"

"Agreed." She bobbed her head.

"But you must apologize to that poor girl. You terrified her."

"I see now that I reacted in haste, but to my justification, I feared the dress was beyond repair. Can the blemish be removed?"

"Oh, yeah." I waved my hand. "Another miracle of the future. We have chemicals that work wonders and machines that will do our laundry for us."

"Truly?"

"Truly." I grinned, making a mental note of all the modern-day conveniences I needed to show her around the house.

Her eyes glossed over. "Am I allowed to attend dinner with you?"

"Sure." I shrugged my shoulders. "I believe you're sorry for your actions, and you won't do it again."

"I won't. Thank you, Katharine. My finest behavior will be paramount, I assure you."

"It has to be." I sighed. "Find a dress for dinner in the wardrobe and I'll seek Anabelle out to help with your hair."

I stepped out of the room and somehow felt a heavy weight lift off my shoulders. Could it possibly be that one of my three problems might be manageable now?

I turned to see Trenton headed in my direction. My heart leapt equally to my broad smile.

"Now this . . ." He smiled back. "This is the Kat I know."

I went to his embrace.

"I've been worried about you. When you didn't return, I inquired of Hennessey who then directed me to Helen."

I pulled back with a grimace, positive he'd heard the full rundown by now. "What did Helen say?"

"Only that you handled the matter with professionalism and for me not to worry my fetching little head about it."

Laughing, I pictured those very words coming out of her mouth. Even more grateful she understood the importance of discretion without me saying a word.

"Thank you." His hands rubbed my arms tenderly.

"For what?" I eyed him suspiciously.

"For treating the staff with the dignity they deserve. It is quite apparent Helen, and the others are most fond of you and that does not come about easy . . . especially as a Yank."

I smacked his chest playfully but left my hand in place. "This Yank will be your bride shortly, so you might as well accept the idea of equality."

"Never!" He chuckled, then sobered the closer he leaned in. His lips nearly touched mine. "You will always be far superior to me." He closed the gap with his soft lips. As his arms engulfed me, my hands slid up to his neck and around his shoulders. What started out as a simple kiss graduated to one that ignited every stirring emotion I had for this man.

When we released, he held my hand up to his lips and kissed my knuckles. "Until dinner, love."

I nodded and watched him walk away. His stride balanced both confidence and contentment, and his very physique took my breath away.

After retrieving Anabelle, I made my way back to the room to get ready myself. When Margaret greeted me with a smile, I froze, puzzled. She appeared genuinely happy. Shaking the confusion from my face, I breathed freely, allowing the respite from contention to seep in. *This might not be so awful after all.*

I retrieved my dress—a rose gold, silk charmeuse that fell gently off my shoulders and hugged my figure beautifully down to my knees. It was one of my favorite dresses . . . Trenton's too.

This time when he met me down the hall, his eyes danced in delight before he drew me against him. The warmth of his body transferred easily to mine. Tickling my ear, he whispered. "How am I so fortunate?"

My cheeks flushed under his skillful charm.

"Hello, Margaret." Trenton released me and greeted her from behind.

She dipped her chin quietly and stepped forward. And like the night before, he raised an elbow for the both of us.

At dinner, I found myself between the two most important men in my life—Trenton and my dad. With the craziness of the last two days, I hardly had a moment to spend with my parents, and although I believed they understood under the circumstances, I missed them.

"Kat, you look stunning."

I leaned over and kissed his cheek. "You're obligated to compliment my dress, you're my dad." I chuckled.

"No, the dress is beautiful, but *you* are stunning. I haven't seen you shine like this for quite some time." He tilted his head forward vying for Trenton's attention. "And I believe I have you to thank for it, Son."

Trenton smiled and wrapped an arm around my shoulders. "It is I who wonders how this delightful creature agreed to be my wife."

I chuckled. "You two can be my dinner partners anytime."

My eyes flitted across the table and down a few chairs where Margaret chatted with Jonah. His eyes lit up every time she engaged him. My heart twinged. *What will happen when she leaves?* She could disappear at any time. If she somehow decided to stay, perhaps get married and have children, what would happen if she took a tumble one day and ended up back in the past. It would break his heart. *She must go back.*

Margaret's eyes darted in my direction as if she knew my thoughts dwelled on her. She smiled that smile again, the one that didn't speak *snake.* Smiling back, I returned to my carrot and ginger soup, somehow more confused *and* pleased than before.

"Mr. Shelton," Trenton leaned forward.

"Yes, Son. I thought we agreed you would call me Dad or Jack?"

"Yes, yes, forgive me. Sometimes when I'm around my family too long, I fall back into what's suitable for them."

My eyebrow arched. "You've never called your father, *dad* before?"

"No. He prefers Mr. Gilford or Sir. Father is occasionally permitted under more intimate circumstances, but no, never dad."

"Hmmm." I couldn't stop my eyes from wandering Mr. Gilford's way. Since Trenton's announcement of open seating, he had claimed the head chair, and though he appeared at ease, he hardly spoke to anyone, including his wife. "I'm sorry. I interrupted you." I reached for a warm roll and some honey then leaned back in my chair to allow them to speak freely, all the while formulating a plan to connect with the senior Mr. Gilford before the week ended.

"Jack?" Trenton smiled. "Will you join me in the morning for a bout of fishing? We didn't have a chance to participate the last time you were here with the weather and all."

"I would love to!" Dad bellowed loudly. He had only fished once before, but from his exuberant expression he seemed thrilled with the idea.

"Brilliant!" Meet me at seven o'clock on the veranda. The river is like glass in the morning, it will be a most peaceful affair."

I turned to Trenton and thanked him. He excelled with my parents, markedly kind and respectful. His lips raised into a half smile. "How else do you think I'm going to learn all about Kat, the child?"

My eyes widened. "You better not," I threatened.

"Oh, I fully intend to get the . . . how is it you say . . . the 411?"

"You do know I can get incriminating information on you as well." I pointed toward his parents.

He smirked. "You really think my mum will divulge anything about me that could shatter her picture-perfect image?" His laugh rumbled low and hearty.

I bit my lip, knowing he had a point, and caught sight of his grandfather across the table. "Grandfather?"

He smiled eagerly my way.

"Would you like to join me for a ride in the morning?" I asked.

His eyes lit up.

I scrunched my nose in Trenton's direction. Then turned back to face his grandfather again, well aware that, even at seventy-four, he still rode horses. Just this morning, he rode out after breakfast.

"I would love it if we rode together tomorrow morning. Would that be okay with you?"

"Yes, Kat, that would be most delightful."

"Clever, clever girl," Trenton mumbled so close to my ear goosebumps rippled down my arms.

I inhaled his manly scent. "Two can play at this game . . . *love*." Then finished my meal with an enormous smile on my face.

Chapter 18

Once we reconvened in the sitting room, like the night before, several games started up amongst the pockets of guests conversing. The most popular were cribbage and chess, neither of which I played, so I purposefully sought out Mrs. Gilford. She occupied one of the two Chelsea wing-back chairs near the hearth. I slid into the second one and smiled my hello. The feather down cushions had recently become a place of retreat for me, but this time, I sat properly near the edge hoping to converse with her.

Startled, she gawked my way. Though I couldn't profess anything remotely close to success yet, I hoped that my persistence in becoming more acquainted with her would soon pay off. Unfortunately, within seconds of me joining her, Justine arrived and sat on the marble accent table between us. Like an odd pair of magnets, the two were entirely inseparable.

I peered past the intrusion and acknowledged Mrs. Gilford. "How are your accommodations thus far?"

With no light in her eyes her voice teetered on annoyance. "They're adequate."

"Is there anything I can do to make your stay more comfortable?"

Her expression remained blank. She glanced over to Justine who met her eyes as if they spoke some foreign language through eye movements. Turning back to me, she sighed. "I would like to spend more time with my son."

My head tipped back, surprised. "I—I'm sure Trenton would enjoy that very much."

She sipped her glass of brandy slowly and deliberately. "Would you be opposed to a mother-son visit after archery tomorrow?"

"No, of course not. I have no intention of keeping him from your company. Have you told him you want to see him more? I am sure he'd be thrilled."

Her lips pursed. "I'm asking you, Katharine. It seems every time I turn around you are clinging to him like flypaper."

"I—uh—I," I couldn't even form words. What does one say to that? *Sorry? I love your son?* My thoughts were immediately disrupted by the keys on the piano. A gentle harmony began and quickly evolved into a lively song. A woman's voice rang out above all the idle chatter and thrust the entire room into complete silence.

I whipped my head around to catch a glimpse of the piano in the corner, a self-assured Margaret pressing on the keys dramatically in a spontaneous performance. A fascinated Jonah stood contentedly next to the instrument and smiled wide. Though I knew Margaret to be talented both in music and song, I didn't expect her to openly engage and act upon those skills here. My eyes flickered over the quiet audience as I bit my bottom lip. I could hardly interrupt her without causing a scene.

"Isn't the talent show slated for next week?" Justine snickered as Mrs. Gilford held her hand against her chest and chuckled brashly.

"I dare say, Katharine—"

"Kat." I corrected Justine.

"*Kat.* Your friend is quite peculiar. Her dinner conversation amused me. I haven't heard half the words she used since my great-grandmother, Pearl, passed away."

"She's an actress, Justine. Actresses are always eccentric and as you can see, her talents lie quite deftly in musical theater." Justine's mouth pulled into a tight bow as if her saliva soured. I brushed a piece of lint off my skirt nonchalantly and continued, "I asked her to share a number with us. Music always compliments the evening's ambiance."

"If you say so," she mumbled and pulled a compact out of her purse and powdered her nose.

Placing a hand on her arm, I labored for the sickly-sweet tone I used next. "But Justine, as your hostess, I would hate for you to feel left out." I tapped her skin lightly before she pulled it away. "If you would prefer to sing next I'm sure your abilities are equal to the task." My lips formed an artificial smile.

"No." She steamed in my direction and placed her compact roughly back into her purse. "No, I will pass. Excuse me." She stood up and eyeballed Mrs. Gilford before she walked away. I savored the satisfaction that blossomed in my chest, but only momentarily, for Mrs. Gilford's piercing stare penetrated my amusement and seemed to say more than her lips did.

"Remember to tell Trenton his mother seeks his companionship in the garden after the archery tournament." She stood to her feet.

"Yes, ma'am." I nodded.

"And do make sure he is unaccompanied." She then joined Justine near the windows, their conspiratorial natures pointed clearly to a coup. Why in the world could she not tell Trenton herself? Why did she insist I do it?

Glancing around the room as the music continued, I feared the other guests viewed Margaret's performance much like Justine.

Taking a steady inhale, I rose and meandered through the groups and watched as they listened. Thankfully as Margaret played, only a positive reaction surfaced and once she finished, she stood to an overwhelming applause. When she curtsied . . . *yes, curtsied*, her cheeks turned a darker shade of pink. With the added confidence, she fluttered her eyelashes wildly toward Jonah, who praised her openly. I laughed. Margaret was thoroughly in her element.

I stepped over to the piano. "Jonah, would you mind if I borrowed the musician for a moment?"

Her smile flattened and she attempted to refuse when Jonah stepped aside and waved his hand for her to follow me. Thankfully, her lady-like upbringing surely prevented her from snapping in front of him.

"Margaret," I led her out the back doors to the veranda. The night air remained temperate, and I prayed it stayed that way for the archery competition tomorrow.

"What Katharine?" She groaned. "What erroneous deed did I partake in tonight?"

I stared at her for longer than necessary. Recalling my first few days in 1878, I made mistake after mistake, and if it weren't for the Gilford children looking out for me, I could have faced dire consequences.

Impatience emerged in the lines of her face. "Pray tell."

"Nothing bad." I shook my head. "I only wanted to say you performed magnificently."

She stared at me with furrowed brows certain to be searching for humor. "Are you unwell?"

"No, actually I'm more relaxed right now than I've been in days." I exhaled slowly to confirm my confession.

Her eyes never left me, but confusion crept in. "Why did you insist I join you here? Couldn't you have complimented me in the parlor?"

I nodded. "Yes, I could have. I just wanted to speak privately is all."

"You're afraid I will say something to humiliate you, isn't that correct?"

My laugh was so light it came out like a smirk. "Honestly, Margaret, I only wanted to tell you that you play and sing wonderfully." I held her gaze until her eyes softened. "I wish I had musical talent like that." I leaned against the stone wall.

"As I recall, you do." Her own shoulders eased, and she moved next to me. "The night Merritt invited you to play first, drove me mad with envy. I wondered why he would ask you over me—his affianced. Then you performed that song and though I detested you, your emotion stunned me. It was a moving piece."

I chuckled.

"What?" She eyed me curiously.

"I'm not an accomplished player by any means, and the only reason I agreed to play was because Merritt had challenged me in a game I taught him called Truth or Dare."

"Truth or Dare?"

"Yes. It's a silly game I played with my brothers growing up. You would choose one or the other, then be asked to share a secret or to do something crazy."

Her expression only confirmed her confusion.

"Like this. Pick Truth or Dare, Margaret."

"What?"

"Just pick one."

"Dare?"

"Okay, so I dare you to run barefoot through the garden, touch the trident on the fountain and run back."

"Whyever would I do something so uncivilized?" She frowned.

"Because that's the game. Then after you're done, you ask me Truth or Dare."

"What if I chose Truth?"

"I would ask you a question you must answer truthfully. Like . . . was Merritt your first kiss?"

She gasped. "What a boorish question!"

I barked a laugh. "Hardly. Was Merritt your first kiss or not?"

Her cheeks blazed a deep red.

"He wasn't." I snickered and peered at her sternly. "You had been kissed before."

"This is a foolish game. I won't play it."

"Relax." I laughed again. "I only explained it to you so you would know why Merritt asked me to play the piano that night."

"What did Merritt choose, Truth or Dare?"

"He chose Truth."

I remembered the day vividly. I ran from the schoolroom and into the trees when Lizzy sent Merritt after me. He may never know the extent of his kindness and how much it helped me overcome the depth of my sadness that day.

"What did he confess?" Her mumble resembled that of a small child. I glanced over to her. *What does she fear?*

"A story from his youth, an indiscretion he regretted."

A gentle sigh escaped her lips. Curiosity built within me over her reaction. Though she knew Merritt didn't love her, I wondered if she feared his public acknowledgement of this would surface.

I thought of Merritt's journals. I read them all. It might be good for her to hear his thoughts. He did have a high opinion of her, of course, until she lied to him about me. She told him that I tried to harm him after the horse accident and then hit her when I didn't succeed. My body stiffened with the memory—one incredibly hard for me to shake.

The next few minutes were spent in silence. The warm air swirled about us from the open door as the twilight stars began to appear. I turned to her. "I've kept you from Jonah much longer than I anticipated, we can talk more later tonight."

Margaret's finger traced a small crack along the stone. She appeared distracted before she shook her head and smiled. "I believe it's always beneficial for a gentleman to pine for a lady." Her smile contradicted the crease that formed between her brows.

"Are you okay?" My inquiry came with sincerity.

She shrugged.

"I know there's a lot of stuff to take in, the way we dress, our mannerisms, the talk, the changes in conveniences. I'm sure it's all a bit confusing."

"Quite."

"Do you have any questions for me?"

She bit her bottom lip and hesitated.

I peered back toward the door. We were entirely alone. "It's okay, Margaret, you can ask me anything."

Her face contorted. "What's the metal case with buttons?" She held out her hands trying to imitate what she'd seen. "People talk into it?"

"Touch and talk into? Oh," I chuckled. "It's a cell phone."

"Cell phone?"

"Yes, a communication device."

The lines deepened on her forehead.

"I'm not certain of the actual date, but I imagine not long after 1878, there will be an invention called a telephone. It won't look anything like what you've seen here, but it will be a way for people in different places, like cities and countries to talk to each other immediately. No more waiting for messages to be delivered, telegrams, or letters that take weeks to arrive. You can hear the other person's voice right through the device."

"Astonishing." Margaret gnawed at her bottom lip. "I've seen people hold it—you, the other guests, Mr. Chapman. He retrieved his several times in the last two days, but I feared touching it, or even inquiring about it. It's such a perplexing object."

"Yes, almost everyone has a cell phone now. For example, when my parents are back home in New York, we can talk to each other on our phones. When we're alone in the bedroom, I'll show you mine. It's an incredible invention. I think you'll like it. Anything else?"

"What about an *air-plane*? This morning, as I took a turn in the garden, something unusual was up in the sky. When I asked the gardener what it was, he answered me with a peculiar look."

"Ah," I smiled. "That's a machine that carries people and flies in the sky."

"A machine that flies? Preposterous."

"No, really, it can take you to other places much faster than a horse or a train. That's how I get back and forth between America and England."

"You don't take a ship?"

"No, I fly in an airplane and I can arrive in about eight hours."

"Eight hours? Gads." Her hand wiped her forehead. "And how can it possibly stay up in the sky?"

"It has high powered engines that thrust it upward."

"That doesn't frighten you?"

"No, I get sick sometimes, but no it doesn't scare me. There are also cars. Do you remember when I pointed them out from the bedroom window? We ride in them instead of carriages. We'll take one when we go to London on Monday." I hesitated, but only for a brief second. "Would you like to come with Kelly, Maria and me?"

Her eyes lit up. "You wish for me to come?"

"I do." The honesty of my words surprised me. "I have to caution you though; the London of today is nothing like the London you remember. It may be a bit distressing."

"As if I haven't been distressed thus far?"

"Not like this." I met her eyes. "I know you lived in London with an Aunt when Merritt went to break off the engagement."

"Yes . . ." her voice trailed off to a whisper. "Yes, I did."

"Why didn't you return with your parents to your country estate? I remember seeing them at Charlock when you were planning the wedding, but after Merritt's injury, I learned you left for London instead of home."

"They are not my parents. It's my father and his wife. My mother died when I was eight. The woman who my father married is a wealthy widow. The means for him to gain land and an entry into society." She sighed heavily. "I detest the woman. She and my father make all my decisions."

"You don't have a say in your life?"

"No."

The reality of her circumstances struck me hard. I couldn't imagine having my parents make all my decisions, despite their good intentions, the choice should be mine.

"Not even in marriage?"

Margaret's eyes glistened in the moonlight. "My brother had once let it slip that my only value in the family is to be peddled to the highest bidder—groomed only to marry for money."

"Marry for money?"

She nodded, then wiped the moisture that grew from the corners of her eyes. "My father and Josiah were adept at pursuing people for their own advantage."

"How?"

"They are quite ambitious and often engaged in subterfuge to accomplish their purposes."

"Such as what?" I placed my hand over hers on the wall.

She tilted her head as she contemplated the question. "Merritt." She took a deep breath. "The day I met Merritt I was driving my gig and the wheel collapsed. He happened to be the first gentleman to arrive and assist me."

I smiled. That was so Merritt like. To do anything for anybody.

"But it wasn't until later, when I overheard my father and Josiah speaking of the incident, that I discovered the truth to their scheme." She sniffled. "Josiah had tinkered with the wheel on purpose with the express intent to snare a gentleman. When it was Merritt who saw me safely home, they were disappointed to discover he lacked a title, but his vast family wealth mollified their discontent."

"You could've been hurt or killed." My shock over the ruse went rampant. "How could they do that to a daughter?" I cried. "A sister?"

"They did not concern themselves with the particulars. In fact, the night I attended Merritt's wedding, the night I fell down the stairs, they arranged for me to meet Lord Gentry *after* he was in his cups."

"Who is Lord Gentry and what does that mean—in his cups?"

"He's a man with no morals." Her emotion hardened. "A man more than twice my age with not an honorable bone in his body, but because he's wealthy, he was to be my next suitor. They wanted the introduction to occur *after* he consumed a great deal of liquor, then trick him into a contract posthaste."

"That's awful."

"It's my duty." She sighed. "Though I never quarreled with them when they chose Merritt . . . he's a good man."

"One of the best." I agreed.

She went silent for a few seconds and though we were alone, she whispered, "Did he . . . uh, was your declaration about Merritt and the slaves truthful?"

"Yes." I tucked a loose strand of hair behind my ear. "He had an arrangement with a man from the woods. He kept the slaves hidden until Merritt could safely secure them passage away from England."

"How did you become aware of this?"

I grinned with the memory. "I actually followed him sneaking out one night. He showed me the cave in his forest where they took shelter. I took Trenton there last year."

"I can't believe he risked himself like that. His reputation, his social standing, his future. He could've been ruined."

"For helping slaves? For freeing children?"

"People have fallen from grace for much less." She sighed. "Society is fickle. Truthfully, they are charlatans, appearing sympathetic to the under-privileged causes, but care little outside of their luxuries."

My expression must've appeared grave. Margaret winced. "I know this because I am one of them." She frowned. "If I had become aware of Merritt's surreptitious deeds, I would've made every effort to convince him to abandon them, regardless of the good he did."

My eyes widened to her honesty. I had warned Merritt of her possible disapproval, but he insisted nothing would change his course. "Initially," I grinned, "I thought he was meeting you secretly under the cover of darkness."

"A clandestine meeting? She gasped. "Me?"

"Yeah," I chuckled. "Of course, now that I'm getting to know you, I realize how ridiculous that thought is."

Her eyes glossed over as she shook her head. "Ours was not a love match, only an arrangement of convenience. We never possessed any feelings of longing for one another. Yet, I discerned early on, with Merritt as my husband, I wouldn't suffer from cruelty."

Everything made sense now, their relationship, Margaret's behavior, even my interaction with Josiah. "If you ever get back,

Margaret, you need to get away from your family." I squeezed her arm. "You should not be forced to marry any man, but especially not an evil one. You deserve to be happy."

"There's no other alternative, Katharine. I am the property of my father until I wed, then I'm another man's property."

"Property?" A hollow pang shuddered in my chest. Memories of Josiah's unsightly appearance emerged. I knew from the moment he spoke to me he was a man of questionable character. *Would they harm her?* "Margaret, we need to devise a plan. You can't leave until we have created a strategy for you. Somehow, we will make this right and if for some reason you don't go back, then we'll help you find the right path here."

Margaret whined, "I simply cannot be an actress. I know nothing of the stage."

I laughed out loud at the sudden turn in our conversation. "Yes, despite your dramatics, I suppose we'd have to explore other options." Though the idea of a plan brought a lift to her eyes, Margaret's overall demeanor remained subdued.

Several more minutes were spent in silence. We both seemed to find comfort in the quiet of the night—crickets chirped, lightning bugs glowed, and a soft breeze carried the various scents of the garden in our direction.

I marveled at the change that arose. The very idea of helping Margaret struck me profoundly. The behavior by her father and brother infuriated me—much like the attacks on the women at ASU. I could not, in good conscience, stand idly by. Though Margaret appeared tough, she faced little protection and no choice. She needed help and it seemed that I might be her only option.

Chapter 19

Sunday, 15 May 2011

The next morning, I awoke early with a smile on my face. Although I couldn't be with my favorite Gilford man, Grandfather Trenton came in at a close third. Merritt, of course, would always be second. I moved quietly in an effort to avoid waking Margaret. She slept soundly aside from her occasional snorts, which tempted me to record it on video solely to use against her later, if it came to it.

Once I donned my riding habit, I made my way to the stables, realizing how much I was looking forward to my ride. I hadn't been on Darby for several days, not since I brought Margaret back to the house, and I missed her and the freedom the rides offered.

Though I arrived on time, Grandfather Trenton was already waiting with the saddled horses when I entered. Clearly he was looking forward to it as well.

"Good morning, Grandfather." I announced as I patted Darby's smooth neck. She neighed and tapped one hoof in her typical morning greeting.

"It is certainly a lovely morning, and I am looking forward to a most invigorating ride as well. Thank you for the invitation, Kat."

Tugging on the saddle, I checked its placement. "You are most welcome, and if somewhere along the way you choose to divulge any bribable information about Trenton, I would not be opposed to it."

He laughed heartily. "It would be my pleasure."

Gripping the horn, I placed one foot in the stirrup and swung my leg over the saddle. Once secure with the reins in hand, I turned to the handsome man next to me. "What do you miss most about Charlock?"

Clicking Achilles forward, he grinned wide. Over the past four days, he switched between Achilles and another steed by the name of Zeus. Both were known to be the strongest and fastest of the lot.

"I miss the library." He waited for me to trot to his side. "I would spend many hours in there reading to my beloved. She claimed no difficulty reading herself, but from the time we married, she loved the sound of my voice, so I read to her every night.

Glancing over to Grandfather's regal appearance, I wondered why he never remarried. When he lost his wife eight years ago, he could've had his pick of many women, being handsome, rich, and energetic for his age.

"What a beautiful memory." I brushed one hand over Darby's mane as she walked to my lead. "Don't you have a library at Summer Hall?" I asked, referring to his home in Nottingham.

"Yes, but nothing like this one. Something about this library always made me feel at home."

I smiled, knowing exactly how he felt. "Why did you move from Charlock? You could've stayed here as long as you wanted."

"We left it to my son, Trenton, when he came of age, as tradition dictates. We desired something smaller, more intimate." He shook his head. "I never believed they would abandon it after only fifteen years, much less transform it into a public reception house."

"You were married here too, correct?"

"Oh, yes. Like my father and his father before him, and so on. You are becoming part of a deep-rooted, traditional family, Kat. I hope you're ready for this."

My smile waned. "I'm not so sure I am. What if I fail?"

He stopped Achilles and gazed at me affectionately. "That, my dear, is entirely impossible. You have already shown your ability to withstand the tempest known as Juliana. You will no doubt continue to rise to the occasion. I see your strength. It's as if you have been faced with great challenges and overcame them."

My eyelashes fought to hold back tears. *Why can't all the Gilford's be like this one?* The comfort that filled my soul knowing someone rallied for me, offered a vital boost of confidence.

"Tell me of your traditions, Kat." Grandfather nudged Achilles forward again and we kept our horses close while we moved toward the open field. "What is important to your family?"

I beamed. Talking about my family had always been a source of happiness. "We are very close." I licked my lips. "When my parents started the deli, everyone jumped in and helped . . . my brothers, uncles, cousins—they all contributed to its success, but this also meant we spent *all* of our time together, good and bad." I chuckled, then grew serious. "Then 9/11 happened."

I took a breath and scanned beyond the wildflowers that swayed to the morning breeze. It was if the tranquility of the scene was foreshadowing something infinitely darker. Though the terrorist attack I experienced as a six-year-old child was life-altering to both me and my parents, what happened on that Tuesday morning in September left our entire family, neighborhood, and city completely askew.

"Yes," Grandfather's voice reflected his kind and gentle nature. "I can only imagine what it must have been like to be in New York on that day."

The memory of that event played out in sequential frames as if it were a slow-motion movie. I shuddered. "We lost friends, customers, a favorite café . . ." I could see all of it quite clearly. "But my dad's two brothers, both cops, and my cousin, Jed, a firefighter . . . well, to say that their deaths truly upended us is an understatement."

My eyes found their way back to Grandfather and I was quite impressed I hadn't dissolved into a sea of tears by now—only a few random ones lined my cheeks. I hadn't noticed, until now, that we had stopped once more, and his gloved hand covered mine.

"What a dreadful ordeal." Grandfather now patted my hand. "I'm sorry for all you lost."

When our eyes met, it was if I saw a mixture of Merritt and Trenton all rolled into one. Though his wrinkled brows dipped with what was sure to be concern, his eyes only conveyed overwhelming empathy.

"Thank you, and I'm sorry. You asked me about our traditions, and I deviated onto another topic entirely." I laughed to cover up my awkwardness.

"And I am grateful you did." He squeezed my fingers before he withdrew them and clasped his reins again. "It allows me see a part of you I suspect you only reveal to your dearest friends." He smiled. "I am honored you trust me with such candor."

My heart swelled in my chest. If Trenton is anything like his grandfather as he ages, which I highly suspect he will be, I have the most wonderful life to look forward to.

He nodded in my direction and I smiled wider in return. "So, back to traditions . . ." I loosened my grip on the leather strap I hadn't realized I held with all my might and flicked it easily. "Up until I left for college, our family spent every holiday together. But hands-down, my favorite was Christmas, not only did we decorate our house and deli to the extreme, there were all the other city sights that I adored—the window displays, the Rockefeller tree, ice skating, and occasionally we had snow and would build a snowman in Central Park, but every Christmas Eve, without a doubt, our favorite activity was putting together gift boxes for the 43rd Street women's shelter."

"Gift boxes?"

"Yes, around twenty of them for the women and their children. They were mostly filled with treats, but toys, books and clothes as well."

Our horses continued forward, but we had slowed so much it felt as if they hadn't moved at all. The warm expression Grandfather exuded so effortlessly, fell upon me once more. "Are you aware of the Gilford House?"

I smiled. *I am much more aware of its existence through reasons I can't share with him.* "Yes, very much so. I was thrilled when Trenton suggested adding our own version of the gift box activity for the wedding week to benefit Martha's orphanage."

Grandfather faced forward again, lifting his chin and smiling. "You have a compassionate heart, dear, much like my lovely Louise." His voice cracked when he said her name.

"Grandfather, you would do us the greatest honor if you came and stayed with us at Charlock. I hate to think of you all alone in your home, surrounded only by memories."

"Thank you." He smiled warily. "But it's her memories that keep me going. I will, however, accept an invitation to visit, now and then."

"The invitation is open for as long as you want."

He nodded courteously and we trotted in silence for several seconds.

"So, as to keep with the intent of divulging incriminating information about my grandson, I will be happy to relinquish one of his follies from boarding school." He chuckled as if he first reminisced the occurrence in his mind. "Thankfully, he called *me* to sort out the predicament. If he had called his parents, he might have been disowned."

"That bad, huh?" I snickered. "Tell me more and don't leave out any of the sordid details."

He laughed aloud. "Let's see, it must've been Trenton's seventh year at Bedford School, which would make him about seventeen. Unlike other Gilfords, he didn't start there until he turned ten."

I struggled with the normalcy of this culture to send children away—this was sure to be one tradition I wouldn't adhere to. The very thought of little Trentons running around Charlock made me smile.

"Trenton's athleticism reached top notch; cricket being his game of choice. As one of the premium bowlers in the sport for his age, many uni's kept their eye on him. But since Oxford has been a Gilford tradition, he didn't entertain any other offers."

Trenton spoke often of his love for cricket but joked nearly as often about his abilities. It was enlightening to hear the truth of his skills from an outside party.

"Hertfordshire, their greatest rivalry in the sport, harbored deep-rooted sentiments against Bedford for many years. Trenton, along with Misters Hastings, Marlowe, and Chapman, whom you're acquainted with—" I grinned, knowing this would be one for the books with the four of them involved. "—had the brilliant plan to organize a prank the night before the championship match."

We stopped our horses at the edge of the woods; my entire being was thoroughly engrossed in his story.

"Hastings managed to acquire a set of keys to Hertfordshire's preparatory hall . . . somehow through a lady, of course. The four of them proceeded to release four goats into the main hall, only these four goats were painted with the numbers, 1, 2, 3, and 5."

I snickered. "Incredible."

"You can only imagine, how long they searched for goat #4. Eventually, long after their win, they were identified as the possible culprits and threatened with expulsion, only the school lacked the evidence. Shortly thereafter, I stepped in and saved his rebellious little hide. After all, it was just harmless fun."

"I love it." I cried. My cheeks ached from the prolonged smiling.

"And I do believe for the longest time, we kept this a secret from his parents." His finger tapped his chin. "Come to think of it, it's possible he has yet to confess."

"Ah . . ." I relished in the moment. "That is one beautifully gift-wrapped piece of blackmail."

He laughed heartily as we turned our horses around.

"Care to race?" His lip lifted on the right side—the trademark devilish smile that ran in the family.

"Absolutely!" I kicked Darby's side into a full run. Achilles' power trumped my mare's stamina by a landslide, but the events of the morning only left me feeling immensely satisfied by the time we reached the stables.

As I dismounted, Grandfather came to my side and lifted my hand. "I hope Trenton appreciates you, Kat. You are exactly the woman he needs in his life."

"I believe we appreciate each other a great deal."

On our walk back to the house, Grandfather shared another little secret, but this one involved Mrs. Gilford and her fear of hounds. "It's precisely why she never allowed the animals to be on the premises." He chuckled. "I can't tell you how pleased I was to see hunting added to the events again. I believe I am quite ready for a good pursuit."

When we reached the entrance, I hugged him right when *my* Trenton opened the door.

"Whoa, hold up. I don't think so, Grandfather." Trenton teased. "Moving in on my girl, indeed."

Grandfather winked at me once more and turned to his grandson. "I say, son, if I was but fifty years younger . . ." We laughed as he excused himself and stepped inside.

"How did fishing go?" I faced him as he reached for both of my hands.

"Your father is a natural fisherman. He caught three trout entirely on his own."

"That's wonderful." I hugged him, although the mixed smell of fish guts and horse flesh made for an awful combination. "I bet he enjoyed it."

"Not as much as I did, I assure you."

I winced. "What did he tell you?"

"That is for me to hold close to my heart until the time comes when I will reveal it at the most advantageous moment."

"Oh really?" I smirked. "I quite enjoyed my most enlightening conversation also. Something to do with goats I believe . . ." I brushed my finger across my bottom lip.

Trenton's mouth dropped. "He didn't!"

"Oh, he most certainly did." I kissed his cheek. "And I will surely enjoy finding a most advantageous moment for my disclosure as well."

Laughing, I stepped around him to go to my room to take a shower. With the widest smile imaginable, my thoughts couldn't help but take pleasure as I envisioned our spirited future together. And though our union emerged from heartache and grief, there was no doubt in my mind, fate had devised its own extraordinary plan.

Chapter 20

"How frequently have you discharged an arrow?" Margaret asked as she entered the bedroom. I had laid down after my shower to rest before the archery tournament.

I shrugged. "Twice in college, and I hardly paid much attention."

"You attended university?"

"Yes, that's kind of how I got this job here at Charlock. My degree is in art and humanities. They were looking for a curator . . . uh, a historian of sorts."

"That's why you were quite knowledgeable as the governess." Her expression lightened with admiration. "I remember Lizzy disclosing details of your lessons. At times, your instruction seemed unfathomable."

I laughed. "That's right. You claimed I lied to the girls about a female professor in America."

She lowered her eyes. "I did more than that, Kat."

I sat up, startled. "You called me Kat!"

"I suppose it's only fitting since everyone else calls you that."

Though using my nickname was a trivial step, I marveled at the transformation happening between us. "Wait, what do you mean *more* than that?"

"I conspired to make you appear unseemly in Mrs. Gilford's eyes." Margaret's rigid stance told me she was not accustomed to confessions. "I told falsehoods and slandered your character whenever possible." She wiped her brow and reached for my hand. "Please forgive me."

"Oh," I froze. She completely caught me off guard. First, she thanked me, then she called me Kat, and now she is asking for forgiveness. *Who is this woman?*

"I am truly regretful for my behavior." She squeezed my hand that still lay motionless within her palm.

"It's fine." I shrugged my shoulders, surprised at how easily a pardon came. "It really doesn't matter now."

"It does to me," she whispered.

My other hand patted over the ones still linked. "It's in the past . . . *literally*." I almost burst out laughing at my own bad joke but didn't. "Honestly, Margaret, I'm fine. Don't worry about it anymore, it's over."

She took a cleansing breath and I stretched both arms above my head before I stood up. "Hey, why did you ask if I've shot an arrow before?

"Oh, yes," she snapped to attention. "On to more essential and present concerns; follow me." She led me to the side window, the one that faced the eastside gardens. My two large windows were part of the reason I loved being in a corner bedroom.

I stepped over and peered out. The vegetation slightly hindered my vision, but off to the left, I spied an archery target. Two arrows were already stuck within the inner ring. *Thump!* A third hit outside of the center ring as I watched. "Who is it?"

"Justine." Margaret sighed. "She is exemplary. I overheard her and Mrs. Gilford whispering in the garden. They are conspiring."

"What else is new?" I yawned.

"No, you must listen. They are scheming to position the champion of the competition to choose their boating partner first. Then each runner-up selects until the last competitor."

"Are you kidding me?" I watched again as another arrow sank close to the third. "If that's the plan, I would end up in a boat with a stableboy."

"Precisely. And to no wonder, Miss Justine spoke only of one *delicious* man."

"Who?" Even when asked, I already knew the answer.

Margaret's forehead wrinkled. "*Your* Mr. Gilford."

"Ugghh, seriously. When is she going to give up?" I groaned. "This is ridiculous! Do they really believe that Trenton is going to simply leave me at the altar?" I paced anxiously before the window. "They must have some belief that he would, or they wouldn't keep trying."

"Enough!" Margaret demanded with her arm outstretched, and her palm facing me, forcing me to stop. "He is utterly, vexatiously in love with you. Everyone has witnessed it."

"But why would they continue to plot?" The question surfaced more internal than anything else. My insecurities were being relentlessly tested.

"Because his mother is an old bitty, and her companion is a slapper. I assure you, she would never be good enough for him."

"That's exactly what they think of me," I mumbled.

"Only because they aren't truly acquainted with you."

My jaw slacked and my mouth parted. "Are you defending me now?"

She tugged me away from the window and gripped both of my forearms as if she were about to shake some sense into me. "Do not expect it to happen frequently." She stared hard, forcing my eyes to meet her piercing gaze. "I do have a suggestion, though, and you must elect to agree or suffer any feasible outcome."

"What?"

"As you are aware, I have many superb qualities, nevertheless, archery is one I am wholly proficient in." She said this with a completely straight-face, but I burst out into a giggle anyway.

"Oh wait, you're not joking."

She shook her head.

"Good to know." I couldn't stop laughing. Margaret's overall character never seemed to lack vanity. "But no matter how proficient you say you are; you won't turn me into *Robin Hood* in two hours."

"No, I dare say that is impossible."

I wrinkled my nose. "Then pray tell, milady," I added a British accent. "What *are* you saying?"

Margaret released my arms and walked back to the window. Her body tensed as if she contemplated something important.

"Margaret, tell me." I urged.

She spun around slowly. "I'm proposing that I win the competition and choose Trenton."

I grimaced. I couldn't even believe we were debating over who should *win* my fiancé. *How did Mrs. Gilford become the authority on the games in the first place?* "So, no matter what, it's a lose-lose for me."

"Kat, tell me . . . who would you trust more with your beloved? Me or Justine?"

I bounced my head back and forth as if the answer were anything but clear. Though I didn't believe Margaret would deceive me any longer, she was a beautiful distraction. Did I really want Trenton spending time alone with her?

"You cannot be in earnest!" She cried at my hesitation, placing both of her fists on her hips.

My smile widened to her obvious offense and doubt over my seriousness.

"Nutter," she quipped. "And you say *I* am wearisome."

This time I laughed out loud, but quickly ceased to her scowl. "Okay all joking aside, Margaret, if I agree to this crazy scheme, will you promise not to flirt with him? It makes me insanely jealous."

"Only a wee bit." Margaret sniggered. This was the first time I had ever seen her react this way, and it brought a smile to my own face. "He is much too fine to forego altogether."

I smirked and playfully raised one threatening eyebrow.

"Very well, I will behave." She huffed and rolled her eyes. "I cannot say the same thing for Justine. She would devise a way to compromise him, and he would be honor-bound to marry her."

"No!" I shook my head vehemently. "That doesn't work anymore. Nobody is forced to marry for something like that . . ." I stopped myself. *How does one explain our relaxed morals?* "Things are more uninhibited now. But you're right, Justine would do anything in her power to manipulate him if they were alone. This I'm sure of." I faced her fully. "Are you certain you can win?"

She grumbled something unintelligible under her breath and pulled me over to the window again. Pointing at the target she said, "If I don't make it into the center circle with *all* of my arrows, I will let you push me down those blasted stairs."

"Hmmm," I muttered. "Now that's a win-win."

She jutted her chin out as if she were offended, but the side of her mouth twitched, telling me otherwise.

That afternoon when Mrs. Gilford announced the twist to the archery tournament, she did so without the approval or consent from Trenton or me. I tried to recall any earlier conversation that gave her permission to take over, however, none came to mind.

"The ladies will compete first." She boldly declared. "And the winner chooses her boating partner for Tuesday's event." Her nod appeared entirely for Justine who stood a few steps behind me. "And the runners up will choose sequentially afterward."

"I don't recall—" Trenton raised his hand to object, but she cut him off in a patronizing manner.

"Not now, Son."

He glanced to me with a grim expression. No wonder he struggled to have a relationship with this woman, she did nothing to build him up or to respect him.

She finished relaying her instructions with a loud and commanding voice, then turned in our direction.

"Is there an issue?"

Trenton kept his voice even and without censure. "I simply do not recall discussing the change in today's event."

She glanced from him to me with the same distinct wrinkle above her nose that has resided there since we met. "I'm sure your fiancé, Son, would find no fault in placating her future mother-in-law's appetite for a variation to the entertainment. It's innocent amusement after all. Isn't that correct, Katharine?"

I smiled tightly in her direction. "Your happiness is my foremost aspiration, Mrs. Gilford."

She smirked soundly and turned to answer another person's question.

Trenton's form stiffened at my side, leaning in, he whispered, "Your happiness is my foremost aspiration?"

My jaw set. "I'm trying to be a peacemaker here."

"Of course, love, and I admire you for that." He frowned. "No offense intended, but you agreed to an arrangement you will not win."

"Don't you think I know that?" I snapped.

Trenton inhaled. "Forgive me. That was rude. It's just that there are very few women present who are as skilled as Justine is at the bow."

My chest tightened at the strange way he pointed out her exceptional talents. "What would you have me do, Trenton?

Disagree with your mother? Be discourteous or disrespectful in front of her family?" My eyes pled for an answer. I had spent so much time the last couple of days trying to please everyone, and to what outcome?

He shook his head. "No, I don't want you to." He ran his hand through his hair. "She is a master manipulator. I suspect this will not be the end of it either—I won't stand for it." His features grew dark once more. "I tire of her treating me like I'm still a child. I'm a grown man for heaven's sake."

Torn between Mrs. Gilford's blatant condescension, and my desire to keep harmony with the woman at the expense of others, I sighed defeatedly. "I don't want to have all this discontent or anger surface right before our wedding. You're her only son, and this is her only chance to see you wed."

Trenton's hand rubbed his chin. New stubble had appeared and given him a more rugged appearance than I was used to, though no less handsome. The way he weighed his thoughts, he seemed clearly bothered. "I just—I just don't want you to get hurt, Kat."

My heartstrings stirred with his sweet confession. I wanted to assure him of its implausibility, but I struggled to find the right words. How strange that my insecurities have materialized more in this week than they had this entire year. He remained silent as he awaited my response. I faced him directly and placed my hand on his scratchy jaw. "Can you promise me that I have nothing to worry about—" I licked my lips and his eyes flickered toward them. "—especially if I'm not the woman in the boat with you?"

Trenton wrapped his arms around me and pulled me against him. His heart pounded against his chest. The whole situation evidently caused him distress. Warmth flooded me. "I know I tell you this often," he whispered, "but I need you to believe it. You, Kat, are everything to me. You must trust me on this."

I took a deep breath myself and moved my hand from his face to his chest. My fingers fiddled with his shirt buttons as I met his eyes. "I know, but it's hard to believe someone as amazing as you . . . would want someone like me when you could have anyone."

His lips parted and, without hesitation, his mouth met mine with a fierce urgency. His kiss articulated his feelings relatively well, leaving my head spinning, and my surroundings blurred.

"That is quite enough!" A shrill voice sounded from nearby. There was no question as to who it belonged to, but Trenton didn't stop. Somewhere in the process of losing myself to him, she moved closer, becoming more persistent. "I don't need to counsel you two on your responsibility to avoid public displays of affection."

We ignored her.

She clapped her hands in a last-ditch effort to get us to separate. "Cease this juvenile behavior!" She cried. "It's as if you are hormonal teenagers."

From behind, Hastings chortled loudly and patted Trenton's back in approval. "He's kissing his lady good luck, Mrs. Gilford, you can't blame the bloke for that."

A mumble from a different direction surfaced, "No doubt she will need it." Justine's biting comment rose barely above the random chatter.

Trenton kissed me once more to assure all who missed it the first time, didn't miss it the second. Whistling and laughter brought the smile back to my face once he released, reminding me not only of the presence of our guests, but that some of those guests actually enjoyed seeing us together.

Trenton squeezed my hand. "We will discuss your irrational doubts, and my undeniable desire for you later." He winked. "For now, do your best, love." He stepped away as I turned to face the wooden rack where a handful of fine bows rested. I knew which one to retrieve only because Margaret gave me a crash course before the others arrived.

All in all, there were seven women competing. Me and Justine of course, Margaret, Kelly, Trenton's twin cousins, Adele and Ashtyn—who were polar opposites, one reserved and quiet, the other needed a muzzle, and his Aunt Beatrice.

We drew numbers to see who would go first. The order went as follows—Aunt Beatrice, Kelly, Adele, me, Justine (of course she would be behind me to accentuate my flaws), Ashtyn, then Margaret. I couldn't have been more thrilled at the idea of Margaret going last. If her abilities fell anywhere near her sureness, she'd surprise them all.

For a woman in her mid-forties, Aunt Beatrice held her own. All three of her arrows hit the target with solid strength, but only one hit the center. Peering around, my fear heightened. Surely, her daughters possessed similar skills. I could possibly be the one anomaly in this event.

Kelly's limited experience paid off. That and Marlowe's instruction these last two days. She hit two of her arrows on the outside circle though the third fell short.

Although I expected an admirable performance, Adele's presentation matched her confidence. She hit nothing. All three arrows struck the ground, but, to her defense, she never lifted her head high enough to even see the target. The girl was either painfully shy or lacked all self-worth. Once she placed her bow back on the rack, she turned to me with a subtle smile as she passed and winked. I glanced back at her confused. *Why did she wink?*

It was my turn. I took a deep breath and focused only on my footsteps as they led me to the starting point. If I attempted to steal a peek at Trenton, his mom, or Justine, I would surely fail. Though I hardly had a chance to win, I refused to fail.

I reached for an arrow, widened my stance, and shifted sideways. When I lifted the bow, I could see my hands shaking. Clutching the grip in my left hand, I raised the bow parallel to my chest. A drop of sweat slid down from my forehead and onto my cheek, and though it tickled my skin, I didn't move to wipe it away. Drawing the string back with my arrow securely placed, I bit my lip, eyed the target with my left eye closed, and right before I released, my arrow swung disobediently outward from its rest.

"No, no, no," I whispered as if my voice could stop it from its wayward defiance. A callous chuckle arose from somewhere behind me, I hardly had to guess at its origin. I lowered the bow and reset the arrow. Repeating the motions, I tried to remember Margaret's coaching. I slipped my two fingers lightly about the feather end and pulled, willing the point to remain on the shelf. Once I reached adequate tension, I eyed the circle carefully again then let go. A slight whoosh slid past my ear as the arrow sailed forward summoning total silence. I closed my eyes. Even the sounds of nature held their breath until a ping echoed from before me. I opened my eyes unsure of what to expect. It could not have hit the target, *that* is a completely different sound.

The spectators responded with varying degrees of surprise. I hit the easel leg the target rested on. A flutter of excitement filled my chest. Though I didn't hit the target, I hit right below it and not a tree five meters behind. *At least it hit something!*

Another grating chuckle emerged from behind. "You are aware it's the round object we are aiming for, correct?"

I wanted to turn around and make Justine my next target but refused to be coaxed into childish banter. She may win this tournament, but I smiled knowing I would walk away with the ultimate prize at the end of the party.

I reached for another arrow with a touch of buoyancy since my last shot. I readied the arrow's position and took an extra moment to focus, then released it. *Thump!* Bottom right, barely on the board, but still on the board.

"Smashing, love." Trenton's voice called out to my left somewhere. My mom and dad hollered in their typical New York fashion and left me smiling. Wiping my brow, I retrieved my last arrow. If I can hit the target once, I can hit it again.

I followed all the previous steps with precision, set the arrow, and pulled the string. At the very moment I let go, something hit my left leg and I jumped, sending the arrow far to the right and into a sea of wildflowers.

The pity came in the form of groans. I stopped myself from cursing aloud and examined the ground near my feet. Nothing seemed amiss. *What forced me off balance?* Must've been an insect of some sort, now long gone.

"Excuse me." Justine smirked and nudged me out of the way. "Child's play is over."

I stepped aside, though irritation hammered inside my chest at her consistently rude conduct, questioning once again my foolish attempt to appease Mrs. Gilford and allow the vixen to remain at the party—*my* wedding party.

As she brushed past me with her smug composure, I couldn't stop a wicked grin from forming. If Margaret really is as good as she says, this battle of superiority might just end up being the most entertaining event of the week.

Chapter 21

After I placed my bow on the rack, I trudged over next to Kelly and Margaret with a heaviness in my step, unsure whether it came from my poor performance or Justine's intimidation.

"You did good." Kelly complimented.

"Yeah, if I was trying to hit the dove sitting on that log over there."

She chuckled. "You can't be good at everything, Kat."

I laughed. "Well, I certainly have proven that point."

Margaret smiled in my direction but quickly turned her attention to Justine. She studied her with careful calculation. Margaret's eyes narrowed and widened to the snap of the bow as Justine took an extended amount of time with each release. Whether she enjoyed all the attention, or she really did take her craft seriously, I wasn't sure. What I did know was that after her three arrows sank, she moved soundly into first place. Two exceptionally close to the center, and one barely inside the center ring. She smiled coyly to the cheers, but when I followed the direction of her eyes, they only fell to one face. *Trenton.*

When Justine returned her bow to the stand, she stood next to me. A whiff of amber assaulted my nose as she leaned in. "Losers never win in the end. It's only a matter of time before I get what I want."

I opened my mouth to speak when a voice cut me off. "I'm most curious, Miss Justine." Margaret turned in her direction with an arched brow. "How many years have you been acquainted with Mr. Gilford, the younger?"

A self-satisfied smirk lifted on Justine's lips. "About twenty-three."

"And in those twenty-three years . . ." Margaret eyed her pointedly. "Precisely how often did he ask for your hand in marriage?"

Justine's cheeks colored bright red while she glanced heatedly between the two of us. I bit the corner of my lip to stop a wide smile, though I allowed a simpler one to slip through. Her mouth gaped open, but the only sound that escaped resembled a squeaky mouse. Lifting her chin defiantly, she spun on her heel and moved several yards away from us.

The satisfaction that bloomed in my chest only came about because of Margaret's quick-wittedness, but before I could whisper my thanks, the puzzling woman had turned and focused her complete attention back to the competition.

Ashtyn's turn went swiftly. She hit all three arrows on the target. Though they marked different parts of the rings, they were still on the board. It forced me to think back to Adele. With a mother and sister quite skilled in archery, how did she fail so miserably? Even *I* hit one arrow on the target.

With only Margaret's turn remaining, the winning order consisted of Justine in 1st place, Aunt Beatrice 2nd, Ashtyn 3rd, Kelly 4th, me 5th, Adele 6th.

Margaret stepped forward then abruptly turned and waved her hand. "I would be most grateful if you all moved back a few steps."

We gazed at her blankly. I knew her to be melodramatic in most things, but why did she need more space than anyone else?

Her eyes narrowed in on Justine. "Flying pebbles seem to appear out of nowhere. I would be most dismayed to see any of you get struck by one."

My mouth flew open. *That had to be it!* The object that hit me and broke my concentration. Margaret must've seen Justine toss a rock at my leg in that split second when everyone watched the target. Of course, when I looked down to find the reason after my turn, there were a half dozen small rocks littered at my feet from the terrain.

My teeth clenched and I clasped my hands tightly at my sides. *As if I'm hardly a threat at the bow.* Apparently finding satisfaction in beating me wasn't enough, Justine needed to take it a step further and humiliate me as well.

Now, not only did I want Margaret to do well, but I also wanted her to obliterate the competition.

Margaret chose her bow and Jonah clapped wildly from the side. Tilting her head slightly, she flashed him a stunning smile before she retrieved an arrow. As I observed them both, I remembered the conversation Trenton and I had the night of the hag party. He mentioned Jonah's complicated love life but seeing him here and the way he doted over Margaret made me wonder if she really could embrace life here in the twenty-first century. Although I didn't know the depth of their conversations, or interaction, it seemed as though they made each other happy. *Would that really be all that bad?*

I refocused the moment her arrow hit the center. Though it could have been disputed by someone with more archery know-how than I, it appeared to be dead center. I heard Mrs. Gilford's distinct gasp from where I stood and found myself sneaking a glance in Justine's direction—her face paled a chalky white.

Margaret's second and third strikes hit in succession directly next to the first. A loud uproar resounded in her favor. I beamed at her success. This time when she curtsied, I hollered "Bravo!"

This result put Margaret at the top of the champion's list and when Mrs. Gilford stood to speak, a slight pang shuddered my insides as I caught sight of Jonah's proud smile. I frowned. He will surely be disappointed if she chooses Trenton as promised. In a hasty decision, I waved my hands in Margaret's direction. *She should choose the way she wished.* Though I wanted Trenton far from Justine's reach, I suddenly recognized my selfishness.

Regardless of my efforts, she didn't glance my way.

"Superior performance, Miss Margaret." Mrs. Gilford spoke as if she chewed on cotton. "You are without a doubt the ladies archery champion and may pick your prize . . . er . . . the gentleman of your choice for the boat ride on Tuesday.

Margaret stepped forward, poised and confident. "I am most grateful for your accolades, Mrs. Gilford, and will surely accept my victory with pride." She stared as if the choice of men was a calculation. They all stood close to one another and didn't seem to mind the thorough examination Margaret offered them.

"I should like to express my gratitude to Mr. Gilford for his generosity and hospitality—" Trenton's father perked up. A broad smile crossed his face to the scowl of his wife. I chuckled at the mistake. "The youngest Mr. Trenton Gilford, if you please."

All eyes fell upon me before they trailed to Trenton. His face didn't hide his own shock, but he quickly straightened his countenance, nodded graciously, and glanced back to me. His eyes pled for forgiveness. I smiled in return. Both Mrs. Gilford and Justine froze in their respective positions. Neither one seemed to get their mouths closed quick enough. I shouldn't have enjoyed the sight as much as I did.

"Justine, dear." Mrs. Gilford practically croaked as she spoke. "Your worthy proficiencies have earned you the next selection."

Once Justine reeled in her disbelief, she chose Marlowe, which I believed to be a direct slap at me through Kelly. When it came to my turn, I chose Jonah. I could not get his surprised face out of my mind. At least this way I could explain the arrangement to him in private without any prying ears. I knew he would understand once he learned the truth.

Shortly afterward, the men showcased their skills with proficiency and admiration. Out of the nine men competing, Trenton barely edged Marlowe out for first place, sinking all three arrows in precise semblance to Margaret's.

"Let us all return to the house for refreshment and rest. I do believe you have all earned it." Mrs. Gilford announced at the end of the tournament.

"May I be your escort, my dear archeress?" Trenton took my hand.

"Only if you promise to never call me that." I laughed. "But you, Mr. Gilford, were sensational."

He smiled and squeezed my hand tighter. "Thank you. I've been partaking in the sport most of my life. It comes quite naturally now." Trenton's gaze always made me feel like the center of his universe. "If you would like, I can teach you. It's entirely my fault I overlooked that responsibility before now. I planned this part of the events, yet failed to prepare you, and that is unforgivable."

"A tragedy to be sure." I chuckled. "But if you insist on making it up to me, I won't refuse your efforts."

He released his hand and moved it around my body, drawing me close to his side as we walked inside. "Would you like tea? I'm sure Mother has already called for it."

"No, thanks. I think I'll rest before dinner."

As we meandered toward my room, I recalled his mother's request from the day before.

"Oh, Trenton, your mother asked me to tell you she would like to spend time with you this afternoon. Only the two of you."

One eyebrow raised. "Why didn't she tell me herself?"

Precisely my question. I shrugged my shoulders, there wasn't much about the woman that I could honestly predict outside of scorn. "Possibly because we were talking last night. I think it will be good for the two of you to visit," I said this with partial honesty, afraid his mother's only intent was to get him alone and try to convince him of my unworthiness to join the family. "She wants you to meet her in the garden."

"Very well, I shall seek her out."

Leaning in, his breath warmed my lips. "I'm sorry you didn't win me today."

I smiled as a tingle ran the length of my spine. "Today is nothing when compared to forever."

His smile matched mine before he kissed me. "I'll see you at dinner, beautiful."

"I can't wait."

I entered the room feeling much lighter than when I left it. Our plan worked only because of Margaret's idea. Her quick thinking kept Trenton out of Justine's talons . . . at least for one day.

Hopefully on the boat ride Margaret will be able to refrain from speaking too oddly. Trenton is smart, it won't take much for him to figure out she's different—really different. Especially with what he knows about time travel here at Charlock. *I should tell him.* He might be upset with me if I didn't. Would he think I didn't trust him? What would telling him really accomplish?

I continued the mental debate for several more minutes convincing myself it was all under control. *I can manage this.* I assured myself. Margaret's head is healing nicely and if things continue to go well, we might be able to experiment shortly with the cellar stairs . . . *or* she could stay here in this time.

Did I really just think that?

The door opened and Margaret walked in with a very self-satisfied air about her. "Now do you believe I'm a diamond of the first water?" She huffed and sat at the dressing table. "…in all capacities," she added as she examined her windswept hair, though she didn't seem to mind as much this time.

"Except humility." I snickered.

She tossed me a severe glance.

"I'm kidding." I stood next to her and studied her reflection in the mirror. "I owe you. I'm sorry I made you sacrifice your time with Jonah to choose Trenton."

"Oh, don't bother yourself, Jonah adores me. He knows Trenton is attached. It's completely harmless."

"He's not upset?"

"Purely a trifle at first, but I agreed to take a walk with him tonight after dinner . . . without a chaperone." She brought her hand to her mouth and tittered uncharacteristically.

"You best be careful, Miss Abbott," I warned teasingly. "You have a reputation to think of."

"That is precisely not on my mind at the moment."

I barked a laugh. "Scandalous!"

She giggled again at my playful accusation then stepped to the lavvy. "I'm going to draw a bath."

I held up my hand to delay her. "Margaret?"

She turned to face me as she reached the door.

"Did Justine throw a rock to startle me on my last arrow?"

She bent her head forward. "What do you presume?"

I sulked. "Exactly what I thought."

Margaret pursed her lips and seemed to gauge her words. "I know she vexes you, Kat, but you truly have nothing to fuss about. You surpass her in every way that matters."

I let her words sink in and smiled. "That sounded like a compliment." She flipped her hair back and closed the door behind her.

As I laid down on the bed, I struggled to fully rest, despite my exhaustion. Every muscle in my body sought relief, partly due to the early morning ride, but mostly from the tension repressed in my body in the hours leading up to and through the tournament.

I shifted to my back and studied the ceiling. My eyes trailed the detailed border trim that ended in each corner with a beige colored center rosette. The carved embellishment could easily be overlooked in comparison to the room's vibrant papered walls, gilded chandelier, and four matching sconces.

I marveled at the fact that there were so many minute details in the house that could be easily missed, except when found in simple contemplation. The ticks of the *Nouvea* figural clock on my mantle somehow grew louder in the quietness of the room and drew my attention from the elegant décor. Similar to my thoughts, each pulse cast additional considerations to my already long list.

First and foremost on my mind was *Margaret.* The fact that I now tolerated this woman, surprised me—the person I had loathed with every fiber of my being in 1878. Then there were the soon to be in-laws—a father-in-law who ignored and evaded me at every turn, and a mother-in-law who exploited my every flaw. *Will I ever make headway with them or will it forever be an impossible task?* My thoughts then turned to the rock that Justine threw. *How far is this spiteful woman willing to go?* And to think she remained here only because I told Trenton not to turn her away as he intended.

After a stint of restlessness, I sat up and moved to the edge of the bed. The orange glow that streamed in through the window hinted an approaching sunset. Two hours to dinner was an hour too long to keep busy without Trenton to spend time with. I needed something to distract my mind, anything to cause a diversion.

After leaving my room and wandering the corridors, I found myself standing on the mezzanine and gazing up to Merritt's image. Memory of the hours before this stunning portrait was painted emerged—the raging lightning storm and the ballroom with its immersive blackness before the lightning exploded off the crystal chandelier and ignited the room with a fearsome brightness. It was there where Merritt comforted me, made me laugh, and shared one of his greatest heartaches—his brother Peter's death.

Today would've been one of those times that I would've sought out his advice, his counsel, and his friendship. I recalled peeking through the sitting room doors to see him standing next to his father in his forest green waistcoat and white cravat, a handsome man with infinite goodness.

I studied him. His very presence always willed strength into me. I considered his determination to the slaves; to right a horrible travesty at the risk of losing everything, including family. His example reinforced my resolve and placated my concern over Mr. and Mrs. Gilford, making my challenges seem trivial compared to people's lives and dignity.

Though he could hardly respond to my one-sided conversation, a sense of obligation crept through me—a desire to not let my trials weigh me down and change who I am. Much like Trenton, Merritt had a way of bringing out the best in me and I owed him . . . to both of them . . .to try harder.

Chapter 22

Leaving the portrait, I entered the library. One step inside told me I found the right place to seek solace. The scent of freshly polished wood and old books rekindled a spark within me. A good book always relaxed my mind, and it'd been way too long since I'd read one.

Stepping up to the shelves, I scanned various titles with my fingers, *Anna Karenina*, *Les Misérables*—both solid possibilities, *The Iliad of Homer*, *Treasure Island* . . .ah, *The Count of Monte Cristo.* Yes, one of my all-time favorite stories of a man who overcame immense injustices to find peace, of course, only after he exacted his revenge. I smiled and retrieved it. Scanning behind me for a seat, I froze. A person sat completely silent on the sofa nearby, her presence so statuesque that I didn't see or hear her upon my entry.

"Oh, Adele, I'm sorry. I didn't mean to disrupt your privacy."

She grinned meekly. "You haven't." An open book rested in her lap. Her eyes darted around the room as she continued, "Though I suspect I'm in here more than any other guest, I can't claim it as my own."

I smiled. "What are you reading?"

"The Flight of Icarus."

"I've not heard of that one." I moved closer, intrigued.

She pointed to the other end of the sofa. "You're welcome to join me." This was, perhaps, the most words exchanged between us since we met. I accepted her invitation and sat down.

"Tell me about your book."

Not only did her smile grow wider, but her entire body wriggled with excitement as she went into detail about the God who'd been given foot wings made of wax. Icarus' father advised him not to fly too high toward the sun or the wax would melt or too low for the salt of the sea to disintegrate them.

"Determined to prove he didn't need to heed the words of his father, Icarus flew too high. Therefore, fell to his death into the sea. Thus, created what we know as the Icarian Sea." Adele sighed. "I do love Greek literature."

"It takes an intelligent person to not only understand it but enjoy it." I paused and tilted my head. "Reading is a worthy pastime, Adele. Why do you hide this side of you?"

She lowered her head and appeared timid again. "It's difficult to rise above my sister's demonstrative nature. She teases me relentlessly for my love of books, so I choose to indulge in my interests in private."

"Well, I for one appreciate your desire to read. It's been weeks since I had the pleasure."

This time her sigh was drawn out. "If I go one day without a verse or a chapter, I'm simply not whole."

I grinned, then paused. "Did you—" I stopped myself in case I interpreted my assumption incorrectly.

She slanted her head in my direction. "Did I what?"

I took a short inhale and justified my pursuit. "Did you fail the archery competition on purpose?"

She evaded my look, but a subtle grin formed. "Why do you ask?"

"Just a guess. This whole family, and friends alike, seem quite adept at the sport."

She glanced toward the large window; the very same window I felt a longtime connection with. "I don't know you very well, Kat, but I'm convinced Trenton adores you." Her eyes returned to me. "I can't tolerate bullies of any kind, even ones that smell like *Chanel*."

My eyebrow arched at her cryptic inference.

One side of her mouth twitched. "I don't like the way you're being treated by my Aunt Juliana and her devious counterpart, Justine."

Both my eyes widened in surprise. So, others have noticed their behavior too. "Do you know Justine?'

"Not well." Her shoulders relaxed. "But she seemed to have found herself in our presence often when our families united for one purpose or another. I've never trusted her." Her eyelashes fluttered, and a frown consumed her pretty face ". . . and I don't trust her now."

I followed her gaze through the glass and stood up. As I neared, bushes of full blossoms shrouded my view until my heart thudded in place. A distinct profile materialized, Justine sitting on a bench. She smiled and giggled with one hand curled cozily through a man's arm.

The man—*Trenton.*

A coldness swept through me as the blood in my limbs seemed to drain and evaporate. With fragmented breath, I placed a hand against my chest, unclear whether oxygen entered my lungs or retreated. My head spun in dizzying circles, but I could not pull my eyes away. Though no action on *his* part led me to believe they were involved in some secret interlude, he didn't appear upset or even attempt to block her rather familiar touch. In fact, he grinned and laughed with her. "He's supposed to be meeting his mother out there." I whispered, but my words were not deliberately censored from Adele. She moved closer to my side.

"Because I'm quiet, I'm often ignored. Unfortunately, I've been privy to the extent of their scheming. This was *not* a chance meeting. Mrs. Gilford planned to claim a headache all along. She asked Justine to inform Trenton of her absence . . . in the garden, of course."

My mouth remained open, though no words came to mind. Heat inched up my neck as I stared. *Have I been played the fool? The dumb American that doesn't know any better?*

I lowered myself back into the chair and fought the tears that threatened to fall. My mind bounced between Justine's earlier threat of getting what she wants and Trenton's words of affirmation. Though I fought to keep his declarations forefront, they slipped easily behind my insecurities.

"They've known each other their whole lives." Adele put an arm around me and squeezed tenderly. "They were never linked romantically that I know of and it's always appeared to me that her fondness for him exceeded his for her." She paused.

I could hear her speaking. A gentle softness lingered in her voice, but mine, when attempted, sounded so foreign—so distant. "I—I don't know what to think."

Her fingers tapped my skin gently. "I'm sorry. I truly didn't intend to hurt you. I only thought you should be aware of her designs."

I appreciated her efforts to calm me, but I couldn't stop the hurt from rising. "I can't fight this," I whispered. "Together they're too strong."

"Who?" Adele's brows furrowed. "Surely you don't mean Trenton and Justine."

I shook my head. Tears bubbled on my lashes as if they were unsure where to go next. "No. Justine and Mrs. Gilford."

Adele's face softened with understanding. "But they are not your beloved." She removed her arm and held my hand. "Trenton loves you."

She said the very words that sent my tears over the edge. "I can't fight his mother's revulsion for me for the rest of my life."

"Ignore her. Ignore Justine." She insisted with more fervency than before. "You'll be with Trenton."

"And when he leaves on business, Adele, will Justine somehow appear at his destination?" I shuddered at the thought of how often he is away and how readily his mother provides Justine with opportunities for them to be together. "What if she finds him in a moment of weakness. She's beautiful . . . staggeringly beautiful."

Adele shook her head. "How can you not see how very beautiful you are?" She lifted one eyebrow. "I've seen your kindness and the way you treat others. And above all, *you* are the woman he chose."

I exhaled. "I think I need to lie down."

She nodded and helped me to my feet. "Would you like me to assist you to your room?"

"No." I wobbled, but quickly collected myself. I just wanted to be alone. Rubbing my forehead, I shielded my eyes from the garden where darkness had already begun to descend. I didn't want to add any more to the image that had etched into my mind only moments ago—one that might never leave. Once I reached the door, I circled around. "Thank you, Adele, for our conversation." My lips struggled to deviate from their rigid line. "It was . . . informative." Then I fled for my room.

Somehow, I made it down the hall without falling. Despite the tears that blurred my eyes at a rapid pace, I located the right door and entered. Rushing to the bed without a word, I pulled the duvet fully overhead.

Margaret stopped primping and paused to watch my antics. "What, pray tell, has you in such a dither?" She asked.

"I—I don't feel well," I mumbled under the comforter.

"You were perfectly fine two hours ago."

"Please, Margaret, leave me alone."

I heard her steps approach the bed. I half expected her to throw the covers off and demand me to get ready for dinner. "Very well." She sighed. "I will have a dinner tray delivered. What would you like me to say to Mr. Gilford?"

"If he asks, just tell him the truth. I don't feel well and went to bed early."

"If he asks?" She scoffed. "Certainly, he will ask. What has happened, Kat?"

"Nothing, please, let me be." I knew if she saw me, she would see the tears, and she would not relent until I confessed. I wanted to disappear, or reel back time, anything to erase the pain that surged from that momentary glance out the window.

"Are you still going to London in the morning?"

Her words shot a dose of reality through me, despite the painful clawing at my chest. Tomorrow was my final wedding dress fitting.

Still speaking beneath the covers, I answered her. "Yes." I tried hard to keep the quiver out of my voice. "Would you please remind Kelly, Maria, and my mom that we will leave around eight in the morning?"

"Certainly." She sounded further away now.

"And Margaret?" My intent to ask her privately if she would be one of my bridesmaids couldn't very well be accomplished with a blanket between us. "Thank you for coming as well."

"I look forward to it."

The sound of the door closing gave me the confidence to peek and confirm her absence. I found myself staring at that same ceiling as I had only hours before, but somehow it lost its charm.

I knew it was Trenton that I was marrying, not his mom, not his friends . . . but what kind of life would I be living if I always questioned his faithfulness or his connection to his past, and especially his mother's hatred for me. As I listed off the items one by one, I found myself agreeing more and more that the weighing scale tipped far too low on the wrong side.

As the room darkened, my mind spun cruelly, and tears continually fell. I tried to sleep, but the lump in my throat kept me awake. A knock came to the door. I quickly and quietly pulled the covers to my forehead.

The door creaked open. "Kat?" Trenton whispered.

I kept completely still and even slowed my breath.

"Are you awake?" Between the sound of movement and the proximity of his voice, he must be close. His hand touched my hair. I fought to control my shudder. His touch never failed to excite upon contact. I bit my lip and pretended to be asleep.

"Sleep well, love," he whispered and walked out.

Love.

After he departed, my cries came harder and longer. I truly love Trenton, but did I have the strength to withstand the pressures weighing against us? *How can I do this?* I would be a crazy person our entire married life. I'm already a crazy person four days into the house party. Would Mrs. Gilford continue to undermine me at every turn? Would she invite Justine to every family function? She evidently didn't oppose creating opportunities for Trenton and Justine to be alone and I can't constantly question Trenton's resolve. He would grow weary of my doubt, but I can't ignore my misgivings either. I wouldn't be true to myself.

I tugged the duvet down to my chin for air. With the wedding now only six days away, and a significant part of the event happening tomorrow, a profound heaviness quelled in my chest as I tried to unravel the mess in my head. The stillness of the room allowed free access for many thoughts. When one suddenly took root, the nervous restlessness in my limbs halted with the significance of this random consideration. Instead of heightened anxiety, as one might experience with such a thought, a burst of clarity spread as I realized the core to this dilemma entailed a mere date—simple numbers on a calendar. Maybe we only needed more time. An exaggerated sigh escaped.

Maybe we should postpone the wedding.

Chapter 23

Monday 16 May 2011

Unaware of the time I finally fell asleep, I imagined it to be late considering how puffy my cheeks felt when I awakened. Sunlight streamed through and, for a brief moment, I silently thanked our good fortune for our pending day in London . . . then somehow the events of the prior day slowly crept in and engulfed me like a black fog.

I sat up and reached for my phone as Margaret shifted on her side of the bed. *Seven o'clock*. My fingers pressed my temples hoping the light pressure might ease the deeper throbbing. Though it had been quite some time since I experienced a hangover, my body, at the moment, knew little difference.

I went to the window first. Scanning the garden did not bring about the same pleasure it usually did. Instead, it produced images of Trenton and Justine enjoying a private moment alone. I winced. Desperate to shake this incumbrance off, I found pleasure in knowing I would be spending the day with my best friends, my mom, and Margaret. I had anticipated its arrival for quite some time, regardless of the recent development.

I knew the men were heading out for their hunt early today and with the possibility of our late return from London, I might not see Trenton until tomorrow. Even then, because of the archery tournament and the fact that we weren't boating partners, it could be well into the afternoon before we would be alone.

What I needed to say could not wait. I hustled to change into my jeans and a t-shirt.

Margaret stirred awake. "Am I delaying the outing? Is it time for us to leave for Town?"

"Oh, no." I waved my hand. "We still have an hour. I want to catch Trenton before they leave for the hunt."

"Ah yes, the kiss that never ends."

I smiled faintly and pulled my hair up into a messy bun before I glanced in the mirror. My eyelids were swollen. I splashed cold water on them and patted them dry. *Maybe he won't notice.*

I rushed down the hall toward the breakfast room. When I entered, only Mrs. Gilford, my mom, and the twins were present. I moved to retreat when my mom called out to me. "Kat, how are you feeling today?"

"Much better, thanks."

Mrs. Gilford's eyes assessed me. "Are you sure you're well? Maybe you need to postpone your trip to London."

"No. I'm fine." My answer was nothing short of curt. Her eyes widened but she didn't respond. I hardly wanted to continue the conversation but maybe she could save me time in locating Trenton. "Have you seen your son this morning?"

"Yes." Mrs. Gilford smeared a large spread of preserves on her toast and didn't look my way when she spoke. "He and Justine took an early ride."

My jaw tightened. Her words only validated my frustrations. "So, he's at the stables?"

"Most likely . . . or gone." She added with little sympathy.

I turned and hustled out to the grounds. Only steps away from the house, Adele caught up with me.

"Are you certain you're truly well, Kat?" Concern lingered heavily in her voice.

"I'm fine." My response was neither warm nor cold. I kept walking.

"What are you going to do?" She didn't need to elaborate on her question. She knew more than anyone the challenges I faced.

"I'm not entirely sure, but I need to talk to Trenton."

"He tried to come see you this morning." She kept pace with me as I walked, but when she said this, I suddenly stopped and faced her.

"He did?"

She nodded.

"Then why didn't he?"

She looked down at her hands clasped in front of her. "Aunt Juliana convinced him otherwise, then insisted he ready her horse for a ride today. Trenton advised her that they have grooms for that exact purpose, but she persisted, claiming she didn't trust them to do the job as well as he." She peered back up with hesitation. "When he departed, Justine followed. I can't say with a surety if they rode together or not, but I wouldn't believe my aunt."

The rumblings in my stomach could have been from hunger, but I suspected they resembled the continued unease from the night before.

This had gone too far.

Not only did Mrs. Gilford arrange to put Justine and Trenton together, but she now also attempted to keep us apart.

"Why are you telling me this?" I questioned warily. For a brief moment, I wondered if Adele played a part in their scheme, sharing these details only to drive me toward losing my mind.

"You know why." She shifted awkwardly. "I don't agree with what's happening here. And if they can conspire to attack . . ." Her mouth lifted into a gentle smile. "Then we can conspire to defend." She touched my arm. "I really like you, Kat. You don't deserve to be treated this way."

My stare softened. I really had no reason to suspect deceit from her. She has only shown me kindness.

Adele's forehead creased as she continued, "Please don't do anything you might regret."

I shook my head. "I honestly don't know what I'm going to do."

"But whatever you do, don't call off the wedding."

I blinked repetitively in her direction. She could not have known my thoughts from the previous night, could it possibly be written all over my face?

"Think of the pain it will cause . . . for both of you."

I moved to leave, but she tightened her hold. "Don't let my aunt and Justine get their way."

"I'm really tired, Adele. I'm tired of the games. It should not be like this. We should be celebrating. We should be happy—and I'm *not* happy."

She now squeezed both of my arms. "Fight for him." Her lips spoke with fervor. When our eyes met, a fire lit like I'd never seen from her. "Fight like all the heroines we've read about in our books. The ones who go through anguish to win the man they love." Adele's cheeks now colored as if the blaze from her eyes spread. "Be like Mercédès, in your book. She never gave up on Edmund. Don't give up on Trenton!"

My eyes widened at her exertion. Even as her fingertips pressed against my skin, they somehow transferred a jolt of electricity through me. If ever I needed a battle cry it would be now, but the person who delivered it could not have been more surprising. Slowly, the flame in her eyes dissipated like the embers of a dying fire, withdrawing back to her passive nature once more.

I absorbed what just happened and, though a fair amount of rigidity remained embedded in my muscles since I left the morning room, I couldn't stop a simple grin from forming in response to Adele's fortitude.

She took a step backward and lowered her eyes. "That's what I think you should do." Then without a response from me, she turned and walked back to the house.

I ran for the stables. Whether the motivation came from her or my fears, I couldn't wait to lay eyes on Trenton.

"Where's Mr. Gilford?" I swiftly scanned for his horse and moved about, not waiting for the grooms to answer. Nothing within confirmed his presence and Achilles' stall lay empty.

"They left, Miss Shelton. Nearly a half hour ago." A stable hand replied.

My heart sank. Now I wouldn't see him until tomorrow. I knew without a doubt, because of this, I'd be spending a lengthy day inside my cynical brain.

Defeated, I walked slowly back to the house. At least I would be sharing the day with those I cared about and especially those who didn't conspire against me.

"The car is ready, Miss Shelton. Are you sure you don't require a driver?" Hennessey met me just inside the doors upon my return.

"No, no driver. Thank you, Hennessey." Though he had ample reason to ask, with my few fender benders amongst one of them, I preferred to have the day exclusively to ourselves. No unwanted ears, led to no unwanted gossip . . . we could speak entirely uninhibited.

Thirty minutes later when I pulled the car away from Charlock Manor, I tried not to think about what could happen with Justine at the house when the men returned from their hunt.

The ease in which my mind played tricks on me grew more exhausting as time passed. I couldn't allow myself to keep venturing to that dark, bitter space. Everything I had felt from last night to this morning left scars in its wake. I needed to force myself to forget it—at least for today.

Chapter 24

Arriving in London, one of the first dramatic sights that catches your eye is the remarkable observation wheel known as the *London Eye* at 135 metres tall. Known as the world's largest ferris wheel, it shadows other familiar London landmarks such as *Big Ben*—the clock tower, and even *Buckingham Palace* in all its royal glory. Though both the tower and the palace stood in Margaret's time, the Millennium wheel, paved roads, and modern buildings, did not.

Before we left this morning, I searched for images on my cell phone of a current London for Margaret. It was imperative to keep her reaction as controlled as possible being that we would not be alone the entire day. She didn't say much. Her eyes only widened in disbelief. I also reminded her that the story of her being an actress in London needed to be believed. If she showed the slightest bit of surprise when we're there, they'd come to know of our deception.

Crossing the legendary tower bridge, Kelly and Maria squealed their delight. Though the Thames was the same one that flowed behind Charlock, it's width nearly tripled in the city.

"How are we possibly going to see everything we want to in one day?" Kelly cried.

"You'll just have to come back." I smiled and turned off the main road leading toward Chelsea. "Things are relatively calm at the house when there isn't a house party."

"These sights probably grow old to you don't they, Margaret?" My mom asked a very silent Margaret in the backseat.

I bit my lip, having learned she could say just about anything.

"No," she whispered. "Never grows old."

I took the breath that I hadn't realized I'd been holding.

"But it is much larger than I recall."

And there she goes . . .

I spoke quickly. "Our appointment at *Phillipa Lepley's* is at eleven o'clock. It might take an hour, but once we're finished, we can explore the city."

"I used to live at my aunt's house right here on Markham Street." Margaret commented and pointed down the street we just passed.

"Used to?" Kelly perked up. "Where do you live now?"

"Uh," she glanced up to me, staring back at her in the rearview mirror. "Westminster."

"Oh, doesn't the queen live there?" Mom gushed. "Isn't Buckingham Palace in Westminster?"

"Yes." Margaret nodded, "But Victoria has become rather private since Albert's death. One rarely catches a glimpse of her."

"Victoria and Albert?" Kelly, of course, would be the one to catch that.

My answer came quickly. "Oh, Margaret is speaking of the book we recently read on early English monarchies. I'm sure she meant Queen Elizabeth." My eyebrow arched Margaret's direction.

"Yes, of course, forgive me." Margaret sulked.

When we arrived at the bridal boutique of one of London's most famous designers, Phillipa Lepley, we were led into a beautiful private showroom. Though I'd been here for fittings twice before, the experience never failed to impress. The women went speechless while their eyes feasted on the expansive luxury of the space.

Like every little girl's dream, the room is designed to immerse you in a fairy tale, from the plush white carpet—the kind you wish you could walk barefoot across—to the multi-faceted chandeliers that illuminated like glitter overhead, flowing diaphanous silver drapes opened to expansive windows, and pearl-colored velvet divans inviting the guests to relax lavishly while they awaited the bride's appearance in her wedding gown.

Though the idea of spending a small fortune for a wedding felt out of place for me, Trenton insisted we have the very best. He even went as far as acquiring Miss Lepley's services himself, with the stipulation that I select nothing short of the dress of my dreams.

Last fall, when I came to London shopping for a wedding gown, I arrived alone. None of my friends or family could be present for the initial search, and of course, I restricted Trenton from seeing it ahead of time. Thankfully, it only took me three attempts before I found *the one.*

While given full carte blanche to personalize each part of my gown, I chose simple elegance. The lavish Italian satin rounded my chest and under my arms, slimmed my waist, and flowed downward in a straight skirt against my hips and thighs, only extending outward at the back several feet. Three-inch strips of white tulle curved the edges of my shoulders loosely, but no other embellishments were found other than the intricately embroidered hem. Never one to be attracted to flashiness, I selected the design not only to flatter my curves, but also because it hinted vintage grace.

When I stepped out of the dressing room and onto the platform where full length mirrors appeared on each side, my entourage exclaimed their approvals.

"Oh, Kat." My mother placed a hand over her mouth, clearly in shock. "I knew you would be beautiful, but this is breathtaking."

I smiled and brushed my hand over the skirt.

"It's the perfect dress," Kelly said, taking a seat. "You're striking."

"Do you really think so?"

Kelly's eyes clouded over. She had been with me when I chose my wedding dress in Arizona . . .and by my side when I returned it. "Absolutely no doubt," she whispered.

My lips trembled as I took in every detail. Though the mirrors surrounding me confirmed I stood upright, my spirit floated as close to an out-of-body experience as one could imagine. My hands brushed between the fabric, and my skin, pinching on occasion to assure myself I was not dreaming. The whole experience overwhelmed me.

Always composed, the practical Maria leapt to her feet. "Now, what accessories do you plan to wear?" She stepped over to a dozen shelves that displayed everything from hair combs and veils to jewelry and shoes.

Margaret leaned against the back wall and watched with wide eyes. She'd been silent since we arrived. I could only imagine what might be going through her head.

"What do you think, Margaret?" I questioned, unsure why her opinion suddenly mattered, but it did.

"Turn around." She lifted her chin. I did as she asked, very slowly, careful to not trip on the train. The tulle straps that draped against the shoulders dropped straight down the back and scooped into a low curve, finishing with a couple dozen buttons.

She sucked in her breath. I turned my head over my shoulder and caught her rubbing her bright red cheeks. Of course, this would be bold for her. "Rather exposed I dare say."

I chuckled.

She stuttered to compose herself once more. "B—but lovely all the same."

I met her smile and nodded my thanks.

The seamstress moved next to me, pinching, and tucking briskly. "A bit loose here." She gripped the sides of my waist. "Not eating?" Her glower fell below her painted eyebrows. "Though I commend you for not obliging me to *expand* the seams, which is typical." Her mouth pulled into a tight bow. "Any last-minute alteration is trying."

"I'm sorry," I whispered. "I've been a bit nervous." I mentally calculated all the missed meals in the last two weeks . . . too many to count.

She tsked and pulled several pins from the cushion on her wrist. "This will need to be brought in, but the length appears adequate. How does it feel?"

"Wonderful." I smiled, glancing back into the mirror. *I can't believe I'm wearing my wedding dress!*

Kelly and Maria appeared before me with different necklaces. I chose a simple teardrop pearl and matching earrings. Once in place, the jewelry complemented the style without drawing too much attention away from the dress.

I stared at the vision before me, fighting to keep any unwanted thoughts at bay. Up until now I had been able to ignore the occasional bristling that nestled in my chest from the night before, but somehow taking in this sight, forced the question—*will I still be a bride on Saturday?*

Before anyone caught sight of my frown, the seamstress ushered me away to change, and additional assistants brought out the bridesmaid's dresses. They were all a light lavender, but varying designs.

When I first asked my friends to be part of the bridal party, I sent them pictures of different styles and let them pick out the one they preferred. I did the same for the mothers, though Mrs. Gilford insisted on using her own designer. I was initially frustrated, but eventually let it go. Now, knowing that her decision allowed us a reprieve from her presence today, her stubbornness earned my gratitude.

Mom first, then Kelly and Maria took their turns in front of the mirrors, with the measurements sent ahead of time, most of the work bordered completion, minus a few final touches, much like my dress.

I turned to Margaret as she took a seat on a divan and watched the others with interest. "I didn't have a chance to formally ask you to be a bridesmaid at my wedding," I sat down next to her. "But I hope you will consider it."

She faced me with a blank expression.

"I'm unsure what that entails," she whispered, honestly.

I reached for her hand. "You would stand with me at my wedding. A member of the bridal party."

"I would wear a dress similar to theirs?" She pointed to the others.

I pointed to the dress that one of the assistants held in her hands. She appeared confused. When I brought Margaret to her feet in front of her, the woman paled.

I cringed. Margaret's shape differed greatly from that of Isabel—my childhood friend from New York. She could not make the wedding due to a family emergency, though she had already picked the dress and sent the measurements before she notified me of the sad news.

"This will not do." The seamstress hustled over and muttered, mostly to herself but loud enough for all of us to hear.

"Is it possible to alter?"

The seamstress peered upward at Margaret. Her thick false eyelashes flickered repetitively. "No. She is much too tall."

My hand wiped my forehead. There wasn't much time, and it wouldn't do to have Margaret stick out any more than she already does.

"It's fine, Kat. I don't need to be included."

I turned to her and, though her countenance undoubtedly appeared calmer than mine, I shook my head. "No, I really *want* you involved. It would mean a lot to me."

Her smile grew, causing the gray in her eyes to sparkle like silver. "Thank you."

I faced the seamstress again. "May we see your existing collection of lavender dresses?"

The woman shook her head. "There isn't much." She scowled. "Lavender seems to be the color of the season." She led us to a barren rack. Nothing remotely matched the shade.

I acceded. "We'll simply have to keep our eyes open as we shop today. There must be something you can wear."

Margaret remained silent. As the others toyed with different accessories themselves, I moved next to her. "Are you alright?"

She bowed her head but said nothing.

"You know it's quite out of character for you to be this quiet."

She glanced around before she faced me again, making sure no one else was within earshot. Her eyes glistened. "What if I'm stuck here forever?"

My heart sank. I remembered wondering that very same thing. My hand reached for hers and squeezed.

"What if I were to never marry or bear children? What if I never find love like bef—" She stopped abruptly. "—Like you."

I moved my arm around her shoulders and leaned in, to whisper. "That's not going to happen, Margaret. Everything will work out the way it's supposed to. If you are meant to stay here, you'll find love again. I never believed I would, but I did."

She looked at me once more. Several tears slid down her cheeks now.

I reached for a tissue in my purse. "And if you're meant to go back, you'll find a man who adores you above all else and marry him. I'm sure of it."

She sniffled. Though my words sounded confident, my spirit lacked assurance. Yet if all I could offer her was willpower, I would.

The Margaret that stood next to me at this moment differed greatly from the Margaret I knew from my time travel experience. She had changed *and* I had changed—and through providential circumstances we now saw each other in a new light.

After the fitting, we spent some time in the area shopping for clothes other than formal wear. All at Trenton's expense—one more thing he insisted upon in the planning stages. Margaret lightened up as we went along, easily falling in love with the art of shopping. Despite the differences in fashion, she had a distinct eye for style.

With a dozen bags in hand, we went to a late lunch at *The Beaufort House* on King's Road. I'd been to the old brick corner restaurant with Trenton once before and the menu boasted an exquisite cuisine of European fare.

We all ordered something different and turned our lunch into a makeshift buffet, much to the displeasure of our waiter. I ordered the honey glazed goat cheese starter for all of us and the fillet with watercress puree, Mom ordered the salmon poke, Kelly chose the lobster linguini, Maria settled on the Panacotta, and Margaret gushed over the oven-baked corn-fed poussin. Each one left a mouth-watering impression, one that would be hard to replace any time soon.

After lunch, we could barely move, yet we forged forward. We refused to waste even one moment in London and continued shopping. Dresses in *Ella Boutique*, summer skirts in *Muse*, pants and blouses in *Trilogy*, and footwear and purses in *Russell and Bromley*. The whole experience was eye candy to the wedding party, and we nibbled quite happily and thoroughly.

Margaret tugged on my sleeve before we entered another boutique. "Please explain the card to me. The one you use when payment of services are requested?"

"Oh," I nodded my head. "That's right, you're accustomed to paper pounds." I reached into my wallet and pulled out a couple of credit cards. "See, my money is in the bank, the financial house, like what your father may have used in your time. This account is Trenton's" I pointed to a blue card. "And this one is mine." I showed her my name embossed on the red one. "When I use the card for payment, the bank pays the retailer directly. I don't need to carry cash everywhere."

"What a brilliant idea." Margaret handled the card. "What freedom you must possess."

I smiled. "Yes, actually it does give me an element of independence."

"I know nothing of my father's finances. He and Helen manage my modiste and wardrobe. I have little control or choice," she whispered. "They are unaware, but I have been saving my pin money for over two years now."

"I remember Lizzy and Abagale referring to pin money . . .an allowance of some sort, correct?"

"Yes, coins to be used not entirely for pins, but ribbons, gloves, even bonnets, but most of those were procured from my modiste budget. I had little need to purchase excess."

"How much do you have?"

"Forty pounds." She laughed. "When I saw the charge for our lunch, I nearly swooned—one hundred and thirty pounds! For one meal no less."

"What are you saving your money for?"

She shrugged. "I don't know. Freedom perhaps." She winked.

I wound my arm through hers and squeezed. No matter what happens to her, whether she stays or goes, I will do everything in my power to help her lead a different life, one of *her* choice. Having lived both in 1878 and modern day, I've come to understand the word *freedom* for a woman was a cherished gift.

As we walked down the street arm and arm, I reflected on how far we'd come. That first day, I wanted nothing more than to strangle her, but each subsequent day, Margaret's character and personality has grown on me. So much so, that I would be entirely okay if she stayed in the twenty-first century.

"A vintage store!" Kelly cried with excitement though no one else truly knew why. Her mother's habit of antiquing must've rubbed off in the year she'd returned home.

The uniqueness of this store transpired in the contradictory window displays. The left half served more of the eccentric artists who descended upon Chelsea and the right half of the store catered to the upscale clientele that appreciated antiquated treasures.

"Should we?" I tipped my head forward. Margaret's eyes widened to each item she paused over in the windows.

I laughed. "If anything, it will be entertaining."

As I wound through the store, my mind wandered. We hadn't found a dress for Margaret yet, surely there must be something useful here.

Margaret's face paled more and more as we continued from rack to rack. "What are we looking for, Kat?"

"Your dress," I whispered back.

"In here?" She grimaced as she fingered a pair of bell-bottom jeans with flower patches sewn on.

"Well not exactly right here." I swatted her hand lightly. "Over there, where the dresses are."

Kelly and Maria happily explored the hippy section while my mother stayed with us.

"I think I understand Margaret's concern." She picked up a bright orange wig. "We should look somewhere else."

I sighed in surrender after scanning through a handful of retro prom dresses with puffed sleeves and obsolete button-up fashion pieces Queen Elizabeth, herself, might wear. "I guess so."

"What about this?"

I spun around to see Margaret pointing to a dress displayed on a mannequin.

Despite the lighter shade of lavender than the other dresses, it's individual features would not detract but compliment them quite well. The high neck and arms were tulle as well as the full-length skirt overlay with a unique embellishment of silver leaves lining the heart shaped satin bodice. A stunning find to say the least.

"I take that back." Mom chuckled.

I ran my finger across the fabric. It must be dated over a half century. "Do you like it, Margaret?" I tried to categorize her expression.

She pinched the tulle. "You don't think it's too telling?"

Though the sheer exposed her shoulders more than I believe she was used to, her chest would be wholly covered.

"Try it on." I suggested. "If you don't like it, we'll keep looking."

She agreed and though the waist exceeded her slim size a tad, I knew the seamstress could manage the adjustments perfectly, if she was willing.

"Well?"

Margaret turned around several times, flaring the skirt before the much smaller mirror this store offered. "It's lovely." She brushed her hand over the shoulders. "You don't presume this to be too brazen?"

"Not for our time," I muttered low enough for only her ears.

She smiled. "Very well, I approve."

I clapped my hands excitedly, but when we approached the counter to pay, I hesitated with my wallet open. Glancing at the cards, I felt an odd tug on my heart strings. Peering up at Margaret, I watched her intently.

In response, her eyebrows nearly met in the middle from the depth they furrowed, but I only chuckled and grabbed the red card—my card. This one would be *my* gift to her.

We returned to the bridal shop only minutes before closing time, and though the seamstress conveyed her displeasure at the idea of altering a dress she didn't have an association with, nor something that belonged in this century, she respected our predicament and the fact that I paid her twice the fee.

"The dresses will be delivered on Thursday." She announced while she finished taking Margaret's measurements. "Please notify us immediately if you have any concerns." Then shooed us out to lock up for the night.

We waved our final goodbyes while I contemplated how fortunate we were in the find. I might have possibly located something in the high-end shops had we kept looking, but to find a dress that so completely spoke of Margaret, thrilled me to no end.

Chapter 25

Later that night, well after midnight, I veered down the road that led to Charlock. The drive home from London remained uneventful. Kelly and my mom fell asleep long before we even left the city. Maria played on her phone and Margaret, once again, fell into quiet contemplation.

I fought hard to stay awake myself. The mental games of the night before left me with little sleep, in addition to driving and spending a full day in London, exhaustion reached its peak the moment I parked.

I woke the sleeping beauties and opened the trunk for everyone to retrieve their purchases. Although I left the house this morning with a clamp on my chest, the fun I experienced from the day trip brought a warmth to my heart and a strange closeness to Margaret, a woman I never believed would ever become a friend.

The house, shrouded in near darkness when we entered, carried an inviting silence—opposite in every way to our day. As the women sluggishly made their way to their rooms, I set my packages down in the entryway, drawn aside by the light coming from the library. It danced at the doorway against the blackness of the corridor as if someone left the hearth aflame. I shuffled in to see my suspicions confirmed. A dwindling fire fluttered within the fireplace, but it was the soft breathing that alerted me to the sofa.

Trenton's long form stretched out past its length. His hair charmingly disheveled, his shirt untucked and partially unbuttoned, and his shoes tossed to the side. I gazed upon him, studying his features with admiration. The peace that appeared on his brow made him astoundingly handsome.

I walked over and touched his cheek. He shook awake. "Kat?" he whispered and wiped his eyes. "You're home."

I smiled and nodded. "What are you doing in here?"

Trenton moved to a sitting position and ran his fingers through his hair. A book fell from his chest when he did this. I stooped to place it on the end table and chuckled. *Crime and Punishment.*

"I wanted to wait up for you." He yawned and squinted his eyes in his effort to awaken. When he tilted his chin upward, the grin that formed on his lips surfaced more like an endearing schoolboy than a man in his prime. A jolt fired through my chest, reminding me of how his attractiveness affects me.

I sat down and snuggled next to him. When I laid my head on his shoulder, the enticing scents of citrus and cinnamon roused me. *Must be from his evening tea.* I leaned back to meet his eyes, wondering if the *talk* we needed to have should happen now or perhaps tomorrow when we'd be more alert.

He rubbed my cheek. "I've missed you."

I grinned weakly, unable to stop my curiosity. "I tried to find you before you left this morning. I went to the stables, but you were gone."

His eyes widened. "You did?"

"Why didn't you come see me before you left?" I hesitated to ask but it ate at me far too long.

"Well, you were ill last night. I checked on you then, but you were asleep." He wiped his eyes again. "Then this morning at breakfast when I suggested visiting you, I—" He took a slow inhale. "I was informed I shouldn't—that women did not appreciate being seen in their bedchamber first thing in the morning."

I stole a deep breath. "Who told you this?" I inquired, even though I already knew the answer.

"My mum."

I bit the inside of my cheek and turned toward the window again, that same window I witnessed his tête-à-tête with Justine. "Trenton, you've come to my room before to wake me. Why question it now?"

He shook his head. "She insisted most adamantly. I didn't want to upset you."

My nose stung. "When have I *not* been happy to see you?"

He looked away. Did he recognize the mistake in listening to his mother, especially since he hasn't heeded her advice for over a decade?

I closed my eyes and shook my head. "I don't have the strength for this."

"What do you mean?" From the tone of his voice, he seemed fully awakened now.

I met his eyes. "I can't fight the games, schemes, and deceit."

"What deceit?" His voice raised. "From me?"

"No." I tried to bring the conversation back to a whisper. "No, not from you—from others."

"Who?"

"You truly don't see it?" Frustration flowed through my limbs.

"I guess not." He snapped.

I instantly regretted bringing this up at this time. We were both tired and not thinking clearly. "Forget it. It's late."

"No, Kat. I'm not going to forget it. You emphatically accused someone of treachery and won't elaborate?"

When I inhaled my nostrils flared. "You honestly don't see what your mother and Justine are doing to me?"

His eyebrows met in the middle. "What are they doing?"

Oh, for heaven's sake. If I had to explain it then this was going to be much harder than I anticipated.

"Okay, I'll start from the beginning. Your mother invited Justine without asking—"

Trenton interrupted. "I offered to send her home, you stopped me."

"Let me finish."

His mouth pulled into a straight line and his jaw flexed, but he nodded.

"Your mother insisted that you sit at the head of the table then placed Justine in the seat to your right."

"I didn't acquiesce, so it didn't happen."

I shot him another look and he went silent.

"Then at the archery competition, again without our permission, announced that the ladies' contest winner got to choose her boating partner, full well knowing Justine is a phenomenal archer so she could choose you and be alone with you on the water. The picnic, where she continually reminded us of how close you and Justine are. The fact that she asked me to have you meet her in the garden but deliberately faked a headache and sent Justine instead to spend an enjoyable moment together, alone."

"I—"

I held one finger up and whispered. "I saw you."

Trenton remained still and unreadable.

"And just this morning, when I went to breakfast looking for you, she told me that you and Justine went out on a ride together.

When I went to the stables you were gone and hadn't thought to come see me before you left."

"I tried, but she told me . . ." He stood up and paced. His thoughts seemed to be fluctuating through the lines that intensified on his face, ending in a deep frown. "This is unfair, Kat."

My mouth parted. "Unfair?" My mind raced with confusion. "To whom?" This sudden deviation left me questioning . . . *everything.*

"I know my mother can be difficult, but she's not malicious." He pinched the bridge of his nose. "And you know Justine and I are old friends. When she came to the garden we only talked." He stopped abruptly and folded his arms across his chest. "Is that what you saw? Us talking?"

I tried to halt the mounting pressure in my chest. "And touching."

"Touching?" His eyes rounded and his arms fell to his side.

I stood to meet him. "You can't be that naïve, Trenton. Women touch when they flirt. It's what they do. And Justine is a master at leaving her mark all over you." I waved my hand from his head down to his feet.

"She has no place in my heart."

"Yet, she has a place at your side."

Trenton shook his hands. His unbuttoned shirt revealed a layer of moisture that spread from his chest to his neck. "I cannot continue to try and convince you of my fidelity." The muscles in his jaw tightened as he opened his mouth several times to speak. "This—this is . . ." He stopped, unable to finish.

"Why didn't you leave the garden when your mom didn't come?"

An icy stare emerged with an ire I'd never seen from him. "Dammit Kat! I didn't do anything wrong."

Tears tingled at the corners of my eyes, threatening to fall at the slightest movement.

"If you don't believe me . . ." His voice rumbled. "How can we share a life together?"

I glanced at the doorway, afraid that our voices alerted someone to our presence. My lips trembled to a plea. "You honestly don't see what games they're playing?" I wiped my eyes. "It seems everyone else in the household can."

With one hand rubbing his chin, the other pointed in my direction. "I won't listen to this." His head shook fiercely, and a wayward strand of hair fell over one eye. He angrily brushed it aside as he turned and walked toward the door. When he gazed back at me, he articulated with concise clarity. "I'm done with this conversation."

I swallowed hard against my dry throat, unable to utter a sound. Confusion gripped my chest like an iron vise . . . its clutch squeezed with each passing second, and though my body longed to be held by him, the chasm that deepened between us implied a hurdle we might never overcome.

He stood in the doorway as rigid as I'd ever seen. "May I escort you to your room?" Even his words were stiff.

I refused to meet his eyes. The ache that spread through my limbs expanded in record haste. Trenton's defensiveness caught me off guard. Earlier when I considered approaching this subject, an entirely different result played out in my head. *Did I overstep or did he have something to hide?* I shook my head. "No, I'm fine. Go ahead and go."

"You're *not* fine." Though his tone had softened, his words still stung. "You haven't been yourself this whole week and now you're making erroneous accusations against people I care about."

My lips parted and I couldn't stop a faint gasp from escaping. He had never said that before. Not about his mother and especially not about Justine.

This must've caught his attention. He rubbed the back of his neck, and a similar uncertainty to mine, flickered across his features. "I'm not even sure what to make of this, it's beyond frustrating."

The tears that hovered on the cusp of my eyes now trailed down my cheeks. "I'm sorry," I whispered and moved toward the window. The enormous glass, ironically, exposed the scene outside that unfolded before me like a cruel joke. The very place I envisioned us taking our vows, was the same place I saw him with Justine, and now it loomed over us, taunting us into irrevocable damage. Folding my arms tightly across my body, I kept my back toward him and attempted to hide my tremble. "Goodnight, Trenton."

Thick, awkward silence prevailed. I sensed him move toward me, hesitate, then walk out.

My hand suppressed my anguished sobs as I crumpled to the floor. I couldn't even recall an argument of this magnitude the entire time we'd been engaged. Even our childish squabbles when we first met never compared to what had just occurred.

Though it pained me to recall, my mind rolled over the conversation repeatedly. I was certain I hadn't imagined the ongoing shots and insults both his mother and Justine directed at me. *Was I wrong to ask?* Shouldn't I be able to inquire anything of my fiancé? *No secrets, right?* Could I have misread what I'd seen and felt in Mrs. Gilford's demeanor? Her sharp comments and condescending retorts? Or even Justine's?

Impossible.

Justine, herself, made it clear—she wants him. Even Kelly and Margaret noticed their pretentious behavior, and Adele confirmed overhearing their schemes.

An unbearable nip of regret burned through my chest and down my body. I glanced back to the empty doorway. Trenton hadn't returned. The painful acknowledgement left me feeling hollow and alone. As the minutes ticked by, the glow of the fire dissipated, forsaking me to the bitter bite of darkness—much like the chill in my heart.

Chapter 26

Tuesday 17 May 2011

The next morning, I slept in.

With the boat ride not scheduled until eleven o'clock I took advantage of the extra time to remain in my bedroom, unseen. I didn't want to face anyone at breakfast . . . especially Trenton. Everyone would learn, if they didn't already, that we argued last night.

I rolled over to find Margaret gone. In the last couple of days, she'd grown quite accustomed to a twenty-first- century lifestyle and seemed to embrace change much easier than I had accepted it in the past. Even in London, her odd comments were few and far between. That might be a good thing, especially if we found she couldn't return.

What if I had never found my way back to the future?

Would I have discovered a way to fit in? Shortly before my second fall, I made the decision to leave the Attwood household and seek out history where I could find it. With some money saved, my intent was to travel to France, to find the celebrated artists of the nineteenth century, to witness their creativity and enjoy a simpler time.

When I found myself back here and with Trenton, my frustration bordered anger. His arrogance, money-driven attitude, and what I believed to be clear disregard for his family history, created an image of a man I could never tolerate, much less care for. Yet, the more I became acquainted with Trenton outside of his stuffy environment, the more he became the man I wanted to spend the rest of my life with.

After losing Jeff, I never believed I could go on, much less love again, but now I couldn't imagine my life without Trenton.

As the late night's events slowly trickled back into my mind, I groaned and smashed my face into the plush pillows. Inhaling the freshly laundered fragrance from my pillowcase, I resigned to the fact that I would happily spend the rest of the day in bed if I could. However, I already used the sick card once . . . if I used it again, I could be seen as weak or fragile. That is not how one *fights for their man* as Adele put it.

Fight for my man.

How exactly am I going to do that? *Did I want to do that?* That question darted in and out of my mind in less than a second . . . of course I will fight for Trenton. *I love him!* Even if it means putting up with his grumpy mother and ignoring Justine . . . anything to rectify what happened. Trenton is everything to me and losing him is not an option.

Reluctantly, I arose and started my day. After my shower, I stood before my wardrobe and considered my options. How does one dress for a boat ride on the Thames and a picnic? Remembering my purchases from London, I pulled the clothes from the bags. Holding up the cotton lawn dress that Margaret convinced me to get, I smiled. The short, breezy, blue skirt with thick straps and white lace applique on the hem seemed like the perfect choice, especially with my white sneakers. In my best mimic of Margaret's voice, I stood before the full-length mirror and held it in front of me. "Absolutely lovely, Kat, you must indulge." So, I bought it.

I curled my hair, darkened my eyelashes, and took one last look in the mirror, grateful to see bursts of the old Kat surface again. Due in part to Trenton in my life and, in a small way, yesterday's jaunt into London with my friends also strengthened me.

That is, until I got home.

I should've listened to the warning bells in my head and not said anything last night. Though the conversation needed to be had, it was quite late, and Trenton and I were tired. Though I don't regret the content of the conversation, I regret the way I handled it. Hopefully, this afternoon, Trenton and I can talk and hopefully he isn't still angry.

Glancing at my phone, I panicked when it showed five minutes before eleven. *Shoot! I can't be late!*

I grabbed my white wide brimmed sunhat and rushed down the hall nearly running into Hennessey. Thank goodness I didn't have my heels on.

"Miss Shelton." He tugged on his lapels. "I was tasked to come find you. I believe you are tardy. The party has already departed for the river."

"Thank you, Hennessey," I said and kissed him on the cheek. I'd only done that once before, but as I glanced back, his smile indicated he didn't seem to mind.

I ran down the steps of the veranda and stopped. Gazing over our "spot," I found myself missing Trenton. Actually, I missed a great deal about our life before the party began, but swiftly reined in my emotion and hustled through the gardens.

As I approached the river, everyone had already dispersed to their individual rowboats or poised themselves to step in from the bank. Mr. and Mrs. Gilford, Kelly and Leo, Justine and Marlowe—although I looked briefly past them—Aunt Beatrice and Uncle

Clarence, Ashtyn and Hastings, Adele and, oh yes, another person I have come to thoroughly adore . . . Grandfather Trenton.

I rushed forward waving my hat. "I'm so sorry I'm late!"

Trenton looked up. His bright eyes matched his smile. I exhaled profoundly and grinned in return, grateful to see that expression once again. He turned to Margaret who boasted a wide smile of her own—probably because of my dress. Then he swiftly tied the boat back up to a nearby post and leaped out with little effort. Wearing a pair of beige slacks and charcoal grey shirt, much too nice for an excursion on the Thames, he reached my side in a handful of strides.

"Kat . . ." He breathed.

I closed my eyes and let the way my name spilled from his lips invoke a thrumming sensation. When he came in for a hug his mouth grazed my ear. Surely, he was aware of the goosebumps developing on my arms, but he didn't pull away.

"Forgive me," he said as he kissed the tender part of my neck. "I'm mortified over how we parted last night." His lips traced the curve of my jaw, caressing my skin until he reached my mouth, shamelessly drawing me in. I wrapped my arms around him and relished in his touch once more.

"Trenton, enough!" His mother snapped. "Must we all be delayed because one chose to dawdle in tardiness?" I opened my eyes over his shoulder to see her pull out a fan and whip it frantically as she sat on one end of her boat with Mr. Gilford II at the other.

"Ignore her," Trenton whispered. I was certain my breath hitched. *What has changed from last night?* I stepped back confused, but Trenton reached for my hand and kissed my knuckles. "You look magnificent by the way. I wish I could steal you away right now."

I smiled. If his heart hurt as much as mine, we could barely stay apart. "I wish you could too."

With a parting kiss on my lips, Trenton returned to Margaret's boat, where the dark beauty sat perfectly poised holding a parasol? I blinked repeatedly as if I had imagined it. *Where in the world did she find a parasol?* I shook my head and laughed then found Jonah with one foot in his boat and one foot out ready to assist me. He extended his hand, and I joined him.

"Welcome aboard, Miss Kat."

"Why thank you, Jonah." I smiled genuinely. Though my heart was tethered to another vessel, I looked forward to this chance to get to know Jonah and how his week has been, *but especially* to find out what he thinks of Margaret.

Mrs. Gilford, who once again commandeered the festivities on her own accord, called out to the party. "Now remember to return here precisely in one hour. A picnic has been arranged for us on the grassy hillside and we mustn't let the food spoil . . ." Her voice faded as her husband rowed them away. I gazed one last time at Margaret, then Trenton, who caught my eye. His simultaneous wink and half-smile sent chills to my toes. If only we had more time this morning . . . if only we hadn't fought last night . . .

"Might we go that way, Jonah?" I pointed in the opposite direction of Mrs. Gilford.

"Certainly." He beamed, revealing perfectly straight teeth and a charming dimple in his right cheek. I had never noticed that before. Of course, to my defense, my attention mainly focused on Trenton and not his friends.

With the sun shining brightly down upon us I adjusted my hat to shade my eyes and settled easily onto the seat as Jonah retrieved the oars. Once he began rowing, the gentle sway of the boat lulled me into a relaxing state. Despite my disappointment of not being with Trenton, I wasn't about to let it dampen the event all together.

As I watched Jonah maneuver the boat, Merritt's silhouette took shape in his place and the memory of our time on the river brought forth a silly grin and a wild idea.

"So, Jonah . . ." I smiled slyly. "The last time I sat in a rowboat on this river, I played a game with a friend of mine."

"Brilliant. What game?"

"Truth or Dare."

His chuckle emerged low and deep. "I do believe that game can instigate conflict."

"Possibly." I kicked off my shoes and wiggled my toes.

He pulled easily back on the oars. "Trenton would have my hide if . . ."

"Jonah!" I sat up. "What exactly are you inferring? I'm only trying to get some answers out of you."

He wiped the sweat off his forehead as if he really believed I could be that forward.

I chortled. "Honestly, who do you think I am?"

"I beg your pardon, Kat, I only recalled playing the game in college where we referred to it as Questions and Commands . . . and to my defense, it's not an innocent game."

"This one will be, I promise. I'll ask first. Truth or dare?"

"Truth."

Good!

"How much do you like Margaret?"

The rowing stopped. His smile began awkwardly then grew to fill half his face.

I laughed.

"Oh, you don't even have to answer that. That tells me everything."

He lowered his head. "My turn."

At that very moment, another boat hit ours and jarred me from my comfortable position. Peering over, I saw Margaret and Trenton beside us.

The excitement that stirred from the sight of them was slightly marred by my shock. "Are you trying to get us turned over?" I hardly wanted to end up in the river. I grasped for the side of the boat and held on as it rocked from the collision.

"Nope!" Trenton stood carefully and threw Jonah a rope which he caught readily.

My eyes widened with curiosity. "What are you doing?"

Both men smiled.

Margaret lifted her parasol and gave me a satisfying look. My brows furrowed at the three of them as they shared knowing expressions. Apparently, I was the only one in the dark.

Jonah tied the rope to an iron hook found barely beneath the bow. Tightening it, he moved to the center and pulled their boat parallel to ours.

"Ready?" Trenton asked while Jonah clutched the sides tightly and steadied himself. Trenton then hopped into our boat and took over Jonah's position while he jumped into their boat with similar success.

"Your timing was impeccable, Gilford." Jonah tugged at his collar and situated himself contentedly across from Margaret. "You saved me from a most uncomfortable game of Questions and Commands." He smirked my way as Trenton's eyes flashed in response. Clearly, he played the same kind of game in college as Jonah.

"I only asked one question and it was hardly difficult." I cried back.

Jonah laughed out loud, but when he turned toward Margaret his cheeks colored a faint red.

Once both men were settled in the opposite boat they started in, Trenton released the rope. Margaret's brief goodbye included a dramatic wink which brought a broad smile to my face. So, the little minx was in on this little subterfuge all along.

I chuckled and shook my head. When my eyes lifted, Trenton's gaze warmed me once more and my heart fluttered with the thrill of being alone with him. Though it dangled under the ploy of deception, anything to have this moment was entirely worth it.

Chapter 27

"I didn't *win* you, Trenton." I glanced around, thankful that the river's length hid our ruse from Mr. and Mrs. Gilford. I didn't want to be the subject of another lecture. "Don't you think *someone* will be upset?"

He shot me a sly smile, dropped the oars, and sat down on the space between the seats. When I peered at him confused, he tugged me down to join him. With one fluid movement, I was beside him. The space in the bottom of the boat allowed our torsos plenty of room but our legs rested above the bench I had occupied a moment ago. A simple blanket served as a pillow.

"Kat." He wrapped his arms around me and nuzzled his face in my hair. "I could not go a second longer listening to Margaret berate me for my selfish behavior. It seems I'm as dense as everyone thinks."

"What do you mean berate you?"

"Evidently, she overheard our argument last night and proceeded to give me the one-two. She called me an *incorrigible cad*."

"Oh," I hid my grin with my hand. This was a term I had heard often in 1878, but it was an uncomplimentary title for a man, much like scoundrel.

"What exactly is that?"

"I'm sorry." I winced, though I wasn't about to tell him. "I truly hoped nobody knew or heard anything." Then I frowned. Maybe his mother did too or worse, Justine.

"Please forgive me." He leaned back, searching my eyes. "It has been thoroughly brought to my attention that you have been mistreated." He cupped my cheek. "I'm truly ashamed of my ignorance."

"Wh—what all did she say?" I feared she'd gone too far.

"Quite enough. Please, accept my apology. I have been in dire straits since last night. I even came to your room twice with the hopes that you, too, were wandering the halls in the early morning, unable to sleep. I hesitated to knock since you weren't alone, but I'm profoundly sorry for my behavior."

"Trenton," I placed my hand over his. "I'm sorry too. I never meant for any of that to happen. I only wanted to express my feelings."

"Which should not be thus disregarded."

"I shouldn't have been so quick to judge," I said, resting my head against his shoulder. Burrowing my face into his neck, I invited his irresistible cologne to entrance me. "When I saw you with Justine, smiling and enjoying yourself, something snapped. I hate it. I don't want to be jealous of the friendship you have with her or anyone."

He kissed my forehead. "Honestly, you have nothing to be jealous about. We were only reminiscing about our other friend, Jonathan."

"Jonathan?"

"Yes, a childhood friend of ours. He lived several kilometers past Wadsworth Hall to the north. He's actually in Afghanistan, right now, fighting with the Royal Air Force."

"I—I didn't know. I'm sorry."

"No, please don't be. I never thought to mention it and Justine simply reminded me of some of our juvenile pastimes with him. I guess that's why I became cross last night. Our conversation was innocent . . . and Kat, it always will be."

A light breeze blew through and chilled my face, alerting me to the moisture that settled around my eyes. I hadn't even realized tears had surfaced. "But that is what concerns me." Uncertainty arose in my whisper. "That she will *always* be a part of your life."

Trenton nudged my chin upward to meet his eyes once more. "Only as a friend, and if I can offer you any peace, our interactions will cease." His thumb brushed my skin tenderly and removed the remnants of moisture. "There is only one woman whose feelings matter, and I fear I have damaged them."

He leaned downward. Pressing his lips against mine, he stole what little breath I owned. My skin tingled under the gentle caressing of his touch.

When I drew back, I sighed. "I worried my accusations went too far last night, and that you'd call off the wedding."

"I would hope you know me better than that. One quarrel will not scare me away. Remember, love, you're stuck with me. Besides, I might provoke you occasionally on purpose." He wiggled one brow teasingly. "I heard making up is most enjoyable."

I punched him playfully in the chest and the boat rocked slightly to the movement. "Do not irritate me intentionally, it will drive me senseless."

"Speaking of senseless . . ." A small crease appeared between Trenton's eyes. "Margaret said the most unusual thing before she scolded me."

I bit my lip. "Wh—what did she say?" *Other than incorrigible cad?* I wondered.

"'That the Thames was quite sullied when Victoria was in the monarchy. I asked her where she read that, assuming it came from a book or an article and she gawked at me as if I wronged her and said, "I'm in earnest, Mr. Gilford, I saw it myself."

"Oh? She said that?" I wrinkled my nose. *I need to tell him.* I could easily remind him of her theatrics, but I shouldn't keep this from him any longer. My pause lengthened while a dozen scenarios raced through my head.

"So," Trenton smiled and changed the subject before I responded. "What is this about Questions and Commands with my mate?"

"Uh, I . . ."

"Shall we carry on then? Whose turn?"

"Um," I debated going back to the subject of Margaret and clearing the air, but I wanted to retain the lightheartedness of the moment.

With Trenton's arm securely around me, his fingers caressed my shoulder. "You first, love."

"Alright," I grinned. "Truth or dare?"

"Hmmm." He glanced upward and hesitated. "Which one would I fear the most with you?" I punched him again as he laughed. We continued to move absolutely nowhere as we snuggled in the bottom of the boat. The clear blue sky above provided a perfect backdrop to this perfect moment. "I choose truth, we'll start easy."

I smiled. "You think it will be easy, huh?"

"I am a paragon of virtue."

I barked a laugh. "Okay, Mr. Paragon . . . where are we going on the yacht?"

"Oh, you're a slick one." He chuckled. "You know that the destinations are strictly confidential."

"You picked truth."

"Very well," He smiled smugly. "We're going to a beach, several actually . . . a casino, a castle, an island, a prison, cliffs, and a monastery."

"Fine." I jokingly stewed, though the mystery naturally thrilled me.

My turn, sweet. Truth or dare."

"Truth." I figured there was nothing I would hide from him.

When he hesitated, my smile faltered.

"What is your greatest fear?" His question should've been simple, yet it ruffled me. I stilled under his touch and waited several moments before I answered.

"I'm afraid I will lose you." My breath hitched. "I'd never known fear until I'd pictured my life without you. Last night when you left—it was like getting a glimpse into this world of nothingness. I don't ever want to go back there, Trenton . . . I need you."

His arms wound tighter, tilting his head enough for me to see his eyes. The green sparkled like jade under the sunlight. "You will *never* lose me." He kissed me again. The salt on his lips singed my tongue and I savored the steady movement of his mouth.

As he pulled away, I whispered, "May I get this reward every time I answer a question?"

His laugh rose heartily. "I think it's time for a dare."

"Okay," I pretended to dwell on it, but knew from the beginning of the game what I would ask. "I believe I have a good one."

"Should I be scared?"

"Most definitely." I chortled from our easy banter.

"Very well, proceed."

"I would love to see you perform something, *anything*, on Friday in the talent show."

"You cannot be serious, Kat! I'm an athlete. You're quite aware I lack the ability to sing or play an instrument."

"You may be as creative as necessary."

Mischief glinted across his façade. "May I recruit my mates?"

"Oh absolutely, I insist." Chuckling, I nestled deeper against his chest still vibrating from laughter.

Trenton cleared his throat. "I believe it's your turn for a dare."

"Now remember," I pleaded. "I am to be your wife, and if you have me do anything humiliating you might regret it."

"I will never regret it." He went silent, and I held my breath wondering what task he would doom me to. "You must showcase your sparring skills at the same talent show."

"No!" I sat up.

"Oh, yes. We are bound by the Truth or Dare rules . . . whatever they may be."

"Trenton, your mother will be mortified. She'll disown me on the spot."

"You should never hide your talents, Kat."

"It's been too long, I'm rusty."

"Well, it just so happens you have a sparring partner on location."

"I don't have the equipment."

"Perfectly attainable. Any other absurd excuses you would like to toss at me?" He squeezed my waist and I let out a cry.

"Oh, this was not supposed to go this way," I cried. "I only tried to get Jonah to confess his feelings for Margaret. You hijacked my amusement."

"*I* am thoroughly amused."

"And I am going to be thoroughly disgraced."

Reaching outside of the boat, I let my fingers dangle deceptively and scooped a handful of water. Before Trenton could figure out my motive, I splashed him with the cool liquid.

He jolted, sending me to the side of the boat as it rocked precariously. I laughed out loud, reaching for the edges to keep from falling overboard.

"Oh, you think you can best me?" He leaned over and took water in both his hands as I reached for my hat that had fallen to the bottom of the boat when I snuggled against him. I pulled it forward to shield my face as he splattered me back. Water drenched the front of my dress. He went for a second round. "You forget love, I've had plenty of practice."

I dodged his aim, threw my hat down, and scooped more water when he grabbed my hands easily with only one of his. My ammunition collapsed in response hitting the wooden bench . . . but his spray hit me right in the face.

"Aahhh." I cried and spat the mouthful of river water out. "I think Margaret was wrong." I choked. "It can't possibly be cleaner, it tastes nasty."

Trenton barked a laugh and let go of my wrists. "I think you have suffered enough for one day." He tugged me close and cleared the moisture off my cheeks.

I flashed my sweetest smile in his direction. "Oh, it's not over, babe. Your revenge will come when you least expect it."

He leaned in and kissed my wet lips. "I look forward to it."

"Oyy!" A holler from across the water brought us both back to sitting upright. Hastings stood at the edge of the bank and waved his hands in our direction. "You two have nearly missed the picnic!"

Trenton glanced at his watch. We, in fact, had been in the boat now nearly an hour over the allotted time. Yet, all in all, I would've been perfectly content to stay in it for an additional two.

Trenton helped me to my seat then picked up the oars. "The only reason we are leaving this perfectly amiable afternoon is because I am thoroughly famished."

I laughed. "And we will be thoroughly scolded upon our late arrival." We were having too much fun with the word *thoroughly* to stop now.

He winked and rowed faster.

As expected, when we strolled up the hill, hand in hand, an hour late to the picnic, we were met with mostly smiles, but one undeniable glower on his mother's face. Lifting her index finger, she shook it vigorously toward us. "You can't even adhere to a simple diversion without breaking the rules, then for the second time today, *Katharine*, you've shown you have a dreadful habit of being late." She pulled her hat lower to block out the sun. "Let's hope you don't make the same mistake at your wedding or I shall have to find a suitable replacement."

My lips parted but Trenton answered first. "I'm the reason she's delayed, Mother, for I could not keep my hands off her." Her face paled. I muffled a laugh. "And if by chance she's late for our wedding, I will wait forever if I must—there *is* no replacement for this one." He smiled down at me once more then led me to the blanket farthest away from her incensed stare.

Chapter 28

Wednesday, 18 May 2011

As the days to the wedding dwindled down, I should've been relieved, but instead, the way the week had splintered in front of me clearly made me more nervous.

I awoke to a knock at the door. Margaret slept soundly through it, but I pulled on my robe and answered it to find no one outside—only a box with a bow rested at my feet. I scanned the hallway and found it completely empty. Smiling, I retrieved it. *Presents are always welcome.*

As I placed it on the bed, Margaret yawned and stretched. "Is that my breakfast?"

"No." I tossed a pillow at her head. The tag attached revealed my name. I turned it over to find a simple message.

Kat,
Don't be afraid of who you are.
Embrace it.
Love, Trenton

My eyebrows pinched together. *What could this possibly be?* I untied the bow and lifted the lid of the box. Looking in, I gasped loud enough for Margaret to shove the duvet aside and peek herself.

She scoffed. "How could a gentleman possibly find this proper?"

I lifted the boxing gloves up and out of the box. Laughing out loud, I shook my head. *Trenton bought boxing gear for me.* How in the world did he know what to buy?

Kelly.

I grinned. Of course, she would support Trenton's addition of boxing in the talent show.

In addition to a pair of leather head guards, I found a second set of gloves within.

I put the gear on and pounded my fists—a perfect fit.

Margaret eyed my every move. "You cannot be in earnest. It's repulsive."

"Do you even know what this is?"

"I'm not daft, Katharine, I do have a brother. One who rather fancied being a pugilist. He mostly fought fisticuffs bare-knuckle but owned a pair of mufflers similar to yours, only he never wore anything on his head."

"Well," I danced in a tight circle. "This is why my right hook left a mark on your eye."

Margaret stuck her tongue out. "You're mistaken. It was I who hit you, remember?" She chuckled.

I pointed to the other set still in the box. "Let's see how the story really ends."

She raised her chin high in the air and walked into the lavvy.

I pounded my fists together. Prior to receiving this gift, part of me hoped that Trenton would forget the dare he assigned me, but now that my hands have slipped into gloves once again, the other part found the idea thrilling. It had been far too long and it felt surprisingly good.

Another knock sounded on the door, and I scrambled to take them off before Kelly entered. She laughed. "I see you have received your gift."

I nodded and playfully punched her in the shoulder.

"He loves you very much. I mean seriously, what fiancé would buy his future bride boxing gear?"

I smiled and set them aside. I practically bowled her over with my hug. "Thank you for helping him."

"How did you know?" She peered at me straight-faced, but her words were laced with sarcasm.

I smirked. "He would not have known the first thing to buy. *Winning* is top of the line, he wouldn't have known that or my glove size."

"You're welcome." She smiled wide.

"But he did send a second set and Margaret insists she is strictly a spectator . . . to my disappointment, of course."

"Of course." Kelly laughed.

"Although," I added, "the temptation to knock some sense into her is quite appealing."

"I heard that." Margaret stepped out of the lavvy. "Concede, Kat. You have high regard for me."

"I wouldn't go that far." I chuckled. "But I don't *dislike* you anymore. How's that."

"Much improved." She stepped over to the armoire while Kelly watched our playful banter with puzzled interest. I forgot much of my connection to Margaret remained unknown to everyone else.

"What's wrong?" I placed the equipment back into the box and turned to find Margaret standing awkwardly before the wardrobe.

She sighed. "I have this odd longing to wear something diverse."

I pointed to the garment bag hanging from a hook on the wall. "There's the new clothes we purchased in London. You looked smashing in that red pencil skirt."

"No . . ." She turned around to face me. Uncertainty marred her perfect complexion. "I think I want to wear some breeches."

Kelly and I went still, though my gasp surely emerged louder than hers. "D—did you say breeches . . . as in pants?"

"Yes." She flicked her hair. "It's not like I'm barmy, I'm inquisitive."

We both dashed to the drawers, eager to help.

Kelly retrieved the first pair she got her hands on. "This one should work. She has long legs."

"Maybe." I said, continuing the search.

We took turns pulling out different pairs of jeans from fashion faded, ripped, loose, or slim fitting,

"Wait, this pair of jeans with the rips will look totally stylish." Kelly held one up.

"No rips." Margaret waved her hand growing more and more cowardly by the minute. "Maybe I spoke out of turn."

"Nope," I cried back. "You're going to wear pants today!"

Margaret started to back away and stumbled against the bed post.

"These are the ones." I held up a pair of black skinny jeans that were not only one size too big, but also too long for me.

"Yep, you're right." Kelly nodded. "Those are perfect."

I sifted through some tops and found a stunning olive chambray blouse. "Go try these on." Then I led her to the door. Leaning in to where only she could hear me, I whispered. "Only one leg in each part and the pockets are the backside."

Small beads of sweat formed on her forehead as she grabbed the clothes but didn't protest.

Once the door closed, I squealed as quietly as I could with Kelly by my side waiting most impatiently for our model to come out.

"Don't you think it's strange that Margaret has never worn pants before?" Kelly shook her head.

I shrugged my shoulders. "I know a lot of women here in England who still consider pants as unrefined."

"Really? Wow, I couldn't live without my jeans."

"Me neither." I laughed.

When she stepped out, her poise reflected such grace as if she'd worn pants her entire life. Until she grabbed the crotch and tugged down. "Why in heaven's name are they so . . . so snug?"

I reached for her hand and dragged her over to the full-length mirror. Turning her around, I pointed to her backside. "Look." Her ample bottom was perfectly rounded.

"Ohhh." She smiled and patted her pockets.

"That's why." I laughed.

We said goodbye to Kelly who left to meet up with Marlowe, and I grabbed my own pair of jeans to wear. "Hey, Margaret," I called to her as she walked awkwardly back and forth before the mirror. I muffled a laugh . . . *she'll grow used to them.* "I have an idea."

"Is that so?" She couldn't pull her eyes from the mirror. "Pray tell."

"Something I think you'll like. Trust me."

I had toyed with the idea of exposing her to the various inventions of our time, though I wasn't sure if it would help or hurt her perspective if she were to return. In the end, I couldn't resist and led her into the laundry area first.

The massive room accommodated large washers and dryers, big enough to manage a great deal of fabric. I showed her the spray that "magically" took the tea stains out of my skirt, then how the washer and dryer work with a simple push of a button.

Margaret played with the knobs, then stuck her whole head inside the dryer. "Fascinating." She shouted into the hollow space. "I rarely spent time with the servants as they toiled over my garments, but I know with a certainty they managed entirely by hand."

"They are the ones we have to thank for the many conveniences of today," I said. "They invented a better way to accomplish simple tasks."

"What's this?"

"An iron. It takes wrinkles out of clothes." I demonstrated under her riveted attention.

"There's more." I chuckled. "Much more."

We approached the kitchen and Margaret stopped. "You forbade me to enter."

"I did, didn't I. Wait here a moment." I stepped inside and spoke briefly with Helen. She confirmed that our presence would not be denied since Margaret attempted to right her wrong.

"Okay, we're good." I quickly retrieved a blender and a half dozen ingredients—strawberries, bananas, blueberries, raspberries, yogurt, and a bowl of ice. "Check this out." I plugged the appliance in, added the fruit, and pressed a button. Margaret startled a bit at the sound, then moved closer to watch intently as the fruits blended together. "Here," I pointed. "You do it."

"Oh, no, I'd rather not."

"Honestly, it's harmless."

She grinned and raised her finger tentatively.

"Go ahead."

She pressed and let go several times before she fully engaged.

I poured the results into two glasses. "It's called a smoothie."

"A smoothie?" She tasted it cautiously, yet it took only mere seconds for her expression to register its approval. "This is delicious."

"I know, right? Bring it with you, there's more."

This time her step came lighter. Instead of apprehension, she seemed eager to discover what came next.

I took her to the office and introduced the computer. Rightly timid at first, she treated the keyboard like piano keys and tapped them softly as if expecting musical notes to sound.

I pointed out the URL bar and typed various words in, then hit *images*. She nearly fell from the chair. Pictures appeared on anything from foods, to fashion, hairstyles, and cars. Everything she asked for, I typed until she found the confidence to do it herself. She searched airplanes, cell phones, and cosmetics, but it wasn't until she found horse breeding that she read everything that crossed her path. I silently questioned its significance but didn't disturb her and continued to watch her childlike captivation go from one extreme to the next for another ten minutes.

"Margaret, come with me. I have something else I want to show you."

"I have not yet concluded my pursuit."

I took quiet satisfaction that I had found something that truly made her happy. Over the course of the week, she had been lucky enough to engage in activities from her own time, like archery, picnics, and cricket, but technology . . . that was something I could offer.

"We'll have plenty of time to do this again." I reached for her arm. "I promise." Leading her out of the house and toward the driveway, she followed obediently, though blindly.

When I stopped at Trenton's car, a puzzled expression transpired. "Get in." I pointed to the passenger side. Once again, she did as I asked.

"Where are we off to?" She settled into the seat and scanned the area around us.

I grinned deviously but didn't answer as I veered down the lane and turned off onto another dirt road. We were still on the property but far from curious eyes.

When I braked and shifted the car into *park*, she glanced at me warily.

I raised one eyebrow. "I thought maybe you'd like to learn how to drive."

Chapter 29

"Drive . . .wh—what?" Margaret stuttered.

I smiled and tilted my head toward the steering wheel.

"Drive a car?" she yelped.

I unbuckled my seatbelt and opened my door to her protests.

"Oh no, no, I mustn't."

"Yes, you can, and you will." I stepped around to her side and attempted to open her door, but she held onto the handle.

"I . . uh, no I mustn't," she shouted through the window. Pressing her hand to her forehead, she moaned, "I'm prone to fits of vapors."

I snorted. "Come on, Margaret." I tugged with enough force to get her to release. She shook her head adamantly. I leaned in and grabbed her sleeve. "This might be your only chance. Even if you returned to 1878, cars don't happen for several decades later."

She bit her lip. When she gazed up, both fear and curiosity flashed through her wide eyes.

"Very well." She seized a deep breath and stood up. "Will you assist me?"

"Yes, I promise." She begrudgingly moved around to the driver's side.

Once she sat down, her cheeks paled. "I—I am most terrified at this precise moment."

I grinned. "Put on your seatbelt." I had shown her how to do this when we went to London. She complied.

The next few minutes I gave her a full rundown on all the necessary parts, although she might've only heard half of it.

"Okay, put your foot on that pedal. It's the brake." I waited for her to do it. "Now grab this lever, push the side button, and bring it down to where the "D" is." She did it slower than I imagined was humanly possible. "That's for *drive.* Right there, stop."

Glancing at me, a chalky gray leaked from her features and her breathing sputtered with exaggeration.

"Margaret, you'll be fine. Don't look at me, look at the road ahead of you. Keep both hands on the steering wheel and slowly let your foot off the brake."

Her knuckles turned white under her grip on the wheel. "Wh—what do I do now?"

Even though she had released the brake, we remained stationary. "The right pedal down there is your gas. Press it lightly."

I knew the moment we lurched forward that she had found her target. Yet, at the same time the car jerked, she screamed and released both the gas pedal and her hands off the wheel.

"Wait, wait, wait, you can't let go." I tried speaking through my laughter. "Try again."

Her lips pulled into a tight line. "This is not amusing." She kept her eyes forward as instructed, but the giggling from my side of the car, undoubtedly, caused the wrinkles that formed across her forehead.

"Try again." I said, biting the inside of my cheek.

This time when she pressed the gas and the car moved forward albeit choppy, her eyes lit up in delight. "Oh," she cried. "Oh, oh, it's moving!"

"Good. Now turn the steering wheel slightly to the left to put us in the center of the road. There wasn't another car anywhere to be found. This was the perfect place for such a lesson.

She turned a bit too far, then panicked and overcorrected to the right, then once more to the left until she let go altogether. The motion felt a lot like the bumper cars I rode at the Coney Island amusement park.

"Steady! Keep your hands on the wheel. It doesn't take much movement to keep it straight." Her foot remained on the gas, lurching us forward again. This time, I grabbed the wheel myself and straightened it out. "Okay, see here, keep the wheel right here."

She placed her hands back on and held tighter if that were even possible.

She stared forward. Small beads of sweat built on her nose. I bit my lip to stop from smiling at her intense concentration. We were hardly going more than five mph . . . it was time to step it up.

"Great, now press the gas a little harder and the car will go a bit faster. We'll stay on this road for a while and then make a turn way down there." I pointed a good kilometer ahead of us.

She shuddered through her labored breaths. I covered my mouth; we were only up to eight mph now.

"You can press a little harder."

She nodded nervously and this time when she pressed the gas, we shot forward a bit too fast, and once again, she let go of everything.

I quickly grabbed the wheel. "Margaret, you need to relax. It's okay to go faster, but don't let go."

"Fine. I will try again." She repeated the steps and this time we inched forward nearly the entire length of the road. While it took us ten minutes to get to the end, a task that would likely have been done by others in one, it was no less an accomplishment.

The muscles in her jaw twitched as we approached the pending turn. The sight of it caused her feet to fumble along the floor and she slammed on the brake just enough to throw me into the dashboard.

I rubbed my ear from the sting. "Why did you stop? You were doing great."

"The—uh, the road, it is ending. What shall I do?"

I leaned back and chuckled. "It's okay, it's simply a turn. You'll rotate the wheel slightly to the left and still press the gas to keep the car going."

Moisture now lined her upper lip and when she spoke, she frowned. "Oh, bother, why did I ever consent to such a foolish endeavor?"

I chuckled. "Because you secretly crave adventure."

Her head whipped in my direction and even though she scowled, it was more in jest this time.

"Keep your eyes forward." I laughed. She wasn't going fast enough for me to worry too much, but it only took a second for her to lose control.

Margaret navigated the turn slowly and this time it wasn't as choppy, although she used the entire width of the road to straighten out once more. The next turn led us back to Charlock and back toward the house. Finally, her shoulders relaxed enough to bring a faint smile to her face and color to her knuckles again.

"You're doing fantastic."

"Oh goodness, oh no, there's something approaching." She cringed.

I peeked forward to see a van approaching us from the opposite direction. It must've delivered something for the wedding since I didn't recognize it.

"Oh, Kat . . . oh my, we are going to collide! This is dreadful." Her eyes went wide.

I placed my hand on her arm. "It's fine, Margaret." I kept my voice calm. "Just stay right here on this side of the road and they will pass us by."

Her breathing elevated to the proximity of the van. "Oh, no." She cried.

"Keep steady."

"I cannot." She screamed the same moment the van passed us by. When she did, she hit the gas a tad too hard and launched the car forward into a sprint.

"Whoa, whoa, Margaret. Press the brake."

"What is the brake?"

Her hands flew off of the wheel, as she covered her eyes.

"No, no, no, Margaret, keep your hands on the wheel!" I scooted closer to her side. *Dang these bucket seats.*

"Press that one!" I pointed to the brake. "That one!"

She screamed again, yanking the wheel to the left and off the road. The crunch of grass and ruffage exploded under the wheels, and the car dipped to the uneven slopes in the ground. I scrambled to direct her leg to the brake, but she had pulled her feet upward as if she retreated from a coiled snake on the floor.

"Margaret, press that pedal!" I pushed her knee down, forcefully attempting to get it closer to the brake, but the rigidity in her muscles held out. I looked up and back over the dash as the car careened toward a tree. *A very large tree.*

"Katharine!" She shrieked as I braced for impact. Within seconds a loud crunching sound brought the car to an abrupt stop.

Shaken, I looked to Margaret first to make sure she was okay. Other than her high-pitched squeaks and quivering torso, she remained unharmed. Then I peered out through the windshield—the tree had not become part of our hood, after all, and sat a good five feet away. From the crashing sound, we hit something for sure, but what it was I didn't know.

Margaret muttered, "Oh, no, what have I done?" Both hands covered her face.

I leaned over and nudged her. When she met my eyes, hers were wider than I'd ever seen.

"Are you hurt?"

She shook her head briskly.

I took a deep breath. "Good. Okay, press that, Margaret." I pointed to the brake once more. When she did, I pushed the gear back into *park*. The car was certainly stuck, but I wanted to be sure it didn't fly over the obstacle and still hit the tree.

Margaret's cheeks were pale, and she wiped the sweat from her forehead. The next look she gave me threw me into a burst of laughter.

"This is not amusing!" Her voice reached an unearthly octave.

"Oh, it most certainly is." I rolled back into my seat and let my head hit the head rest, laughing louder than I had in a long time.

Her cheeks turned bright red. "I could've been killed."

"Margaret! You just drove a car." I beamed in her direction. "How cool is that?"

"Cool?" She shook her head, unlocked her seat belt, and threw the door open. "I don't see how you find this so diverting; I am quite anguished over the matter." She stomped away from the car.

I unlocked my seat belt and stepped out of the car.

Glancing underneath, I saw the reason we didn't collide with the tree. A decent sized boulder fit snuggly under the front bumper. I winced at the minor damage and the fact that this might be the time I have to tell Trenton his beloved Mercedes needed repairs.

Margaret lowered to her knees and joined me in assessing the problem. "This is a dreary lot. Your beloved is going to be most cross with me."

"It will be fine. I'll pay for the damage."

"What gave you the slightest provocation I should commence in this atrocious pastime?"

I laughed again and grabbed both her hands, raising her to her feet. "Don't you realize, Margaret, you did something that nobody in your time has *ever* done."

She blinked repeatedly. Her brows slowly separated, and her mind seemed to calculate my words with careful consideration.

"I did, didn't I?" Her fingers went to her mouth in astonishment. She moved around the front of the car and took in the whole scene. Finally, a wide smile covered her face. "I drove a car . . . not a phaeton, not a barouche . . . a car!"

I giggled as I wrapped my arm through hers and led her toward the road. "We should probably get back to the house." I nodded to the structure a short distance away. "I imagine the party is anxious to begin the horse race."

"What about the car?"

I briefly glanced back to it. "I'll send someone to retrieve it."

"What will Mr. Gilford think when he hears of our incident?"

I bit my inner cheek. "Hopefully, he won't." I tapped my other hand against my lips. "If the same guy from before is available, it will be fixed in a matter of hours."

"Before?" She came to a sudden halt. "You've done this before?"

I grimaced, debating my wisdom in confessing. "Not this exact thing, but yes, I did hit a tree last winter. I slid off the icy road."

She began walking again. Her muscles tightened within our hold. "That must've been terrifying."

I grimaced again. "Yes, and no, the one before that was worse."

Her mouth flew open. "And to think I put my welfare in your very *incapable* hands."

"I'm quite capable," I declared. "It only took me a bit longer to get used to driving in icy conditions." Though I experienced snow in New York, I never drove in it. "That . . . and driving on the opposite side of the road." I chuckled.

Margaret appeared confused.

"Never mind," I assured her, and we continued to walk in silence. Seeing the manor from this view turned out to be quite a site. I had always approached the entrance from inside a car, so going at the snail's pace that we were, offered the chance to truly enjoy the splendor of Charlock.

I remembered my initial arrival. How intimidated I was by the size, the brilliance, and the sheer grandeur of the estate. I recalled sitting on my suitcase when I first arrived, fearing my next move. Now, looking back, I had no idea how drastically my life would change for the better.

"Thankfully," Margaret sighed and stirred me from my musings, "considering your history . . . our next mode of transportation is a horse."

I barked a laugh. "Well, aren't we a bit snarky today?"

She smirked and ignored my comment. "Regarding the horses, what am I to wear for the race?"

"Your jeans are fine. This way you don't have to worry about sitting astride around men. It's totally normal in pants."

"Will you wear your breeches?"

"Yes, I'll wear my *breeches*." Though I loved my riding habit, there were many times I took a ride in my jeans.

Margaret stared upward. "It appears as though the sunlight has deserted us."

I followed the tilt of her head upward and frowned as a scattering of darkened clouds now crept across the sky. "This can't be good." The intrusion swallowed the clear horizon at an alarming rate. The horse race was our final outdoor event, and everyone looked forward to it with an abundant amount of enthusiasm. I tugged on Margaret's sleeve to rush her forward. "We should find the others and figure out what to do."

"What do you mean?"

"It's not safe to ride in a storm."

"I've ridden in the elements before, a little rain is hardly dangerous."

"But what if it's not only a little rain?" I questioned realistically.

Once Margaret and I stepped through the main entryway, my first order of business was to make arrangements for Trenton's car.

"Margaret, you can go locate the others, I just need to find Hennessey first, and then I'll meet up with you."

She nodded and walked away. Within minutes, I located the dutiful butler working as hard as ever in the office.

"Hennessey, I'm sorry to bother you."

He clasped his hands together and nodded. "What can I do for you, Miss Shelton?" Though I insisted on him using my first name, he never relinquished due to his genteel professionalism.

I grimaced. "I need to have Trenton's car retrieved from up the road." My smile emerged strained. "I had a little accident."

Hennessey's left eyebrow rose shamelessly. I tried to appear remorseful but whenever he shot me that look—which was often—it always made me chuckle.

"What, pray tell, has occurred *this* time?"

"I didn't drive on the wrong side of the road if that's what you're referring to." I retorted. "I—uh, I just hit a large rock."

"On the road?" He tipped his head sideways.

"No . . . off the road."

He sighed.

"It might take two people to retrieve it." I added. "One to drive in reverse and one to push the car back." My hands gestured the motions. "And if you don't mind . . . please see to it that the work is completed as soon as possible . . . and by the same technician as last time."

"Not a problem, Miss Shelton, I happen to have him on speed dial." Hennessey's lips pulled tight. Though he was skilled in hiding his smile, the light in his eyes told me he found humor in the situation.

I smiled wide and squeezed his arm. "Thank you so much, also, um, can we keep this between us?"

"You really should consider acquiring your own bumper car to toy with."

My head fell back in a full laugh this time. "It's only the third time, Hennessey, but yes I believe I will. Oh, and do you know where Trenton and the others might be right now?"

"They are assembled in the dining room at the moment."

"Thank you." I hollered as I hustled down the corridor. Once I entered the room, I found that most of the party had gathered within. Their lively conversation was debating at odds over the safety of the race with the impending storm.

"I am certain it will pass. It always does." Mrs. Gilford waved her hand in the air. She wasn't even going to be on a horse, she would be watching from the veranda.

"It could develop quite quickly into something worse than what we see now." William argued.

"What if we postponed it to tomorrow?" Ashtyn suggested from a far corner.

"It will be perfectly fine." Justine insisted.

"I'm not sure if we should chance it, Trenton." When I spoke I alerted them to my arrival. A few disappointed groans made their way around the table.

Justine took a few steps in my direction and placed her hands on her hips. "If you feel you are inept at riding through a few raindrops, maybe you should stay back with the spectators."

"I'm not inept, Justine, I'm cautious."

She lifted her chin and sneered. "Seems more like the response of a frightened child to me." Her contempt was no longer veiled behind her phony politeness. "Allow the adults to come to their own conclusion."

I moved forward myself and narrowed my eyes. "I'm thinking of the safety of our guests."

Trenton stood between us and faced me. "What if we shorten the length of the competition?"

I exhaled faintly. "I'm not trying to be difficult, Trenton, just reasonable. What if someone got hurt?"

Hastings walked over to the window and peered out. "I imagine it appears much worse than it is. If we cut through the forest instead of going around it, we could shorten the route by three kilometers."

Marlowe chimed in. "Excellent suggestion, mate. A compromise . . .what do you say, Kat?"

I glanced around at all the hopeful faces before me, avoiding the glaring ones, then glimpsed out the window myself. The dark clouds did seem to be moving the opposite direction.

"Okay. Let's do it."

The room erupted in cheers.

I spoke quickly. "So, if we cut through the forest, it should reduce the race by at least thirty minutes. Everyone should be back and checked in before three o'clock. Does that sound alright?"

"Yes. That's plenty of time." Trenton turned to the doorway where Hennessey appeared, awaiting direction. "Please notify the grooms to prepare the horses."

"Are we sure about this?" I whispered in Trenton's ear.

He wrapped an arm around me and leaned in. "Most everyone here rides exceptionally well, yourself included, and those who don't, have opted to remain back at the house to watch." He kissed my cheek then snickered. "Besides, I placed a heavy wager on three of the bets."

"Which ones?"

He lifted the small notebook that made its way around the group last night after dinner. Pointing to the entries, I chuckled.

Will Trenton and Kat get lost on purpose? Will Kat punch someone before the ride is over? And *How many times will Mrs. Gilford tell Trenton and Kat to stop kissing before and after the ride?*

I ripped it from his grasp. "Did you bet for or against?"

He bellowed, "For of course! Except for the third one, it required a number. I chose ten."

I chuckled and read over the other friendly bets and the amount attached—most wagers were a five-pound note nicknamed a *fiver.*

Will Jonah get lost?/a fiver.
Will Marlowe and Kelly get lost on purpose?/ a fiver.
Will Hastings fall off his horse?/a fiver.
Will Margaret take a parasol on her horse?/a fiver.
Will Justine use a bow and arrow to knock Kat off her horse?/a fiver.
Will Grandfather Trenton win the race?/ a fiver.
Will Charles fall asleep on his horse?/a fiver.
Will Jonah and Trenton trade horses before the race is over?/ a fiver.
Will William ride to the closest pub instead?/ a fiver.

This was only the first page. The friendly competition brought forth some of the silly encounters that had occurred over the course of the week in an amusing way.

"Well, we can't have you losing." I wrapped my arms fully around him and kissed him in a way that was sure to draw attention.

"Utterly disrespectful, I tell you." Mrs. Gilford huffed and walked out of the room.

My lips formed a smile next to Trenton's. I whispered, "I think that counts for number 1."

He laughed, then bellowed to the group. "And we're off!"

Chapter 30

Sitting atop Darby, I examined the sun's failed attempt to shine behind the scattering of gloomy clouds. My brows creased trying to discern if they were multiplying or if my mind was simply playing tricks on me. Either way, a hint of unease rippled beneath the light hoodie I wore and my torso involuntarily shivered.

Though I didn't entirely agree with the plan, I took comfort in the shortened route . . . and the current lack of rain. If all goes as planned, the group will return within the hour, and all will be inside sipping salted caramel tea or hot chocolate before the storm unleashed the brunt of its fury.

I regarded the riders and their horses on each side of me. Most were lined up parallel to one another waiting for Mr. Gilford to ring the traditional cowbell. Trenton, on my right, smiled as he gripped the reins to Achilles. Grandfather managed Zeus on his other side, and down the line it went as follows . . . Kelly on Bella, Marlowe on Hawk, Margaret on Legacy, and Jonah on Chet. To my left sat Uncle Charles on Tuck, William on Temper, Henry on King, Ashtyn on Raven and Justine on Whisper. Mr. and Mrs. Gilford remained on the veranda with Aunts Beatrice and Tabitha, Uncle Clarence, Roger, Adele, Maria, Grace, and Leo.

Zeus, Darby, Achilles, and Raven all resided at Charlock Manor permanently, the others were brought to the manor on loan from the closest equestrian farm, apart from Whisper, who Mrs. Gilford purchased a month prior. Trenton said this is not the first time his mother had purchased a horse, sight unseen, and he imagined it wouldn't be the last. Though she never clarified her intentions on where Whisper would go after her visit to Charlock, based on her stellar communication skills, we might safely assume the mare will remain under our care at the manor.

Shortly before we gathered, we'd all been given a map of the terrain and the route which we were to take. The one variation allowed us to cut through the forest instead of rounding the border's edge. Once inside the sprawling grove, we could then choose any path as long as it brought us back out to the eastside clearing and straight back to the stables.

All the horses pranced and whinnied in the small vicinity until the clink of the cowbell rang loud and clear, then many were quick to start. With the varying skills of the riders and their horses, distances materialized swiftly.

The majority of us charged forward while Marlowe trotted with Kelly at a much slower pace. Darby could not claim breakneck speed, but her robustness as a seasoned horse kept her in the mass. Within seconds, however, it quickly became apparent that Trenton had entered a three-way battle for first with his grandfather and Hastings. *Ever the competitors.*

By the time we reached the open fields, Darby paced neck and neck with Margaret's horse, Legacy, and Ashtyn's horse, Raven. Henry's horse effortlessly passed us on the right and launched into line with William and Jonah who disappeared over the crest of the hill. I could no longer see Trenton or his grandfather before me—they were long gone.

On the descent of that first peak, Margaret edged ahead of me with Ashtyn close behind. When we finally reached the valley, Darby inadvertently fell a good ten meters behind both.

The momentum of the race left little time to enjoy the surroundings. The earthy aroma of wild grass floated about as repetitive hooves tramped them down. Despite the darkening skies, there was an element of freshness that came as the breeze whipped at my face, and although I had only ventured down limited parts of this trail, the ride remained relatively calm and uneventful.

Navigating the additional hills, Margaret and Ashtyn maintained a clear distance ahead and when we grew closer to the shaded woods, I struggled to harness my misgivings.

Glimpsing the opponents far up front, I caught the tail end of the three fastest as they darted into the forest, followed by William, Jonah, and Henry close on their heels. The moment I stole a peek behind, Charles passed me on the outside. That left very few riders in the rear—Marlowe and Kelly, who appeared like tiny blots of color and Justine somewhere in between.

Under Mrs. Gilford's insistence, Justine was the only one allowed to ride her newest acquisition, who from the beginning of the race seemed quite difficult to manage. Now, Whisper was more than making up for the initial delay as she topped the first hill.

I smiled at my timely luck. If I could only stay ahead of Justine, that would make my whole day.

"Come on, girl." I nudged Darby faster at the same time a few raindrops splattered against my leather gloves. I gazed upward; the blackness spread with a grim purpose. Looking forward again, both Margaret and Ashtyn disappeared headlong into the trees leaving me far behind.

The Gilford's lands were expansive, with many acres separating them from the nearest estate. Though I knew a smidgen of the woods, the race breached the trees from the unfamiliar western direction and moved eastward versus the other way around. My grassy patch of paradise near the Thames marked the tip of the same dense forest I had followed Merritt into the night he shared his secret about the slaves, but I now found myself at the farthest opposite end.

Upon entry, the murky skies dimmed tenfold while the increasing rain seemed to be the only thing that penetrated the thick vegetation. I struggled to see any remnants of the paths made by the previous horses. I slowed Darby down to listen—certain that the common sounds of horses' hooves would emerge. I even stilled my breath. Yes, they were *somewhere* in the woods.

My unfamiliarity seemed to heighten Darby's own unease. Despite my attempts to keep her moving at a swift pace, she slowed. "Let's go, girl." I kicked her forward.

The *clip clop* from her hooves faded rapidly to the sounds of nature—birds called in frantic flight to the pelting rain, and the swooshing of leaves amplified from the wind's commands. Very little light shone through, but even that emitted gloom. The deeper we went, the darker it grew.

A sudden rustling from behind startled me, until I realized a rider swiftly approached. Justine, Marlowe, and Kelly were the only ones at the rear, but somehow even knowing this, brought an element of comfort to me. *I'm no longer alone.*

Whisper's tan hide came into view.

"Justine!" I hollered back in her direction. This might be the only time in my life I'd be grateful to see her. She increased her speed as she approached and showed no signs of slowing down. Her countenance appeared hard and focused. "Slow down!" I shouted the moment she narrowly passed by.

Whether it was Whisper grazing Darby or the cackle of thunder that exploded overhead, my normally calm mare reared anxiously in response. I scrambled for a tighter hold on the reins as she bolted heatedly to the right.

"Justine!" I yelled her way. "Help—" My words were lost in the sound of another boom of thunder.

Though I struggled to see her reaction clearly while grasping hold of my horse, she must've known I faced distress. When I whipped around to the front again, Darby broke into a wild frenzy, neighing, bucking, and blasting through any shrubs that stood in her way. The loose reins didn't offer me much security, so I clutched her thrashing mane with my other hand. Underneath me, Darby's agitation magnified in the strained muscles of her body. If I fell now, no doubt, I would be injured.

"Whoa, Darby. Come on, girl. Please slow down." I tried to keep my voice calm, but it came out high and panicked. The increasing deluge offered no mercy as it soaked everything in its path and drowned out additional attempts to soothe my horse. I pulled the reins now with both hands but didn't make much headway. When the bucking stopped, the sliding began.

We're slipping downward!

I dug my boots into her sides trying to slow her and find some footing for myself, but she lost control. My thoughts flickered to Merritt and his story about his father's horse. I could not let that happen to Darby. To lose her would be devastating.

Lightning flashed above long enough for me to see how steep the incline was. With only a few yards to go, I gripped the horn and slid off her back hoping the lesser weight would ease her fear. I hit the ground hard, smacking my knee on a rock as I rolled to a stop.

Groaning in place for mere seconds, I reached for a low hanging branch of the nearest tree to help me stand and ignored the throbbing that intensified. Scrambling in an urgency to get to Darby, I pulled my hood over my head with a faint attempt to shield myself from the onslaught, though it hardly mattered when the rain fell in this manner.

The outline of my restless horse appeared at the bottom of the slope. Though she no longer jumped or kicked, she trotted with comparable stress in the confined space.

I stumbled my way down the remaining distance and approached her cautiously. Though she would not harm me intentionally, one kick could render me lifeless. She neighed angrily. I raised my hands and tiptoed closer to soothe my advance. When I reached her, I patted her wet hide gently with one hand and gripped the halter tightly with the other. The blustery elements didn't help, but Darby calmed significantly under my touch. I leaned forward and kissed her nose. "I'm sorry, sweet girl."

Wiping the moisture from my eyes, I peered around. Nothing looked familiar. The narrowness of the ravine assured me that climbing out would be difficult, at least until the rain stopped.

I called out. "Hello?"

Stepping away from Darby momentarily, I screamed louder. "Can anybody hear me?" I didn't want to spook her any more than she already was.

Thunder drowned my words with my second attempt. The crack reverberated off the trunks of the trees and pounded against my chest. I regained a solid hold on Darby, the fear that she might bolt once more without me was significantly more consequential . . . for us both.

Sludging onward, my leather boots were now caked in mud, and every piece of wet clothing clung to my body. My teeth chattered readily as the cold now seeped through the thin layers and reached my skin. Pushing the wet strands of hair off my face, I tucked them behind my ears and contemplated my next move. *Keep moving forward* . . . or what I believed was forward. Having been turned around, the direction of the Thames, Charlock, or

Wadsworth Hall, were unclear, especially now that the gully walls restricted my view considerably.

I stopped again, hoping a familiar sound would emerge, but the angry sky didn't cooperate. Another flash of lightning exploded above me, but before it disappeared, a spark of recognition materialized.

The ravine!

This had to be the ravine that led to the cave. I paused long enough to get a bearing on my surroundings. *It should be right around this bend.* Another crack of thunder bellowed right overhead and rattled Darby. I nudged her forward hastily to locate the entrance.

The cave!

Tying Darby to a nearby branch, I fiercely kicked down the vines that shrouded the space. Dead branches caught on my hands and snagged my clothes, but I disregarded the pain. I wiped my face crudely against my sleeve and continued. Though the soaked material did little more than remove the excess moisture, I could see better to some degree.

With the thick overgrowth removed from its entry, I reflected on my last visit. It was a year ago—July. Trenton had asked me to show him Merritt's cave. We hadn't been back since and a brief jolt of panic entered my thoughts—*Will it be empty?*

I seized a deep breath and entered cautiously. The eerie blackness pressed against me, but no sound came forth . . . no heavy breathing, no shuffling of feet or paws, and no rotten smells. I exhaled evenly then stepped back out to retrieve my horse.

"Come on, Darby." I untied her and tugged her headfirst, but she fought the move. "We need to get out of the rain." I patted her neck and whispered with a gentleness she softened to, though her eyes remained wide and wary. "Please, girl. Let's go inside."

Reaching for the carrot in my jeans pocket, I lifted the damp vegetable up to tempt her to enter. Thankfully, I always carried one to reward her at the end of our rides. Its existence became a useful source of bribery in this crucial moment.

Once she stepped inside, I took my first normal breath. Patting my way toward a side wall, I guided her body against it, hoping the dryness would offer some comfort. I knew the cave wasn't too deep, but outside of the occasional bursts of lightning, the sheer blackness was unnerving.

With the shortness of the ride, I didn't think to bring my cell phone, resulting in nothing to light the space or the ability to call for help. I knelt to the ground, recalling the fire pit from before that centered the cave.

Though the circumstances weren't ideal, I wasn't frightened by my predicament. The rain *will* eventually cease. Even if I remained stuck here for a few hours, I would no doubt find my way back, but for now my concerns fell to Trenton—he will most certainly come looking for me. His worry would heighten with the storm, and he wouldn't stop until he found me. The cave, however, might possibly be the last place he looks—unless Justine pointed out where Darby got spooked when we parted ways—though that was highly unlikely.

I fingered the rocks that formed the makeshift fire pit and hoped somehow a match would be found, but there wasn't, or at least none I located. Darby remained against the wall, unmoved, with only an occasional whinny or tap to validate her presence. At least I wasn't alone.

Wrapping my arms tightly around my legs, I took deep breaths to slow the trembling of my body. I'd lived in the freezing temperatures of the east coast most of my life. I knew enough about the cold to know its danger.

Listening for a break in the rain, my eyes grew weary with the hypnotic sounds. That first year after Jeff passed, my inability to sleep reached all-time highs. In her attempts to help, Kelly played these CDs that imitated falling rain. They were meant to soothe, but all they did was cause a mental chill. She switched to ones with ocean waves, and not only did it initiate warmth as if I psychologically laid on a beach, but the rolling seas effectively calmed. I tried to imagine those waves over the pounding rain, though it proved to be difficult.

Chilled, I removed my soaked gloves and pulled my arms inward from my wet sleeves and wrapped them close to my bare torso, hoping my body heat warmed enough to get by.

Eventually, my eyelids drooped and my body curled tightly against the dirt until everything around me disappeared.

"Kat!" An anxious voice stirred me awake. "She's here!" The loud cry caused me to shudder. Darkness smothered me except for a bright light that shone in my face.

"Kat, love." A warm hand went to my cheek.

"Trenton?" I squinted to see past the beam. I recognized the voice but failed to recognize my whereabouts. "What's going on?"

More loud shouting and more voices joined in.

"Peanut!" A heavy breath was exhaled nearby. "Are you alright?"

"Dad?" I blinked. A thin layer of moisture coated my skin and I shivered nearly uncontrollably. *Did I have another nightmare?* I couldn't recall the last time I did.

"I—I . . ."

Hands slipped underneath me and lifted me up. Spice. *Trenton.* I let my head fall against his chest. His heart thumped rapidly.

Why?

When his lips brushed my forehead, a heated trail blazed across my icy skin. "You scared me." He breathed.

Why? I wondered again. I didn't understand.

Trenton's arms brought me out into colder elements. My trembling graduated into a full shake. More voices transpired and more hands touched my head and arms. Dad leaned in. "Don't ever do that to us again."

"Wh—what diii—did I do?" I stuttered.

"Get me a blanket—she's frozen through."

Trenton set me down on a wet, cold surface. My fingers brushed the damp leaves beneath me. *Leaves?*

Someone draped a wool blanket across my shoulders and tucked it in front. Trenton kneeled before me, holding it tight. His breath closed in. "Are you injured?"

I tried to hold his gaze. He appeared fuzzy and distorted. "I—I . . ."

"Get Darby!" Someone hollered. Trenton's scent returned; he must be close though my sight dimmed.

"Quick, I'll get on Achilles, hand her up to me."

Trenton's warmth disappeared. I leaned forward. Though my eyes were not fully opened, what little light prevailed was being swallowed rapidly until my face hit the ground.

Chapter 31

Thursday 19 May 2011

My eyes fluttered open with a struggle. The light in the room forced them closed again.

"Kat?" The tone that materialized conveyed familiarity mixed with anxiousness.

I pulled one arm over my eyes to shield the light as I attempted to open them again. The muscles in my limb screamed in protest to the move. "Ow," I moaned.

"Oh, Kat." Trenton's face came into view. He leaned over me.

I attempted to smile, at least I thought my lips curved upward.

Trenton bent down and kissed my forehead. "You're awake!"

"Why . . .why wouldn't I be?" The words fought to come forth. I wrinkled my brow trying to piece together my last memory.

Trenton's face remained over mine. Concern held his handsome features captive.

"What happened?" I peered around the room, then my head shot to the empty side of the bed. "Did something happen to Margaret?"

He shook his head. "Margaret's fine. You don't recall?"

"I—I'm not sure."

Trenton sat down and reached for my hand. "Do you remember the horse race yesterday?"

"Horse race, yes." My eyes widened. "Yesterday?" *I lost an entire day?*

He nodded. "Then the storm came."

I bit my lip. My head hurt to think, but pieces of the event slowly materialized. The rain, the darkness, lightning, thunder, Darby. . . the ravine.

"Oh . . ." The rest of the puzzle flooded at once. "The cave."

"Do you remember when we found you?"

"Very little." I reached for his hand. His strong fingers wrapped around mine and when he squeezed, his touch conveyed his fear. I met his eyes. "I knew it was you. I smelled your cologne." I brought his hand to my lips and breathed in the familiar scent. "How did you know to check there?"

"I didn't right away." His angst was evident in every line on his face. "When you didn't return and the skies unleashed, I went out looking. I was stark raving mad, unable to find you. I returned after an hour and recruited the others."

My nose wrinkled. "Justine didn't tell you what happened or where to look?"

"Justine?" His eyes narrowed. "Why? Did she know something?"

The sudden anger that coursed through his pupils startled me. "I—I thought she saw my horse buck and tear off." At least, I was certain she saw it. She turned in my direction when it happened.

Trenton's jaw tightened. "I will return shortly." His touch shifted quickly from softness to rigid stone.

"No, please." I clenched his hand tighter. "Don't leave me." I held on until his frame eased.

"You could've been injured."

"But I'm not." I shifted in the bed. At least I didn't think I was—my muscles begged to differ.

"If we hadn't found you when we did, you could've become severely ill from exposure." He frowned. "She should have told me if she had the slightest inkling of where you might be. This behavior is unacceptable."

Though I warmed at Trenton's defensiveness, I didn't want to see him get in the middle of this ridiculous squabble—despite the fact that he was at the center of it all. "How long was I gone?"

"Five hours."

"Five?" My lips parted. "It felt like minutes."

"You must've fallen asleep, but your body was ice cold when I found you."

"Is that why I'm so sore?"

"Most likely." Trenton leaned down and nuzzled his face into my neck. "I've never been more terrified in my entire life," he whispered.

My fingers threaded through his hair at the back of his head. "I'm sorry."

"It is entirely my fault. I didn't heed your initial caution and then my obsession with beating Hastings and my grandfather caused me to neglect you." Trenton's voice quivered as he continued. "It was selfish of me. I could've lost you."

I lifted his head to face me. "But you didn't. You saved me."

"It was only when we scoured nearly every path that Margaret mentioned a cave. Oddly enough, she spoke of Merritt and a cave where he kept slaves safe, though she didn't know where it was located."

My lips parted. *Margaret remembered what I said about Merritt.*

"I didn't know she was aware of that story, but grateful she mentioned it. It was smart of you to take shelter there. I don't want to even consider the alternative. You could've been much worse off."

"But I'm not."

"I'm sorry."

"Trenton, please don't. It's over. You found me and that's all that matters." I smiled warmly. "Besides, Darby handled the terrain and weather much better than I imagine any other horse would." I sat forward in a rush, though my head hardly complied. "Darby! How is she?"

Trenton gently laid my head back down on the pillow. "She's a strong female, much like the woman who rides her. She is fortunate to have you looking out for her."

"Has she been checked for injuries?"

"Yes. I assure you, she's fine. And you, love, must worry about your own recovery. Dr. Kymball visited last night. In his early assessment, he believed you sustained only mild trauma, but he's returning today to be sure."

"Oh, great." I chuckled. "The only times I've met the man are when I'm unconscious and delirious."

Trenton's laugh came easier—almost as if he allowed himself a reprieve from the torment he put himself through.

I placed my palm on his cheek. "I will be a good patient if you will let this go. It was an accident. I only thought Justine might've seen me, it's entirely possible she didn't." I fibbed. Even once Justine learned of my absence, it was apparent she chose to say nothing. "I promise I'm fine, and now we can go on with the activities as planned."

"You, my love, are going to stay in bed all day."

"But the charity work. What will happen with that?"

"It's already in motion. Your mother has kindly taken over, under the direction of my mother, of course." He chuckled. "And I'm to remain by your side."

"Really?" I grinned mischievously. "Right by my side?"

His warm normal laugh filled the room. "Not in that sense . . . not yet anyway. We must restore your health to its natural state, then when the time does come . . ." He winked. "You have all the energy necessary."

I smiled.

Trenton kissed my hand. "Today, I'm at your every whim."

My lips curved playfully. "Really? You'll do anything for me?"

"Anything." He answered confidently. I grinned wide, and he quickly backtracked. "Almost anything."

I chuckled. "Would you read to me?"

"Read to you?"

I nodded and pointed to the book on the side table.

"*The Count of Monte Cristo*, huh?" Trenton picked it up. "You've been talking to my grandfather."

"Yes." I snuggled under the covers. "He's a wonderful man."

"I heartily agree." He pulled one foot up to rest on his opposite knee and opened the book. "Where would you like me to start?"

"The beginning."

Trenton stayed with me the rest of the day. Occasionally he stepped out to check on the guests and their progress with the activity, but otherwise he remained by my side.

My mom and dad, Kelly, Maria, and Margaret all made short appearances and filled me in on any pending drama. Kelly especially gave a rousing recap of my mom and Mrs. Gilford's conflicting ideas on what an orphan would find entertaining . . . Mrs. Gilford insisted on putting CDs of *The Marriage of Figaro* by Mozart in the boxes, while my mom claimed a doll or a pickup truck would suffice. I laughed, wishing I could have witnessed it myself.

Dr. Kymball stopped by before dinner and gave me another thorough check up at Trenton's request. His assessment assured me that I suffered shock from the moisture and chill but nothing more serious.

"You are perfectly fine to join the others tomorrow." He patted my hand. "What revelry do you have planned?"

I glanced between both men. "Uh, boxing actually."

The doctor snorted, then grew serious when he realized I wasn't joking. He cleared his throat. "I don't believe that is the best activity to participate in."

"I'm only demonstrating." I brushed my hands across the duvet. "It's harmless." At least that's all I was willing to divulge. I deliberately omitted the part about sparring with a partner.

"Very well, Miss Shelton." He picked up his instruments. "I will see you at the wedding."

"Thank you, Doctor Kymball."

When Trenton returned from seeing the doctor out, he announced that our guests successfully compiled thirty boxes for the Gilford house occupants and an additional thirty for another London house for orphaned children.

As sad as I was for not participating, I was equally thrilled for Martha Gilford. Her legacy of caring for others would continue for as long as we could do something about it.

Trenton moved to the edge of the bed. "Would you like me to read some more?"

I nestled eagerly into my pillows and brought the duvet to my chin. "Yes, please." I smiled. "Unless you're too tired."

"Never." He grinned and settled himself on the chair beside me once more.

Trenton's smooth voice brought the story of Edmund Dantes to life like I'd never heard, and we were close to the part where he would use the priest as a ruse to escape the Chateau d'if prison in Marseille.

When I awoke again, darkness filled the room. Even the windows were draped in an eerie blackness from the night sky. I glanced to where Trenton sat earlier, however, only the book remained, open and upside down.

I don't remember him leaving. I rubbed my face, struggling to orient myself and my surroundings. I rolled onto my back and stared at the ceiling. My stomach rumbled with hunger. Though meals were requested twice, I claimed little appetite until now.

Feeling the other side of the bed, I realized it was empty. Margaret hadn't returned yet either. Stretching for my phone, I found the time. *10:21 p.m.* Surely Helen wouldn't mind if I scavenged up something more substantial than cold soup to carry me over for the night. Though much of my strength returned, my stomach growled sharply.

Pressing the flashlight on my phone, I located my robe lying over a nearby chair. In a moment of weakness, I flashed it briefly toward the mirror, catching a glimpse of my reflection. I hadn't paid any attention to my appearance all day and though it wasn't frightening, I was hardly fit to be seen.

I threaded my messy hair into a loose braid that hung over my shoulder and called it good. If I were careful, I could avoid the sitting room or any number of lingering guests still out socializing. Slipping into the kitchen stealthily, I could make a sandwich and return unnoticed within minutes.

I tiptoed down the hallway. Though a few sconces lit the space, it was pleasantly dim for most of my covert cover. I rounded the corner and headed toward the kitchen but pulled back when voices came from the library. I surely didn't want to come upon any clandestine meeting. Both Kelly and Maria warned me several days ago that they enjoyed the company of Hastings and Marlowe well after the others said goodnight. They could've easily slipped into the room for additional privacy.

"You could not have possibly forgotten." Justine's voice dripped like honey.

I cringed at the very sound. *Why* m*ust she be everywhere?*

She continued, seemingly unaware of inquisitive ears. "Every time I see a football match I'm reminded of that night."

Leaning my back against the wall, I scooted closer to the door. The light in my hands still beamed. I quickly turned it off and scanned the hall behind me. I feared being caught eavesdropping, but somehow her words sparked a curiosity within. *Who is she with?*

"It was years ago."

Panic seared through me. *Trenton!*

She's talking to Trenton! Are they alone? I bit my bottom lip and inched to where I was nearly flush with the door frame. Fragments of our last argument materialized. I held my breath steady, determined *not* to make the same mistake as before and jump to any misread conclusions.

"Oscar has never spoken to me since." Justine whispered, but I still heard her words clearly.

"It wasn't your fault, Justine," Trenton said. "We'd been drinking way too much that night. For Pete's sake, *Manu* was unstoppable that season. We were celebrating,"

She chuckled. "I don't recall ever seeing you drink that much, but you kept going pint after pint."

"It was a disaster waiting to happen." His tone quieted.

I bit my lip as silence lapsed in their conversation. "I don't believe the concluding result was a disaster at all." Justine's voice emerged low and breathy. I fought my desire to peek around the doorway. Her proximity must be close from the way she spoke. "It was fate, Trenton. Oscar and I were never well suited . . . you and

I—" I missed part of her words. "—are you afraid of remembering?"

My heart thumped rapidly. *I should leave.* I needed to leave. This conversation was not for my ears, yet I remained glued in place.

"I don't recall much." Trenton's voice sobered. A hint of remorse hung clear. "I only know where I was when I woke up."

"And do you regret where you woke up?"

A piercing sensation stabbed my chest. *No, no, no, no. I can't be hearing this correctly.* My hand flew over my mouth to stop my gasp from taking flight.

"Justine, this is not a conversation I should be having right before I wed."

"Then when should we have this conversation because we *never* talked about it." Slight desperation suddenly surfaced in Justine's voice. "I can't stop thinking about it."

My head spun. *This cannot be happening. It's a mistake. Something could not have happened between them—Trenton assured me.* The ground seemed to roll beneath my feet as I stumbled away from the door and clumsily into a wall table. A sleek white vase filled with charlock rocked awkwardly, then crashed to the floor. Like watching a slow-motion movie, I froze as it scattered into hundreds of pieces around my feet. I choked a sob. My sight blurred as tears trailed down my cheeks and fell in large droplets upon the ceramic shards and broken petals.

"Kat?" I glanced back to see a fuzzy Trenton at the doorway. The way he said my name undoubtedly communicated shock. Justine stood behind him.

I shook my head and ran—fleeing toward the back door with all the strength I could muster but with no actual plan. I only needed to get out of this house, to get as far away as I possibly could. It wasn't just the words that speared my heart, it was everything about this week that ravaged my insides and finally erupted with unnatural force.

"Kat!" Trenton's voice thundered somewhere behind me, but the darkness took pity on me. I could hear footsteps somewhere in the distance as I scurried through the garden paths, winding around the decorated trees, fountains, and trellises.

Stumbling over rocks and scattered branches, I ignored the state of my bare feet or the sting of unfamiliar terrain underneath as I disappeared deeper into the vegetation. Moving behind a large lattice covered in cats claw vines, I hid against the perimeter wall. My heart physically grieved. Sinking lower, I pulled my knees against my heaving chest and cried.

What did I hear? What was the unspoken shame between his words? Unquestionably, something I wasn't meant to hear. Trenton told me he never kissed her! No, apparently it was much more than that! And all this time she was here to remind him of that night.

"I can't do this!" I whispered between sobs. "I'll always wonder . . .always question."

Every agonizing frustration clambered through my body and strangled me. I couldn't breathe or think.

Footsteps rustled from somewhere in the garden. "Kat, please?" Trenton's voice called out. I could hear the regret in every syllable, but was it regret from the action or me stumbling upon his confession?

Why didn't he tell me? Why did I have to find out this way, just two days before our wedding? Wiping my nose, I calmed myself, but found comfort huddled against the wall. "Better to have known now than after."

More calls rang out, additional voices joined his, possibly his friends. *They must've heard the commotion in the hall when the vase broke.* I hardly expected Justine to come looking. She, most likely, enjoyed the show. This was exactly what she sought. Every strategic move she made this week wedged me farther away from Trenton, and now I was giving her exactly what she wanted. Nevertheless, my pride failed to relinquish. Trenton *should not* have kept this from me.

My body tightened, envisioning her self-satisfied smirk. At this very moment she was probably sharing her successes with his mother. I imagined the two of them huddled in happiness at the night's events, finally achieving their intended mission.

This is ridiculous. I chided myself. I can't hide from every challenge that comes at me. I took several deep breaths and stood to my feet. A piece of glass lodged in my foot from the broken vase and a trickle of blood lined my ankle, but it paled in comparison to the lacerations that now marked my skin from the barbed bushes. My legs trembled underneath my robe as I gathered the strength to step forward.

I spent nearly all of my time running after Jeff passed away. I ran from everything. The running only stopped when I made the decision to return to the wedding "ball" and return to Trenton. How childish and ironic it felt now since it was him, I was currently fleeing from.

Though I had no clue as to how I would handle what faced me, it didn't take away the fact that I still needed to face it. I stepped away from my sanctuary and when I emerged, it was Trenton who saw me first. He ran to my side and grabbed my arms. I stilled at his touch, when my eyes reached his, I could physically feel the ice form in my stare.

"I need to explain."

"No." My body tensed. "Not now." I shook free of him. "I'm going inside."

"Kat, please? We should discuss this."

I spun around. "Why now?" Every muscle in my body pulsated. "You didn't think this was important enough to tell me *before* she came to stay for the week?"

"She wasn't supposed to be here. This wasn't supposed to happen."

"The truth?" My teeth gritted, fighting the words that would surely cause harm if spewed. "The *truth* wasn't supposed to happen?" I pointed my finger at him. "You should've told me."

He raked both hands through his hair. Though I rarely saw his hair less than perfect, a raw youthfulness transpired.

"Please?" He pleaded, trying to stop me again. "Remember it was you who refused to send Justine home, not me."

I exhaled slowly, then glared hard. "Yes, Trenton, you're right. This is all my fault."

"No, no, that's not what I meant."

"Goodnight." I walked past the handful of guests who ventured out, each turned away to offer a minuscule portion of privacy as we spoke. *Impossible.* They all witnessed our exchange. I briefly stared in their direction but kept walking and didn't turn around until I reached my room where I dropped weakly to the bed.

My heart ached—like a jagged scar had been reopened from a frail suture. The pain seared with unforgiving exactness, but no new tears came forth. Instead, anger arose and gripped my chest like an iron clamp.

"Kat?"

The weight shifted next to me on the bed. I hadn't even heard the door open. Margaret's hand brushed my hair off my cheek. "Do you wish to speak of it?"

I shook my head. *I don't want to even think about it.*

"Very well. We will speak in the morning."

Sleep didn't come until the early hours of the morning. Even though Margaret slept soundly on her side, and the noises of the night were calm, my nerves were wrecked. I replayed the conversation between Trenton and Justine over and over in my head until it pounded unceasingly.

What am I to do now? The same question haunted repeatedly through the troubling length of the night and as the blackness faded to purple then gray, and finally a sliver of orange peeked through, I realized my wedding was now one day away and I was no closer to knowing what to do than the night before.

Chapter 32

Friday 20 May 2011

By full sunrise, I could feel every bit of my rough night in each turn of my body compounded by the tightness and pain from the earlier incident. The little sleep I received showed no mercy in the tenderness in and around my eyes. Anger and exhaustion consumed me and my feet stung from my careless flight.

When I turned over, I came face to face with Margaret. Her eyes lifted to mine and she wasted no time in her interrogation. "What occurred to cause Trenton to seek you outside after dark?"

I pinched my nose. A tender throbbing poked my forehead. "I overheard Trenton and Justine speaking in the library. They inferred an event that had occurred between them. I panicked and ran."

"Inferred?"

"They spoke of a compromising situation they were in."

"Oh." Margaret's mouth bowed. "I'm sorry."

"I'm hurt, and I feel like an idiot."

"Did this happen recently?"

"It sounds like years ago, but Trenton told me there was *nothing* between them."

"He loves you."

"But he lied."

"Did he?"

"He said there was nothing between them, but there had been."

"As in the past?"

"Yes."

"Then it's the past."

I blinked repeatedly at her trivial comment. "How can I trust him?" A fresh set of tears tried to break through. "How will I ever know if he's telling me the truth?"

Margaret leaned back. Her eyes scanned the ceiling meticulously. "You simply know." My eyebrows curved as I watched her. "Your heart affirms it."

"My heart is currently muddled."

Margaret continued staring at the ceiling. "I'm in love with a man named Jacob Hardy."

My mouth fell open. "I knew it." Though she didn't glance in my direction. "We met at a dinner party held by his aunt, a wealthy and well-known social climber. Jacob wasn't truly invited until an eleventh-hour cancellation from one of her guests occurred. She merely fretted over the imbalance of her dining numbers than her regard for her own family. He's a horse breeder, not titled or wealthy but a hard worker with a dream of becoming more."

Margaret's complexion flushed as she spoke of him. "We met secretly for months, until my brother discovered us. I don't know what occurred, but Jacob stopped coming, stopped seeking me out. When I found the courage to address him, he told me he didn't love me."

"That must've been devastating."

Margaret finally faced me. "It would be if it were the truth."

"You didn't believe him?"

"It was his eyes." She sighed. "They revealed everything . . .the fondness, devotion, and affection he had for me."

"You saw that in his eyes?"

"His eyes, his touch, his heart . . . they betrayed his words. He loves me, Kat. Its truth is indisputable, yet I can do nothing." A tear rolled across her nose and hit the pillowcase. "Even if Jacob asked for my hand, my father would refuse him. We would have to elope . . . can you imagine what that would do to my reputation—an elopement?"

I smiled fully now.

"What, pray tell, could be so diverting from that wretched tale?" Margaret sneered and brushed the line of moisture from her nose.

"You're in love," I whispered. "Margaret Abbott is thoroughly head over heels for a man."

"Did you not hear me?" She snapped. "It's to no avail. We can never wed." She turned away again.

I tugged on her arm until she looked back at me. "I'm sorry, Margaret." More tears built in her eyes. "You should be with Jacob." I reached for her hand. "Shouldn't your happiness be worth more than your reputation?"

She fell deep in thought.

"Even if I went back, I wouldn't know where to find him. My brother boasted about scaring him off."

"There has to be a way."

"I can only wish."

"Merritt would help you," I offered.

She shook her head. "I couldn't impose. He recently married. It wouldn't be proper."

"No, Margaret. You know he would help, he's a good man."

"We are discussing this as if I will be returning." Margaret exhaled.

She was correct. We had no guarantees on how she could or would go back or even what day she'd arrive.

I watched her carefully. She no longer epitomized everything I hated. In fact, a warmth in my chest led me to believe I'd grown fond of her and liked her—she might even be considered one of my closest friends. "Do you want to return?" I almost hesitated to ask.

Her eyes speared mine but not in the way I feared from before. They were contemplative and childlike.

"I—I don't know."

Tears trailed down her face. It was the first time I'd ever seen her fully cry. I squeezed her hand tighter.

"I fear my return will force me into a harsh, loveless marriage."

"Margaret," I adjusted to a sitting position. "I'll do anything to help you. If you want to stay, we'll make arrangements for you here. If you want to leave, I'll write a letter to Merritt asking for his help. Please keep it on you before you . . ." I struggled to finish the sentence. Her falling down the stairs no longer brought the pleasure from before.

"You would do that for me?"

I nodded. "Yes, anything."

"Do you think Jacob would have me after all that has happened? The engagement to Merritt, my family, and . . ."

"None of it should matter if you're truly in love."

Margaret paused then shifted to face me better. "You're right, Kat." She arched one eyebrow. "It shouldn't." The heat of her pointed words singed me. I didn't need her to elaborate to know what she implied.

"This is different."

"It most certainly is not." She smirked.

"Trenton should've told me."

"Yes, he should have, but whether he did or didn't, has your love for him altered?"

I searched my soul. *Did my pain change my feelings for him?*

"Don't be so blinded by foolishness that you can't see what we all see, Kat. Trenton is most ardently in love with you."

My chest stirred. "It's not him." The truth of my sadness finally reached the surface. "It's those who are working tirelessly to see us break apart."

"Then why are you allowing them to succeed?"

Stunned at her words, I stilled. They contained nothing that hadn't been said before, but somehow, they hit their mark more accurately now.

Why am I?

Chapter 33

This afternoon was to be our last group event before the wedding. While nothing was said about whether the nuptials would go on or be postponed, Margaret sent word through Gretchen that the talent show event was still a go.

Although I hadn't spoken to anyone besides Margaret since the night before, it wasn't for a lack of effort. While I engaged in a long and recuperating bath and tended to the cuts on my feet, Margaret—the ever-defensive guard dog—refused entry to everyone including my mom, Kelly, and Trenton several times.

The door to the lavvy remained closed, nevertheless, the connecting wall was thin enough to overhear nearly everything.

"Margaret," my mom persisted. "I'm sure she wants to speak with me."

"I'm certain of that, Mrs. Shelton, but she's quite occupied at the moment."

Kelly's request came shortly after Mom's but with less gentleness. "Margaret! Let me pass."

Margaret's well practiced spurns kept Kelly from entering. "She is indisposed. She will seek you out when she is so inclined."

The next voice to surface had attempted access twice already. "Please, Margaret, please?" The anguish in Trenton's tone was difficult to hear. "I need to see her."

"Mr. Gilford . . ." Though Margaret's voice revealed a fair amount of sympathy, she stood her ground. "You should know, sir, she has much to ruminate over."

"That's what I fear." When his voice cracked, my heart hurt. My avoidance didn't come as the result of intentional punishment, it arose from my need to be alone . . . to think—to process everything that had occurred.

I held extra still in the bathtub to hear the rest of the conversation.

"What can I do?" He pled. I visualized him running his hand through his hair, something he did more often as of late.

"Rest assured, Mr. Gilford, Kat is an intelligent woman. She, no doubt, will make a wise decision."

Trenton's tone seemed laced with pain. "Will you tell her I came by, again?"

"Certainly." There was a significant pause in the exchange. "Anything else you might wish to convey?" I couldn't help but wonder if Margaret deliberately probed for my benefit. She had to have known I was listening—not a sound came forth from the lavvy.

His sigh came loud and long. "Tell Kat, how much I love her."

I imagined Margaret's self-satisfied grin surfacing from her machination. "Though I have no doubt she is well aware and thus reciprocates it, I will reiterate your sentiments forthwith, sir."

The door clicked shut.

Alone in my thoughts for the next thirty minutes, a ridiculous scheme came to mind. Not only would it provide a way to free me from the confines of the house and the faces I wasn't ready to see, but it allowed a way for me to do something special for

Margaret—something that might communicate my gratitude to her in a most unusual manner.

After dressing, I stepped back into the bedroom with a wide smile on my face. "Margaret, would you mind going somewhere with me?"

She glanced up from her book with a startled look on her face. "I suppose." The sight of a small lift from her mouth encouraged me. She had grown to be more of an adventurer than I ever pegged her for.

"We have to leave the house carefully."

Margaret sighed and set her book aside. "You know you cannot circumvent them forever."

I winced. That wasn't my only intent, but I could see how she believed that. "I have somewhere to be and wondered if you wanted to come, that's all."

I glanced away, but not after Margaret's stare burrowed through me. "I'm quite aware you were privy to Mr. Gilford's utterances."

My eyes settled on the windowpane, though nothing truly registered in my view. I felt her sharp eyes penetrate my back.

"However," she continued, "should there be any doubt in his devotion, I could relay his words for you once more." I circled around and met her eyes. "Your betrothed is quite besotted with you."

I nodded. "Thank you, Margaret." Tears pricked behind my eyes. "Thank you for being so kind to him."

She stepped closer and placed a hand on my arm. "So, what, pray tell, is our destination?"

I smiled slyly. "Not all of my time spent in the lavvy was in the tub. I have concocted a plan. You will have to wait and see." I laughed. "It's a surprise."

She grinned in response, no cheekiness or sass, and I found myself watching her as she retrieved a sweater. I could no longer deny that my nineteenth-century nemesis had come to mean a great deal to me.

Through careful maneuvering, we exited the house and within minutes we were safely inside Trenton's car once more. The polished exterior shone as if nothing destructive had occurred two days prior.

I smiled at the memory of Hennessey's face when Margaret and I came back from her driving lesson. I led him to believe it was I who caused the damage only to spare Margaret the embarrassment, but truthfully, considering my track record, it wasn't a hard sell. Despite Hennessey's prim and proper role, I discovered him to be a gem of a man, abounding in integrity, loyalty, and goodness, everything befitting a close ally and friend.

I felt above the visor and retrieved Trenton's keys and though my intent was to leave my tangled thoughts of him far behind today, the musky scent of his cologne emitted freely from the leather upholstery. A pleasurable inducement to be sure, but not if I was trying to keep a clear head.

As I drove down the road and away from Charlock, my smile returned as I contemplated the events surrounding Margaret's surprise. If all went as planned, it would surely lift both of our spirits.

"When you were at Charlock, Lizzy informed me that you were in love," Margaret said shifting in the passenger seat to avoid the sun shining upon her.

I handed her a pair of sunglasses. "Try these." She observed how I wore mine and copied it. I smiled at her twenty-first-century profile in her jeans and shades and imagined the force she would be if she remained in our time.

I considered her comment, then thought back to my conversations with Lizzy. They were brief. It was Merritt and Joanne who knew all the details surrounding Jeff.

I nodded. "Yes, I was."

She looked over to me, but I kept my eyes forward. "I assumed that your designs were upon Merritt at the time."

I laughed. "Well, yes I imagine that would happen. We were together often."

"Without a chaperone." she scoffed.

"I didn't know that was necessary. Seriously, give me a break, I didn't know any of the customs or proper behavior."

"Merritt did."

"He was being kind to an awkward foreigner. He never said or did anything to make me feel bad," I said as I recalled our cherished moments together. "Well, that's not true." I backtracked and proceeded to tell her what happened in the library when she came upon us, and I was crying. That was the only time Merritt really upset me. Of course, it was all over an imaginary Johnna, and worked itself all out. "Regardless of propriety, Margaret, or lack thereof, Merritt was always a gentleman."

"So, this man you loved? Was it Mr. Trenton Gilford?"

"No."

In my peripheral vision her mouth gaped open. "You loved another?"

I nodded. "His name was Jeff." I waited for the sharp pains to come. *They didn't.* "He was from my time but a few years ago. We were engaged to be married until he was killed in a car accident."

"A—a car, such as this one?" Margaret's cheeks paled as she gripped the side of the door. "So, my presumption was factual. I could've been killed driving the other day."

The side of my mouth lifted partway. I would truly miss her dramatics if she left.

"Yes, it was a car like this one, but no, you were hardly going fast enough to be injured." I inhaled. "This accident happened in America and it . . ." a hollow pang surfaced in my chest. "It was my fault he died."

Margaret peered over to me. Her eyes grew wide, waiting for clarification.

"He was driving, like I am now, and well, I was teasing him. Playing with his hair, touching his cheek. I leaned in to kiss him and he became distracted." My voice quivered. "He drove into the path of an oncoming truck." I pointed to the vehicles that passed us on the right. "Something like that."

Very few people knew the truth. Why I felt the need to explain to Margaret, I wasn't sure, but I did. My mouth suddenly felt dry. "We were to wed a couple of months later."

Margaret's hand went to mine on the steering wheel, and she squeezed lightly. "It must've been tormenting," she whispered.

I licked my upper lip. "I believed I had nothing to live for."

"You're a resilient woman, Kat."

I turned my head. "Why do you say that?"

"Because you found a way to live *and* love again."

Looking back at my path from that day, there were many times I wanted to give up, many days I refused to get out of bed, and many times I considered ending my own life, but she was right. Had I not continued forward, I would not have been lucky enough to meet Trenton.

The more I focused on her words the more I realized how reckless it would be to let such insignificant stupidity from his past derail our happiness now. I peered over to thank her but watched her grow rigid as her eyes darted about the landscape out the window.

"Are you okay?"

"I know these roads . . ." Margaret's eyes widened. Th—this l—land." She stuttered. "It belonged to Helen . . . and my father."

I nodded. After my bath this morning, I researched her family estate. A portion of it remained in the Abbott name, and I stealthily contacted them for a visit.

As we pulled down a long drive, Margaret's behavior concerned me. She clasped her hands in her lap and rubbed them raw. When she turned to look at me, her cheeks were deathly pale.

"I did some checking this morning." I spoke carefully, watching her intently. "The woman who still lives here, is an Abbott. According to the woman I spoke to on the phone, a Mrs. Henry, she told me that Miss Abbott never married or had children." Margaret's breath came a half tick faster than before. "She's your relative, Margaret. I'm unsure exactly how, but isn't this amazing?" I wanted to believe the shock on her face was in response to my news, but a gnawing at my insides told me otherwise. That and what she said next.

"We should not be here." Margaret warned.

"Why not?" I cringed at the bitterness in her tone.

"It's not proper. We have not been introduced and we are coming uninvited. It's possible it's not her at-home day for callers."

"No, we've been invited. When I reached out to them, Mrs. Henry said the mistress would be quite pleased with visitors. She never gets any."

"What could I possibly say to her?" Margaret's face and neck now had a slight sheen across her skin. She seemed legitimately nervous.

I shrugged my shoulders as I parked the car near the front of the house. "She's seventy-eight years old, I imagine a simple conversation will be perfectly fine."

We both paused to study the structure. It was a lovely two-story cottage home. Beautifully carved eaves hung over a half-dozen plated windows. Large white rose bushes lined a brick path to the front door and another row of rose bushes, this time bright pink, lined the foundation on both sides of the door. I half expected seven dwarfs to come marching out the door.

"Is this the right home?" I questioned, expecting a grander estate. Glancing back at my notes, I double checked the location.

Margaret choked. "This was my mother's home . . . my home."

My mouth parted in surprise.

"At least it was until she passed." Tears bubbled on her lashes. "When my father wed Helen Tilly, they rented this home to a different tenant family and we moved to the main house." She pointed over a hill where only the uppermost crown of a larger structure could be seen.

My eyebrows nearly met in the middle. "Wait, Mrs. Tilly was your landlord?"

She peered down at her fidgeting hands. "My father was employed as her steward. When my mother became ill, Mrs. Tilly took an interest in me and sent me away to one of her relatives until I was old enough for finishing school."

"Why were you sent away?"

"Once they were wed, my future was decided. I had been informed on more than one occasion that suitable training was required to become a proper lady. They insisted it was my only chance at obtaining a worthy husband."

"I'm confused, Margaret."

"What?" She snapped. This distressed her more than I expected.

"Why would a wealthy widow take interest in one of her employees and his family? I don't know a lot about the nineteenth-century hierarchy, but I do know that conduct like this would have caused some sort of an uproar."

Margaret's jaw tensed. "There was a bit of tongue-wag in the beginning, but widows have more freedom when it comes to society's rules."

"But why *your* father?"

Margaret's stiff posture proved her unease with this topic. "He pleased her."

"Wait . . . this happened before your mother passed?"

She nodded solemnly. "I wasn't permitted to be present when she died."

"What a lousy piece of—"

"Enough!" She slammed her hand on the dashboard. "I care not to discuss it any longer."

The car grew very silent. Regardless of my good intentions and bringing Margaret here to thank her, it appeared to be a terrible mistake.

"I'm sorry Margaret. I didn't mean to pry. Every family has their secrets, and I have forced yours from you unintentionally."

She shrugged.

"We should go." I placed my hand on the gear shift, but Margaret stayed my wrist.

"Wait." A mixture of fear and curiosity consumed her stormy eyes. "Maybe we should go in." She bit her lip. "I admit, I *am* curious."

"Really?" I searched her face for honesty. "I don't want this to upset you."

"I imagine emotion will come either way, but since we have already arrived . . ."

"Okay." I turned off the car and joined Margaret on the other side. Reaching for her hand, it trembled under my touch.

Our steps toward the front entrance were slow and teemed with doubt, however, any trepidation I felt dissipated quickly when the front door flew open before we even knocked.

Chapter 34

"Please, please come in." An older woman with auburn hair and a smattering of freckles appeared. "Welcome!" Clapping her hands excitedly, she introduced herself as Mrs. Henry, the housekeeper and companion to Miss Ellie Abbott. "I was a tad gobsmacked to receive your call, to say the least," she said, all in one breath. "But Miss Abbott has chatted of nothing else since."

I glanced at Margaret. Her skin turned pallid.

"My name is Kat Shelton, and this is my friend Margaret Ab—" I faltered. *What if Margaret doesn't want them to know?*

Margaret's hand shot forward clumsily and shook Mrs. Henry's. "I am Margaret Abbott, a very distant relation to Miss Abbott. I am pleased to make your acquaintance."

My eyes widened as she shook hands in a fairly normal way with our host. She has come so far in such a short amount of time. I chuckled lightly in remembrance of our first few difficult days.

Mrs. Henry led us into a small but quaint parlor. I watched as Margaret's countenance fluctuated in emotion as she scanned the room. Several large windows in the back opened to a lush green garden where the intoxicating scent of jasmine floated in and made it seem as though the flowery wallpaper was but an extension of the flora and fauna.

While Margaret toyed with the hem of her shirt, I studied the walls where dozens of pictures of cats in various poses were displayed. Several of them even had props like hats and bowties, and one, in particular, wore a crown and royal mantle. A dark tabby cat wound its way through my legs and rubbed against my jeans. I covered my mouth to keep from crying out, startled by its sudden appearance.

I swallowed hard. *Margaret's family member is the epitome of an old cat lady.*

"Might I introduce Miss Ellie Abbott." Mrs. Henry pointed to a woman sitting properly upon a teal-colored sofa in the center of the room, an inviting hearth centered behind her and an antique piano enhanced a far corner. Her snowy white hair had been pulled back into a fine bun and, though she never made eye contact with us, her baby blue eyes carried a gentleness in them.

"Ma'am, Miss Shelton and Miss Abbott have arrived." Then she pointed to us. "Please, have a seat, ladies, I'll get you all a cuppa and some nosh." Then she swiftly departed from the room to retrieve the refreshment.

We sat down on the sofa directly across from Miss Abbott and I found myself staring at this perfectly poised woman before us. Her slim hands rested gently on the lap of her rose-colored skirt and she tucked one leg gracefully behind the other, yet something seemed off.

"Thank you, Miss Abbott," I spoke first. "Thank you for allowing us to stop in at the last moment."

She smiled warmly and tipped her head in my direction, but her eyes never met mine. It was then that I realized my suspicions were correct.

Miss Abbott was most assuredly blind.

I glanced to Margaret and pointed to my eyes trying to inform her, if she hadn't already noticed. It seemed to only take a second for my motions to click.

"I'm most grateful for your phone call," Miss Abbott said, moving her head so ever slightly side to side while her smile never wavered. "I understand one of you is a relation of some sort?"

"Yes," Margaret squeaked at first. Then cleared her throat "It is I."

Miss Abbott's face now turned to Margaret's voice, but again her eyes remained unattached to anything or anyone.

"And how might we be related?"

I winced, unsure of how this question could be answered truthfully, but Margaret's years of cordiality arose at a timely pace.

"My family is through the William and Sarah Abbott's line who first dwelt here in the 1870's."

"Oh," Miss Abbott tittered joyfully. "What a coincidence. As am I. Their son Josiah is my second great-grandfather." The woman clapped her hands daintily. "Esther?" She called. Her companion rushed from another part of the house and poked her head in the room.

"Yes, ma'am?"

"Would you retrieve my book? The family one?"

"Certainly."

Within seconds she stepped back in carrying a large book with thick binding and placed it on the table between us.

"What would you like me to show them?" Mrs. Henry tenderly touched her shoulder. The ease in which they connected was impressive.

"The photographs of Josiah's family."

Mrs. Henry flipped through several pages and found the aged black and white photographs tucked into the crease between other pictures. When she laid them out, Margaret gasped.

Mrs. Henry peered up. Her eyes narrowed a bit. "Are you well?"

Margaret nodded. We shared a quick glance before she answered. "I just haven't seen these before."

I leaned over to take a better look.

Josiah. I pursed my lips together. It was the same man I remembered, both at the church and the Gilford ball. I fought the grin that wanted to come forth when I recalled our last encounter. I swiftly covered my mouth with my hand, but the way Margaret looked oddly at me, she had to know I was laughing.

"Later," I whispered. "I'll explain later."

I picked up a picture of him, with who I assumed to be his wife, the poor woman, and two children. So, the awful man produced offspring? *Of course, he did, we are currently conversing with one.*

Thankfully, it seemed as though none of his conniving traits seemed to filter down the bloodline. I glanced back to Miss Abbott as she stared at the wall over our heads. The wrinkles that formed upward at the corners of her mouth proved her tendency to smile often. There was no doubt in my mind she was a pleasure to be around.

"Why do you not live in the estate house?" Margaret inquired with some hesitation.

"I was the sole heir but had no need for such an enormous residence. I sold it to my cousin who has graciously allowed me to live in this cottage for the last decade. I didn't want to be a burden to anyone since I never married."

So many questions spun in my mind, probably not unlike Margaret, but I restrained myself. This was her moment.

"Would you mind disclosing more about your ancestor, Josiah and his family?" Margaret queried.

"Not at all." She smiled again. "Josiah had three sons that lived and lost another two children at birth. His oldest son, Geoffrey, was my first great grandfather, then William, my grandfather, and his oldest son, Leo, was my father."

I smiled, quite impressed this woman knew her lineage so well. Margaret must've thought the same thing for her eyes only grew wider.

Margaret cleared her throat. "My namesake is Josiah's sister, Margaret."

I grinned over to her, pleased with her quick thinking.

"What might you know of her circumstances?" She continued her inquisition.

Miss Abbott sighed heavily. "Not as much, I'm afraid." She pointed in the general direction of the book. "Very little was written on her behalf in the family records."

Disappointment marred Margaret's expression. Curiosity strangled me. Could this be because Margaret never returns to the past?

"Might I examine the contents of this book?"

"Oh, certainly dear, help yourself."

Margaret scooted closer and turned each page slowly. Some she spent a lengthier time on than others. It was filled with documents, pedigree charts, and photographs. It was a wealth of information and Margaret was thoroughly captivated.

When she neared the end, she froze. The page rattled slightly under her shaky fingers. I glanced over as she picked up a certificate of marriage. The edges were crinkled and torn, the paper itself had a yellowing fragility to it, but when Margaret handled it, she did so as if it were a brittle piece of glass.

The names, ***Sarah Eleanor Green*** and ***William Martin Abbott*** appeared on the front above the bold words "joined in a union of Holy Matrimony" with additional signatures at the bottom. It was dated 23 July 1853.

"My parents." She mouthed. Then traced her index finger over her mother's faded signature.

"Would you mind if I took a picture of a document in your book, Miss Abbott?"

"Oh, not at all." She waved her hand still staring at the wall behind us. How sad it must be for her to not be able to see her precious cat images any longer. Though a real one, different from the tabby, had now taken up residence next to her on the sofa. The animal stretched out and its white fluffy tail bounced against her thigh repeatedly. I smiled; they must bring her so much comfort.

"Thank you," I said, and proceeded to take a picture of the certificate. Margaret flinched in confusion. Phone camera—just another thing to explain on the drive home.

Mrs. Henry entered the room with a tray of tea and sandwiches and quickly set about to fixing a cup for Miss Abbott first. Even after she lifted the woman's dainty hand and placed the cup tenderly within her palm, she never referenced her employer's disability, and I found that fascinating.

After Miss Abbott took several sips, she felt for the edge of the table and set her cup down. Lifting her finger, she pointed toward the hearth behind her. The one sole picture in the room of an actual human being was a large stately photograph of a man in uniform. "Did you know, my grandfather William, fought in the Great War?"

Margaret paused with her cup next to her lips and mumbled, "What great war?" She stared between us with wide eyes.

"World War I, my dear." Miss Abbott's hearing certainly bore no limitations. She continued, "I know many believe World War II to be a more honorable battle, but the actions of many of our beloved countrymen, simply by a request from King George V to assist France, were most admirable. Their battle to prevent

Germany from becoming a potentially global threat was indeed God's plan."

A new fear clouded Margaret's eyes, and she mouthed silently, afraid to be heard a second time. "Two world wars?"

I offered a subtle nod then whispered back, "I'll explain that later, too."

As late morning turned to early afternoon, I watched with growing fascination as Miss Abbott shared numerous family stories that had been passed down through the descendants over time. Margaret asked many questions and hung onto every word she said. It became quite apparent in the short time that the two women were forging a deep connection.

"You say you are here for a wedding?" Miss Abbott questioned.

"Yes," Margaret pointed to me, though our hostess could hardly see the gesture. "My lovely friend, Kat here, is getting married tomorrow."

I was quite taken back by her words that I missed what the elder Miss Abbott said next. Margaret nudged me to answer.

"I'm sorry, what did you ask?"

"Are you marrying an Englishman, dear?"

"Yes, I am. His family has an estate not too far from here, Charlock Manor, near the Thames. His name is Trenton Gilford."

"Gilford? Oh yes, a fine family I should say. I knew a Mr. Trenton Gilford many years ago." She chuckled. "It could hardly be the same man."

I beamed. "No, but it could possibly be my fiancé's grandfather, Mr. Trenton Gilford the first," I added. "He's such a wonderful man. I'm sure he would hardly be forgotten."

She laughed. Even her laugh was graceful. "We were acquainted through friends, although I lost contact with him quite some time ago. Congratulations on your good fortune, young lady. You must be delighted."

My smile broadened. "I am." And I really was happy when my thoughts dwelt only on Trenton. I knew everything else that transpired this week should be ignored. "I would love for you to attend the wedding tomorrow, Miss Abbott. You could be reacquainted with Mr. Gilford once more."

"Oh," she waved her hand. "I hardly leave the house." She paused, and her eyes seemed to sparkle. "But it would be good to visit with him again."

I smiled. "Mrs. Henry, if you have a piece of paper, I could write down the details. It would be wonderful, really, if you both would come."

Mrs. Henry quickly retrieved a paper and pen. Her rush and fluster indicated she recognized the significance of her employer's interest.

"Now, my dear." Miss Abbott turned quite serious in my direction. "You are aware, are you not, that every young bride must adhere to certain stipulations."

"Stipulations?" I gasped lightly, remembering the comment Mrs. Gilford made about severe consequences occurring when traditions aren't observed. Had I missed something else in the British handbook on *What you need to know when you marry an Englishman*? There actually wasn't a book like that that I knew of, though I held my breath waiting for her to elaborate.

"Traditions, of course." She chuckled.

"Esther, will you retrieve my jewelry case. The gilded one?"

What is Miss Abbott thinking? I searched Margaret's face for an answer, but she appeared as confused as me.

"I'm certain you've heard the term . . .something old, something new, something borrowed, something blue."

"Yes, yes I have." I exhaled with relief.

"Well, have you secured your items?"

I shook my head. "No, actually I haven't had the time. This week has been a bit overwhelming."

Mrs. Henry walked in with a beautifully crafted gold box.

"Consider my gift to represent the 'old', my dear."

"Oh, no I couldn't." I waved my hand, but Miss Abbott appeared quite determined. She felt for the lid, raised it, and fumbled around within.

"Ah, yes. Here it is." She pulled out a jeweled stick pin.

I gasped. "Miss Abbott, that is stunning. I really cannot take this from you."

"Oh, posh." She objected. "Here. Open your hand."

She reached out in the air between us and waited for me to meet her fingers. Once she turned my hand over face up, she placed the jewel securely in my palm. It was a one-inch silver stick with a dazzling blue butterfly at the tip.

"Sapphire is my birthstone," she whispered, "but I can no longer gaze upon its beauty."

"Was this your mothers?" I inquired, still startled by the gesture.

"Yes, but given to her by my father's grandmother. This has been passed down from long ago, it's original owner unknown."

Margaret and I wore similar expressions of astonishment, but I was certain her eyes took on a sadder mien.

"Oh, Miss Abbott, I can't accept such a cherished gift."

"Please." She waved my protest aside. "I'm nearly in the grave and have no daughter of my own to give this to. I would be truly honored if you were to wear it on your wedding day."

I pinched the jewelry between my fingers and examined the delicate detailed wings of the butterfly. The eyes shone clear like diamonds, but the rest was entirely in varying shades of blue. "It's breathtaking."

I handed it to Margaret who received it with tenderness. Tears trailed her cheeks. I watched as she traced it in reverence. Then swiftly handed it back, folding her hands in her lap.

Within the hour we said our goodbyes and made promises to visit again. I could very well enjoy coming here often when in residence at Charlock. It was only a forty-five-minute drive.

Once inside the car, I drove down the lane slowly. The hovering silence that lingered drew me to pull over and face Margaret. Her tears had never really stopped though she blinked them away quite effectively.

"You recognize this jewel, don't you?" I lifted it up.

She nodded slowly. "It was my mother's."

"I thought so." I handed it to her.

"No. I cannot take it. It was a gift to you."

"It does not belong to me." I lifted her hand and placed it in her palm. "Your mother would want you to have it."

She held it lovingly in her fingers. "My mother owned few possessions, but this was one of them. She wore it to church every Sunday."

I marveled at the miracle of how an object this small and precious found its way back to her. She was quite young when her mother passed, but it was apparent that the memories she did have were cherished ones. It seemed this little jaunt turned out to be more of a blessing than expected.

As I drove back to the house, a lightness washed over me. The frustration I carried over Justine and Mrs. Gilford seemed minute compared to the challenges Margaret faced—to stay here, try to return, find Jacob, elope? A wave of embarrassment crept in as I realized my struggles were in no way a comparison to hers.

Once in the driveway, I reached over and hugged Margaret. She stiffened at first, then allowed her arms to encircle me as well. "I don't think I could've gotten through this week without you," I confessed. "I don't believe your appearance in my life at this time was a mistake, for me, it was more like a miracle."

She released and lowered her eyes to the jewel once more. I imagine her mind was trying to wrap itself around the day's events. "It is I who should be thanking you, Kat." She peered up. "I would not have fared well in this state without you."

I smiled and glanced at my watch. "Are you ready to blow the audience away again with the piano?"

Her forehead creased severely. "Blow the audience away?"

I laughed. "Sorry, I meant to ask . . . are you ready to amaze the guests with your musical gift?"

She grimaced. "I nearly forgot about the talent performance."

"You will still play, won't you?"

"Yes." She twirled the jeweled stick between her fingers. "I will play my mother's favorite—*La Prière d'une Vierge* by Badarczewska."

"A Maiden's prayer." I whispered. I embraced every opportunity to use my French, which wasn't often enough.

She smiled in return. "My mother sang that song to me. I learned to play it on my own after she died."

I squeezed her hand. "I can't wait to hear it."

Chapter 35

A short time later, on my way to the ballroom for the talent show, I was steered without warning to the side of the staircase. The move came so quickly I had little time to react. When Trenton faced me, my pulse should've slowed, but it only increased.

An unfamiliar emotion flickered across his face . . . unease or irritation, it was difficult to identify. He ran a hand down his face and his voice strained with an unmistakable rasp. "Why are you avoiding me?"

I peered down. "I—I needed time to process everything."

"We need to talk."

I nodded. "But they're waiting for us." I pointed to the guests entering the ballroom. "We'll be late."

"I don't care about that." The intensity in his eyes sharpened. "I only care about us."

Hastings looked over from the ballroom entrance, our conversation was anything but private.

"Not here." I pleaded.

Trenton grabbed my hand and pulled me into the deep coat closet underneath the staircase and closed the door. When he flicked the light on, the empty space expanded.

My back pressed weightily against the door. The musty aroma of a handful of abandoned coats from a nearby rack floated about the substantial space. Trenton paced uncomfortably before me. His movements surfaced unnatural and pained.

"Stop." I placed a hand on his arm. "Please?"

He raked a hand through his hair, letting his dark waves fall across his forehead. "Will you forgive me, Kat?"

My head lowered. He wasn't the only one that required forgiveness. My conduct last night showed immaturity and much of the way I behaved this week bordered selfishness.

When I glanced back up, he had resumed his unsettled strides. "I have been a complete bugger this entire week."

"Not the whole week." I chuckled at my terrible attempt to lighten the situation.

He stopped and in one stride stood before me. Both of his hands pressed against the door on each side of my head. My breath caught as he leaned forward. His proximity always left me wanting, but it was the intensity in his ivy green eyes that paralyzed me. He seemed to be searching for something. I closed my eyes and inhaled his scent . . . spice and something outdoors.

Opening them again, I could practically see his mind spinning. "Trenton, I—"

Someone knocked.

"What?" Trenton said past my ear.

Hastings spoke through the door. "Sorry to interrupt, chap, but your mother insists we promptly begin the event." He must've seen where we disappeared to.

"In a moment." Trenton's gruff tone sent his friend a clear message.

He turned back to me. His determination seized my movement. "Tell me I haven't lost you."

My heart pounded.

Another knock.

The muscles in Trenton's jaw tightened. If I angled forward but an inch, my lips would meet his, only the angst in his face kept me distant. *When had that ever happened before?* I lifted one hand and cupped his cheek. The heat from his skin easily filled my palm as he leaned into it.

"Sorry, mate . . ." Hastings' voice penetrated the wood. "I do apologize, but I believe your mother will have my head if I don't retrieve you, and I rather like it attached."

I dropped my hand to my side and spoke quickly. "Would you have dinner with me tonight?"

He moved closer until his whisper tickled my lips, fostering a sensational reaction. "Only the two of us?"

The temptation to pull him into me surged. "Yes, alone . . . on the veranda."

His lips parted as he searched my eyes. "Is that truly what you want?"

I nodded.

His soft exhale confirmed his relief. "I will be there."

Trenton's eyes slowly scanned the contours of my face, then paused at my mouth. Though the strength of the pull between us was undeniable, I sensed his trepidation. He must feel like he doesn't have the right to kiss me at will any longer.

When he withdrew, his warmth disappeared with him. Despite the unknown that hovered between us, my heart belonged to this man. I clutched his shirt and brought him back to me. His lips easily found mine and every ounce of pent-up frustration surfaced in the desperation of our kiss. His fingers found their way to my waist, tightening and releasing to the pace of his mouth, dispelling any earlier caution for there was nothing tentative about him or his touch.

Hastings stirred on the other side of the door. "Take as much time as you need, Gilford. I will appease your mum."

When Trenton drew back, the calm that now smoothed his brow had effectively replaced his grim countenance. Reaching for my hand, he kissed my knuckles. "Thank you, Kat." His acute exhale warmed my fingers. "This means everything to me."

"Me too." I smiled warmly then winced. "How mad do you think your mom will be?"

Trenton's response took less than a second. "It doesn't even matter."

I grinned and held fast to his arm as he opened the door and led us back out.

Chapter 36

When we entered the ballroom at ten minutes past four o'clock, the room carried a heaviness that hadn't been present earlier in the week. I knew Trenton and I were solely responsible for the added weight. Much had happened in the last forty-eight hours to generate their grim expressions, but I refused to let that settle for our last casual night together.

I stood before the group in my tight-fitting training pants and an equally form-fitting tank top. Despite the glare from one person in particular, I wore this precisely for my talent. I wasn't entirely sure what triggered my confidence, but I would no longer be ashamed of any side of me.

"Thank you for being here." I took a deep breath. "I would personally like to apologize to you all for any discomfort that may have arisen recently. It has been an unusual week—"

"To be sure . . ." Mrs. Gilford muttered from the front.

I forced a smile in return. "But please don't let any misgivings affect your enjoyment tonight. I promise you; you will not be disappointed." I shot a peek at Trenton as his eyes studied me curiously. The memory of our recent kiss brought a flame to my cheeks. I quickly cleared my head. "If you all wouldn't mind taking a seat, I'm thrilled to introduce the talented guests amongst us."

As everyone shuffled to the seats provided, I waited a few moments to finish the announcement. "I hope you're as excited as I am to see the varying talents of our friends and family." I unfolded my notes and read from the list. "The order will begin as follows—Margaret will play on the piano and sing, *La Prière d'une Vierge* by Badarczewska. Hastings and his lovely assistant, Maria, will entertain us with a magic show—"

"Excuse me," Hastings interrupted. "That is . . .the elusive Mr. Slytof Hand and his enchanting assistant Miss Boom Shaka Laka." Though he said this with a completely straight face, my head tipped back in a full laugh along with everyone else. "My apologies Mr. Slytof Hand." I grinned effortlessly. The refreshing turn in the atmosphere brought a well-deserved wink in his direction.

I continued, "Ashtyn will delight us in *Sibelius* on the violin. My dad will play *Stand by Me* on the harmonica." I grinned his way. "Uncle Clarence will recite the poem *City of the Sky Gondolas* by Jules Verne. Justine will play *La Vida Breve* on the harp." A loud cough sounded from the audience, but I didn't glance up. "Trenton, Marlowe, and Jonah will impress us with M&M's—please don't ask me to elaborate because I cannot." The group roared once more before I took one last profound inhale. "And *I* will be . . ." I glanced at Trenton, and he nodded his encouragement. "I will be sharing some boxing insights and tips with my friend Kelly."

I heard a gasp but refused to locate the source and slipped quietly into an empty chair in the back of the room—eager to have the attention off me.

I peered over to Kelly nearby as she spoke to Marlowe. She only agreed to be my sparring partner if I promised not to leave a mark. Jonah, sitting a row ahead of me, agreed to be my pretend attacker only moments before Trenton whisked me off to the closet. This didn't leave me any time to relay my instructions, though I appreciated his willingness regardless.

Once the talent show officially began, any earlier unease dissipated to an entranced captive audience. I sighed my relief that this afternoon's event might be salvaged after all.

When Margaret engaged in her spontaneous performance a few nights ago, the piece she chose was no less beautiful than what she played today, however, the passion that surfaced in this silent tribute to her mother was unparalleled. Her extraordinary execution brought every emotion of the week to the surface. Once finished, she curtsied to a rousing display of appreciation and that's when I noticed two distinct things—the tears in her eyes, and the butterfly stick pin on her bodice front. When she looked in my direction, the pride that swelled within me arose unparalleled.

Next, Hastings and Maria's magic show did exactly what I hoped for and delivered a limitless amount of comic relief. While most of their tricks were sabotaged on purpose and embellished for a dramatic flair, the banter between Mr. Slytof Hand and Miss Boom Shaka Laka, had the group nearly in stitches.

"That was awesome," I whispered to Kelly.

She laughed. "They came up with this yesterday." Then she stopped and looked at me carefully. "Are you okay? I've been really worried about you."

"I'm alright. It's been a tough week."

She leaned in, whispering low. "I heard some things . . . you know, from Marlowe."

"Yeah, I can only imagine what is being said."

She tipped her head closer. "He said you're the best thing that has ever happened to Trenton, and he hoped he hadn't screwed it up."

I smiled genuinely. "Thank you for that."

"So, is there a wedding tomorrow?"

I nodded. "I believe so."

She sighed. "Better be, because I look exquisite in my dress."

I laughed. "Yes, yes you do."

She wrapped one arm around me and pulled me next to her. "I love you, Kat."

"I love you too, Kelly."

After Ashtyn finished, my dad performed a song I had heard a thousand times, but in my mind that was never enough. I missed hearing him play the harmonica at night from the store below our apartment. Many memories were tied up in those words . . . *Stand by Me.* It had come to be an even greater significance after 9/11 and the loss of his two brothers and nephew. Only mom and I recognized the rare tears in his eyes when he ended.

Uncle Clarence's poem reciting went off without a hitch, and once the room scaled back their concluding praise, the audience fell completely silent. All eyes went to the front where the harp stood empty. I glanced around and then back at Kelly who shrugged her shoulders. When Trenton and his friends stood up, nothing was said about Justine's absence, and they carried on as if they were the next ones on the list.

By the time the men finished their flying M&Ms slapstick routine, which appeared something akin to a vaudeville act, circus music and all, the entire room was practically floored with laughter. Everything about this afternoon was not only much needed, but it was also a perfect conclusion to the week's events.

When I stood up to close out the talents, the room grew quiet once more, and I wished I had the foresight to switch the order of the presentations.

My legs trembled as I moved to the front and took several cleansing breaths. I shook out my hands anxiously. It was reckless for me to show any signs of uncertainty even in something as simple as a spar. Part of my training is control—controlling my mind, breathing, and execution.

My first presentation involved Kelly. After putting our gear on, I talked through my stances and moves, especially careful not to cause harm. I apologized to the group for my rustiness, having only sparred once this week.

"Don't hold back," Kelly muttered as she faced me.

"I thought you wanted me to take it easy."

"I don't want you to appear weak either."

My lips curved shrewdly, and I took a few insignificant shots, but Kelly continued to taunt. "Is that all you got, Softy?"

It was all good and fun, but as I sidestepped around her, I popped off several decent strikes in response.

"Ohhh." Hastings cupped his mouth and cried aloud.

Marlowe chirped a quick rebuttal. "You've got this, Kelly."

She smiled wide, and we juked a bit more. Though the audience clearly enjoyed the bout, a series of scathing remarks surfaced. I didn't need to look to guess their origin.

Stepping the intensity up a notch, Kelly hooked, and I cross punched.

"Smashing, love!" Trenton cried.

"Okay, okay, I'm kidding." Kelly said as she ducked my next swing, but because I followed up as a one-two, I got her on the uppercut.

"I think you've proven your point." She snickered.

I backed off. Turning to the audience, I explained some of the more common moves for a boxer, both in offense and defense and with a little less realism.

"Thanks, Kelly."

She tossed the headgear and gloves aside on her way back to her seat to a solid applause. "I don't think two years is long enough." She chuckled. "She's hardly forgotten anything." Then took her seat again where Marlowe proudly wrapped one arm around her shoulders.

Pointing to the space next to me, I called for my next volunteer. "Jonah?"

"Yes, I do believe I've changed my mind." Everyone laughed, but he still stood up.

When I removed my gloves, confusion marred his stoic face. "Don't you need those?"

I smiled. "Not for this one."

"Okay, this next part is only an example of how I would react if I were attacked." I turned to Jonah. "Come at me from behind."

"I can't do that." He scoffed.

I placed my hand on my hip and looked to Trenton to give his approval. It was more than apparent that Jonah wouldn't budge until he did.

"It's fine." Trenton encouraged with a hearty laugh. "I'm more worried about *your* safety than hers."

Jonah seemed to take that as a personal challenge. He walked a good twenty paces behind me and stealthily bounced forward as if he could creep up from behind. His arms wound around me quickly and tightened his hold. A good six inches taller and much broader, Jonah paralyzed me—exactly what I aimed for.

In a swift move, I jerked my head backward and hit Jonah square in the chin.

"Ahhh, bloody he—." As his hands went to shield his face, it muffled his string of curse words, but also left his weaker points vulnerable. I could've easily kneed him in the groin for the illustration, but wouldn't be that ruthless, so I grabbed his wrist, twisted his palm upward, and forced it downward. This pulled him completely off balance and to his knees. Once on the ground, I pushed him flat with my foot and onto his stomach.

The reactions from the audience varied. Of course, leave it to the men to respond boisterously, but I specifically picked Jonah for his height and build to prove that with the right moves, any woman could free herself from danger.

I squatted near him. "Are you okay?"

Jonah shook his head. "I am certainly humbled."

I chuckled and held out a hand to assist him upward. He stood to his feet and continued to rub his chin. I never intended on hitting him hard enough for it to bleed, only to surprise him.

"Remind me to never bloody well volunteer for anything again." Jonah cried with a hint of humor.

"Watch your mouth, young man." Mrs. Gilford huffed. "I ignored it the first time, but if you continue, I shall have you removed."

"Forgive me, Mrs. Gilford." Jonah took his seat.

She waved her hand in the air with disgust. "The whole display is utterly appalling. I am simply mortified at the belief that this is appropriate in any way."

"Give it a rest, Juliana." Mr. Gilford faced his wife for the first time I had ever seen. He not only joined our conversation, but he also openly chastised her.

"I beg your pardon?" She blustered. "What have I done to deserve your bitter censure?"

Mr. Gilford's jaw tightened as he pointed in my direction. "Kat is showcasing her hard-earned skills and does not deserve to be rebuked by you. There is no doubt you have made your disapproval abundantly clear . . . all week!"

She gasped and held her hand to her heart. "Well, I never—"

"And furthermore, we *both* could be kinder to our daughter-in-law. She has only shown us the height of decorum in return."

"They are not married yet." She barked.

"They are getting married tomorrow. Do you truly intend on stopping this union in one day?"

She stammered. "I—I am not . . ."

"Cease this behavior." Mr. Gilford's voice commanded the room. Not one utterance sounded outside of his. "I am on the brink of exhaustion from your criticisms. Trenton has chosen his bride and you would do best to accept it if you ever want to see your grandchildren."

Mrs. Gilford's mouth went slack and from the color of her cheeks, she must've realized that everyone had stopped to listen to their most public conversation.

"Please proceed, Kat." Mr. Gilford turned away from Mrs. Gilford and her mortified countenance. "I apologize profusely for our disrespectful interruption."

Taken aback, I stood motionless before the group until I stumbled through my next sentence.

"C—can I get a new v—volunteer for the next part?"

Trenton stood quickly and reached for my hand. His unsteady touch confirmed he shared my surprise in the recent turn of events. Neither one of us expected such a protective outburst from his father but were appreciative all the same.

When I didn't speak, Trenton took over. "Many of you might not know this . . ." He addressed the audience yet only looked at me. "But Kat has taught hundreds of women how to protect themselves from such attacks. A lot of women successfully avoided harm because of what she's shared."

I smiled in his direction.

"I am entirely at your disposal." He chuckled nervously, then whispered only to me through tight lips. "You won't really hurt me though, will you love?"

"Only if it's deserved."

"Well then I am most concerned," he murmured. "I more than deserve your wrath."

For a brief moment, I lost myself in his gaze. His eyes revealed all the pain we'd endured in the last couple of days and all the subsequent regret. The temptation to end the talent show as is and run off with him nipped at my thoughts.

"Anytime now, chap." Hastings hollered. "I'm going to find this part quite entertaining."

Trenton drew his eyes away and snickered. "Would you like to trade places, mate?"

Hastings leaned back in his chair and folded his arms over his chest. "When hell freezes over."

Trenton chuckled again then faced me. "Now what would you have me do?"

"Stand right here and place your arms around me like Jonah did." Trenton moved into position. This felt so much better this time.

Though the awkward display between my future in-laws had initially thrown off my composure, it didn't take long to fall back into rhythm. I addressed the audience again. "So, now if your attacker is taller than you which is typical, a head butt might not work as effectively."

"I wholly disagree," Jonah shouted to a smattering of chortles. My smile in his direction was more out of sympathy. I really should've warned him.

I continued, "One option is to lower yourself to the ground and slip out of the hold, the other is to poke at the attacker's eyes, or punch him in the throat. Both moves will induce pain and stall the attack momentarily, but don't cease the onslaught." My next words were solely for Trenton. "Hold onto me as tightly as you can."

"Absolutely." The playfulness in his tone returned.

I waited until his grip seemed unbreakable, then wiggled my way down and out. Once free, I only pretended to show the audience the following moves. "Next take advantage of the weak moment and grab a finger and twist it back even to the point it breaks, or by far the most effective move now is to render your attacker immobile by a solid knee to the groin." I lifted my knee slowly in the false motion.

Trenton swiftly turned his back. "Please don't make me sterile."

I chuckled at the rambunctious response from our friends.

"I would never." My look softened. "Thank you for helping me."

He kissed my hand. "My pleasure."

I faced the group again. "Well, those are the basics on protecting yourself. Are there any questions?"

Ashtyn raised her hand. "Have you ever used those moves on someone before? For real?"

I couldn't stop my eyes from glancing at Margaret, then quickly back to Ashtyn. "Not so much my defensive moves, as an occasional punch in the eye."

Margaret's eyes widened to my grin.

Adele now spoke out. "How many women did you teach self-defense to?"

"Well over 200."

Her eyes widened. "That's so incredible, Kat!"

Grandfather stood and clapped enthusiastically. This brought most of the others to their feet as well. Heat tinged my cheeks as they gave me a sound ovation for something I never really considered to be a talent before.

"Thank you." I shifted awkwardly. "Please, let's offer an applause to everyone who participated tonight in the talent show. We have been immensely entertained."

Once the praise subsided, I glanced at my watch. "It appears that we have an hour before dinner. Feel free to visit amongst yourselves or do whatever you choose. The dining room will be open at seven."

Trenton reached over and pulled me close in a loving embrace. "I look forward to *our* dinner, love." He kissed my cheek and nodded. "Until then."

Rushing back to my room, I waited for Margaret to arrive. I had never been so nervous in devising a plan before.

"Well, Kat . . ." She entered the room with her usual flair and closed the door. "I presume you are speculating as to why your friend, Justine, has suddenly vanished."

"You know she's not my friend." I snapped. "But yes, I am curious. Do you know what happened?"

Her smile curved into the snakelike smile from my memory. "Yes, I do."

I waited impatiently, shifting weight from one hip to the other. "And . . ."

"Oh, I do love intrigue." She sighed and practically sashayed to the dressing table.

"Margaret . . ." I groaned.

"You know, I'm not one to be a gossipmonger." Her smile returned.

I lifted one eyebrow as I waited.

"Very well." She chuckled. "In our absence this morning, your beloved Trenton evidently confronted Justine most ardently. He practically packed her belongings and expedited her departure, posthaste."

"He kicked her out?" I choked.

"I doubt there was any kicking, as you say, but Mr. Chapman told me Trenton rang for a ride and showed her the door."

"Wow." I sat on the bed. "I didn't want it to come to that."

"He did it for you, Kat. It's apparent he's trying most devotedly to win your heart back."

"He never lost it. I just . . ." My eyes flashed at the memory of our earlier conversation and the rawness of his emotion clearly displayed in his features. "I need your help." I announced as I threw the wardrobe open and slid several hangers aside until I found what I searched for.

"My help?"

I turned around and faced her. "I need to set things right."

She clapped her hands and smiled wickedly. "What might that entail?"

"Will you help me *fight for my man*?"

Her face beamed. "I am entirely at your service."

Chapter 37

My hands nervously pressed against my stomach to settle the unease that fluttered about like a girl going on a date with her high school crush. I wasn't exactly sure why my nerves tingled so close to the skin, but it was apparent I felt anything but confident.

Fidgeting with the fabric of my taupe lace gown, I followed the length of my dress as it embraced my curves and graced the floor. Only the silver tips of my new shoes poked out from the hem at the bottom. I had never worn this dress before, having saved it for the honeymoon, but this evening's purpose called for something striking and bold.

As I waited for Trenton's arrival, I scanned my surroundings. The full moon offered passable light for our intimate table tucked into a private corner of the veranda. The white rose vine in which Trenton had plucked a flower off a year ago and presented it as a gesture of peace bloomed near the balustrade. I paused over the satin tablecloth, brilliant crystal, and fine china. I wanted everything to be perfect. One vase of pale pink lilies arose amidst two sleek silver candlesticks, each with a fervent flame. The flowers, so fresh that their scent wafted up and about in an enticing aroma under a nearly perfect evening sky.

Another deep breath unearthed my courage.

When Trenton appeared, my heart leapt. Though he was dressed in a midnight blue, slim suit and undoubtedly handsome from head to toe, there was a similar nervousness that exuded from him. When my smile reached him, his approach surfaced more certain and his stride more natural.

"You look positively . . ." The right side of his lips lifted, and he shook his head. "Perfect."

Though I continued to fidget subtly, I smiled under his stare. "Thank you. You look amazing yourself, Trenton."

"I'm most grateful for the invitation." He rubbed the back of his neck. "However, I would be lying if I said I didn't fear what you have to say."

I closed the distance between us and wound my arms around his neck. Barely a breath away, my eyes met his with a resulting calmness. "I love you, Trenton. My heart belongs to you, and nothing will ever change that."

He exhaled openly then cupped my neck with his hands. His thumbs rubbed my jaw tenderly. Placing a soft kiss on my top lip, his breath stirred my heart wildly when my name came forth. "Oh, Kat," he whispered.

"But," I added quietly. "We do need to talk." His emerald eyes flickered with an emotion that resembled his struggle from earlier. When he stepped back, I met his hands with mine in between us. "Do you recall the first time we had a dinner similar to this?"

He nodded. "You had just returned from New York."

I smiled to the sweet memory. "You told me that you canceled the sale of Charlock and shared Merritt's journal with me."

"I could never forget it." Trenton shook his head.

"A lot of truths came to light that night." I paused, "And I wondered if we repeated it, the result would be similar." I held his gaze. "I think you'll agree that we need to be open about anything and everything."

He squeezed my hands and nodded. "I promise. I'll answer anything you ask with complete honesty."

My eyes closed momentarily, then opened. "It's not only you who must be truthful. I have some things to say as well."

Surprise flashed across his features, but he quickly smoothed his face and pulled out my chair for me. "Might I go first?" He scooted his chair closer to mine.

I nodded.

"I must tell you, Kat," The earlier strength in Trenton's voice diminished. His eyes fastened to mine, and I saw how difficult this was for him. "I honestly don't know what happened between Justine and I."

I winced at her name. This conversation needed to happen, yet I still braced for the possibility of heartache.

"I was not fully honest when I said I never kissed her. I should've said I've never *willingly* or *consciously* kissed her. I've never wanted anything more than friendship with Justine, though I know she has always desired more." His forehead wrinkled. "What you overheard, was us talking about a night three years ago. A group of us met together to watch a championship match. I drank more than my fair share and somehow woke up the next morning in her bed. I don't recall anything . . . not kissing her, not—"

I held my breath and tears pricked behind my eyes. I promised myself to give him every opportunity to say whatever he needed to . . . even if it hurt.

He reached over the table. "Please take my hand."

I met it. His thumb rubbed my skin tenderly. "I can't change what happened, though I loathe to know the details. I can't change my past—a past that has some rather impish behavior, I'm afraid. But please know this, I will do everything in my power to prove my love to you every day forthwith."

His sincerity stirred my soul and my heart overflowed with love for this man. I met his eyes and the bind that drew us together magnified as if a tangible cord itself proved unbreakable. "I promise to do the same."

At that moment, Margaret appeared. The first course of our dinner rested securely in her hands. Trenton gasped with visible astonishment. Looking at me, he pointed to her. "What is she doing?"

Margaret rolled her eyes and lifted her chin. If she heard his question, she ignored it. "Mr. Gilford, Miss Shelton." She nodded as if she had serving experience, though I highly doubted she did. "Your *London Particular.*" She set the steaming bowls of ham hock and bacon soup before us and wiped her hands on the borrowed white apron tied around her hips.

I smiled wide. When Margaret insisted on serving us, I tried to deter her plan, but when she persisted in allowing us the utmost privacy away from any and all ears, I essentially agreed. She knew our only sure way to speak openly was if none of the staff or guests overheard our innately private conversation. Her astuteness never failed to surprise me.

Before she departed, Margaret winked in a way only I would have seen and smiled her approval.

Reaching for his spoon, Trenton tilted his head in my direction before he took his first bite. "Now what could you possibly have to confess to, Kat?"

I bit my bottom lip and glanced down, placing my napkin on my lap. "Well, for starters," I peered back over to him. "I've, um . . . crashed your car three times."

"Three?" He nearly choked on his food.

I winced. "Truthfully, only twice." As if that would make the admission easier. "Margaret did the third one."

"Margaret? She was driving my car?"

"I was teaching her how."

"In an $70,000 vehicle?" He shook his head.

I chuckled. "Maybe not one of my brightest moments, but you should've seen her face, it was priceless."

"Wait. Why wouldn't she know how to drive? She must be twenty-two, twenty-three?"

My lips parted, but nothing came out. Then before I could gather the courage to answer, he jumped to his next question. "How did I not know of or see this so-called damage?"

"Um," I grimaced. "Hennessey and I, kind of, have this arrangement with a mobile vehicle technician."

Trenton's mouth fell open, but his eyes lit up with a lightness I had missed. "Hennessey is in on this?"

I wrinkled my nose, though secretly my spirit soared, recognizing the playfulness of our relationship from before. Trenton tried hard to look upset but the creases next to his eyes gave him away.

"I'm sorry," I entreated. "I probably should buy your car from you."

He snickered out loud. "I have a better idea. How about I just give it to you as a wedding present."

"I would feel bad."

"It's either that or I will buy you a new one." He laughed out loud. "You can't drive my car anymore."

"Fine." I attempted to appear miffed, but my smile broke through.

Trenton leaned back, resting his elbow on the armrest. A half smile teased his lips while his fingers rubbed his chin. "Anything else I should know?"

As the night progressed and Trenton and I revealed everything, a deep connection transpired. Not that we hadn't already shared a special closeness, but our raw honesty allowed for us to reach a new level of trust and understanding.

After a couple of hours, Margaret brought out the last course of the night—a berry trifle dessert. Though the fruit and cream tempted me to indulge, I paused and gazed between the two of them. A thousand thoughts invaded my mind in a matter of seconds. Since the first moment Margaret appeared in the stables, her trusty pitchfork in hand, until now, standing before me with her ever so familiar arched brow—so much had transpired in the last nine days that it was hard for me to put the emotion I felt into words.

"Um, Trenton, there is one last thing I must confess."

He set his fork down and faced me. With the conversation we just had, there was certainly nothing that could surprise him . . . or so it seemed.

"You can tell me anything, Kat, and I mean *anything*." Though his words matched the intensity of his countenance, his eyes revealed a hair's breadth of hesitation.

I took a lengthy breath and grinned awkwardly. "Okay."

Margaret started to walk away. "No, Margaret, wait." I held my hand out to stop her as she spun around slowly. From the look on her face, it seemed as though she knew what was coming. "Please?"

I stole another breath. You would think that the similarities in this conversation to the one I'd had before with Trenton would ease its entry, but it didn't. "Trenton, Margaret is . . ." I hesitated. My throat suddenly grew very dry. I quickly took a sip of my drink. "She is, uh . . ."

Margaret placed one hand on her hip and huffed brashly. "I'm from the past, Mr. Gilford."

Trenton's eyes bounced between the two of us. He was clearly confused and waiting for further explanation. When one didn't come, he lifted his hands. "What does that mean exactly?"

"She's from Merritt's time." I blurted out.

His brows furrowed in continued uncertainty.

I reached for Merritt's journal that rested on the edge of the table. "Here, maybe this will help explain it better." Opening it to the pages I previously marked, I pointed to several specific entries. "Remember? These were the same writings you showed me back when you realized I was the Katharine from Merritt's accounts."

He blinked several times in blank recognition and took the book from my hands and read it.

I watched him as his eyes flowed down the page with varying degrees of measure.

23 August 1878.

Mum is in her element. The preparation for this year's ball is above remarkable.

Naturally, it will be the grandest event in the county once again. However, the most astounding affair occurred yesterday when Miss Katharine arranged for the four of us to retire from our labor momentarily and picnic in the country. It had been ages since we had that much time to relax and converse. Once Mum finally agreed to unwind, it was most enjoyable. The girls shared what they are learning in their studies and Mum was impressed with their increasing knowledge. I surprised them all when I presented the engagement ring I plan to present to Margaret the night of the ball. It's a stunning jewel, but pales in comparison to Miss Abbott's beauty.

"And this one . . ." I turned the page.

18 Oct, 1878

My first entry in two weeks. I cannot begin to tell you what has occurred. I fell off of Captain, my most esteemed horse. Thankfully, he did not experience any prolonged injury as I have. I was unconscious for an undetermined amount of time, and since my injuries were near fatal, the wedding plans were postponed. Miss Abbott returned to her family's residence while I rehabilitated. I would have preferred her presence at my side during this most burdensome time, but she had great difficulty seeing me in such a wounded state and vowed to return upon my recuperation. I fear complete recovery will never occur. I may always require the use of my walking cane.

At the time I awoke, Miss Abbott shared a horrifying recollection that has me quite perplexed. Her face bore the mark of a ghastly offense. She was bruised and bled from what she says was at the hands of Miss Katharine. Miss Katharine, the governess! Margaret relayed the details after my fall, insisting that Katharine attempted to assault me most disturbingly when Captain had not completed the task. Then, when Margaret attempted to protect me from further harm, she was attacked maliciously by Katharine. I am severely troubled by this disclosure; I have no knowledge to contradict its truthfulness. My conscience tells me this cannot be factual, knowing what I do about Miss Katharine, but unfortunately, she has left our employ. She is gone, and I have no inkling where I may find her.

His eyes flickered from me to Margaret, and his mouth opened several times to speak but words struggled to come forth. Laying the book down before him, he ran one hand down his face and rubbed his jaw.

Shaking his head, he glanced back over to Margaret. "I don't even know what to say." He released a loud exhale. "You're *that* Margaret?"

She had stood in the same stance this entire time and only shifted uncomfortably under his stare. Though she remained silent, her mouth tightened in a bow. This, I had come to know as her impatient face.

"This explains so much!" His hand slapped the table causing us both to jump at his exertion. He quickly held a hand up. "Sorry, I didn't mean for it to be that loud." His mind seemed to mentally recall all of his interactions with her throughout the week. "It's all starting to make sense."

I barked a laugh.

Margaret scowled.

"So, you . . ." His eyes lit up. "You time-traveled to the future. Here, here in this house?"

Margaret tensed, but nodded affirmatively.

"She fell the same way I did. Down the cellar steps."

He shook his head noticeably baffled. "When?"

"That first night. The night of the hag party." I gestured toward the house. "I thought I saw something strange in the hallway and left the dinner."

"I remember." His eyes flashed as if recollections came quickly. He tapped his forehead and pointed to me. "She was the person you were trying to help the morning of our ride and why the horses were left in the garden."

I nodded.

He glanced between us both, then his smile waned. "Wait, I thought you hated her?"

My own smile grew when my gaze fell upon Margaret. She had said nothing this entire time. When she met my eyes, a distinctive awareness sparked. Ten days ago, she undoubtedly claimed the title for the person I disliked the most on earth. Tonight, she was nowhere near that—tonight, she had become a sister.

"A lot has changed this week," I whispered.

Trenton shook his head again. "I have to say this is all really overwhelming."

Margaret's eyes lit, and she snapped in his direction. "For whom?"

He laughed easily. "Forgive me. I'm sure this is quite difficult for you, Margaret. Please, sit." He stood up and pointed to his chair. "Tell me everything."

She jutted out her chin. "No, thank you, sir, I have no intention of encroaching on your private assignation." She turned to me. "I will let you manage the colloquy without me, Kat." With that she walked out.

Once we were alone again, Trenton reclaimed his seat, and I shared every detail of what had occurred from the moment I crossed her path in the stables to today and visiting her relative.

The more I relived the experiences through my disclosure, the more the events took on a realistic milieu. I didn't leave anything out. I divulged Margaret's plan for the archery tournament, her first time wearing pants, her introduction to technology, and my personal favorite . . . her mother's butterfly stick pin miraculously returned to her. Throughout the entire revelation, Trenton remained speechless, outside of an occasional query. It was all so much to digest and once again, if I hadn't lived it, I might not have believed it myself, the whole experience was beyond extraordinary to be sure.

"So, what now?" He asked the question I'd been asking myself since the beginning.

"I don't know, I imagine she must go back." In an instant, the strangest thought entered my mind—*am I okay with her leaving?* I had grown so accustomed to her being around, that the thought of her absence somehow generated sadness.

"Does she want to go back?"

I lifted one shoulder. "I believe she's torn. She's in love with a man back there, Jacob Hardy, but her father and brother refuse to let her marry him. She has few liberties, if any."

"That can't be promising." Trenton bit his bottom lip. His mind seemed to be spinning solutions as fast as mine.

My mouth fell open. "I think I have an idea." I didn't wait for Trenton to respond. "Merritt could help." I had touched on the thought previously, but now calculated the possibility with more credence. "If I could somehow let him know, he would be more than willing, I'm sure of it."

"One moment, Kat. I'm trying to wrap my head around this." Trenton took a sip of his drink. "You're talking about asking a man who has been dead for a hundred years if he can help?"

"He isn't dead if she goes back to the same time."

Trenton reached for my hand. His touch instantly soothed. "What are our assurances she would even get back to her own time if she fell down the stairs?"

Tears built in the corners of my eyes as I considered the risks. "Nothing. We have no guarantees of anything."

"Then maybe she should stay here. We could help her."

I pulled Trenton's hand to my chest and squeezed. "You would do that?"

"Of course." He smiled, appearing slightly confused that I would question him. "We could set her up so she would be comfortable. She could pursue a life of freedom, maybe marry and have children without being forced by her father."

My heart swelled at his kind considerations, grateful that I had found the courage to share her predicament. It was a burden that neither she nor I should bear alone. Knowing what kind of life awaited her in the past, I hoped she would choose to stay, but I also understood the stakes of losing the one you love. I sighed. "Whatever the choice, it must be hers."

Trenton seemed deep in concentration. Silence embraced us momentarily as his eyes pierced mine. "And what of your choice, Miss Shelton?" He stood up and came to my side, then knelt with one knee. As both of his hands reached for mine, he beheld me with loving trepidation. "Will you still do me the honor and marry me tomorrow?"

I smiled without a second of hesitation. "Yes, Mr. Gilford." I wrapped my arms lovingly around his neck and drew him in. "I honestly want nothing more."

Chapter 38

Saturday 21 May 2011

Last night's dinner with Trenton went exactly how I hoped. We were inseparable, rarely interrupted, and talked late into the night. Once I returned to my room, I realized this was the strongest I'd felt all week. Now, *nothing* came between us—our night of confessions and truths had brought a wave of emotion from good to challenging, but in the end, the affirmations were cleansing.

Taking a deep breath, I smiled upon my circumstances. No matter what my future held, I would no longer be alone. Trenton and I would be embarking on our new married life with no questions and no doubts.

When morning came, it was as if I awakened from a dream—one of those curious moments where you're unclear of what exactly filled your mind while asleep but felt peace and serenity regardless. There was no nightmare, anger, pain, or revenge. The only thing lacking perfection was Trenton beside me, but after tonight, even that would be amended.

I peered around the room. With the sunshine pouring in, my prayers were answered. *No rain.* The dresses arrived a couple of days ago without a hitch and all hung in garment bags scattered around my bedroom—Mom's, Kelly's, Maria's, Margaret's, and mine. Today's singular significance still hadn't quite sunk in.

I rolled over to find a scribbled note atop Margaret's pillow. We hadn't spoken after dinner and since my return had come so late—more like early in the morning—she must've recognized my need to sleep in.

> *Kat,*
> *I have given the directive to leave you undisturbed today with only a breakfast tray arriving at noon.*
> *We will be in promptly at four to assist and ready you properly for this most wonderful day.*
> *Margaret*

Peeking at my watch, breakfast was surely over . . . it would be more like lunch by the time I ate, though as noted, my tray arrived precisely on time and only minutes after putting my robe on.

"Thank you, Gretchen." I smiled at her as she set it down on the table.

Her bright eyes danced as she reached for my hands. "Are you utterly chuffed?"

My excitement easily matched hers. "More than ever."

"I can't wait to see you all dolled up." She winked. "Do you need anything?"

I glanced around the room. "No, I believe everything is covered, but thank you."

"I'll return in an hour for the tray." She squeezed my fingers and giggled. "What a day it's going to be."

I closed the door behind her and eyed the tray. The presentation on the silver platter had clearly been arranged by someone who knew my love for Charlock. *Which could be anyone by now.* Three stunning yellow blooms wrapped in a deep blue ribbon, graced the meal. Their floral scent and appeal more than surpassed the smell of the bacon, if that were possible.

After nibbling on a piece of toast and sipping the orange juice, I found the rumblings in my stomach prevented me from eating anything else, regardless of how tempting the food looked.

Pacing anxiously around the room, I found it much more refreshing to have the fluttering in my stomach, abuzz with delight, rather than the serious torments my body had endured this past week. Nevertheless, I found it difficult to focus on anything, except what lay ahead, now only a few short hours away.

Glancing at my watch, the wedding was set to begin precisely at seven o'clock, right when the glowing descent of the sun will be challenged by the dazzling lights on the trees. Thankfully, when my thoughts finally settled on Trenton, they brought an element of tranquility with them. I couldn't stop the smile that formed on my lips knowing in a little over five hours, he would officially be my husband.

After my invigorating shower and before my friends were scheduled to arrive, I sat down at the small corner desk in my room and retrieved a paper and pen. Since expressing my desire to help Margaret last night with Trenton, I had considered the words I would write with much sincerity. Whether Margaret ever delivered this letter to Merritt or not was irrelevant . . .she would have it regardless.

To my dearest friend
Mr. Merritt Gilford,
First and foremost, let me tell you how much I miss you and your family. I think of you, Joanne, Lizzy, and Abby quite often. You may never know how much your influence changed me. Your kindness and love helped to heal some very open wounds on my heart,

and I fear I had never told you thank you for that.

I am writing this letter to you from a distant place with a special request. Recently, I crossed paths with Margaret Abbott and surprisingly it was not a terrible reunion. In fact, it might shock you to know we have become good friends. But as one of my friends, she is in dire need of help that I cannot offer. I am no longer within reach to assist her, so I turn to you, my dear friend. You were correct in your assumptions regarding Margaret's father and brother. They are not good men and intend to use Margaret in a way that would only benefit them financially. They have no intention of considering her feelings or future. Perhaps you may already be aware of the arrangement for her to meet Lord Gentry. I understand he is not an honorable man and has little regard for women.

I am not entirely sure what you can do to help her, and I know it may seem unusual for me to ask, but Margaret needs your help. I have done all I can, and I beg you, as my sweet friend, to help her seek out the man she truly loves, a man by the name of Jacob Hardy. He is a horse breeder by trade, and a good, honest man, but has been driven away by her family.

Please, please do what you can to help her locate him and through your influence and position somehow help them reunite and (if it be their wish) to marry as well, even if it means an elopement. She recognizes the risks, and I'm certain she will do whatever you ask of her. Please I beg of your assistance. I would not have asked if I didn't already know your heart and goodness. You are a great man, Merritt, helping many who cannot help themselves.

Congratulations on your wedding. I cannot tell you how pleased I was to hear you have wed my beautiful friend, Joanne. Give her, Lizzy, and Abby my love. I miss you all dearly, but please know I am happy and content in my life and future. In fact, I myself, am to be married soon. I have found a gentleman who is much like you—kind, generous and loving. His name is Trenton. And in a strange twist of fate, there is much about him that reminds me of you. I wish you the very best.

Your friend, Miss Katharine Shelton

I folded the letter in quarters and titled the outside, *Mr. Merritt Gilford.* Since I had only suggested contacting Merritt for help, I had not yet informed Margaret of this intent, so I left it on the desk for later. If she decided it was time for her to return, I would be sure to have her carry it on her body before she fell.

With an hour before my friends were due to arrive, I settled myself down on the settee and opened my book. It was not the same without Trenton's smooth vocals and charming accent but allowed me to become immersed in someone else's trials for a time.

"Knock, knock." The door swung wide open, and Kelly and Maria entered, each holding an end of a dressing table.

"Oh, let me clear an area." Rearranging the furniture to allow for two dressing tables and two full-length mirrors was a comical experience, but what really brought forth my biggest laugh was when Maria emptied a case filled with hair tools and products onto the bed. . . most assuredly one of every type ever made.

"Did you bring all this with you?" I arched a brow Maria's direction.

Kelly paused and answered for her. "What do you think?"

I laughed out loud. Of course, she did, she doesn't go anywhere without her glamour arsenal.

Upon strict bridal guidelines, according to my friends, one does not manage one's own hair for your own wedding, so once Margaret and my mom arrived with Anabelle in tow, the fun was sure to begin.

First my hair was curled, then the sides were interwoven into several relaxed twists and folded up into a loose chignon at the nape of my neck. I watched through the vanity mirror as Margaret moved naturally around me, tugging free several wisps of hair, both in the back, and a few bordering my face. My forehead creased in response, knowing she had used the services of Anabelle her entire time at Charlock.

"What?" she shrugged her shoulders with a grin. "I'm completely capable of managing one strand of hair."

I laughed.

Anabelle then took the curling iron and arched them to perfect position. Kelly took her turn next, tucking a few clusters of baby's breath blossoms into the folds of my hair at the back and my mother turned my chair around and held a hand mirror up, so I could follow the progress. It wasn't until everyone stepped back that I realized they had finished.

"Breathtaking." Anabelle chimed as she spun me gently around for all to see. A chill slid down my arms. The realization that today was my wedding day hadn't quite hit me this powerfully until now.

I'm getting married, today!

Those thoughts stunned me silent. There was a time that I genuinely believed it would never happen. Looking back, it was hard for me to imagine I could love someone as deeply and thoroughly as Jeff, yet if anything, the heart has proven time and time again, it holds no bounds.

"Time for your makeup." Maria announced, pulling me from my musings while opening yet a different large case.

"What didn't you bring with you to England, Maria?" I chuckled.

She wrinkled her nose. "My car."

Since Maria was unquestionably the beautifying expert, having worked at a high-end cosmetic counter for most of her college years, Anabelle took advantage of the time and assisted the others with their hair—however they wished it done.

"You have such great skin tone, Kat." Maria brushed a light layer of powder on my checks and forehead. Nobody understood tones, shades, and color like she did. Thankfully, she respected my desire to find the right balance between simple and bridal elegance, and once she was finished, I gazed into the mirror, astounded at the transformation.

Staring at every inch of my face with critical precision, she smiled wide. "You're the most beautiful bride I have ever seen." Tossing her make-up brush back into the case, she shook her head with attitude. "And I don't give compliments easily."

I laughed at her honesty. *This was true.*

Next, it was time for the dress. Kelly, Maria, and Margaret each held a section of the fabric and carefully guided it over my head and down my body, being extra careful not to touch my hair. My mom directed its success from the side.

"Oh, that's good." She'd say one minute. "Oh, no, no, careful, it will snag." The next. I couldn't stop my smile from forming as I watched the reflection of each woman's various personality emerge through their facial features.

Once the skirt reached the ground, they took turns joining the incessant line of buttons on my lower back and behind. After an adequate amount of nipping and tucking, I stood, once more, in my wedding gown before the most important women in my life.

My skin rippled with goose bumps and my heart pounded with undeniable joy recognizing the depth of this one moment—this one tick of time, never to be relived in exactness ever again.

"Oh, Kat." My mother squeezed my shoulders from behind as she viewed me through the full-length mirror. "You are lovely."

In the brief moment our eyes met, we were both on the brink of tears. She had spent a lifetime worrying over me, and I'm sure, wondering if I would ever be the same. In truth, I never would be. Some events in our lives don't ever leave us . . . they simply become part of us.

"Thank you, Mom." I placed a hand over hers and squeezed. "Thank you for everything."

"Now, don't cry and mess up my work." Maria teased and held out a tissue, but I could see she was dabbing another one on her own cheeks.

I turned around to face the rest of my friends as they stood back and glowed with admiration.

"It's even more perfect than I remembered." I brushed my hand down the front of my bodice and turned slightly toward the mirror to see the back.

"Trenton is going to go nuts when he sees you." Kelly cried as she located my shoes.

"I hope so," I whispered.

She rolled her eyes. "No doubt." Then slipped the simple white slippers onto my feet. I opted early on to avoid heels in the garden. If anyone were to make a mess of things moving down the aisle, such as a stiletto stuck in the mud, it would be me.

"Have you seen the gardens yet?" My question went out to anyone that could answer as my eyes flitted to the window. The sun had begun its descent. Though I had seen over fifty weddings in various forms at Charlock, Felicia, the wedding planner, assured me ours would be unprecedented.

"Yes, they're exquisite." Margaret stepped to my side. "I have never been privy to anything quite like it."

My mother nodded. "There are more lights out there than half of England, I believe. The whole garden is lit up and the arch . . ." Mom placed a hand to her heart. "The sight is simply remarkable." My eyes fell upon her warmly once more as I reached for her hand and held on.

"Thank you all for being here," I said as I continued the fight to keep my makeup moisture-free.

"We wouldn't be anywhere else." Kelly was the first to hug me, but everyone else followed shortly after.

"Okay, Kat." Mom reached for her garment bag. "We need to get dressed now, but Margaret will be here. Let us know if you need anything. And Margaret . . ." She pointed sternly toward the door. "Do not, under any circumstances, let Trenton anywhere near her."

Her eyebrows rose.

"He can't see the bride before the wedding, it's bad luck."

"Ohhh." She grinned wickedly. "You have my word, Mrs. Shelton. I shall not relinquish."

When the door closed, Margaret returned to my side. Her eyes regarded me tenderly. "I have never beheld a bride as enchanting as you, Kat."

I smiled in return. "It's because you haven't gotten married yet. You're bound to be breathtaking yourself."

I followed her eyes as she lowered them to her hands. Though her lips still turned upward, there was an element of sadness in her composure.

I placed my hand on her arm. "Are you alright?"

She lifted her chin and smiled wide again, only this time she held up what she was toying with in her hands.

"Would you wear this for me?" The butterfly stick pin was pinched between her fingers.

I regarded her. A softness rarely witnessed from her, emerged. Her eyes clearly conveyed the depth of how much it would mean to her if I did.

"Yes, of course." I squeezed her arm. "I will wear it for the ceremony, as long as I can give it back to you afterward."

"Agreed." She turned me around and nestled it into my chignon. It was most likely meant to be worn on fabric, but it fit nicely in my hair. Only the wings could be seen through a cluster of baby breath.

"Thank you, Margaret." I held both her hands in front of me. "Thank you for being here."

"You are most welcome." She embraced me gently.

I chuckled lightly, wondering what Lizzy would have thought seeing us here together like this. "Okay, get dressed." I cried, once again forcing the tears back. "I can't wait to see your dress on you."

She smiled wide and went into the lavvy to change.

When she emerged, my mouth separated on its own accord. Between her dress, and Anabelle's hair magic, Margaret appeared as if she stepped off the page of a glamour magazine—she was gorgeous and she knew it—placing a hand on her hip, it almost appeared as if she struck a pose as she walked.

"Wow, Margaret." I whistled to her broad smile. "Jonah will not be able to think of anything but you, tonight."

Her smile faltered and her eyes fell to the floor.

"What?" I gripped her wrist lightly to get her to look back up at me.

She lifted her head. "Nothing. All is well." The smile reappeared; however, it never reached her eyes.

"Look, Margaret," I tried to get the real smile back. "When I told my friends that you had nowhere to go while we were on our honeymoon, they all offered for you to go home with them. Kelly lives in her own apartment in California. Maria has an extra bedroom at her place in Arizona and my mom even said you can go back to New York with them."

"New York?" Margaret gasped. She most likely heard the same stories Merritt had about how uncivilized the city was.

I laughed. "It's modern, much like London. You can go to the theater, shopping, sightseeing. I would let you stay here, but Trenton's parents will be here during the month we're gone, and I wouldn't make anyone suffer through that." I tried to get her to look at me. "Trenton has also offered to pay for you to stay in London if that's what you prefer. He'll cover any expenses to make you comfortable in any part of the world."

She smiled. "That is very generous and kind of him . . . of them all." Margaret's eyes took on a faraway look, one that I was all too familiar with.

"But you're unsure, aren't you?"

She closed her eyes and when she opened them again, several tears slipped down her cheeks. "I miss my home. Not so much my dad and brother, but everything else." She sniffled. "I miss my time—my extravagant gowns, handsome carriages, intimate soirees, elaborate balls . . . but most of all, I miss Jacob."

I dabbed a tissue on her cheeks. "I'm sorry, Margaret" I put the tissue down and held her hand. "Please tell me how I can help? I'll do anything."

She shrugged her shoulders. "Truthfully, I know of nothing to alter my circumstances other than what we've discussed." She took a deep breath. "But let's not dwell on it for now, it's your wedding day, after all."

I lifted my chin. "Regardless, when the wedding is over, you and I, and Trenton, will sit down and come up with a plan. Whatever you decide, we'll help. I promise."

She smiled. "I believe you." And this time it reached her eyes.

A soft knock on the door brought my mother inside. "It's time, Kat." She let out a small squeal. "Your future is about to begin, sweetheart."

I took a deep breath and grinned. "I am quite ready."

Chapter 39

It was nothing short of a miracle that I made it to the back doors of the veranda on two feet, my legs shook so much. Dad met me inside while the wedding party lined up on the terrace. He looked handsome in his black tuxedo, lavender tie, and white *Calla Lily* boutonniere. When he reached for me with both hands, he held them tight. "You're lovely, Peanut." He kissed my cheek then handed me my simple orchid bouquet. When he faced me again, his eyes were filled with tears. "It's your time to shine, kiddo."

As the wedding march began and the bridal party stepped forward couple by couple, I stole another deep breath and waited for the announcement to come.

The booming voice of the pastor surfaced loud and clear. "Please, all rise for the bride."

This was our cue. Hennessey and Gretchen opened the doors wide and waited for our exit. When Dad held out his arm, I wrapped mine within and gave him a squeeze. "I love you, Dad."

"Love you, Kat."

From this position, I could not see the guests, the arch or anything else other than the lights twinkling on every available branch, but the sight still stirred my soul. A small string quartet played the music on our approach—its gentle chords matched my every step along the pathway.

Once in view, I peered anxiously past the chairs, guests, and the rose petals that lined the aisle, until my eyes found Trenton. Dressed in a charcoal gray tuxedo suit, light gray vest, and a handsome lavender tie—he took my breath away.

My father leaned in and kissed my cheek once more and reached out and shook Trenton's hand before passing it to mine.

Though I was entirely aware others were nearby, my world only beheld Trenton. As he faced me and held my hands, everything but him blurred into oblivion. Even as the pastor spoke words of love and affirmation, I lost myself in the moment, only rousing to attention when I was asked—apparently for a second time—if I took Trenton for my husband.

"Yes! Yes, I do." I cried, to a scattering of chuckles. Trenton's mouth curved wide showing his straight teeth and his amusement in the situation.

"Thank you," he mouthed, evidently relieved.

I wrinkled my nose and tried much harder to pay attention from that point on, but to my defense, Trenton remained a fine-looking distraction.

"You may now kiss the bride."

Without hesitation, Trenton reached one hand around my waist and pulled me against him. His lips easily found mine in a sound kiss to an explosion of cheers.

"I present to you the newest Mr. and Mrs. Trenton Gilford."

As we faced our family and friends, Trenton raised our clasped hands high between us and pumped them in the air. "We did it, love." He whispered to me.

"Yes, we did." Husband and wife. *We are husband and wife!*

The realization of the truth to those words pounded steadily to my rapid heartbeat as we moved down the aisle and to a different part of the garden to greet our guests. The whole moment seemed so surreal.

Mom and Dad were the first to descend upon us and their excitement nearly bowled us over. Mr. Gilford, Trenton's father, came next and showed more interest in our exchange than ever before. Though Mrs. Gilford never met my eyes directly, she congratulated us without a smirk on her face and, in hindsight, that was quite the accomplishment. Grandfather stepped up next and, in his regal manner, lifted my hand and kissed my knuckles. Bowing slightly, he welcomed me to the family and gave his grandson a robust hug.

Hugs and kisses were shared with the bridal party and each of Trenton's friends took their turn giving me sound advice on managing their now married mate.

When I faced Margaret, I slipped the butterfly pin from my hair and pressed it into her palm. "Thank you for letting me borrow this."

She clasped her hand closed. "It meant a lot to me, Kat. *Thank you.*"

I leaned in and hugged her tightly. "You are a wonderful friend." Then I kissed her cheek.

Her mouth parted as she touched her skin. Who would have ever guessed how much I would grow to care for this woman? Her eyes followed mine until I was tugged the opposite direction. Her hand swiftly reached over and clutched my wrist bringing me to a stop before her once more.

She threw her arms around me and held tight. "Thank you for showing me how to love." When we released, tears flowed easily down her cheeks.

The next couple of hours passed as if it were mere minutes. Congratulations came in all forms. And to my special delight, Miss Ellie Abbott arrived on the arm of Mrs. Henry. Nearly as quickly as they appeared, I endeavored to reacquaint her with our sweet grandfather. The two hardly separated after that, seemingly engaged in a most diverting conversation.

"*Whit a spacial nicht, lassie.*" A familiar voice surprised me from behind. I turned to face a fully embellished hat with nearly as many flowers adorning it as were planted in the gardens. Peering below the brim, I found the loving eyes of Miss Campbell appear.

"Pauline! I'm so glad you made it."

"*Aye, bonny deary, I wouldn't hae missed tis fur tae wurld.*" She embraced me then shook a stern finger in my direction. "*Ah knew yer be sometin' braw.*"

I laughed. "You aren't surprised things turned out this way?"

"*Och! Naw wee bit.*"

She turned to Trenton as he leaned down to hug his former curator. The one he had confessed was responsible for hiring me.

"*Yer merit tae bonny lass, Boy*!" She patted his cheek like a child.

He towered over her petite frame, but his voice rang loud. "Yes, I married her, Miss Campbell." He shot me a teasing look. "Though I'm not sure she knows what she's gotten herself into."

Pauline laughed out loud, kissed our cheeks, then said her goodbyes, or what I assumed was a goodbye. "*Lang may yer lum reek.*"

As the hours carried on, we laughed, visited, ate amazing foods courtesy of Helen and Laura, and enjoyed every moment of our celebration. When it came time to cut the luxurious cake, Trenton was a perfect gentleman and spared me the embarrassment of frosting up my nose . . . for the first bite. The second turned into something akin to an icing snowball fight.

"Mind if I steal your bride?" Kelly chuckled. "I think we need to get her presentable again."

Trenton grinned and swiped a chunk of cake off my cheek. "Certainly, but only for a moment."

She wrapped her arm through mine and led me to the nearest washroom.

"Thanks, Kelly." I laughed. "I hardly need dried cake in my hair for the rest of the night."

She smiled and handed me a wet wipe for my face. Thankfully, she carried a mini makeup kit in her purse. I hadn't thought that far in advance. After she fixed my makeup, hair and cleared any remnants of pastry off my dress, she stood behind and wrapped her arms around me.

"Kat, I'm so proud of you."

I glanced at her through the reflection and exhaled. "There were times, Kelly, I wasn't sure I would make it."

"Same here—" She chortled and moved to the side. "—But you have always impressed me with your fortitude."

"I'm not only referring to this week, but before . . . you know when I couldn't see past the grief."

She licked her lips and sighed. "When you called me from the top of Flatiron after Jeff's death . . .you scared me."

A few random tears filled my eyes. Sometimes there are moments that will never leave us. I bit the inside of my cheek. "It was the hardest call I've ever made in my life."

"You chose *life* that day." The tears that trailed her cheek mixed with mine "And look at where it has led you." She leaned back and smiled.

"Thank you, Kelly. Thank you for always being there for me."

"And I always will be, but now, now you have someone else that will be by your side for the rest of your life."

A knock sounded on the door.

"Our dance has been announced, love. Are you ready?"

The bride and groom's first dance.

Kelly swung the door wide open. "Go, you wild lovebirds. This is what we've all been waiting for." She winked at me as Trenton held out his hand and brought me to his side.

Once outside and back in the garden, he took me in his arms and the music for *Somebody's Me* by Enrique Iglesias slowly materialized. Finding my place next to him, my heart thumped in an indispensable rhythm. This, right here, was the final puzzle piece—fitting seamlessly into my blank void and erasing all evidence of emptiness. I was complete.

Trenton's chin nestled against my neck as he whispered the words of the song in my ear. Everything about this night was perfect. Even when the large window from the library came into view, the vision of the woman who used to stand there on the other side and grieve faded before me. I blinked away the tears, closing a chapter in my life that no longer held me bound.

I drew my head back and moved my arms from Trenton's shoulders to his face. With a long loving kiss, I began anew.

As the night dwindled down, I searched out my friends to thank them for their role in this night and my life. It could not have gone as flawlessly without them. Maria and Hastings sipped wine from a secluded table, snuggling and whispering. Kelly and Marlowe danced, and Jonah . . . Jonah stood under the bough of a willowy aspen. His hand cupped a champagne chute, but he drank alone.

My head whipped nervously around. "Jonah?" When he stared in my direction there was no question, he wore the look of heartbreak. "Where is she?"

His lips quivered. "She's gone."

"What do you mean gone?"

His stare pierced me with a deliberate gaze, but he said nothing. *Could he possibly know?*

Many of the guests had since departed, so despite my frantic search for Margaret, it didn't take long for me to locate Trenton instead. When I reached him conversing with his uncle, I couldn't mask the trepidation in my voice. "May I speak to you for a moment?"

Uncle Clarence dipped his head and excused himself. I pursed my lips, fighting the tears that had already built in the corners of my eyes.

When Trenton gazed upon me, his expression clearly spoke of compassion for he knew *something*. He reached for my hand. "Will you come inside with me?"

I nodded. The sudden somberness of the moment stole any calm I claimed from earlier in the night. Trenton wrapped one arm securely around me as he led me straight into the library. Unsure why he chose this particular location, other than for the privacy it afforded, I glanced around before I was drawn back to his features. We were alone. A hint of sadness surfaced in his countenance. I lifted my hand to his brow and brushed his forehead tenderly as if I could brush his sorrow away as well. *What hurt lies behind this perfect face?* I wondered. His lips pulled tight, as if he struggled to say his next words.

"What's wrong?" I whispered. A small stir in my chest began to rise with this unusual demeanor.

He shook his head, then his eyes flickered toward the nearby alcove. I followed his line of sight. My heart thudded in my chest. "No." Lifting my wedding skirt, I rushed to the corner. The cellar door hung open. Sputtered breaths came in between my words as tears easily sprung forth. "No, no please no."

Trenton came behind me.

"Where is she?" I cried. "Where's Margaret?"

I went to step down when Trenton caught me around the waist and pulled me against his chest. I could feel his heart pounding as fast as mine. "She didn't want you to see her go."

"When?" I mumbled.

"She sought me out when you went to clean up with Kelly."

Muffled cries stung my throat. I buried my face against his shoulder. "I didn't get to say goodbye."

Trenton rubbed my back for several seconds before he held me out to face him. His eyes hurt for me. Wiping my tears with his thumbs, he whispered, "She feared having the strength to leave if she saw you."

My nose tingled. "Are you certain she's gone?"

"Yes." Trenton cupped my neck. "After she fell, I checked the stairs, the room, everything. She's gone."

I turned to leave. "But she didn't get the letter. How will she make it all alone?"

Trenton held me close as we walked back to the center of the library. I stopped abruptly. "I wrote a letter to Merritt." Alarm filled my chest again. "I left it on the desk in my room. I didn't have a chance to tell her about it."

Trenton held me in his arms. "She has it, Kat. She showed me. She also wanted me to tell you thank you, thank you for everything."

I buried my head in his shoulder and couldn't stop the tears from flowing. "Do you think she returned to the same night? The night of Merritt and Joanne's wedding?"

"I hope so." He rubbed my back again. "Don't worry. From what I've seen, she left a stronger person than when she arrived. She'll be okay."

"How will I know for sure?" I lifted my skirt again. "I need to get to a computer." My mind suddenly went into overdrive. I desperately needed to know what happened to her.

"Actually . . ." Trenton fell into stride next to me and pointed up the stairs versus down the hallway to the office. His countenance showed an unusual mixture of curiosity and determination. "Follow me, love."

I took his hand as he led me upstairs and into one of the family bedchambers, Abagale's old room. He pushed the door open and flicked on the light.

"What are we doing in here?" I glanced down the hallway before I stepped inside. Its emptiness assured me that the family was still celebrating in the gardens . . . everyone except the bride and groom, of course.

"Grandfather gave me permission to enter earlier when I told him I needed to retrieve something."

"I don't understand. Why are we here?"

He smiled and went to the panel where Abby hid her dolls—the very same place my ring necklace was returned to me. When he popped open the panel, he reached carefully inside and retrieved a folded paper. He smiled widely and handed it to me.

The label addressed my name . . .

Miss Katharine Shelton or might I say Mrs. Trenton Gilford.

I gasped. The sheet of paper was yellowed, covered in dust and the ink somewhat faded. I turned to Trenton for an explanation.

He smiled. "Before Margaret departed, I showed her this nook and asked only one favor of her, that she let us know how her life fared. I'm guessing this letter will be our answer."

I went to the nearest settee and sat down as Trenton took his place by my side. I carefully unfolded the parchment.

To my dear friend Kat,

Today is the 15th of June 1902. It has been twenty-four years since I returned and yes, I returned the very night of Merritt Gilford's wedding only several hours later following my fall and another dreadful headache. Fortunately, my father and brother had already returned home. I assume this occurred when they were unable to locate me at Charlock, presuming I left on my own accord.

Kat, please forgive me for being intrusive, but I discovered your letter to Merritt on the desk as we readied for your wedding. I read it and placed it within my clothing. I thank you dearly for your words. They were the very strength I needed to accomplish my feat. They also gave me the courage to find a moment to speak to the bride and groom privately.

Just as you insisted, both Merritt and Joanne were kind and generous to me. Once they read your letter, they immediately set forth to assist, even going as far as providing shelter for me until Jacob was located a fortnight later. As fate would have it, I successfully eluded both my father and brother for many years.

Jacob and I wed on the 10th of March 1879, and with the Gilford's assistance, we purchased property in Bristol where my husband continued his occupational trade. We have two beautiful children, Jacob Jr. who is eighteen, and Katharine who is fifteen and she is every bit as lovely as the woman she is named after—you my dear friend. Thank you, Kat for giving me the courage to follow my heart. If it weren't for you, I would not have found the happiness I am proffered.

When Mr. Trenton Gilford asked that I write to inform you of my life, I believed it to be an odd request given the distance of our time, but acquiesced. I apologize it has taken me this many years to write of my progress, but as I put this to paper, it is quite possible you won't even find it for many years to come. This is all quite overwhelming to puzzle together. Jacob knows of my time journey, but like you have cautioned me, it is an experience few will understand.

I have struggled to wait patiently for some of the inventions to come forth that I witnessed in your day, though they may very well not happen in my lifetime. I know one day, my children or grandchildren will be riding in cars and airplanes and taking showers instead of baths. I do miss the ease of instantaneous warm water and you might be pleased to learn I have found a way to blend my own fruit drink though it is not quite what you might consider to be a smoothie. And just between us, and Jacob of course, I have worn breeches a time or two and find them quite comfortable.

Though I know little of the parameters of time travel, I have shared some of the foreknowledge I learned on the computer regarding horses with my beloved. Jacob has used some of this wisdom in his horse trade and it has become a profitable venture. He is now considered to be one of the finest breeders in all of Gloucestershire.

Tonight, we are here at Charlock Manor to celebrate the wedding of Merritt and Joanne's oldest son, Mr. Merritt Frederick Gilford. I found a moment after the ceremony to slip into Abagale's old room (unused now that she is married and a mother herself) and place a missive in the very place Mr. Gilford asked me to. He said you would be anxiously forlorn without news of my existence.

Fear not, sweet Kat, I am alive, well, and exceedingly happy thanks to you and to the goodness of those around me.

To your own future, I wish you both the very best. Perhaps our paths shall cross again one day.

With love and regards,
Mrs. Jacob Hardy.

I read it again, only this time with not as many tears blurring the words. *Margaret found her Jacob!* She found her happiness, and I could not have imagined a more wonderful outcome.

Silence lingered as we descended the main stairs. Though it came with a touch of peace, I marveled at the complexities.

Pausing on the mezzanine below the portrait that played a significant role in my life, I faced Trenton. "Thank you for asking her to do this. I wouldn't have been able to stop worrying about her."

The warmth of his hands transferred to mine the moment he held them. Leaning down, he encouraged me to meet his eyes. "I know she has become one of your dearest friends. I'm grateful she listened." He grinned. "And I'm sorry she's gone."

I smiled up at him with a sense of contentment that instantly flooded my soul. Though this week splintered in every wayward direction possible, it ultimately became the most profound experience since my own time travel . . . and much like the result of that journey, I am changed because of another.

Trenton cupped my face tenderly. "Thank you for marrying me."

I wrapped my arms around his neck and pressed my forehead against his. "You are everything to me. Thank you for taking a chance on me."

"A chance, Mrs. Gilford?" He chuckled. His breath warmed my lips. "I'm nothing without you, love."

Then kissed me *thoroughly*.

Epilogue

"I'm certain I saw someone come in here." Trenton winked in my direction as we tiptoed into the library. A childish giggle floated up from the direction of the desk.

"Did you hear that?" I smiled his way and moved toward the bookshelves." I think it came from over here." I glanced behind the pillar with the Shakespeare bust. "Nope, nothing here."

He bent down to the fireplace and looked up the chimney. "Maybe in here." Then stood and dusted off his pants. "Certainly not there, either."

I peered over to the alcove and the bookcase that now covered the fated cellar door. We had once considered sealing the door entirely shut but feared the thought that someone would be stuck down there if they fell from a different time and had no outlet. It was strange to think of that room as some sort of time travel portal, offering a glimpse into another era, past or future.

My curiosity piqued over the possibility that others may have experienced a fall in time but kept silent, fearing the consequence of sharing such an ordeal. In the end, we opted for the assurance that nobody from *our* family could fall down the stairs or vanish, so a bookshelf was crafted specifically to hide the door from any inquisitive eyes. Now, only Trenton and I and a hand full of staff knew of its existence.

Another giggle surfaced.

"Maybe here?" I peered behind a large tapestry against the wall. "Or here?" I looked underneath the sofa.

Trenton clapped his hands together. "Well, love, I guess we'll have to go on the boat ride without them then."

"Nooo!" Two little bodies popped up from beneath the antique desk.

Abby's curly brown pigtails bounced in the sunlight as it streamed through the back window. Her petite five-year-old form could hardly contain her excitement. "Don't leave us!" She cried.

Merritt launched easily into Trenton's arms. "Me too! Me too!" He patted his father's scruffy jaw. "Me too, Daddy!" Trenton nuzzled our youngest child with a warm tenderness. Even at three, he was the spitting image of his dad—dark wavy hair and bold green eyes.

"Are Grandpa and Grandma coming?" Abby asked.

"I believe they are on their way here."

"Let's go outside to the veranda and wait for them." Trenton suggested.

Abby grabbed my hand and pulled me easily through the house. Once we stepped through the back doors, more squeals of delight burst around us.

Merritt wiggled out of Trenton's arms and rushed joyfully into Grandpa's. "Papa, go boats."

"Yes!" My dad swung him high and caught him as he giggled hard.

Abby rushed forward "My turn. Swing me too, Papa."

Trenton wrapped an arm around my waist as we watched the kids move giddily from my mom to my dad. "Who would have ever thought . . ." He chuckled.

I peered at him warily. "They are not the grandparents who have surprised me the most."

A door flew open behind us. "Where's my hug?" Juliana appeared, tossing her handbag to the ground, and freeing her hands in preparation for a little body to fill them. Abby squealed and ran to her grandma. I turned to face the woman who, at one time, could have been sculpted from ice more than the malleable warmth that emitted from her now.

"Glad you could make it, mum, father." Trenton greeted his parents and shook his father's hand.

"I would not have missed this for the world." His mom laughed as she snuggled the two littles in her lap. "It's not every day your granddaughter turns five."

Mr. Gilford reached out and took a wiggly Merritt into his arms and lifted him onto his shoulders. Merritt's titters over being taller than the rest of us could surely be heard throughout the grounds.

"Okay, Abby." Trenton pointed to her. "It's your turn to be in Mema and Papa Shelton's boat and Merritt, son, you go with Grandma and Grandpa Gilford this time." Trenton paused and turned in my direction "And you…" He pulled me close and nuzzled his chin into my neck. "You, love, are with me."

Juliana clucked her tongue. "And don't get *lost* this time, Trenton." She raised a skeptical eyebrow. "Or we'll just have our picnic without you."

Trenton's roguish grin emerged. "Why do you think we enjoy having both grandparents here for a visit?" He winked at me. "I quite like getting lost with my wife."

My mom laughed out loud. "The truth comes out."

I chuckled and shrugged my shoulders. We do love having the family together but having the kids thoroughly entertained . . . well, who would pass that up?"

"Oh, never mind," Juliana flicked her hand. "Do what you please; I quite enjoy having the children without you."

Trenton snickered. "As you wish, mum." His fingers playfully pinched my waist while he leaned closer. "I do believe I have permission to kiss you."

I squirmed under his tickle and laughed. "Wait until we're at least in the boat, Trenton."

"Very well," His eyes roamed my face. "But not a moment longer."

Sliding his hand into mine, we watched our parents walk and balance the children down the path toward the Thames. I sighed contentedly over the sight, as my chest swelled with overwhelming warmth and peace.

We had come so far since that unforgettable wedding week . . . eight years, next month, to be exact, and though there were times I wasn't sure the scene before us might ever happen, its truthfulness emerged with little doubt.

I smiled broadly at the recollection of the events and those who played a significant role in our happiness—Merritt, Lizzy, Abby, and Margaret—friends long since departed, but not without leaving their loving imprints on my heart.

I peered over to Trenton as we sauntered slowly behind the group. He met my glance and lifted one eyebrow in mischief, tugging me in the opposite direction and to a stop with my back against the thick trunk of an old willow. He leaned in and his eyes settled devilishly on my mouth. "On second thought . . ." His lips parted. "I'd rather *not* wait."

Printed in Great Britain
by Amazon

10499526R10222